THE HANDFASTED WIFE

THE HANDFASTED WIFE

The story of Edith Swan-Neck,
beloved of Harold Godwin

Carol McGrath

Published by Accent Press Ltd – 2014

ISBN 9781909520479

Printed and bound in the UK

For Patrick

Acknowledgements

My sincere thanks to Jennifer Neville and Douglas Cowie of Royal Holloway, University of London, for their time and valuable advice, and to Jay, my editor – you are simply indispensable!

Godwins Family Tree

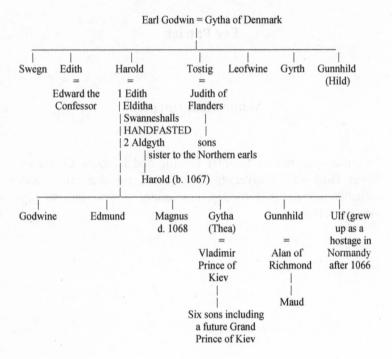

Earl Godwin = Gytha of Denmark

Swegn	Edith	Harold	Tostig	Leofwine	Gyrth	Gunnhild (Hild)

Edith = Edward the Confessor

Harold =
1 Edith
| Elditha
| Swanneshalls
| HANDFASTED
| 2 Aldgyth
| sister to the Northern earls

Tostig =
Judith of Flanders

sons

Harold (b. 1067)

Godwine	Edmund	Magnus d. 1068	Gytha (Thea)	Gunnhild	Ulf (grew up as a hostage in Normandy after 1066

Gytha (Thea) =
Vladimir Prince of Kiev

Gunnhild =
Alan of Richmond

Maud

Six sons including a future Grand Prince of Kiev

Les Heures Bénédictines

Matins Between 2.30 and 3.00 in the morning

Lauds Between 5.00 and 6.00 in the morning

Prime Around 7.30 or shortly before daybreak

Terce 9.00 in the morning

Sext Noon

Nones 2.00 and 3.00 in the afternoon

Vespers Late afternoon

Compline Before 7.00 as soon after that the monks retire

Angelus Bells Midnight

Glossary

Hippocras – a sweet honey wine

Thegne – an Anglo-Saxon nobleman of middling rank

Villein – peasant

House coerl – the elite corps attached to an earl's household

Palisade – the protective fence that circles the estate buildings

Seax – a short Anglo-Saxon knife sometimes double sharpened

Skald – a poet but one of Viking origin

Relics – saints' relics were an important part of Christianity from the seventh century onwards

Old English riddles – short poems

Burgh – town

PART ONE

The Burning House

My dress is silent when I tread the ground
Or stay at home or stir upon the waters
Sometimes my trappings and the lofty air
Rouse me above the dwelling place of men
And then the power of clouds carries me far
Above the people; and my ornaments
Loudly resound, send forth a melody
And clearly sing, when I am not in touch
With earth or water, but a flying spirit.

An Anglo-Saxon riddle, *A Swan,* translated by Richard Hamer

Prologue

Tell us a story, you say. Then let us sit by our frames and listen to a tale while we work. Here is a story for you, sisters. Its characters: a king, his mother, his lady, a queen and a stolen child. We have adventures to embroider, a broken promise, a great treasure and riddles to resolve. Charcoal glows in the brazier. The afternoon draws in, so listen carefully as my tale unfolds.

Do you recall the Godwin estate at Reredfelle? No? Let me tell you about this place. Reredfelle was a sprawling territory of ash, beech and oak only a day's ride from Canterbury. On its southernmost edge, where the forest opened up into parkland, fields and hamlets, Earl Godwin of Wessex built his new, two-storey hall, a magnificent thatched building. The long side walls were painted with great hunting birds and in the centre of the front short wall an oak door led into an aisled room with a raised central hearth. Upstairs, Earl Godwin had his private rooms, an antechamber and, through a doorway hung with a curtain of crimson and blue tapestry, his own bedchamber. Here, he had two windows of glass, like those in the old minsters, set into deep oak frames; so you see, his wealth was great and he was not shy of showing it.

A wide track meandered past the women's bower, a kitchen, stores and barns to a three-barred gate set into a palisade which protected the hall, its outer buildings, herb gardens, dovecote, an orchard and the Chapel to our Lady. The same track curved from the gate, through parkland loved by huntsmen, and disappeared into the encroaching forest beyond. There was, however, a secret way in and out of Reredfelle. A small latched door was set into the orchard wall, concealed by fruit trees, which were shaped to arch over and conceal it. On the other side of the wall, a shaded path curled down through undergrowth to a riverbed.

Reredfelle was loved by the canny old Earl, who came there to hunt and scheme; its desolation began after his death. The countryside was gripped by a festering plague. The population in the villages shrank and the estate was deserted except for the reeve who watched over the fields, and an odd collection of servants. The painted birds on the outside walls of the hall faded. The herb garden grew wild. Barns lay empty. The bower was silent. Tapestries gathered dust and the glass windows dulled. Years slipped by until King Edward himself passed away and Earl Harold, Godwin's son, was elected as England's new king.

Now, sisters, this is not King Harold's story. That one you already know. My tale follows the fortunes of the woman whom Harold loved, and who passionately loved him back; his handfasted wife, Edith, she of the elegant swan's neck. But let us call her Elditha, for in this story there is a second Edith, and names can confuse. After he became king he betrayed Elditha and sent her away. But that is not the end of her story. It is but a beginning.

1

Westminster
December 1065

Through snowflakes that floated out of heaven's pale circle she heard voices crying. Closer to the palace they became the greetings of women, the shouts of noblemen, their children's shrieks, the snorts and stamping of horses. She could hear the earls and bishops and their families, their grooms and servants who were arriving at the Palace of Westminster for King Edward's winter crowning.

Elditha had ridden in from the east on her mare, Eglantine. She raised her hand to stop the guards that trotted beside her and the wagons that followed. The new stone minster rose up behind St Peter's monastery, its white walls merging with the snow-clad ground, its tall towers silent in the pale afternoon light. She nudged the mare's flanks and, urging the creature forward, she walked it into the palace yard, her retinue of wagons and her guard trailing behind.

Grooms rushed to help her dismount. Breathing clouds of icy breath, her younger children, Ulf and Gunnhild, jumped from the first wagon and raced to her side while Thea slowly climbed down after them. Elditha told her guards to go find stable space for the horses, if any was to be had.

'Elditha!' The shout came from the great hall behind them. She spun round. Harold's brother, Earl Leofwine, was striding towards them, clapping his hands and calling, 'Elditha, welcome, welcome. Come into the Hall. The servants are throwing cloths on the tables. You are in time for dinner.'

Sensing that his joviality was only half-felt she hesitated. All was not well here. She frowned, shook the snow off her mantle and glanced up again, smiling and composed. 'Leofwine, it's good to see you.' Then, lowering her voice so that others could not hear them, she added, 'But, cousin, is it true that the King is unwell?'

'No, no. The old man may yet recover. Edith and my mother are with him. Physicians are hopeful.' He seized Elditha's gloved hands and, holding them tight, stood back from her. 'Look at you. Holy Madeline, Elditha, my brother is a fortunate man. You are as unchanging as the Queen of Heaven; you are indeed a true winter queen in that ermine-trimmed mantle.' He dropped her hands and studied her face. 'Eyes, what are they today, emeralds or jade, or have they changed to wild wood hazel! So, lady sorceress, how was your journey?'

'Come, come, and don't let the Queen hear you spin such fairy tales, Leofwine. As for the journey, well, let us just say it was a long one,' she said, trying to look serious. 'Enormous snow drifts; wolves howling from the woods, terrifying; monsters were ready to devour us ... but,' she waved her hand towards the Hall door, 'here we are at last and we shall put it behind us.'

'You look none the worse for the ordeal,' Leofwine remarked, smiling now.

'We were sheltered and cared for. Still, this year it took us two whole days to get through those woods.'

'Then, cousin, let us get you settled. You have your usual chamber. The boys are sharing hall space with my lads. Your girls, Ulf and the nurse will have a room to themselves behind the bower hall, your ladies in the bower.' He spoke quietly. 'Elditha, it is the biggest gathering in years. The greatest earls and bishops are here for this Christmas feast. They fear for the King's health.' He held her eyes with a warning look and she slowly inclined her head. It was best to watch everyone and say nothing.

Her servants were already unloading their luggage. She directed them to carry her belongings to a chamber in the East Hall, to unpack the clothing chests and hang her wall tapestries. 'We will all need to change into fresh garments,' she warned

Ursula, her chief lady. 'See that our clothing is aired.' As the women scurried off to do her bidding she said, 'Leofwine, can you take the children into the hall? I wish to give thanks for our safe delivery, and to pray for the King's recovery.'

Leofwine took Ulf's tiny hand in his great bear's paw and made a sweeping gesture with the other towards the tall towers and arches beyond the gates. 'Isn't it the most beautiful building in the world?'

'It must be. I have never seen a building like it.' And so, here she was, once again in the heart of the King and Queen's world. She bit her lip. A woman of 32 summers and as excited as the children; still, it was Christmas, the most magnificent season of all. If King Edward recovered all would be well, but if King Edward sank into a deep, dreamless sleep, what then? The sour taste of fear rose in her mouth. Who would be crowned in his stead?

'May I come too, Mama?' Gunnhild was tugging at her cloak.

'Yes, of course, if you wish.' She turned to her older daughter. 'Thea, would you like to see inside the new minster?'

'No, I will wait for grandmother in the hall, if I may.' Thea was watching a young thane who was saddling a beautiful Arab horse with a jewel-encrusted saddle, kicking up a flurry of snow as he circled the beast. 'Is that him, Mama – is that Earl Waltheof?'

'Yes, but stop staring, Thea,' Elditha said.

'Come with me,' Leofwine said quickly. 'Your grandmother may have left the King's chamber already.' He looked down at Ulf. 'And you, Ulf, too, you must meet our little prince from Hungary. His name is Edgar. Your Aunt Edith and the King have adopted him.' He hesitated. 'And his mother and his two sisters.'

So this was the boy who might inherit England, this young son of Prince Edward who had fled into exile after Danish Canute killed his father, King Edmund Ironside, all those years ago. She touched Thea's arm and fixed her eldest daughter with a stern look. 'Do not move from the hall until I return.'

'Of course not, Mother.' Thea tossed her copper curls and stomped off through the snow behind Earl Leofwine and her brother. Elditha called after them, pulling her mantle more tightly around her shoulders, 'And have your maid braid your hair. That will not do here, Thea.' She turned to Gunnhild. 'Come, follow me and careful where you step. We don't want your new boots ruined.'

With Gunnhild following closely after her, Elditha made her way along the swept path into the abbey's grounds. Sweepers paused and waited for her to pass. Snow was piled in fat heaps under the skeletal ash trees. Thankfully, the track ways were clear. She grasped Gunnhild's hand. 'Be careful now, the ground is slippery.' The murmur of prayer filtered out of the opened door into the afternoon. A knot of young men bowed to her as they brushed past and hurried out. Still grasping Gunnhild's hand Elditha entered the new doorway and walked along the apse, through an abbey that was full of faces – many familiar ones, who acknowledged her as she passed – until she had almost reached the front. There, a group of noble ladies turned to stare at her. She recognised them. They were from the north – Earl Morcar's family. Could they be staring at her so boldly because she was a handfasted wife?

She smiled at them, wishing no one ill-will, but the looks they gave her back were distinctly chilly. Elditha felt her eyes widen as she recognised one who continued to stare coldly at her. Surely that was Aldgyth of Wales? Harold had only a few years before been responsible for her husband Gyffud's death and something about that look was unsettling.

She held her head proudly and moved away from them and closer to the great altar. 'Kneel, Gunnhild,' she whispered and pulled her child down beside her, her back rigid. These days everyone talked of how important a church wedding was, the priest listening to vows exchanged in the church porch and then blessing the marriage. Harold, her lord, was the greatest noble in England and ruled the land for King Edward. So what if they had been handfasted in the old way? Their wedding ceremony had been held in her father's meade-hall up in the flatlands of

Norfolk and they had sworn their oaths there, clasping each other's hands on the great silver-and-gold whetstone that was placed at the hall's entrance. But though she was Harold's handfasted wife and the mother of his six children, she never could forget that she was also his cousin thrice removed. It was that which impeded any renewal of their vows in a church wedding.

As she knelt on the cold stone floor, she stared ahead at the flickering candles, trying to concentrate on prayer. The scent of new wood emanated from the elaborate pillar carvings mingling with the scent of beeswax candles, a smell that drifted towards them as soothing as summer. No sooner had she begun to feel peace again than there was a rustling of robes close by. The chanting of prayer in the nave hushed. She raised her head. A choir of monks was gathering in their stalls.

'*Tu autem Domine miserere nobis*,' the precentor intoned loudly, his voice echoing through the nave.

'Gunnhild, we shall find a quiet chapel,' she said softly and, hurriedly rising, taking her daughter's hand again, she guided Gunnhild back through the nave into a small side-chapel halfway along it. 'The most magnificent church in Christendom,' she whispered as they sank to their knees again in the seclusion of the alcove. Elditha touched Gunnhild's golden head. The child seemed lost in the murmur of prayer. Elditha folded her hands and gave thanks to St Christopher for their safe deliverance from the icy roads and snowdrifts that had threatened their journey. She prayed for the ailing King, for the Queen, her sister-in-law, and for Gytha the Countess, who was Edith and Harold's mother. She prayed that Harold would have a safe journey to Thorney Island from the distant Midlands.

When she rose again, Nones had finished. The northern women were filing past them out of the church. Aldgyth, she now observed, was really quite plain despite her thin, silver-edged linen veil and gold fillet. Then, the answer to why the widowed woman was at Edward's Christmas court occurred to her. She was here because her ambitious younger brothers were hopeful of finding their sister another noble husband.

Two days later, Earl Harold sailed down the Thames to Thorney Island, the magnificent Wessex Dragon flying in the prow of his ship. London merchants walked through white fields and across frozen streams to cheer him on to the wharf. When he strode into the courtyard, it was his sister, Queen Edith, and her retinue of noblemen, who hurried out through the palace door to greet him. For an instant Elditha's forehead creased as she waited with the other women inside the hall, as Edith had rushed past them. Today, the cold-eyed Queen's attention was all for Harold. Elditha swallowed her pride and smiled and told Thea to smile too; that was until she saw that the girl was boldly watching the young nobles who waited to greet her father. Irritated, she found herself frowning again and snapping, 'We are on show, Thea. Stop staring.'

At that moment, with a trumpet announcing his arrival, Harold entered the hall. He spoke to the noblemen who had gathered by the door. Elditha stepped forward, but before he could greet her, Edith took her brother's arm, swept past them and led Harold straight up the stairs towards King Edward's chamber. Elditha noticed her boys among Harold's retinue and raised her hand to acknowledge them. They, unlike their father, pushed out of the throng towards her. Magnus, the youngest at 13, grasped her hands and kissed her.

Edmund, two years older, said, 'Lady Mother, we are here now too, and you look lovelier than all of the other ladies at King Edward's court.' Then he turned to elbow his younger brother out of the way to embrace Thea.

Glowing with his praise Elditha smiled and turned to Godwin, who was the eldest of her sons. He knelt before her and said simply, 'It is good to see you, Mother.' She raised him up and said quietly, 'Godwin, I fear all is not well here.'

'The King, I know. Father says …' She never heard what Harold had said about King Edward because Leofwine emerged from the great press of people, made a fuss of the boys and rushed them away, saying, 'You will all be housed with your cousins, and they will be excited to see you, all three of you.' He turned to Elditha. 'May I?'

10

'Of course, Leofwine, I am sure they are just as pleased to see their cousins too.'

Thea said after Leofwine disappeared with her brothers through the press of courtiers, 'That was quick. They hardly noticed me. As for father, he never even spoke to us.'

The gathering nobles and their ladies began to disperse, conversing in lowered tones and as the crowd thinned Elditha saw that they were almost alone in the middle of the vast great hall.

Elditha turned to her daughter. 'Never mind, Thea. There is a tapestry to be worked. Your father will greet us later.' She guided Thea to a side door that led from the great hall to the women's building, with a servant scurrying in front of them to move back the tapestry and usher them through. Outside, they crossed the snowy yard, winding around drifts and abandoned storage wagons to the bower hall which lay peacefully under its glittering white covering. As they were shaking snow from their cloaks inside the doorway, Thea clapped a hand over her mouth. 'Oh, Mother, I nearly forgot. Grandmother Gytha says that she needs to talk to you.'

'I see.' Elditha surveyed the long room. Candles burned and spluttered in their sconces. An enormous log hissed and glowed in the central hearth, but otherwise the hall was quiet today, the large tapestry frame deserted and the stools before it empty. The northern women had absented themselves and only a few women from their own lands of Wessex were talking quietly in corners as they spun wool. She nodded to them, sat Thea down to sort threads into colours and, when the girl was settled, she asked quietly, 'And why is that? Does your grandmother need to speak about you, Thea?'

Thea must not upset Gytha. None of them must: not Thea, not her either, nor any of her other children – especially her three boys all older and, hopefully, gaining sense. She sighed. For how long would they remain a family? The boys would soon be off to King Dairmaid's court in Dublinia, but Thea was to go to her grandmother's household to learn responsibility from Grandmother Gytha and to prepare for marriage. Her

11

grandmother would train her to be a wife and mother, to learn other ways of running a household: brewing, understanding herbs, making cheese, churning butter, organising maids. 'Thea, if you upset your grandmother you will be spending the feast of St Stephen here sorting those threads and without company except for your maid. Do you understand?' She pointed at the box of threads.

Thea bowed her head. 'I do not think that Grandmother Gytha is angry with me. She just said that she must find time to speak with you.' Thea looked down at the box of threads on her knee.

'Well, then, behave and you will enjoy Christmas after all.'

Young Gytha, known to them all as Thea, since Harold's mother possessed the same name, was developing into a provocative girl of 14 who dwelled in a world of new gowns and ribbons, gazing into her silver mirror and preening. Yet for all Thea's faults, Elditha loved her beautiful elder daughter's spirit, and she would miss her terribly. In a year's time her child would be married.

She sighed. Any talk with the family matriarch could be daunting. Gytha had wasted no time in putting Elditha firmly in her place as a wife and mother. When she had been a new wife – Thea's age, young and inexperienced – it was Gytha who had befriended, protected and guided her, but when she had confided worries about Harold's fidelity to her, Gytha told her, 'A soldier needs comfort at night when a wife is not there to provide it.' Elditha had bristled at those words and from that day on she could not help wondering which ladies had slept with her husband, even though Gytha had meant soldiers' women, never noblewomen.

Gradually the bower hall filled up and, as the afternoon light grew into twilight, there was the comforting hum of female conversation. The ladies ate dinner in the bower so that their husbands could discuss the King's illness. With great thumps the servant boy turned the sand clock over and over as the afternoon passed. Elditha longed to see Harold but he did not attend the evening service either. Perhaps he was waiting for her to come to their chamber. She said her goodnights to the other women early, returned to their apartment, her three women trailing behind in case they were needed, but she sent her ladies away to her children and sat alone sewing by candlelight.

Towards midnight, just as she began to think he would not come to her, he swept into their antechamber. Wearily, he pulled off his mantle. 'I am sorry to make you wait, Elditha, my love, but it bodes ill. King Edward is weak. Edith says he won't eat. Now he only wants clergymen by his bed. We can do nothing more for him.'

She set aside her embroidery, rose and took his mantle, folded it and laid it neatly over the wide arms of her sewing chair with a comforting and familiar gesture.

'So, then, husband, which will it be: Christmas banquet or a funeral feast?'

'Edith says that he wants us to carry on without him and the physicians tell us that he may yet recover. Who knows? We can do nothing more but wait and pray. It's in God's hands now.' He caught her waist and drew her close to him. 'But I am sorry, my love. How have you passed your time here? Come here and tell me.'

His presence filled the room. She adored him and she knew he still loved her too. 'Well, we are mostly with your mother, our own cousins and our women. Thea adores her grandmother. But Gytha wants to speak to me about something. I wonder if it is about Thea.'

'Probably the arrangements for Thea to be in her household, and that is good, don't you think?' He reached up and pulled her veil away and tossed it onto the cloak.

Elditha kissed him and, anticipating what was coming now, began to loosen her thick plait's binding. 'Well then, your mother has set up a tapestry for us to embroider, a hanging depicting the Garden of Eden. It is for the new cathedral. Thea avoids it when she can. I am working on Eve. And appropriately enough Gytha is embroidering the apple.'

'Ah, I suppose you have left the serpent for my sister? Here

13

let me. I love to loosen this.' He was undoing her pale hair and shaking it out. She was aware of it dropping in thick swathes about her shoulders.

She composed her face into a picture of serenity. 'Of course not, though she can be domineering. We never see Edith these days. There are so many ladies working on the tapestry. We move around it. It keeps us occupied. We talk together.'

Now he was untying the laces of her overgown. His hands moved over her body and to her it felt as good as it had always felt. Nothing had changed, nothing; and as usual she was beginning to soften at his touch. 'Ah, so what do you talk about?' he asked in a teasing tone as her overgown slid to the floor.

She drew back, took a deep breath, exhaled and said, 'Harold, everyone speculates about everything, about the King, about us. There is whispering in corners. What will happen if he dies?' She clasped his arms but he gently removed her hands, pulled her back and continued to unlace her gown. 'Who will be king?' she said.

'Let us not think of that now, my love. Tell me about Thea and the others.' Her gown slid to the floor and she was in her linen undergown. He turned her round and parted her loose hair and began to kiss the back of her neck. 'No one can ever hold a candle to you, my Edith.' He whispered the words into her hair. 'Don't ever forget it.'

She kissed him passionately, seeking out his tongue with her own, before breaking away to say, 'The boys are well, of course. Ulf is very, very mischievous and Gunnhild is serious.' She sank down on a stool and tugged off her deerskin boots, fondling them for a moment before setting them neatly by the bed. 'Thea is growing up quickly. Betrothal is all she can think of. She teases Earl Waltheof, but then she tells your mother that he is not good enough for her. Our Thea wants a prince.'

Harold raised his head and said sharply, 'She'll take who she is given. None of us can choose.'

'We did.'

'We were fortunate. We have love,' he said but there was,

she noticed, a momentary pause. He took her in his arms again and laid his chin on her head.

It was an old familiar gesture, but she twisted out of his grasp and studied his face. 'When you are by my side, yes, we have love. When you are not ... The women here, they talk among themselves about you and other women ... I cannot help but hear them ...'

He put a finger to her lips. 'Enough, Elditha, they are of no consequence.' He drew her close again. He smelled of the sea, of the earth and, slightly, of the musk oil with which he sometimes anointed his hair. He was her husband and she had loved him since she was 15 years old and he had so gently taken her maidenhead. She loved him still. He buried his face in her hair. 'Not now,' he murmured. 'Come with me. How I have missed you. Perhaps we can ride tomorrow.' He led her to the bed and they tumbled onto the goose-feathered mattress and he loved her until she made herself forgive him all his passing infidelities.

Snow fell heavily during the night and that made riding impossible. The women passed the following day closed inside Queen Edith's bower hall. Servants carried great pitchers of hippocras and plates of honey cakes into the bower and, as she nibbled on cakes and sipped the sweet wine, and tried to keep warm, Elditha would glance over at the northern widow who sat with her frosty relatives. Sometimes she caught Aldgyth watching her too. She had noticed how Harold greeted the brothers Morcar and Edwin in such a friendly manner, how he had turned to Aldgyth, their sister – once a lady of Mercia and a queen of Wales – when they had been in the hall that morning, for a moment giving her his full attention, his grey eyes seeking hers. Aldgyth had modestly looked down, but when he moved on around the great hearth talking to others, Elditha had noticed how her eyes had followed him.

All morning the women worked on Gytha's tapestry. They talked about the King's illness. Would he die or would he recover? In the afternoon they sewed gifts for each other, purses and belts, and as they stitched they tried to pretend that everything was normal, though nothing was. Everything creaked. A chill wind rocked the timbers of the wooden hall; the dark skeleton branches of trees outside bent under great plops of snowfall; conversations in the bower hall became in turn knife-edged or dreary. Elditha wished now that she had remained at Nazeing this Christmas, where she would not have had to see the northern women who gathered about the ex-queen of Wales, as though she were a queen bee in the hive. Aldgyth sat close by her, quietly stitching on a length of fine white linen. It seemed to be a man's new shirt with extravagant gold and silver embroidery creeping around the neck opening. Elditha wondered who it could possibly be for. She tipped a pitcher and poured wine into a cup for Gytha and said in a low voice, hoping that Aldgyth could not overhear, 'Thea mentioned that you wished to speak to me?'

Gytha leaned forward in her chair and lowered her voice to match Elditha's own. 'Elditha, if King Edward dies there will be an election and they could decide that Harold must rule. It's a pity that King Edward and Edith have no children of their own.'

Elditha pricked her finger. A drop of blood showed crimson on her embroidery. And I could be queen, she mused. She sucked the blood away.

'What about Edgar?' she said. 'He may not be his son, but he is the nearest living relative and it was Harold who brought the family back from Hungary. Do you not think, Gytha, that now his father has died, Edgar will be king when Edward dies?'

Gytha gave a low laugh. 'The country needs more than a boy to save it from the scavengers, my dear.'

'Duke William?'

'Others too. Harald of Norway and Sweyn of Denmark.' Gytha sniffed, lifted her long sleeve and wiped her nose on it. She nursed her hippocras for a moment, slowly turned the cup and then sipped from it. 'Still, we all know that that William, the bastard son of a washer-woman, is the worst of the locust princes. Edward's mother always wanted Duke William to be England's heir.' She sat her cup down and glanced over at

Aldgyth. Elditha followed Gytha's sharp eyes. Aldgyth immediately raised her head from the shirt she was stitching. Gytha placed a finger on her lips and lifted up a linen fillet that she was embroidering with tiny blue flowers. 'I think Thea will like this,' she remarked. She paused then added, 'Blue will go with the red hair.' She snipped a pale blue thread with her scissors and rethreaded her needle. In and out her needle slipped, making tiny stitches, her eyesight very keen for a woman who had three score years.

Aldgyth of Mercia, the widowed Queen of Wales, bent her head again and seemed absorbed in a section of work about the shirt collar. 'It's not surprising, of course, that Edward's mother wanted William to be the heir; he is her own nephew,' Elditha said in a whisper.

'Emma was a schemer. King Edward hated his mother for abandoning him and marrying Canute. After all, Canute killed the father and married the mother. What do you expect? That woman hated us Godwins too, but she couldn't do without us in those days.'

'Emma is long dead, Gytha.'

'But now, Elditha, that bastard William wants England's throne when her son is dead. What about that claim he made about Harold's promise to him?' Gytha's lips pursed.

'It will certainly cause trouble that both Edgar and William consider that they have a claim.'

'Even so, my dear, the earls won't have either of them. The boy is too young and the bastard's a foreigner, a liar and a thief.'

'Duke William claims ...'

'... that Harold promised to uphold his claim over relics gathered from all over in churches in Normandy. Well, he told me that those reliquary boxes were empty. Some trick.'

Aldgyth stood up, came closer and lifted the warm pitcher and a cup from the hearth. Elditha bent her head over her embroidery. Harold had told her another version of that story. He had confessed to her in bed that he'd been given a choice of becoming William's vassal or of remaining William's hostage.

He had made the only choice he could; but when he'd made his oath of fealty to William in the church at Bonneville-sur-Touques, his hand had been firmly placed on reliquaries.

'It's different, you see,' he had whispered into her ear, 'all fealty means is that I will help the Duke if he is in difficulty. I owe him that loyalty at least: he saved me from the pirates when I'd been shipwrecked when I went over there to get our family hostages from him. I never swore that I would be a kingmaker. I, Harold, Earl of Wessex, will never support any claim by William of Normandy to the throne of England. And so I got my nephew back from him.'

Frowning, Elditha pulled the gold thread through the linen on her lap. 'The earls will declare for the Atheling,' she heard herself saying.

'No, they will not,' Gytha said. 'Edgar's father, had he lived, would have been a fine king, but it won't be that young boy who follows his uncle nor the bastard – nor will it be any other prince who has been elf-shot with greed. It will be an English earl. And what I have wanted to say to you, Elditha, is that Thea will have greater prospects than young Earl Waltheof. Now, where is my thimble?'

Elditha pulled a thimble from the purse hanging from her girdle and dropped it into Gytha's lap. She spoke her thoughts aloud. 'Edward will not choose a Godwin. He will want Alfred's descendants …' Before she had a chance to say anything else, the bower door creaked open, blowing a flurry of snow inside and Queen Edith herself swept into the hall with four of her ladies following. Now, Elditha thought grimly as she dropped her sewing, there really will be an end to any Christmas festivities.

All the women seated in the hall rose and bowed their heads. The children stopped playing. Aldgyth was nearest to the door rummaging in the silks basket for a fresh thread. She sank onto her knees. But, to Elditha's surprise, Edith just smiled and gestured to them all to sit again. She raised Aldgyth to her feet and shooed her back to her embroidery with a thin smile. Then she approached Gytha, bent over and kissed her mother's cheek in greeting. Turning to her women, she sent them off to work on the tapestry frame saying, 'I wish to speak to my mother.'

The queen's dark-cloaked women scurried off to the Adam and Eve embroidery, seeking empty stools. The others made room for them and threaded needles for them. Sitting opposite each other in pairs, they began to stitch the flowered border, talking in hushed voices. Elditha rose again, thinking to join them but Edith said, 'No, Elditha, stay. You may listen to this too.'

Edith sat by Gytha on a cushioned chair and arranged the heavy folds of her blue cloak. 'Edward may yet recover,' she said, smiling her thin smile. 'We must hold the Christmas feast as usual. Nothing must appear amiss. The King will attend.'

'And if there is a relapse?' Gytha's face was anxious.

'There will be no relapse, Mother. The King must show the world that he is recovering. If we all pray for him, God may spare His most faithful son.' She paused, looked round at the other Godwin women who were listening and raised her tone. 'So, since you are all listening, I come to say that we women, all of us, and the families, must attend a nightly vigil in the new Abbey Church, asking God to spare our king.'

'The children, Edith,' Elditha said, dismayed. 'Should they attend the services? Some of them are so young.' She looked over to where the nurse, Margaret, was playing a game with Ulf and the other young children, thinking how harsh her sister-in-law could be, but surely she would not insist on the younger children observing the vigil?

'As you wish, sister; but they ought to understand the value of humility and the importance of such prayer. The King is, after all, their uncle.'

'Of course my children will pray too, Edith,' Elditha said quickly, not wishing to cause offence. How would her four-year-old Ulf stay awake?

Nightly, as the moon hung above the abbey, the women and children joined the monks for the midnight vigil. On the fourth evening, when Elditha picked up her cloak, Harold said

19

impatiently, as if this had been her idea and not his sister's, 'Not again. Not the children as well. Not my mother.'

'Edith has insisted. We should all pray for his recovery – you too.'

'But not my mother; she is so old. Her nightly vigil must stop.'

'She will not stop.'

'Let us hope her prayers are answered. By the by, I am told that you are crowning young Edgar Atheling king already, Elditha.' She could hear the gathering chill in his voice.

'I was not wishing the King's death, my lord.'

'That is not what I have heard.'

'From Gytha?'

'No, but you must guard your conversation, Elditha. There are ears everywhere.'

Only one person would have reported that particular conversation and twisted it into something she had clearly not intended. She did not wait to ask what he had heard. She lifted the latch, allowed it to crash down behind her and headed out into the cold courtyard alone. So Aldgyth had lied to her brother, Morcar, who had repeated the lie to Harold. It was the only explanation.

That night God listened to their prayers. The following morning, Edith's steward announced that the King would attend the Christmas festivities, and following that announcement a sense of levity returned to the court. Elditha pushed Aldgyth from her mind. She riffled through the gowns hung neatly on her clothing pole until, after much indecision, she selected a fine woollen overgown to wear. It was dyed a shade of green that complemented her eyes; its gold embroidery the richness of her heavy plaits. She owned a green mantle of the same wool and a curving brooch pin of gold studded with garnets, a present from Harold. He would be pleased to see her wear it. Although she chose to ignore his accusation, she could not but continue to notice his glances towards the one whom she suspected had tried to come between them.

Determined to enjoy the Christmas festivities she sat in the bower and strummed on her harp. The girls and their cousins practised their dancing steps. Elditha showed them all a new dance with high leaps and swirls that turned as fast as the weather-cock spinning atop a church steeple on a windy day. She laughed when her sons came to the bower to tease them and tell jokes, relieved that the vigil was over. But, often, she felt a pair of pale blue eyes watching her when they dined in the hall. She sensed them following her from the shadows of the nave in the cathedral, where Aldgyth's pasty countenance would suddenly appear from behind pillars. Most annoying of all was when that mousey head popped up smiling from the shirt she was embroidering, and which she seemed to thrust forward menacingly every time Elditha passed by.

2

Christmas 1065

And King Edward came to Westminster towards midwinter, and had consecrated there that Minster which he himself built to the glory of God and St Peter and all God's saints ... and he passed away on the eve of Twelfth Night and was buried on Twelfth Night in the same Minster.

> *The Anglo-Saxon Chronicles,* January 1066, Worcester
> Manuscript, edited and translated by Michael Swanton

Elditha peered into the hall on her way to the bower. It bustled with preparations. She clapped her hands with delight and sent her lady, Ursula, to fetch Gunnhild and Ulf and the nurse from their sleeping chamber so the children could see the fun. Servants rushed about the hall with baskets of greenery, table coverings, napkins, silver candlesticks and an enormous Yule log for the hearth. They hung the richest tapestries behind the dais. They decorated every spare wall space with wreaths of holly. They strewed the floor with fresh rushes and dried chamomile and set up trestles with linen cloth. Above in the gallery, musicians practised on drums, pipes and harps. In alcoves, skalds, the palace poets, rehearsed stories and fools tried out their antics on anyone who strayed their way.

For a few minutes they watched, their excitement mounting, until Elditha said, 'Enough for now. Your grandmother and sister will be in the church already.' She urged the children away, fussing about their cloaks and then marching them outside into the frosty morning and along freshly swept pathways to the cathedral. They would not break their fast until they had given thanks to the one who had saved their Uncle

Edward's life.

Harold burst into the bower after midday service anxious to escort his family into King Edward's feasting hall. Elditha frowned and tried not to care as the women eyed him when he passed through. He smiled through long moustaches that were, this Christmas, tinged with grey. Her husband was still handsome despite his 40 years, utterly resplendent in a fine new woollen mantle and linen tunic of blue as deep as a summer sky. He paused and bowed before Aldgyth. Maids blushed and flustered around the woman tidying her gown and brushing her shoes. Harold lingered for a moment and whispered something, a compliment Elditha supposed, and then passed on to his own family. Gunnhild was waiting for Elditha to pin a small amethyst brooch on her cloak while Ulf danced up and down in new shoes, unable to stand still. Harold called a greeting to her, kissed his mother and helped her from her chair. Elditha glanced over at Aldgyth. She must rise above the sense of unease she felt in the presence of this younger woman. Jealousy was a shoddy feeling, and though Aldgyth was plain, her eyes small and set too close together, she did manage a regal bearing. Tonight in a red cloak with squirrel trimmings the northern widow looked impressive. Elditha took Ulf's hand and gently pushed him onto a stool. She asked Ursula to use her comb on the boy's hair but as she handed it over she felt a shadow descending, as if it had come from nowhere.

'We are ready, my lord,' she called to Harold. He was wearing a new belt, her gift to him. She had known that he would wear it, but it was not just the belt that she noticed. A new silver dagger hung from it, the hilt set with amber. She leaned forward and touched the stone. 'I've never seen a piece of amber as large as a goose egg before. Where does this come from, Harold?'

'Morcar, Lady Aldgyth's brother – an offer of friendship.' He looked away and would not meet her eyes.

She said softly, so that Aldgyth could not hear, 'Morcar shows you friendship? His sister ignores me.'

'Morcar holds the north and he is grateful for that position.

Come, my dear, no ill-will, today of all days. You too, Mother. Here's your stick. We must not keep King Edward waiting.'

Gytha raised a thin eyebrow. She touched Elditha's arm and shook her head. 'Don't let Aldgyth upset you,' she muttered to Elditha when Harold turned away and pushed Ulf and Gunnhild before them. 'What must be, will be, Elditha.' There was a chill in those muttered words but Elditha, undaunted, managed to offer Gytha her help.

The old woman shook her head. 'I have my stick and thankfully, my dear, my eyes.'

Together they crossed the palace yard, walking slowly so that Gytha, who was stiff from the nights of prayer in the chill cathedral, could keep up. The King's steward separated them at the opened door into the hall. Harold, Elditha and the Countess slid into their places at the high table, beside the empty chairs left for the King and Queen. The rest of the family were dispersed about the lower trestles that stretched down either side of a huge double hearth where an enormous Yule log blazed.

Harold remarked, 'Look at our sons just across from us here. We Godwins are well placed tonight.'

No wonder Harold was pleased. All three of their older boys sat with their uncles and young Prince Edgar. Elditha now sought out their two daughters and little Ulf. They were seated far away, with distant aunts and female cousins.

Trumpets sounded. The King's bailiff tapped his staff. She looked towards the staircase at the back of the huge hall. Everyone stood as the snow-bearded old King appeared on the stairs, supported by his wife and surrounded by priests. He tottered down and shuffled towards his centrally placed chair at the high table. His own household followed in a procession. They waited until his personal steward helped him into his chair before they sought their own places.

Elditha smiled as the Queen adjusted a cushion behind the King, and greeted Harold and her mother. She inclined her head momentarily to Elditha. Elditha nodded and looked at the King.

He seemed not to recognise any of them. His eyes were pale and misted over like the insides of oyster shells. He who had once been good-sighted was now turning blind. There was another bustle as people relaxed back onto their benches. Side doors opened and a parade of cooks carried in great trays of food from the kitchens. Female servants poured wine and beer into cups. A boar's head arrived. Venison, peacocks and small birds followed. Blackbirds and partridges, woodcocks, pheasants and geese were all carried to the King in a stately procession. He waved them away. As course followed course, Queen Edith attended to his every whim. She washed his fingers, arranged his napkin, filled his drinking cup and mopped the dribbles from his beard. Elditha sadly noticed that he ate no more than the pickings of a thrush's wing.

Harold placed small portions of meat onto their shared silver plate but they ate slowly, without conversation. Elditha searched the board right and left for the red cloak and the headdress, the golden fillet studded with jewels and a veil of snowy linen. Then at last she saw Aldgyth's plaits lie darkly against the red of her gown and mantle. She glanced sideways to see if Harold was watching Aldgyth too. Harold was not paying the widow any attention at all. He was speaking quietly to the King, whose response was limited to an odd grunt. Edith tried to persuade her husband to sip spiced wine from a silver-and-glass goblet, but he shook his head. Fools came to the table and told riddles and a storyteller began to strum his harp and recite an old tale. King Edward managed a weak smile but he looked tired and strained, as if it was all too much to bear.

'He shouldn't be here,' she whispered to Harold. 'Speak to him. Tell Edith if you can't tell him. He is exhausted.'

Harold shook his head. 'He likes the storyteller. This time Edith knows best.'

Elditha was sure that the King was worse than his physicians were prepared to admit. 'I must say something to Edith, even if you do not. This is cruel.'

'Don't you dare utter a word.'

Course followed course and servers came and went. The hall

grew steamy. Mantles were cast aside. Servers returned and held aloft a pastry model of the palace decorated with confections and nuts. King Edward croaked at his wife to break off a honeyed turret for him. Raising his shaky hand, he nibbled at a corner. He tried to speak, but suddenly his mouth twisted and contorted, so that not a word came from it. His left arm jerked out and the piece of pastry flew up and then dropped onto his wife's lap. He began to slump, falling forward past her, onto the table, where he clutched at the cloth with claw-like hands, bringing silver plates clattering down and glassware tumbling. Red wine splashed onto the rushes. Harold leapt to his feet. Edith cried out. The storyteller ceased strumming. The steward and the royal physician raced to the King's side. Edith and Harold raised him into his chair again. The physician listened to the King's chest through a horn and held a small mirror to his mouth, raised his head and proclaimed, 'He lives. The King lives. Carry him to his chamber.'

I knew it, Elditha thought. He has not recovered, not at all. Retainers cleared a pathway. The steward, the physician and courtiers lifted the frail old man up the staircase, through the wide gallery above the hall, vanishing into the apartments above. Queen Edith raised her hand and bade the storyteller to continue. She asked Harold to accompany her. They followed the King's physicians and courtiers up the staircase.

She heard Gytha's voice say as if it was sliding through a thickening mist, 'Elditha. We cannot stay now.' For a moment she could not move, nor did words form in her mouth. She felt imprisoned, as though sewn into a shroud. This was it. England would be adrift and the locusts would descend. And what now? She felt danger sliding closer and closer to them, towards Harold and herself. Did she not want this? Before, as Harold rose to become the first earl in England she had enjoyed the importance she and their children had, but something worried her now – something she could not quite grasp. She glanced down the hall. Seeing Aldgyth studying her again through those pale little eyes, Elditha signalled to her ladies. When Ursula hurried to her, she sent the girl to gather up her younger children, and with them by her side – confused but obedient – she swept from the hall and returned to her own apartment.

In the freezing courtyards around the palace, groups of young nobles gathered in tight knots waiting for news. In the galleries, by the curtains of private chambers and on staircases up into the towers, Elditha observed bishops and earls muttering. One thought hung on everyone's mind. Who would be fit to rule if the King died; local earl or foreign atheling? Not Harold, she prayed on her knees on the hard, icy pavements of the abbey's many alcoves, prostrating herself before the abbey's multitude of saints. *Not my husband.*

Days passed and it seemed to her that the King lingered, his soul suspended as if hovering on a lightly feathered angel's wing. Harold consulted with physicians. He comforted the Queen or became entrenched in the council room where he reported on the King's progress. He never returned to his own chamber but remained close to King Edward. Elditha quietly embroidered and waited patiently for news.

On the day before Epiphany Gytha tapped her way along the gallery to Elditha's chamber. Leaning on her jewelled, hooded walking stick, she requested thread of gold from Elditha for the new tapestry. As she hunted it out from the box in her chair Gytha suddenly said, 'The corpse serpent is gnawing at the roots of Yggdrasil.'

'Edward is finally dying?'

Gytha lowered her voice. 'His spinners have ceased their spinning. He will not last out the night.'

'In time, the serpent arrives at the tree of life for us all,' Elditha said gently.

She heard before morning that the corpse serpent slid into the room that very night as the King was sleeping. His spinners had spun their last. Harold came to her and took her hands. 'It is over, Elditha. Now all is to change.' She did not need to ask him what was changing because the changes had been happening since the morning she had ridden on Eglantine to Thorney Island. A king was dying and a plain young widow waited in the shadows to take Harold from her. She asked him how the King had died. Harold sank into a chair, buried his head in his arms for a moment, then raised his head and said, 'He was just a dying old man; he had become a great fetid stench that lurked beneath the smell of wax and unguents.'

'What about Edith?'

'Edith held his feet and caressed them. Archbishop Stigand was muttering prayers. Then just as it seemed that if he would never speak again, his lips began to move.' Harold took a long deep breath. 'It was the strangest thing. Edward's voice as clear as the ringing of Angelus bells; he cried out, "England will enter a terrible time."'

'What did he mean?' Elditha whispered. She shuddered. Edward had been, in truth, an obsessive and quite unpleasant old man. Rumour had it that he had never slept with Edith and that he admired young men, or perhaps, since there was no evidence of that, he was a virgin.

'I said, "What is this, Your Grace?" The Queen kissed his forehead and he opened his eyes. He looked straight at Edith and stretched out his right hand, touched my arm and said to me, "I place my kingdom into your care." And that was it, Elditha. After that, he said not another word. But don't you see, he has given me the kingdom and we all know that any wish spoken by a dying king must be granted.'

'So does this mean you are to be king?'

'If the Council says so then, it seems that I am, and Elditha, not a word of this to anyone. There is too much to do, to arrange.' Harold snatched a cup of wine from her, gulped it back, shook his unkempt head and rose to his feet. He dropped a perfunctory kiss on her forehead and hurried out into the darkening evening. Bewildered, she sank into the chair that was still warm from Harold, lifted her mending, then put it down and called for Ursula. 'Bring me my mantle and my boots. I need air.'

'Do you wish for company?' she heard Ursula's small voice saying.

Elditha shook her head. 'Not tonight. Go and rest. King Edward is dead. The morning will be busy. You and Margaret must keep the children hushed, and we must all pray for his soul.'

Around midnight, Elditha picked her way through grim mourners kneeling in huddled groups around the hall, chanting prayers. She climbed the staircase to the gallery and slipped into an empty alcove. She flung open the shutters of a window overlooking the river. A full moon glowed and the water below reflected stars, appearing as if it was filled with shoals of silver fish. Smoke from riverside huts twisted upwards into the night. As she leaned on the sill, Elditha wondered if the King's soul had already sped into the heavens. She listened to the lapping water, the cries of mourners and the chanting of prayers until these sounds faded into the background. Closing the shutters again she thought that she could hear voices close by. She followed the wall to where the leather hanging concealed the entrance to the King's antechamber. Leaning her ear against it, she could hear Harold and Edith talking. Their voices rising, they weren't just talking. They were arguing.

'Edward sent for Edgar's family. You fetched them back from Hungary yourself. We adopted the boy after his father died.'

'Sister, you heard Edward give the kingdom into my care. A dying king's wish is sanctified and must be obeyed. Morcar and Edwin will not have that child for king.'

'But, brother, Edward meant that you were to care for the kingdom in Edgar's name.'

'Archbishop Stigand does not agree. Tomorrow Edward will be interred. I shall be crowned king.'

'Then, I shall retire to my convent at Wilton.'

'No, you were Edward's queen and tomorrow you will show them all that you support my kingship.'

'And who will be *your* queen, brother? Aldgyth of Mercia? You have been plotting this for weeks.'

Elditha clutched the folds of her mantle, turned on her heel and fled back along the corridor. She rushed into her apartment. There was no sign of her women. She sat alone in the dark as the candles burned low. There, as bells cried out through the long night for the safety of Edward's soul, she brooded over what she had overheard. Next to Harold, Morcar and Edwin were the most powerful earls in the kingdom. She understood it all now: the looks, the snubs, the snide whispering as she passed.

When the charcoal dimmed in the brazier she climbed into the empty space that had been their bed here for 17 years and, heartsore, sobbed angrily into the pillows. He would betray their love for a kingdom. And he had not returned to their chamber since Christmas night. This was not the way it should be. Before the Christmas feast they had made love. Before King Edward had died they had been a family. As morning dawned fear paralysed her, but she could do nothing; not yet. She was not to be queen – but what about their children? Would they be princesses and their sons, athelings, heirs to the throne?

Epiphany, the day of Edward's funeral and Harold's coronation, turned out to be bitter, the skies shedding icy sleet. Elditha froze anyone who came close to her. She silently walked with her children and beside Gytha and Edith to the great minster. The Thames was crowded with boats and many stood patiently in the broad space around the palace and on the river, huddled in their cloaks watching. They followed the procession of nobles and clergy that swept from church to palace after the King's interment, and then a few hours later swept back again for Harold's coronation. She sensed that both Gytha and Edith looked at her more with pity than joy and she held her head high, determined not to show the weakness she felt. This was Harold's greatest day and she should be happy, but she could have wept with despair.

She stood with the others in the nave and watched with them as Harold, the earls' choice, slowly descended the platform and stood by the altar. He made a threefold promise to the archbishop and to his people, promising to protect the church, maintain good laws and abolish the bad, and dispense justice to all.

31

'What justice will you dispense to me and ours?' she whispered to herself, clutching Ulf's hand tight.

'What are they putting on my father's head?' she heard the child ask.

She looked down at him and said tensely, 'Sanctified oil, a sign that your father is king and you, Ulf, are now an atheling – a prince, a king's son – so never, ever do you forget it.'

When the ceremony drew to a close and the clergy began to process out of the great church, Elditha saw the northern ladies standing together on the opposite side of the nave. The Lady Aldgyth stood in their midst. She thought bitterly: it has happened before when a king has had a handfasted wife. He will put me aside. She closed her eyes and prayed to her name-day saint, 'I have anger in my heart for him, please help me to contain it. I have pride and I envy that dull girl. Please, dear St Cecilia, beg the good Lord to have pity on your daughter. Help her to face this cruelty. God help us all now.'

Harold moved into the royal apartments without her. They spoke little to each other. The closeness that they had shared only weeks before had frozen like the bitter earth outside. When the court came to dine in the hall after Harold's crowning, she watched the demure smiles Lady Aldgyth gave Harold, and she noticed those he bestowed upon that lady in return, while all the time he spoke pleasantly to Elditha, passing the salt cellar or placing morsels of fowl on her plate, choosing her a sweetmeat.

'Harold, we must talk,' she said when they met in the hall on the following day at dinner.

He touched her arm, smiled at her sadly and said, 'Not at the moment. There is so much to do. Soon, Elditha, soon we shall talk.' Then he hurried away to some earl or other who wanted his attention.

Gytha tried to comfort her by saying, 'He will come to you soon. We are the new royal family, my dear. You should rejoice.' But Gytha knew, and Elditha knew that she knew.

Again she tried to talk to Harold, and he dismissed her saying, 'I am burdened with arrangements, my dear. There is no time for anything else, not now.' But he had time for the pasty-faced widow who had once been wed to Gyffud, a king of the Welsh.

Three miserable days slid by and then the widowed threat travelled back to the north. Elditha rejoiced, hoping that Harold would be drawn back to her, now that Aldgyth was gone. Her sons came into her chamber for her blessing daily and often they joined her in the minster for evening Vespers. They were filled with excitement lately, not because they were the sons of a king, but because King Dairmaid of Dublin had invited them to reside at his court. They were important now and all their friends and cousins admired them. She realised this but was glad that they were modest too. They made her proud to be their mother. She happily practised her harp, spent time with her children, helped Thea with her embroidery and returned to the bower hall to work on the Garden of Eden tapestry. When she tired of this she encouraged her ladies to fill her own apartment with the clatter of dropping spindles and chatter.

A few days later, as she was preparing for sleep, she heard Harold's footstep outside her chamber. She sent Ursula to see if he was there. Ursula returned smiling. 'The King is on his way, my lady.'

At last, and what will he say now? 'Go to the bower hall,' she barked at her women, and they fled through the doorway curtain like a flock of migrating birds. Harold pushed in as they left and thrust his hands towards the brazier.

She took a breath and composed herself as she poured him a cup of wine, keeping her hand firm. He accepted and sipped slowly. She poured some for herself, though she would not drink it. She must be measured. She would not keep him with soured words. Yet the Devil perched on her shoulder, urging her to give him a look so sharp her eyes could have sliced through his bones. 'Why, my lord, has it taken so long for you to remember you have a wife?' There, it was out.

He placed his cup on a low table and opened his palms in a supplicant's gesture. Time froze. She noticed a new gold garnet-studded cross rise and fall on his breast. He said slowly,

'In the spring I shall ride north and tour the kingdom.' He sipped the wine. It was a deliberate pause, she thought. At last he said, 'Elditha, I will speak frankly. In York, I shall wed the Lady Aldgyth. I must, not for love, but for the kingdom.'

She set her cup on the table, her hand shaking. Red wine splashed over the cloth. She spun round to face him again. He was kneeling before her. 'I beg you, Elditha, do not make a fuss.'

'Get up, Harold. You do not kneel before me to beg my forgiveness.'

He stood up and grasped the chair. He was shaking as he shook his head. 'Elditha, listen to me ...'

'No, my lord, I have watched you woo her in front of the whole court. You have betrayed me and our children. Tomorrow, I shall return to Nazeing.'

He reached out and touched her face. She drew back, frightened, hurt and angry beyond words. She swallowed. She must not weep. There was silence. She waited. 'Elditha,' he said at last, 'I need this alliance. Without the support of Aldgyth's brothers the kingdom is divided. Without them we are all lost.'

'Why? They cannot make you do this.'

'Yes, they can. We are cousins thrice removed and were handfasted because of it.' He sank onto their bed, his head in his hands. 'I am the King now, Elditha, and although I am King, you still remain the mother of our children, but,' he paused; she waited. 'You cannot be my queen. And, though I may not wish it, I must wed with Aldgyth.' His next words were spoken with gentleness, but they cut deeply. 'A king needs a queen approved of by the Church.'

She had been thinking for days of what she would say if he brought this up. 'Then appeal to the Pope. Build him a minster as Duke William did when he wed Matilda of Flanders. They were cousins something removed.'

'Duke William is closer to the Pope than we are here. It is different. Can you not see that I don't have any taste for this marriage, but marry her, I must. It is only an arrangement.'

She snapped back at him, 'An arrangement with Morcar is more important than your own children? Our sons, our daughters too – what will happen to them and to me?'

'Our sons will go to King Dairmaid's court in Ireland. They will learn to be princes. Thea will remain with her grandmother, where she can prepare for marriage. Ulf and Gunnhild will dwell with you, though soon, perhaps, Gunnhild will join Edith in Wilton for her education.'

'What?' She was about to retort that Gunnhild would not go to Edith's household to become a nun – not ever – but he was running on ahead of her.

'Elditha, my dear, for the sake of our children – for us – we must both accept this change in our lives. Others have done so in the past.' He lifted her hands and held them tight. She felt his strength and she felt her own fragility. She knew that she must make a bargain with him, for the sake of their children and for her own sake too. Theirs had been a long and loving marriage. Slowly, she nodded. 'But our children must take precedence over her children. You will swear it to me.' She lifted her prayer book and thrust it into his hands. 'Swear it upon this, on St Cuthbert's prayers. I am not going to quietly vanish into a nunnery. Don't you think that, my lord.'

'Of course not, the very thought of it, Elditha. Godwin will inherit my kingdom. I swear it.' He held the prayer book and touched the cross that hung on his breast as if to confirm his oath. He lifted it to his lips and kissed it. 'I swear it on the holy cross. Godwin will follow me. Elditha, we too can continue if you will still have me.'

She shook her head. 'And how is that possible, my lord?'

She felt him study her and heard him say quietly, 'Do you remember Reredfelle?'

'How could I forget it? It was the place of our first summer. We conceived Godwin there.'

He was still holding the prayer book. He laid it down and looked up at her. For a moment everything was still, frozen in the air. She saw a glistening, a gathering of tears, in his great blue eyes. Then he spoke again. 'And it has been neglected. Do not return to Nazeing. Go to Reredfelle and make it what it used to be. Consider it as one of your own estates, and I will come to you there.'

'When will you come, my lord?'

'I cannot promise a visit soon, but I do promise that I shall come when I can.'

Promises, crosses and relics betrayed; sinking down beside him on the embroidered coverlet for a moment she watched the brazier glow and the candles flicker. She searched his face. He looked tired. He was weary with the burden of kingship already. The Devil fled from her shoulder and her heart ceased to beat like that of a frightened bird. 'My estates are in good order. I will do the same for Reredfelle,' she managed to say with dignity.

He reached out for her and though she held back, he pulled her into his arms and kissed her. 'That is it, my swan, my love. Do not leave me. Our lives are, for now, buffeted by rough seas.' He smiled down on her through moist eyes and said, 'I have gifts.' He pulled a pouch from his cloak and pressed it into her hand. 'Conceal this in a safe place. Padar, my skald, will accompany you to Reredfelle. If you need me, send him.'

She untied the purse cord and drew out six sapphires. They shone pale blue against her linen. She dropped them into her lap. 'Padar the skald and baubles. I would rather have had you, my lord,' she said, feeling a monstrous sadness sweep over her and devour her. Tears bit the back of her eyes. She must not allow them to flow.

'And I you,' he whispered. He withdrew a small, leather-bound book from the lining of his cloak. 'Whilst we are parted, this will amuse you. See, here is your riddle.'

She began to smile. Riddles had been a secret language between them. He read the verse about a swan that he had always said was for her. She had drawn strength from that poem. 'Forgive me,' he whispered into her hair, but she could not forgive; forgive him she would never bring herself to do. For the sake of their family she must accept his proposal, but she was not so easy with her heart.

She laid the book of verse aside, stood up, walked to the chair and lifted his mantle. There was surprise on his face as she gave it to him. 'Go, Harold, and God go with you.' She turned away from him. The room had become chill and the candles had burned low in their sconces. She felt a draught as the tapestry moved. She turned around and he was gone. In that moment of final separation, she knew that she must learn the lessons of loneliness.

On the day dedicated to St Valentine her cavalcade gathered in the yard. She sat proudly on her mare, wrapped in her ermine-lined cloak. Deep in her saddle-bag she had concealed a precious silver-plated, bone casket containing Harold's gifts and her collection of ivory figurines of female saints. Over these treasures she had folded the christening robe which she had used for her children, and which, one day, she prayed that she would use again.

Ulf and Gunnhild peered out of their wagon at the small gathering which had collected to wave them farewell: three brothers, who had tears in their eyes as they watched their departure, Thea and Gytha. As their cart trundled towards the gate leaving tracks in the snow, they turned back and waved again to their grandmother, their cousins and their brothers and their elder sister. Elditha turned and scanned the watching faces, but their father was not there to say goodbye.

3

March 1066

Then throughout all England, a sign such as men never saw
before was seen in the heavens. Some men declared it was the
star comet, which some men called the haired star.
  The Anglo-Saxon Chronicles, March 1066, Worcester
  Manuscript, edited and translated by Michael Swanton

Elditha's company took on a festive mood as they rode through
villages that were strung out along the old Roman road south of
the river. Padar trotted on a small pony by her side, telling jokes
and stories, making her laugh. A heavy cloak of seal skins lined
with fur fell over his pony's rump and halfway down his shins
and a sword hilt protruded just above his belt. Every time her
eye caught its gleam she felt safe. Why would I not, she
whispered to herself, as she trotted on Eglantine along the
snow-packed road; there is a warrior bard on one side. She
glanced sideways, and on my other an armour-clad Norfolk
thane. Osgod was his name, she remembered, a loyal Godwin
servant too. Furthermore 30 of Harold's own house-ceorls rode
close to the 20 long-wagons carrying her children, her ladies,
her house-ceorls' families, her servants, cooks, grooms and
even a beekeeper and a gardener; in others there were her
tapestries and furniture, including the oak bed and feather
mattress that she had shared with Harold.

From time to time, Padar rode up and down this line of
lumbering carts, chivvying their drivers and checking the snow-
packed road for obstacles. The sun climbed high in the winter
sky, and the ceorls munched bread as they sat in their saddles,
drank ale from leather flasks and threw pennies to peasants they

encountered in villages. Thankful for these, the villagers called blessings and greetings to the company as they passed.

Her children shared a covered long-wagon with their nurse, Margaret, and Elditha's three ladies. In the afternoon a light snow fell and, for a while, the children leaned out to catch the flakes and watch them melt on their fingers, but soon they became too cold and retreated into the fur-piled depths of their wagon.

The cavalcade entered the wild wood where trees closed in on them. It was difficult to drive the carts forward on the frozen, rutted woodland paths. Deeper into the wood, the light faded to grey and it grew very cold. Soon they were lost. The children in the convoy began to whine that they were hungry and Elditha's ladies complained saying that they must stop, that the wives, children and servants, all needed to rest. Osgod rode ahead. Eventually he cantered back pointing through the trees, 'There it is. I knew there was an old hunting hall here. It is our stopping place. Back to the fork! We have missed the track in.'

It was not easy to turn all the cumbersome wagons back along the track, but slowly and carefully, one by one they were turned around and they returned the few miles to where the road had forked. The long thatched hall nestled in a large clearing. Through the fading twilight Elditha saw a simple timbered building with tiny shuttered windows. Huts were clustered around the main hall and piles of wood were stacked in every open space. Smoke twisted into the darkening sky.

As they approached the buildings, a wolf began to howl. Another echoed the first and another, their cries so mournful and prolonged that the children clutched each other's cloaks, her ladies shrieked and her ceorls froze in their saddles. Elditha shuddered, tried hard not to be frightened and turned her mare's head, thinking to reassure her children. Here they were open to the trees and the dangers that lurked among them.

Padar reached out and touched her arm. 'There is a pack of wolves out in those woods but never worry, my lady, they are far off.' He lifted his hand to signal the carts to follow them into the compound. Once the wagons filled every open space close to the hall, he said, 'We'll set fires and a guard on the horses tonight.'

Their horses snorted, breathing clouds of steam and restlessly stamping their hooves in the snow. The charcoal-burners that lived in the huts surrounding the old hall came hurrying from the trees carrying torches. They stared first at the gleaming mail of the house-ceorls and then they gazed at the fur-cloaked lady who was seated on her mare, her flaxen plaits bound with rich jewels. Osgod broke the silence. 'This is your King's lady. We need shelter.'

Their leader waved his flaming torch towards the long building behind. 'My lady, the hall is warm and dry. I care for it for Lord Athelwold when he is at his Winchester house. There are alcoves curtained off at the back. Our fare is simple ... a stew of grain and onions ...' he started to say, 'but what we have –'

She broke in, 'We have food in our carts and servants to cook it. You must save your stew for your wives and children.'

'Thank you, my lady.'

The thane called for the servants to make fires in the open. Soon they had a pottage of meal, salted beef, herbs and onions bubbling in a dozen cooking pots. They ate inside the long building, sitting on the hearth benches. After supper, Elditha sang her children to sleep in the curtained chamber to the back of the hall. She drifted out into the hall again and over to the hearth, where Padar had been strumming his harp. She was too awake to sleep. The wolves' howls had long since ceased and a woodsman said that the creatures must have moved deeper into the forest away from the fires. Lady Ursula asked if anyone in their company had seen a wolf. 'Of course, how do you think we get wolf skin rugs for our halls?' was the reply.

Then one said, 'There is nothing finer than a silver wolf cloak, Lady Ursula. One day I shall find you one, if you wed me.'

Elditha took Ursula's hand in her own when Ursula looked down, embarrassed by the man's attention. Padar strummed his harp. He stopped after a few moments and said, 'But, of course, a wolf can be dangerous. It is two-faced, just like many people I have known.' He glanced sharply about the faces that were illuminated by firelight. 'You all seem loyal to your lady, though if any of you were not I would feed you to those wolves myself.' Then he chuckled at his own joke.

How like Padar to be suspicious. Elditha placed her arm protectively around Ursula. The fire blazed high. These were thanes, the men who held land from both herself and Harold and who protected and guarded them, trained warriors whose first loyalty was to fight for their lord. She had known these men for years, and their wives and ladies whom she had long kept by her side. These were the people whom she trusted. They would be her strength during the difficult months that lay ahead. 'Tell us a story, Padar,' she heard herself saying. That would distract those who glowered at the skald's insulting jest. He laughed, strummed his harp and began to recite a part of the tale of the great warrior Beowulf; the best part, the fight with the monster. As he reached the end he stopped strumming and rose up and managed a growl.

"'I had done no evil to him, but the furious demon wanted to force me and many others into a bag – but it was not to be. I got to my feet in a blind fury. It would take me too long to tell how I repaid the terror of the land for the lives he stole. And even though he got away to enjoy the pleasures of life for a while longer, his right hand stayed behind him in Heorot, evidence of his miserable overthrow as he dived into murk on the mere-bottom.'"

His audience clapped and begged for more and he began a story of a silkie, a mermaid who shed her tail and lured fishermen from their wives. Ursula yawned. Elditha rose. 'Time to rest. It will be a hard ride tomorrow,' she said softly. 'Take the pallet close to ours, Ursula.'

As Elditha crept into Lord Athelwold's great bed, with its soft feather mattress, beside her children, she fancied that she could live for ever in a wood, hidden from the world of palaces and kings. As she drifted into sleep she knew that just like the she-wolf who guarded her cubs she too would watch over her children's destinies no matter what lay ahead of them.

The next afternoon they rode out of the woods south-west of Canterbury and into the parkland surrounding Reredfelle. They entered Reredfelle itself through a palisade gate that lay wide open. That was not unusual at all, but there were no guards or farm workers in the yard and everywhere fences were broken and the barns were crumbling. She sent her servants to find firewood and to make what barns they could into a refuge for her wagons and horses. Then she led a procession of women and children into the hall. There, she took one look at the two shabbily dressed and surprised servants left to watch over Reredfelle's hall and despaired. The hall was bitterly cold. She spoke sharply to them, and ordered them to build the hearth fire higher. Then they must show her cooks the kitchen house. Her ladies wrinkled their noses as they swept through the building and out through the side entrance at the back into the bower hall. On their return Ursula said brightly, 'We can clean it up, my lady. The bower hall looks out towards the rising sun and we can sew there in the mornings.'

Elditha cautioned Margaret to watch over Ulf and Gunnhild, who were chasing a skinny three-legged dog around the hall. She called her ladies to follow her and they climbed the narrow staircase to the upper chamber. They stood in a pool of green light by the windows that Earl Godwin had put into the wall of his sleeping chamber. Maud fingered the dust on the glass windows and recoiled. 'As well there is another with shutters. You would suffocate in here in summer.'

Elditha said, 'It is beautiful. Vinegar and water will clean it up. And, you, Maud, must supervise the task. See to it.' Maud obediently ran back through the antechamber and down the stairs to ask the cooks for a bucket of vinegar and water. Elditha insisted that her other two ladies follow her down and into the chambers behind the hall. She sneezed as dust rose off ancient chests but wiped away the cobwebs with her elbow and opened the lids. Some coffers were empty and would be useful for storage. She opened another lid, drew out an ancient linen garment, coughed as dust spiralled out of it, threw it back in and slammed down the lid. They must see if these things were worth mending. But no sooner had she the thought than it blew away from her. There was so much more to do.

The chambers needed sweeping and the white-painted walls that were grey with dirt must be washed down. She chose Freya, another of her ladies, to supervise that, saying, 'These will be for the children and their nurse.' She wanted it clean by nightfall, she added. The woman nodded and hurried off to find servants to help with the task.

Finally, Elditha delegated the task of cleaning out the bower hall to Ursula, who said she loved the old bower hall already and that by tomorrow they would be able to set up their looms. Elditha then summoned the hall servants and ordered every hearth bench washed down and fresh rushes and dried lavender spread on the hall's hard-packed earth and lime floor.

Two house-ceorls lugged Godwin's bed down the staircase to the chamber behind the curtain where the children would sleep. Once Elditha had overseen her maids sweep and wash the floors and walls, she installed her own bed in the upper chamber in its place. She hung her cloaks on pegs, cleaned out two old chests and placed linen in them. Soon, the plain garments that she wore daily hung from the rafters. The maids folded others into a coffer, secreting plump linen bags filled with dried fennel among them to keep moths away. When she was alone, she unpacked the contents of her saddle-bag. She looked up into the roof, climbed onto her mattress, reached up and placed the bone-plated silver box containing her treasures carefully beside her shoe collection on a wide rafter above her bed. Harold's sapphires were protected, concealed under a christening gown, with her ivory statuettes. She touched the tiny silver key that hung on a thin chain nestled between her breasts. The gleaming blue stones were her safety net, just in case. Just in case what? The words echoed in her mind. Just in case, just in case, but she couldn't think why she had such a presentiment.

During the weeks that followed, Elditha's thanes rode into the village and persuaded the villagers to return to the estate. When

44

she sent to Canterbury to the monastery of St Augustine for an over-seer, the monks obliged and gave her an experienced reeve of their own. Guthlac, her new man, persuaded the villagers to plough the great fields and encouraged them to plant their own gardens. The villagers came back to the estate because it was their duty, but they also came because Elditha promised them rewards. She called a meeting in the hall, and sitting in old Godwin's great oak chair, she announced, 'This year, there will be a bountiful harvest. If you work hard, your families will eat well, and until crops grow, I shall purchase grain to feed you all.'

As if they did not believe her, they melted away like sullen though obedient hounds back to their hovels. Though they knew their place in the order of things, they could still feel resentment at an overlord who was a woman. A week later, the promised grain arrived and the result was that they worked harder. Under Guthlac's direction, the villagers set up hen coops and cleaned out the dairy. Her cooks organised kitchens and stores. The roof thatch was repaired and the hall's interior and exterior walls were freshly white-washed, until not a trace of lichen clung to them. A painter came from Hastings and touched up the hunting birds that decorated the outside walls. He painted their feathers and beaks in bright yellow, red, green, touches of deep blues and precious black. They became her symbol of prosperity, and a beacon to anyone who rode out of the wood into Reredfelle.

As the household settled into a daily rhythm the children roamed around their new home exploring, and inventing games. They skated on the frozen pond with sharpened bones tied to their shoes; indulged by the milking maids, they drank cups of warm milk from the dairy whenever they pleased; they disappeared for hours into camps they created in the hay barn. Gunnhild and Ulf appeared to forget that their father was now the king and she wanted to forget him entirely too, but she could not. Memories would creep up on her at unexpected moments, a look from Gunnhild whose cornflower eyes resembled Harold's own or Ulf's ability to climb trees, more daring every time. Although Ulf's face resembled her face, her hair, her eyes and her height – slim and tall already for a five-year-old – he would be physically strong and he was adventurous like his father. Then, there was another reminder. It crept in one night in the guise of a long-tailed star that appeared in the heavens, glowering down at them, ominously hanging above them for weeks.

On the evening that it first appeared, Mass was held as usual in the estate's decaying chapel by Father Egbert, the village priest. After Vespers, Elditha sent her children off with Margaret and Ursula for their supper while she lingered by the herb garden, pushing back weeds and poking at the ground with a stick. The time had come to clear this wilderness and grow new plants, parsley here, rosemary there, sage, fennel, thyme and rose: always her favourite. Night still dropped early and as darkness gathered and the stars appeared, she was at the orchard gate. She stood still and stared up at the heavens. The stars appeared brighter than was usual. There were those that she knew and loved, those that could be angels' haloes. She caught her breath and looked harder. One star appeared even brighter than the others and seemed to be growing a long colourful extremity.

'My lady, look at it!' She started and looked around her to see where this disembodied voice had come from. She saw the skald, Padar, leaning on the newly mended wattle fence farther along. He was gazing upwards, his hand shading his eyes. She glanced up again and saw that the long-tailed star flew across the night sky like a dragon spitting silver flames.

'What is it, do you think, Padar? It's not an angel. Maybe it is some creature that unseen sails over us from one end of the Earth to the other.'

He shook his head. 'I don't know, my lady. Perhaps there are, as some might think, other worlds up there woven through the air between the heavens and the Earth we know. In any case, it is an evil omen. You should come away from it now.'

Elditha followed Padar back through the garden and across the swath towards the hall's warmth. The skald often talked of things that were best not to dwell on. He filled their minds with stories of creatures called dog-heads, ungodly monsters which dwelled in houses and villages just like their own, spoke and talked as did human-kind but were evil – representations of the Devil himself. And though he laughed and said they were only notions, nonetheless many of her people believed in them. He told his stories by firelight, striking fear deep into her people's hearts, yet sometimes she had to laugh at the absurdity of his tales of men who married two-tailed mermaids. As they approached the hall's entrance a crowd had gathered to watch the sky. Osgod announced, 'Mark this, my friends, it is a warning. There will be trouble in King Harold's kingdom.'

She stopped the thane's talk. 'That is nonsense, Osgod,' she said sharply and swept past them inside the hall. She told her maids that she would take supper alone that night, in her antechamber. She did not want to listen to them discuss that star.

She tried not to think of the strange dragon-spitting star that hung in the night sky. Villagers frowned at it. The house-ceorls were edgy and sharpened their weapons; as if that would protect them from a dragon star. As the month passed and the long-tailed star continued to reign above Reredfelle, she wondered if it could, in truth, foreshadow a terrible change in the kingdom and in their lives. At night, alone in her great bed, she knew sure as the seasons' turnings, that Harold had forsaken them. She had not heard a word from him. He had abandoned them and ridden north, simply leaving instructions that she was to have a great household for Reredfelle. Gytha and Edith had been solicitous, bringing her tapestries, sewing threads, linens. And they never spoke of that woman in her presence. At Westminster the older boys had spent evenings playing chess in her chambers and her daughters had danced for her, stitched with her, packed travelling coffers with her and accompanied her to services. At Westminster the new court had treated her with reverence, because she was the mother of the King's sons, but she knew a court to be fickle; they would switch loyalties as quickly as threading a needle. As for their sons, by now they would be preparing to make their journey to Ireland.

48

4

Here is the remedy, how you may better your land, if it will not grow well or if some harmful thing has been done to it by a sorcerer or by a poisoner.

A Field Remedy Ritual in Karen Louise Jolly, *Popular Religion in Late Saxon England*

'The people would like you, my lady, to scatter the first seeds into the ground,' Guthlac said as they settled down to discuss the estate's accounts in her antechamber.

She raised an eyebrow. 'What does Father Egbert say?' she asked, carefully, as she peered at the neat writing in Guthlac's accounting book.

These old ways were not approved of by the Church. She knew the ceremony well, had often watched it but there were those who thought that her soul would be in mortal danger if she took part in one. Nonsense! Her soul could not possibly be in danger just because she prayed and placed a loaf of bread blessed by a priest along with a cellar of salt, the herb of fennel, powder of incense and soft ash soap into the earth to cleanse the soil and encourage crops to grow.

'Father Egbert will be in charge, he says,' Guthlac persisted. 'My lady, it would be a way to win the villagers to us. They are frightened of that star in the night sky. If you bless our land the crops will be fruitful and there will be no famine. That is what they are saying.' He hesitated before adding, 'And, of course, Lady Elditha, you are the mother of King Harold's children and that matters to them.'

She turned away at that reminder. Still, if they wanted a field blessing she would oblige. No harm could come of it and maybe, as Guthlac pointed out, much good. She touched his sleeve and said, 'When would you wish it, Guthlac?'

'On Friday?'

On Friday morning, Elditha wrapped herself in her mantle against the brisk March wind and wore her hair in two thick, golden plaits. Followed by her whole household, she rode out to the fields. She climbed down from Eglantine's back and handed the reins to Padar. He looked at her suspiciously and said that he would wait with the horses. As she marched into the meadow she could see that Father Egbert carried a prayer book and Guthlac was standing by a garlanded plough holding a linen sack. They were surrounded by villagers. When she reached them, she knelt, whispered a short prayer, rose, then said that she was ready to begin.

Father Egbert raised his right arm in blessing. Today, she represented older beliefs and he the love of Christ and the holy saints. Together they would bind both into one. As he chanted prayers she repeated his words. That was what she knew she must do – follow his lead. She lifted her arms and the wide sleeves of her green gown fell back. Her blue cloak and her pale veil flew behind her in streaming pennants. She raised her head to the heavens and her long plaits swung free of her veil, bright against the green of her gown, but there was no time to push them back. She began to call out the ancient wyrd, an age-old chant:

I may this charm by the gift of the Lord open with my teeth.
Sanctus, sanctus, sanctus.

She stretched out her arms towards the earth and then the sky as Father Egbert followed this with the *Benedicte* and the *Magnificat* and two *Pater Nosters* over a plough that was strung with winter greenery and plaits of barley. As the prayers ended Elditha looked ahead and noticed that a strange figure – a skinny, dark Benedictine monk – was watching her from a sycamore tree. He was standing apart from the villagers. There was something she recognised as disgust on his face. He clutched a satchel close to his chest. She observed him for a moment. His lips were moving. She was sure of it: he was praying. Guthlac nudged her and pointed down. She took the

50

things he had drawn from his sack and dropped all four objects into a prepared hole in the earth. The reeve nudged her again. 'My lady,' he whispered in her ear. 'Your blessing.' She began to chant the words that were always spoken before the planting:

'Tall shafts, bright crops,
And broad barley crops
And white wheat crops.'

Guthlac handed her the bread. She knelt, her pale, thick plaits swinging over the ground and placed the loaf into the hole. It had been kneaded with milk and holy water and earlier had been blessed by Father Egbert. Nestling beside the stalk of dried fennel, the squishy soap, salt from the Reredfelle cellar and incense from the Lady Chapel it would lie under the first furrow. As she rose again she felt her eyes drawn back to the sycamore tree. The strange monk was still there, standing as if he were joined to the tree, holding his satchel in one hand and wiping perspiration away with his sleeve. She turned to ask Father Egbert if she needed to do more, say more. He shook his head. She looked back and the figure had gone.

Gathering her cloak around her, followed by her servants, she marched back over the field to where Padar was guarding the horses. She climbed onto Eglantine and cantered to a gap in the hedge. Moments later she was back on the track that edged the great field, with her band of servants and ladies around her. She kept turning her mare from side to side as she glanced backwards but the stranger had vanished. The villagers – men and women – were dragging ploughs from the hedgerow. Oxen were brought forward, their necks garlanded with straw. She turned Eglantine towards Reredfelle, pleased at the sight. Today her people had acknowledged her as their lady. That evening all who came into her hall would eat well and drink beer. It was Lent and they would dine simply on fish and pastries, savoury breads and eggs, pease pottage and honey cakes, but they would nonetheless eat well.

She was dabbing her face with a damp towel when a servant

bustling into her bower hall saying, 'My lady, there is a
from Canterbury asking for you.' She dropped the towel
the basin of rose-scented water and lifted a linen drying
. 'I am on my way,' she said. Her ladies were peeking up
their work with concerned and inquisitive eyes. 'Curiosity
ught out the cat,' she said. 'Carry on with your spinning. You
vill find out soon enough.'

She pulled her cloak from the peg by the door and set out
from the bower to the hall, wondering who had sent the monk.
As she came into the back of the hall she saw that her children
had dressed up in the moth-eaten old clothes that had lain in a
chest belonging to the old Earl. Ulf strutted in a red cape which
would have just covered Godwin's shoulders but enveloped his
child's frame and trailed in the floor rushes. On his head he
wore a woman's black-plaited fillet into which he had stuck
three yellowing ears of wheat. Gunnhild trailed after him,
wearing something very long and musty-smelling. Elditha made
a mental note to have all the clothing in that chest washed,
mended and distributed to the poor, and the chest dusted with
flea-bane.

The monk was sitting by the hearth drinking a bowl of milk.
'My lady,' he said, preparing to stand. He appeared lanky inside
the voluminous folds of his black habit. His face was stern and
his eyes were set into his lean face like beaten down nails.

'Do not raise yourself, monk. Finish your milk. What brings
you here to our quiet hall in the middle of Lent?'

'I come to open the chapel and to be tutor to your son.'

'Sent by whom – the King?'

The monk was frowning at her. 'The Archbishop, who, of
course, has the King's ear.' He put his bowl aside and folded
his hands into his lap, 'My lady, I fear you are being led astray
here. I saw today ...'

Elditha swallowed. Who knew what tales this Archbishop's
man might carry back with him to Canterbury? 'What you may
or may not have seen today does not concern you, Brother ...'

'Francis. But it does, my lady. I am concerned for your
children, for you, for the villagers here. The Church finds

52

practices such as I saw today questionable. These are the very kinds of sorceries that lead God's flock away from their faith.'

'I think that God would want to see His people eat, don't you?'

'My lady, I fear you are misguided. The village priest should know better. I see it is for me to bring an understanding of what it is to be a Christian to Reredfelle.'

'Brother Francis, you are welcome here, but you will restrict your mission to the chapel and the education of the King's son. As for the village priest and his family, do not meddle. I have worked hard these past two months to gain the love and support of my reeve, the priest and my villagers. Tread softly.'

'But the Archbishop would not approve.'

'The Archbishop knows me well. I would never do anything misguided. The Archbishop of Canterbury leaves us to our own ways; these are the same Christian practices that we have observed with devotion since the time of King Alfred.'

'As you wish, my lady.'

The words slipped from his mouth like spider's silk. But she saw by his thin-lipped grimace that he did not mean to do as she wished at all. She would show him that they were observant of the liturgy at Reredfelle. 'We have already opened our chapel here. Father Egbert, the village priest, comes to us every day.' She folded her hands. 'Brother Francis, I will have the priest's house made ready for you at once. I can provide you with one of my own servants, a freed slave who refuses her freedom. She will be happy to serve you.' Brother Francis bowed his head. She went on, 'This afternoon you must dine with us. We have fish from our own ponds, pottage and sweet pastries ...' Her sentence went unfinished. She heard her children shriek. Not now. She rose to her feet. 'Excuse me a moment, Brother Francis, the children ...'

Too late; Ulf and Gunnhild were racing into the hall, Ulf chasing his sister. Gunnhild flew up to her and clutched her cloak and then, as she tried to unpeel her daughter, to her horror Elditha saw that what she was wearing was in fact a vestment. Before she could speak, Gunnhild had turned to Brother Francis

53

and was saying in a solemn voice, 'Can you betroth us?'

'Hush, Gunnhild,' Elditha said.

Brother Francis looked both children up and down. Elditha could feel his censure of her and her children. She heard the chill in his voice as he said, 'I am come to Reredfelle for other purposes, certainly not to betroth brother and sister. Perhaps the children could show me the chapel.' He pointed at Gunnhild. 'And then we can return that garment to its rightful home.' He removed his eyes from Gunnhild to her and lifted a box that sat by his side on the bench. He added, 'Lady Elditha, the Archbishop himself has sent this relic as a gift for Reredfelle's chapel.' He shuddered dramatically. 'And I do think, my lady, that here we are sorely in need of St Benedict's help.'

'St Benedict?' She reached out for the box but as she went to touch it, he pulled it away.

'His finger bone. You must provide a more fitting reliquary for it: a crystal shrine decorated with gold and jewels – sapphires, perhaps, the colour of the Virgin's veil – but for now it remains in this box created from the cedars of Lebanon.'

'A moment please, Brother Francis.' Elditha leaned down and placed her hands on her daughter's shoulders. 'Gunnhild, and Ulf, you too.' She looked at him sternly. 'Put those garments back into the coffer where they belong. And fetch Margaret to me. She really must be more attentive to your play acting. Then we shall show Brother Francis our chapel.' She turned to the monk. 'The vestments will be cleaned carefully and restored to your care. They were in an old chest behind the hall.' Elditha spoke again to the children. 'No more silliness. We shall wait here by the hearth until you return. Go at once.' They slowly trailed off and she shook her head and sighed. If God could forgive Harold the setting aside of a wife, then he must forgive her need to love and even spoil her children. 'Well, Brother Francis,' she said, scanning the monk's countenance, 'I hope you will be content with us.'

The Reredfelle chapel was built of stone. It was a small and plain structure that possessed a simple chancel and nave and high, glazed, arched windows. Despite glass windows that kept out rain and wind, the inside was always cool. If God's sanctuary at Reredfelle was the resting place for an important and travelled relic, Brother Francis soon made it clear to Elditha and anyone else who would listen that he was determined to make the chapel worthy of it.

Determined not to antagonise him further, Elditha allowed Brother Francis to supervise the painter from Hastings as he painted the stone chapel's inside walls. He would create a world's doom painting on the chapel walls. Oswald set to work. Brother Francis designed the wall paintings. All the painter had to do was sketch with charcoal and paint in the demons and angels. Elditha watched the work's progress, bemused. Perhaps Oswald hoped that Brother Francis would recommend him as a church painter to the Archbishop himself. He seemed so creeping, so determined to please the priest. The painter was to be found working in the chapel by day and night in simple rush light. He flew insect-like along ladders and scaffolding that now covered the east wall. Brother Francis supervised, driving the project on. He was passionate. Then, two weeks before Easter, he told Elditha that the first wall painting would be revealed on Easter Friday. She showed her pleasure, saying, 'You have done well, Brother Francis. Ulf enjoys your teaching too. And it keeps him out of mischief.'

'And I think he is an able student. He knows many of his letters already, just in the space of a fortnight.' But Brother Francis swung out his dark cloak which puffed up in the breeze, a little like himself. She politely said back, 'It must be the teaching.'

Gunnhild seemed bereft. She complained that she wanted to learn to read and write as well, and hung about the priest's cottage. Occasionally, Brother Francis allowed her to scratch letters on a wax tablet, but more often he sent her back to Elditha to learn how to spin, saying, 'Little girl, learn to run a household. You do not need writing.'

Gunnhild ran to her mother complaining. Elditha shook her head. Since her own writing ability was lacking, she must find someone else to tutor her daughter. If Gunnhild wanted to learn, she must not stand in her way. She should, after all, spend a few years, but only two years, at Wilton, which was the only abbey that taught daughters of the nobility to read and write as well as the art of fine English embroidery that was admired everywhere in the world.

'I shall write to your father. Perhaps you can go to Wilton for a while.'

'Please, please. I like Aunt Edith. I do want to go to Wilton.'

5

That you, bejewelled should yourself recall
In your secret heart the vows and oaths you both made
in former times together, when you might still together
live in festive cities and dwell in one land.
The Husband's Message, in *A Choice of Anglo-Saxon Verse*,
edited and translated by Richard Hamer

Soon after his arrival on the estate, Brother Francis took to passing time in the wooden village church waiting to catch hold of Father Egbert, who was always conveniently elsewhere. When Father Egbert eventually reappeared, Brother Francis questioned him about his faith, asking him how many services the villagers attended, seeking confirmation that they were observing Lent and saints' days, and then he confronted him with the fact that the Archbishop now disapproved of priests taking wives. Father Egbert shrugged and replied that until the Archbishop deigned to come to the village, he would decide what was best for the villagers, and for him.

Shortly after this encounter with Father Egbert, Brother Francis noticed the estate's butcher outside his hut busy at work. Partridge hung from the eaves along with a brace of ducks. A pungent-smelling steam coiled up into the cold air. He angled his long nose into the crisp April air and sniffed. Then he saw it. A pig had just been slaughtered and it was dropped from a ghastly hook on the cottage gable, where blood and entrails spilled into a large vat. He stopped and watched for a moment. 'Why have you butchered that pig? It is not the right season. I hope you are observing the last days of Lent.'

The butcher wiped bloodied hands on his leather apron, studied the pallid-faced monk and said, 'It's a wild hog from the woods. When Lent is over we'll all be glad of a blood sausage, you included.' His woman raised an eyebrow and began collecting the blood into a pitcher. Brother Francis was sure that she had made a rude gesture behind his back, twirling a finger by her head and dropping it just as he glanced back. He hurried along the track, determined to report the villagers' disrespectful practices to the Archbishop. As he passed through Reredfelle's opened palisade gate, Lady Elditha's skald was sitting on a tree stump. Above, crows cawed and careered across the clouded sky.

'Good afternoon, Brother Francis.' Padar lifted a small harp and began to sing. 'There's been a killing in the woods. There'll be a wild partridge for supper and a pig is on the way.'

'Partridge in Lent,' Brother Francis repeated. He shuddered and hurried off. There was no doubt that the spitting star hung in the night sky because God was angry with England's sinners – men and women like Lady Elditha's villagers and servants. He would have to speak about this heathenish estate with the Archbishop himself.

Later that week Ursula brought a messenger up to the antechamber where Elditha sat by the green glass window. Brother Francis was recording the coinage she had spent on seed for the great fields. He had taken this task from Guthlac, who was now busy supervising the sowing of grain. The visitor was one of Harold's personal messengers.

He bowed and said, 'My lady, I bring a letter.'

'So I see. Well, give me what he has to say.' Brother Francis's eyes widened. Noticing, she said quickly, 'Ursula, take this man to the hall and see that he is fed and has a sleeping place for the night.'

She then placed the small scroll on top of her sewing chair. 'Now back to work, Brother Francis. I want this done well before noon. I have to hang up our cheeses later.'

The candle burned the hour away. Elditha tried to concentrate, but her eyes kept returning to the scroll that lay so temptingly on her chair. At last, she closed the ledger with a thump. 'It is done for today, Brother Francis. Go to my son. He is playing in the yard with the other children.'

The priest's eyes slid away from hers to the scroll. 'Would you like me to read that to you, my lady, and scribe your reply?' he asked smoothly.

She raised an eyebrow. Really, the monk was insufferable. This unpleasant man would never see her personal correspondence and certainly nothing written by the King.

'No, I can read, Brother Francis, as well you know. If there is to be a reply, the skald will take it. Go, Ulf must work on his letters for at least an hour this morning. Put the ledger in that chest.' She handed over a key from the collection that fell from her belt.

He lifted the heavy book, secured it in the coffer and returned the key to her. She watched and waited as his dark robe trailed through the heavy blue curtain and on to the landing. He stooped as he passed under the lintel. What a tall, thin man, she thought, and so little about him to like. At last she felt she could pick up the scroll. She examined it first, turning it over in her hands and peering at it cautiously. The seal had been tampered with and there were two extra cord tags on it, dropping from a second seal. She frowned as she realised whose tags these were. Puzzled, Elditha unrolled the scroll and read the curt message it contained. The messenger had travelled from the north all the way to Queen Edith in Winchester first and only after that had he travelled on to Reredfelle. Harold, too, clearly wanted his youngest daughter to be educated at the abbey at Wilton. It was one thing for her to request this, another for him to pre-empt the request.

Elditha summoned Padar to her antechamber. When he pushed through the curtain she spun round. She had been pacing and thinking.

'My lady, you sent for me?' he said standing just inside the doorway.

'Padar. I need advice and there are few that I trust with it.' She waved the letter. 'First, my husband sends us our Brother Francis, a monk who is obsessed by Pope Alexander's reforms;

a zeal that is, no doubt, popular with our Norman enemies. Now read it.' She pushed the letter into his hands.

Padar read slowly. He frowned and handed the scroll back without a word.

'Padar, what am I to do? Gunnhild wants to go to her aunt.'

Padar looked up at her. 'Let her go. Your daughter will thrive with her aunt at Wilton. It is where many of our noble girls learn to write and speak in tongues other than our own and that will prepare her for a great future. My lady, he misses you and promises to come soon.'

She turned from him at that and glanced out of the opened window towards her garden. Margaret's loud voice drifted up, telling Gunnhild to fetch a jug of cream from the dairy. She had learned to live alone but sometimes she missed him. Some nights, when she slept beneath the green glass window, her heart yearned for him. They had bedded each other here during the first summer of their marriage and they had conceived Godwin beneath this window. And now Harold was putting the affairs of state before her whom he had loved and declared he loved more than lands or even, he had said then, more than a kingdom itself.

But she must look to the future of her children, not dwell on the past. Gunnhild should go and learn the things men learned, so that she could find her way in the world. If she desired the Church, so be it, though many a nun went blind embroidering God's work. She turned back to Padar. 'Padar, you must ride to London and tell my husband that, yes, he is missed. If he is not in London, discover his whereabouts. Find out where he will pass Easter. Ask him if he remembers he has a son here and a wife. And I want to know, Padar, if he has yet wed with that pasty-faced widow.' She added in a quiet voice, 'And say to him that Gunnhild will go to Wilton.'

She summoned the messenger and ordered him back to Winchester, to Queen Edith to inform her that Gunnhild would travel after the Easter feast. When Elditha told her daughter that she was to go to her Aunt Edith and that she must choose two of the older maids as companions to accompany her, she could see by Gunnhild's happy face that she had made the right decision. 'And, of course, I shall come to visit you in Wilton once you are settled. Meantime, my sweet, we have much to do: gowns to stitch, shoes and a coffer to fill. And we must send gifts with you to your aunt. We have only three weeks to prepare.' As she spoke, Gunnhild's eyes grew wide with excitement.

'May I bring Lise and Greta?'

'You may, but they must only stay with you until you are settled.'

How she would miss this lovely, dutiful daughter.

A few days later Guthlac brought Elditha the slaughtered pig. She was in the kitchen when he arrived, filling little bags with fennel for Gunnhild's coffers. Clay bottles were waiting for her to pour unguents and healing potions into them, all gifts for Edith. The pig was, Guthlac told her, a gift from the village. She filled the last linen bag as he waited and tied a cord around it. Everyone wanted to eat flesh again instead of the fast-day diet of bread, worts, pease pottage and salted herring.

'But, Guthlac, the village has more need of this pig than we do here.'

'Wild pigs are plentiful now. We have already slaughtered several more.'

She nodded. 'You are right, the woods yield food even if the fields have suffered neglect. My thanes hunt the deer there. At least we have sides of venison hanging in our stores.' She added cautiously, thinking of Brother Francis and his disapproval of her people. 'So how do my villagers fare?'

'Well, my lady, but we have had visitors.'

She raised an eyebrow and set down a small flask she was holding. 'Really, who would bother us?'

Guthlac told her about two strangers who had ridden through the village that week and who had stopped and asked questions. He added, 'And claiming to be merchants on their way south to Hastings.'

She chewed at her lower lip. 'Maybe they are as they say.

They never came to my hall, though. That is odd. The only stranger to come here in recent days has been the messenger from Queen Edith.'

'My lady, these were no ordinary merchants. They were more interested in gathering information than the selling of buckles. They poked their noses into everything. They asked if the King was wed again. They enquired if his children are with Lady Elditha at Reredfelle. They claimed that they wanted to purchase wool from your manor. My lady, has anyone come to purchase wool? No.'

'Guthlac,' she said, dragging off the enormous linen apron she had wrapped around herself to protect her gown as she worked with herbs and oils. 'Walk with me. I need some air. Come and see my garden.' She pulled on her mantle and led her reeve away from the hall. In the garden seeds were already pushing up shoots. She could breathe here. The newly turned soil calmed her. The sun was shining and, as they glanced up at the pale blue sky, a flock of long-necked birds flew overhead.

'Wild geese,' Guthlac remarked. 'Ah, the garden looks good.' He walked up and down admiring her neat rows of planting. 'By summer this will yield us great baskets of vegetables.'

'Thank you. My ladies have helped me.' It was pleasing that a man whose life belonged to the soil had admired her efforts here. 'Guthlac, I've seen no merchants in Reredfelle,' she said. 'Tell me more.'

'My lady, they did not know the value of anything. They knew nothing of the quality of linen and wool. Their own cloth was too fine for that of merchants. There were swords under their cloaks and they spoke in a foreign tongue.'

She stopped sharply. 'As they would if they come from Normandy. What have you told them?'

'We said that it was too early in the season for us to trade and that they should go to Canterbury. All we have anyway is old wool. Our own women are using what we have. My lady, we sent them packing.'

'You did well to send them away before they found a loose

tongue in Brother Francis.'

'Ah, and this is another thing; Brother Francis is meddling again.'

'How?' She sighed and began to walk again. Not this too; but it was no more than she had expected.

'On Easter Day, my lady, on Easter Day he wants to process the relic into our village church and back again, us all following it, like they do in the towns. And he wants to say the Mass for the villagers. But Father Egbert always said our Easter Day Mass before, and we are used to him.'

'We must reach a compromise.' They had come full circle around the garden and were back by the chapel gate where they had started. Elditha thanked Guthlac for the villagers' gift, saying she was glad of it. 'I will speak to Brother Francis,' she added.

That afternoon she sought out Gunnhild from the bower, and told her that they would supervise the salting of the bacon. She could take some as a gift to Winchester. Gunnhild jumped up, laid her sewing neatly in her sewing basket and pulled her mantle from its peg.

In the kitchen house the cook was already overseeing the chopping up of the carcass. With a big smile on his face, he gave Gunnhild the pig's trotters.

'Mama, what must I do?'

'Watch me and pay attention. We can steep the trotters in verjuice to tenderise and preserve them.' Elditha sought out a pot of verjuice from the shelves at the back of the kitchen. She lifted it out, set it on a bench and cut away the wax seal with her knife. Gunnhild wrinkled her nose. 'So sour.'

'You get used to it. You pour.' She supervised as Gunnhild tipped the vinegar into a bowl. 'Throw these sage leaves in too,' Elditha said, trying to think of the task and not the parting that would come all too soon. The meat would be delicious. The rest of the pig, including the head, could be eaten on the Easter Day feast. She sent Gunnhild to the cook for cuts of flesh. Taking a key from the ring on her belt she opened up a small store behind the kitchen and brought out a wooden box full of salt. She would use a lot of it today and, although they produced salt in the Wessex salt pans near Winchester, it was precious. They barrelled the greater portion of the meat and set aside one of the two barrels of salted pork for Gunnhild to take to Winchester.

'Your Aunt Edith will see that you learn everything quickly,' Elditha said, knowing full well that Edith was not in the least interested in the arts of a kitchen. In Wilton Gunnhild would learn to read and write in foreign tongues and hopefully, one day, she would become a princess of whom her father would be proud, rather than an abbess to please Edith.

Elditha began to choose garments for Gunnhild's travelling chest. The village shoemaker made two new pairs of leather shoes. Her women chose woollen cloth from lengths that Elditha had ordered from Canterbury and commenced work on a new cloak. They promised Gunnhild silver threadwork on the hem. Gunnhild hemmed her own shifts perfectly and then set stitches on fine linen for a veil for her aunt, begging the leftover silvered thread the women had used for her cloak so that she could embroider it.

'I'll miss you, Mama,' Gunnhild whispered as they sewed in the antechamber together surrounded by Elditha's women.

Easter would come and go and then Gunnhild would go too. She grasped Gunnhild's hands. 'You will learn many new things in Wilton, my love,' she whispered back.

6

Easter Day

> Now must we praise the Guardian of Heaven
> *Caedmon's Hymn*

As Elditha's eyes adjusted to the chapel's dimness she saw that the ladders had been removed and the scaffolding taken down. Now she could see the finished wall painting behind the altar showing Christ's agony on the cross. Elditha stared at the painting, thinking it was different to anything she had ever beheld before. Below the Passion, the Devil shied away, banished from Christ's presence. Christ's face, though fair, was sardonic and His mouth held the hint of a sarcastic smile. His blue eyes were hooded. She saw Brother Francis himself in that face. She looked down at the Devil and realised that although he spat fire and wore horns as always, he possessed a pigtail and features that uncannily resembled those of Padar the skald. Sighing, she closed her eyes. She heard everyone present gasp and fearing the worst opened her eyes again. This time she noticed that a star painted above Christ was uncannily similar to the long-tailed dragon star. Her household was mesmerised. The villagers stood outside Reredfelle's newly decorated chapel shivering in the chill morning but her household had crowded inside, coughing and sneezing in a cramped space where the air was thick with incense, and were staring at the wall painting.

Brother Francis turned and pointed at the star. He began to speak 'That star is a warning to the people of England. We must follow the laws laid down by the Church. Saints' days are to be observed with reverence and not with profligate feasting and coupling.'

An angry murmuring quivered through the small chapel. Brother Francis raised his voice as the murmuring grew louder, 'In future, there will be fasts on Wednesdays, Fridays and Saturdays and on those days Christ's flock must remain celibate, as the Church decrees.' He lifted his arms and appealed to his flock. 'We must all make sacrifices ... for the sake of our souls ...'

Elditha's Norfolk thane, Osgod, called out, 'Be careful of your own soul, Priest, and we can mind ours.' Osgod shoved past the others back through the crowd and out of the chapel into the gathering of servants who began to cheer. Elditha pushed after him to the chapel entrance and said, 'There will be peace among us and respect for the monk's words. Osgod, you will do penance for your arrogance.' It was enough. The others fell silent. And inside the small chapel Brother Francis began to chant the Easter Friday prayers.

No one remarked on the paintings and she wondered if only she could see any likeness. Then she remembered Father Egbert speaking with the painter. He knew something of this. As for the painter, he had returned to his own home. On Easter Day Brother Francis carried the reliquary before him. Elditha and her children dutifully walked behind him, wearing their richest embroidered clothes and gold bracelets. Reredfelle's house-ceorls and their women and children followed with their heads bowed. Elditha firmly insisted that Osgod walk barefoot among them, clad only in a white shift. Finally, a group of estate workers and servants trailed in their wake. Then, as they slowly entered the village, she saw the skald galloping along the track-way. He had returned. She stopped the procession and signalled to him. Padar reined up sharply.

'I have news, my lady!'

'That must wait, Padar.' She looked over at Brother Francis, who had paused the procession. 'But join us and give thanks.'

The skald fell in behind the procession. When they reached the great winnowing barn near the wooden church, he stopped alongside the blacksmith.

'Where is Father Egbert? Why are we processing behind Brother Francis?' he asked.

'He had his way over that relic,' the man whispered. 'But the villagers love Lady Elditha. They'll obey her. Look, the wheat is coming up – barley too. See how it shines green on the earth. Be a good harvest this summer. They'll eat from her hand, see.' He stopped speaking and shook his head. 'But that black monk bodes ill. They all distrust him. Father Egbert is inside the church but the monk is running things there.'

Padar snorted, wheeled his horse around and returned to the manor.

After a brief sermon from Father Egbert, Brother Francis spoke on how the Reredfelle relic would be returned to the Chapel to Our Lady where soon he hoped it was to be placed in a crystal reliquary with silver decoration, a gift from the Archbishop. Though her villagers seemed impressed today, Elditha knew they really couldn't care less whether the relic was revered or not. What mattered to them was a good harvest, an end to Lent and a generous Easter Day feast.

Then it was over and the household strolled back through the noonday sunshine. There was to be a feast in her hall. Elditha took her place in Godwin's chair halfway along the table, under her own swan banner. Beside this she had hung a copy of Harold's fighting man. She might be angry with him but he was her husband and the father of her children. Also he was their king, so she honoured him by hanging his banner beside her own. Servants poured jugs of mead and ale. After the first course was served, she passed the pepper-horn and salt cellar down the table. Eating of flesh after a long fast always created excitement. Dish after dish came to the table and the centrepiece was the great boar's head that the villagers had given her, their lady, as their Easter gift. She noticed Padar slipping into the hall. He took a place along the side with her thanes and, after they had eaten, Padar entertained them with stories. Even Brother Francis chuckled at his tales and laughed at his riddles. She studied him. The monk thinks he has subdued my people. For how long will the truce last?

Later Padar came to her antechamber carrying two large leather saddle-bags he said were crammed with gifts.

'What have you brought us?' she asked pointing to the table. 'Put them there.'

Padar fished deep into the leather bags and withdrew a collection of parcels. 'My lady, these are from the King, the Countess and your daughter.'

He laid them on the oak table side by side, lumpy packages wrapped in soft leather and tied with plaited cords. She wondered who had prepared these gifts or if they were afterthoughts, tempting morsels thrown at those who were hungry and, were, like Lent itself, contrived to purge Harold's guilty conscience. 'Why does he send us gifts but does not come?' She looked sternly at the skald waiting for his response. There were deep shadows beneath his eyes. She realised that he had ridden hard through the night to bring the parcels to her.

Padar pulled at his wisp of a beard before replying. 'My lady, the King says that he would come if he could but he cannot.'

She reached for the soft leather wrapping of the gift nearest to her. 'Why is that?' She lifted the parcel and turned it over but did not untie the leather cord that bound it. She gave him a piercing look. 'And do not lie to me.'

Padar shifted uncomfortably. 'The King has married in York and has held his Easter Court at Westminster. The northern lords have come south with their sister. Countess Gytha was present, along with Lady Thea and many noble ladies. The King cannot leave London, my lady.'

Elditha dropped the package back onto the table as if it had scorched her fingers. 'Go and rest. Thank you, Padar, for riding so hard to us with these ... gifts.' She added as an afterthought, 'And for your honesty.'

After he pushed out through the curtain, she stared at the package. Her future with Harold looked as glum as those gargoyles circling the great abbey in London. Slowly, one by one, she untied the cords that bound the gifts. She recognised the valuable herbal that had belonged to Gytha – one that she had admired in their companionable days, now past. Sighing, she recollected that together they had once poured over its delicate drawings of plants. 'Just as I am planting my own garden,' she said aloud. Gytha had also sent a prayer book for Gunnhild. Written on its first vellum page was Gunnhild's name. Clearly it had been a commission since written in it were prayers to Gunnhild's favourite saints. She opened the remaining gifts. Thea had stitched a linen tunic for Ulf. It was a fine shirt, just the perfect size for her little brother. 'So Thea has settled down to her needlework at last,' she said aloud, though there was no one to hear her.

Her fingers trembled as she opened the last packages. These were wrapped in fine deer skins soft as wool. She lifted an accompanying note scribed by one of Harold's priests. He had sent gold cloak pins shaped like sparrowhawks for the children, a purse for Gunnhild containing gold coin stamped with Harold's own head, a small wooden Noah's Ark for Ulf with tiny carved animals, a pair of silver bracelets for Elditha engraved with doves, and for a summer undergown, the scribe had written, a length of blue silk cloth. Despite herself, despite him, she was pleased with the gifts. They had been carefully chosen. She fingered the silk, thinking of all the Spanish worms who had provided it and the dyers who had so delicately given it such a wondrous colour – the shade of the Virgin's veil.

She summoned Ursula and showed her the gifts. 'Retie the parcels that were intended for the children. It will be a joy for them to discover the contents for themselves.'

Ursula gasped when Elditha held up the silk cloth, allowing the material to float in the air in a blue rippling cloud of silk. 'My lady, it is a fabric of such beauty. Look how it catches the light. It is like butterflies' wings.'

'Catch a butterfly and it will die,' Elditha said. 'This silk has come from lands far away.' In the candlelight, as she held it up, the silk reflected blues, greens and gold.

'He must love you very much.'

'Enough to wed another, it seems. The children are asleep,

but tomorrow they shall have their presents and know that their father remembers them.'

When later she lay down to sleep she twisted her pillow and thumped it over and over. The earls and their wives, all the great in the land who had once admired her as the wife of the Earl of Wessex, now gave their loyalty to a queen called Aldgyth. Unable to sleep, she climbed out of her bed and pulled on her boots. Wrapping her mantle around her, she stole past Ursula, who was fast asleep on her pallet in the antechamber, and climbed down the stairway. She slipped out through the hall's back entrance to look up at the sky. There was no longer a dragon star spitting its wrath through the heavens. That night, as mysteriously as it had appeared, the dragon-tailed star had vanished from the sky. Perhaps, she thought hopefully, perhaps, if I pray hard, all will be well. I shall send Padar with our thanks after he returns from Winchester and with news of Gunnhild's journey, but I shall never ask him to come to us. That, he must decide.

7

May 1066

> Fate is the mightiest; winter is the coldest,
> Spring the most frosty, it is longest cold,
> Summer most bright with sun, the heavens hottest.
> *Gnomic Verses,* in *A Choice of Anglo-Saxon Verse*, edited and
> translated by Richard Hamer

Elditha folded the delicately stitched veil that Gunnhild had
created as a gift for her Aunt Edith. She wrapped it in soft cloth
and secreted it deep in Gunnhild's saddle-bag. Her new clothes
and shoes lay in a travelling chest that was crafted from pale
ash wood. So Gunnhild set out for Winchester with her two
ladies, escorted by Padar and protected by a small band of
Elditha's thanes.

She said a tearful goodbye to Gunnhild but quickly, after the
parting, told herself that life must continue. She sent again to
Hastings for the painter and insisted that he erase the Devil's
pigtail, though she ignored the Christ. He must re-create the star
into a firmament of stars. Brother Francis continued to lead
services in the chapel. Elditha thought him more moderate in
his homilies than before, but her villagers' discontent with the
monk was ever present, though never spoken. Though her
thanes and house ceorls ignored him, Ulf liked Brother Francis
and for that she was grateful.

Padar returned from Winchester to Reredfelle in May, when
she was setting bee skeps in the orchard, the woven hives and
bleached cloth lying in the grass ready to be placed on stoops
beneath the trees the moment a swarm arrived. When she saw
the skald pushing his way through the garden gate, she signalled

to him with a wave of her hand. Looking anxiously at the skeps, Padar hurriedly began to garble his news.

'Gunnhild is happy with her aunt,' he said.

'Is there other news?' Elditha asked impatiently, her attention on the palisade.

'Queen Edith has Norman monks committing King Edward's life to vellum. Already Edith allows the child to sharpen quills and dabble with inks.'

'She will soon know more than her mother, for although I can read, I cannot write more than my name.'

'Writing is monks' work.'

Elditha spun around and gave him a stern look. She said fiercely, 'The work of men, Padar; the work of priests and scribes. There was a time when ladies of the Church wrote too, you know. Oh, of course, naturally, when a clever idea catches on it becomes the prerogative of men.'

A stray bee buzzed around them. She smiled as Padar remained very still.

'And my husband, have you news of him?'

For a moment Padar didn't speak. He twitched as a bee flew close to his face and flicked it away with the back of his hand.

'You don't like them?'

'No, my lady.' He looked uneasy. 'My lady, I heard in Winchester that the Countess has returned to Waltham. The King is arranging Lady Thea's betrothal.'

'So then, he arranges and I agree, though I am not consulted. To whom?'

'Earl Waltheof.'

'Ah, we spoke of that at Christmas; a good match. Well then, I am sure in time, he will think to send me word of it.' She bit her lip, determined not to show her irritation in front of the skald. She shrugged. Why should she be sad when summer was coming and the countryside was so beautiful? Yet there was a pain in her heart – a sense of something lost, as if for her, love had had its season, and passed away.

'Yes, Lady Elditha.' Padar cleared his throat.

'Padar, is there anything else?'

'Brother Francis is unpopular with the thanes, your house-ceorls and the villagers. The guard complained the whole way to and from Winchester.'

'So what is new about that?'

'Your thanes think he is a spy.'

Elditha lifted her eyes from the palisade and turned to face Padar. 'Why so? He is loyal to Archbishop Stigand and the Archbishop is loyal to the King.'

'He creeps around listening.'

'He is the monk here, but eavesdropping is a serious accusation, though I have wondered.' She frowned. Every time she spoke about the estate to Guthlac the monk was there too, hovering at her elbow.

'And before Eastertide there were those merchants who went around the village gathering information. You are watched, my lady. I wonder if you should travel to Canterbury this Whitsun? The weather is perfect for travel.' At that they both looked up at the flawless sky. She did not reply. He added, 'The Pentecost services at St Augustine would be a change to those led by Brother Francis here. Why not take Brother Francis with you to Canterbury?'

She shook her head and looked towards the sky again. 'Here they come,' she called out to her bee-keeper and her women. A cloud made up of a multitude of dark spots appeared from the direction of the woods. 'My bees are here.' She lowered her voice, 'So who do they think he spies for, Padar? Pope Alexander?'

'The Bastard of Normandy, of course.'

His words were drowned by a cheer from the ladies as the bees arrived in the orchard. The swarm descended into an apple tree and then hung in a tightly packed clump from a bough. The leaves rustled, their branch sighed and bent as it carried the new weight. Elditha's women raced to open up a sheet of bleached linen and set it under the tree. Two of them lifted the skep and placed it close to the boughs, hoping to tempt the queen inside. One woman beat at the branch with a willow switch to make the bees drop onto the sheet, the stick swishing backwards and forwards, whistling as it caught the air.

Elditha turned back to Padar. 'Brother Francis was sent here by Archbishop Stigand, whom we trust.' She considered for a moment. 'Yes, on second thoughts, you are right. The idea really does please me, Padar. We shall set out later this week. I shall visit the Archbishop and ask him to punish our spy.' She laughed. 'Go into the hall. I see that you dislike my bees, though I have observed that you enjoy honey on your bread.'

She smiled to herself as she watched his red cloak flee through the garden. He was a loyal friend and she was glad that Padar was part of her household; he was the best gift Harold had bestowed on her.

A week later, early in the morning, she rode out for Canterbury with Padar, Brother Francis, Ulf and a group of her women. They had an escort of house-ceorls and thanes, all of whom were glad of a change from Reredfelle. The atmosphere was festive and the weather was perfect. She could not wish for a better day to ride through the woods that surrounded the estate. Occasionally they caught a glimpse of a deer darting through the trees, or a kingfisher near a stream. They sang as they rode, old songs, rounds, and when they were tired of that Padar entertained Ulf with his mermaid stories.

Padar left Elditha's train on the road that led north to London. He said that he had heard that Earl Tostig was sailing ships towards England from Flanders. He would convey her Pentecost greetings to the King, and visit his own friends in London.

'Tell the King that I have not heard of our older boys since February. Thank him for our Easter gifts.' Despite her best intentions not to, she said, 'And say to him that Ulf needs to see his father. As for me, I am well, as you can see, and after the Reredfelle harvest is in I shall visit my Norfolk estates. I am neglecting them. We shall pass the winter there, where I was born and bred.'

Padar reached over and lightly touched her arm. 'He will come to see you both, my lady. It has all been more difficult than he ever thought it could be.'

She shrugged. She was busy and would remain so. Padar kicked his horse's flanks and galloped off, his long pigtail flying and his red summer cloak caught by the wind he'd created, his small frame lifted momentarily off the animal's back. She glanced back at him. He raised his arm in a backwards wave and was gone. She wiped a tear away with her gloved hand and moved her mare forward. Ulf refused to sit before Osgod, who lifted him onto his own saddle and, managing Elf, his pony, well, he trotted behind his mother.

As they entered through the gates of the town, Brother Francis left her retinue too. When they parted at the monastery of St Augustine, the monk remarked that he had news for the Archbishop.

'I have much to report on Egbert,' he said in a supercilious tone, his face long and lean with the sharp eyes of a rat.

'That is not advisable,' said Elditha. 'Not if you want to remain with us. Besides, there is nothing to report.'

'He is married.'

'That is not as yet forbidden for priests.'

'We shall see what is now forbidden,' retorted Brother Francis, as he turned his nag into the monastery courtyard.

She nudged Eglantine's flanks harder than she normally would and turned the mare towards her own properties.

Elditha owned two large, double-storied houses enclosed by fencing in Canterbury. A higgledy scattering of huts and workshops devoted to dyeing and weaving occupied the yard of the most spacious of her houses. She rode past them into the paved courtyard, stopped in front of the great weaving shed and jumped off Eglantine, as if the long journey had been nothing to her. After handing Ulf's reins to a waiting stable boy, she lifted her son down from his pony. Towards the end of the journey he had been falling over Elf's mane, clutching it to steady himself, insisting that he could still ride. Now, on firm ground again, he clung to her mantle.

The servants fell to their knees before Elditha. She thanked them for their care of her house and bade them rise and go about their work. After a few words with the hall steward, she prised Ulf away from her cloak. 'Take him inside,' she said to Margaret, who had clambered out of a covered cart. 'Bathe him and then have servants make ready a bathtub for me as well. First, though, I must visit my weaving sheds and examine my cloth.' Her three ladies, who had climbed down after Margaret, nodded their enthusiasm. It had been months since they had looked at bolts of newly woven wool. She smiled at their longing for new clothes.

She hurried into the barn-like room, followed by her women, and spoke with the weavers. She examined their looms carefully, watching as they pedalled and wound fabric onto the rollers in front of them. Then she selected the finest cloth to be transformed into plain shifts for herself and her ladies. The weaver promised that the garments would be made up by a seamstress before they departed from Canterbury. Elditha made a final search among the bolts of linen, turning them over and looking closely for something special. She held samples up to the rays of summer light that shone through the windows. She had servants carry bolts of cloth out into the yard so that she could examine them more carefully. At last, she discovered a cloth the colour of emeralds.

'Like grass glistening after summer rain.'

'Best green in years. This came out of the vat bright like jewels, my lady.'

'Send me the seamstress. I shall have a new gown.'

'My lady, it will be done.' Smiling, the weaver bowed low.

As evening dropped Elditha soaked in a herb-strewn bath, concealed behind hanging sheets. She trailed her hand over her belly, allowing the water to fall through her fingers. Her skin was white and smooth, despite many years of childbearing. Her breasts were small, high and firm. She was still narrow-hipped and flat-bellied. Children had slipped from them with ease. Her hair fell onto the water, rippling and flaxen. Though she was now past 30 years old, there was no sign of grey in it yet.

She lay back, closed her eyes for a few moments, remembering how, as an Anglo-Danish heiress of only 14 summers, she had been given to Harold, Earl of Anglia – how willingly she had pledged herself to Godwin's second son and allowed the ribbons to be tied about their hands, joining his to hers, his heart to her own. Their marriage feast had glittered with jewels and gleamed with the gold- and silver-embroidered cloth worn by the Earl's brothers and his sisters and his friends. Harold Godwin had already been a great warrior. She had been proud to become his wife, and even prouder when he had fallen in love with her.

She conceived their children easily – one after the other, all strong and healthy; all excepting Emma, who seven years before had taken ill with an incurable disease. Elditha and Harold had buried this golden, happy child in the church at Bosham. Elditha retained such unhappy memories of Bosham that after her daughter's death she had never wanted to live there again. Within a year, they had conceived again. Ulf slid from his mother as easily as a snake sheds its skin and soon, though she loved them all, this youngest boy had become the most precious of her brood.

The scoop of soap that was balanced on the board across the tub plopped onto her belly. Its musky scent was the one she enjoyed in particular. She stretched her arms over the side and reflected sadly that what had happened to their marriage was more powerful than she.

Yet here in Canterbury she was a queen. Her every need was tended to but, still, she was incomplete without his love. She pushed this thought to the back of her mind and listened drowsily to her ladies laughing and talking in the room beyond the sheets. She called for Ursula to come and soap her back, and for Freya to wash her hair, and told them both to rinse it with water steeped with flowers of chamomile. It would brighten it. Afterwards her ladies took it in turns to comb out her hair, dry it with linen towels and plait it so that by morning her loosened tresses would fall around her once again in rippling waves.

That night Elditha lay in the upper room with Ulf by her

side. It was pleasant to be back in Canterbury. Perhaps they should stay on here through the summer. Then she thought of all there was to do back on the estate before they set off for Norfolk in November. It must not become neglected. She would return to Reredfelle by summer again and make sure it continued to prosper. Meanwhile, Guthlac would see that the villagers planted the fields and tended the orchards.

Somewhere among the pear trees in the garden an owl hooted. The bells for Compline tolled from St Augustine's. Then suddenly there came a loud knocking on the outside door. All at once she was wide awake, sitting up. Then, the shuffling of the porter as he hurried into the porch. He was calling out, 'I'm coming, coming.' Grumbles of, 'Let us sleep.' The front door was dragged open. She lay back against her pillow. If it was a messenger they would speak in the morning. A little talking below, a hound's bark and gradually the night eased back into quiet. She drifted into sleep curled protectively around her boy.

Shortly after dawn, when she had climbed down into the hall to break her fast, she discovered the cause of the midnight disturbance.

'Earl Tostig is raiding along the coast,' the king's man announced. 'The King is raising a fleet and he is on his way to meet it. He will lodge here tonight and ride on to Bosham tomorrow.'

'He knows that I am here?'

'He is concerned for your safety, noble lady. The royal estate of Reredfelle is less than a day's ride from the sea. Earl Tostig is on the island of Wight with a fleet. He is harrying villages. He takes what he can thieve to feed his soldiers.'

'How does the King know I am here?' Of course, Padar, she realised after she had said it.

'We met the skald on the Great Road. King Harold is calling up the fyrd from Kent to join him to send Tostig back to whence he came, be it Normandy or Flanders. The King has already sent his fleet south.'

'It is Pentecost tomorrow. Everyone will be with families.'

'The King must ride on, no matter what day tomorrow is,' the messenger said.

By mid-morning the messenger had galloped out of the gate and was on his way to rejoin the King. How quickly everything changed. Ulf would see his father and his father would see his son. As for her, well, that remained to be seen. What would they say to each other now?

Elditha gave orders for her house to be cleansed and for a feast to be prepared. She threw on her mantle ready to accompany her ladies to the Whitsun market always held on a field near to St Augustine. For days, since she had told them they were going to Canterbury, they had talked about nothing else but this great market.

Just before they climbed onto their horses and prepared to ride through the town, she noted how the preparations for the King's visit were already underway in her hall. There were baskets of strewing herbs waiting by the porch door. The cook had purchased fish from the monks in a nearby monastery which had already arrived. Hens squawked in their runs as kitchen women pursued them, caught the birds and wrung their necks on the spot. Elditha turned her head away, and gathering her reins in her hands, rode out of the gate with her bridle bells jingling and her retinue following behind her.

As she rode through the narrow streets she reflected on the omen that had caused them all such anxiety. Had the star foreshadowed Tostig's attack on their coasts? If so, Duke William would follow. After all, Tostig was married to Judith of Flanders, the Duke's own sister-in-law. 'St Cecilia,' she whispered, 'stop them. He never promised England to Duke William.' She flicked Eglantine's reins. The Godwins had seen enemies off before and would do so again, even if the enemy turned out to be one of their own.

The market became a pleasing distraction. They dismounted. The guard strode on in front of Elditha and her three women, leading their horses. Townspeople pressed to the sides making room for them to pass through the narrow lanes. After a short while, they reached an open space where merchants with the most valuable goods had erected large circular tents. These were guarded by fierce-looking Norwegians wearing breastplates, helmets of steel with broad nose-guards and carrying huge swords with decorated hilts. The lesser merchants had set out their wares on trestles that looked like small ships with awnings, crude coverings against the possibility of rain, fashioned from heavy bleached sacking like sails.

Trays of bone and antler ornaments were set out close to strings of coloured stone and glass beads. Another stall had purses with ivory ornament. She picked one out and examined it closely. Surely this was elephant tusk ornamentation? It would make a pretty betrothal gift for Thea. She told Ursula to go and barter for it. The girl came back smiling with the purse. 'It is elephant tusk and I only paid him half of what he asked.'

The purse was made of soft linen cloth that was of a blue hue and gathered at the neck with silk threads. The treasure lay there. Its twisted silk tassels were ended with several delicately carved ornaments of ivory. 'You have done well, Ursula. Thea will be delighted. It is rare to find such unusual ornament.'

Although the hour was early, well before Nones, everywhere was busy. She pushed further into the market, her women following. Their guards were caught in the stream of people far behind them. Everywhere people spoke in foreign tongues. Merchants had travelled from distant lands to trade, and spoke in many languages, some of which Elditha recognised. She spoke French and had an understanding of Norse. Pie sellers walked the lanes with trays. Bakers called out that they had spice cakes and honey buns for sale. The light scent of perfumes distilled from flowers mingled with the heavy pungent smell of animal dung, reminding Elditha to warn her ladies to watch where they stepped.

At last, a twisting path brought her nearer to the goods they wanted most: needles and thread. There was little silk thread left in the seat of her velvet cushioned sewing chair and hardly any woollen threads for them to work into tapestry for her chapel's altar hanging. Her ladies constantly paused now, lifting up merchandise, seeking the price of ribbons or feeling the quality of silk. As she wound her way around the stalls, people glanced up, murmured and stared at her with curiosity. Others recognised her and whispered to each other. Elditha adjusted her veil to cover more of her face, held her head high and hurried past, until all of a sudden she was arrested by an unfamiliar voice calling her name.

'Lady Elditha!'

She looked around for the voice that had called. The accent was of Ireland. A warrior clad in an overshirt of mail, clearly of noble birth, stepped forward. His hand was resting by his seax and she looked back anxiously for her guard, but she could not see them at all through the press of people in the narrow lanes and her ladies were engrossed in searching through a selection of glass beads laid out on the next trestle.

'Who are you?' she demanded of the stranger, fixing him with a furious stare.

The rogue bowed. 'Connor, Earl of Meath. I had care of your three sons when they sailed from London to the King in Dublin. I have seen you at King Edward's court and I never forget a remarkable face.'

'Earl Connor of Meath, if you wish to speak to me, seek a proper introduction. Do not accost me here among the people of Canterbury at their Whitsun Fair.'

She called out to her ladies. Seeing the intruder they hurried to her, closing about her protectively, stretching their cloaks outwards like colourful wings. Her guards, bobbing through the crowd, were dragging Eglantine and the three other horses with them. At last they saw the trembling ladies with outstretched arms, left the horses by a stall and pushed through a band of ragged children towards the stranger.

Raising her arm, she turned her disapproval on the guards who were now accosting the earl, prodding him with their daggers and cursing him. 'Leave him alone. He claims that he is an earl. I need you by me, not watching the womenfolk over there.' She threw a purse of coin at one of her men. 'Pay this woman what she wants for my ladies' purchases and have the threads and ribbons sent to my house.' The Earl of Meath watched her performance with a surprised look of admiration on his face. Then he bowed and moved away.

Surrounded by her women and her guards, one of whom followed closely behind them holding Eglantine's reins, Elditha hurried away from the glass beads and leather pouches, and to the grander pavilions where they would find expensive threads of gold and silver. Her eyes burrowed through the crowds, searching and thinking if only she had asked the rude warrior about her sons. She kept peering through the lanes for him again but he had vanished.

Harold did not come for the Whitsun Feast. She asked her steward if the messenger had returned with news of him.

He shook his head. 'The King must still be recruiting support in the north of the county, my lady.'

'Have the cooks prepare a smaller feast today. We may have company tomorrow.'

She threw herself into supervising the preparations in her hall, but although she concealed her feelings carefully, her ladies sensed her anxiety and trod softly, not wishing to disturb her. She consoled herself with the thought that he would arrive after Pentecost.

On Pentecost Sunday she attended three services at St Augustine. This church was fat with relics – sealed treasure boxes with saints' knucklebones and splinters of holy wood and it was filled with wall images of saints, Madonnas, infant saviours and many devils. While its walls and pillars were splashed with colour, darkness gathered in drifts in the many side chapels and there was everywhere the constant press of people. Still, Archbishop Stigand did not call on her, nor had he invited her into his presence, even though she had sent him a Pentecost gift of fine cloth from her looms.

The following day Harold arrived in Canterbury preceded by silken embroidered banners and followed by an army of warriors, and when he rode through the North Gate he sat proudly on a stallion as the crowds cheered him. Looking down from a window set high into the gable of her hall, Elditha and her women watched the procession pass and, seeing him looking so regal, her spirits soared.

Leofwine, the Earl of Kent, rode by his side and Gyrth, the youngest of Harold's brothers, trotted on a grey horse close behind. Harold wore a gold circlet and his armour shone in the sunlight. He paused and raised his hand, causing his followers to rein back their horses, bent down and spoke to a small boy who leaned on a crutch and waved a hollyhock. The crippled child handed the flower up to the King, who immediately produced a purse and gave it to the woman standing with the child. The woman kissed his hand with gratitude. Elditha found herself softening.

Padar rode behind the royal party. In the few days since Elditha had seen him, the skald had undergone his own transformation. He was now wearing a mail breastplate which gleamed beneath his cloak and he was seated on top of a handsome black gelding. Then her eyes followed Padar to the front of the second column where a stocky fighter with tow-coloured hair rode with Harold's house-ceorls on a pale-coloured, high-stepping Arab horse. She gripped Ulf's hand so hard that he squeaked and turned to her ladies. 'That rude Irishman is riding a horse that surpasses my husband's stallion.'

The three ladies smiled and clucked together, 'But the King looks so majestic.'

Accompanied by Archbishop Stigand, Harold came to Elditha as the evening shadows began to fall. He embraced her at the entrance to her hall. She knelt and ceremoniously bathed his feet as was the custom, while Lady Ursula, as her favourite lady, attended to the Archbishop. Now she saw what she had not recognised that afternoon. Harold had aged in the months since she had been at Reredfelle. His drooping moustaches were greyer than at Christmastide and there were fresh lines carved deep into his face.

'Elditha,' he said and reached towards her veil. Then he dropped his hand and he was the king again, aloof and

83

untouchable. The moment had passed. They proceeded into the hall where trestles were laid with fine cloth and silver bowls.

Elditha had made sure that supper would be plentiful. On the religious day before, they had only eaten fish and pies filled with meal and herbs, but today meat was permitted. The appetising smell of roasting flesh, herbs and onions had been drifting out of Elditha's cookhouse all day long, since Harold's entry into Canterbury.

For an old man, the Archbishop stood steadily. He slowly traced the cross in the air with an aged paw and then blessed the food and wine. Servants buzzed around like busy summer bees. Her army of cooks anxiously sent forward the many dishes they had prepared. Course followed course, doves and pigeon, pottage of beef brawn, suckling pork, meat pies and beef, as well as dishes of new peas and carrots from the garden. Although wine was plentiful, Elditha held on to her cup, determined not to have it refilled. Harold addressed his conversation both to the Archbishop on one side and Elditha on the other. The talk was of war. Now that he had raised his fleet, England could stop any invasion from across the Channel.

He smiled his reassurance at Elditha. 'The rebels will have flown by summer's end like swallows, though unlike swallows they will never return.'

She wondered if the unspoken closeness of before – the ease they once felt in each other's company – was now absent. Children who had meant so much to her were no longer in either of their households and as yet Harold had not asked after his youngest son who *was* in her household, though Ulf, of course, had asked to see his father. 'He will come to you in the morning,' she promised Ulf before Margaret hurried her charge off to sleep in his own chamber, rather than beside his mother. Even if she had to waken the boy, Harold would see his son.

Harold's brothers lodged in the town. They arrived to the feast late and departed early, saying that they needed to rest with their men. As Leofwine kissed Archbishop Stigand's jewelled hand he promised, 'Our soldiers will not behave badly in Canterbury, nor will they drink to excess, destroy property or attack the townspeople. Gyrth and I will go now and see to it ourselves.'

After he spoke to Archbishop Stigand, Leofwine raised Elditha from her chair, held her in a close embrace and asked how all went with her. She smiled up at him and said, with as much neutrality in her voice as she could manage, 'Indeed, I am well, cousin. The estate thrives, as have done all my other properties. Come soon and see for yourself.'

'Dear sorceress, nothing would please me more.' He turned to Harold. 'Do you stay, brother?'

'I shall rest in Elditha's hall tonight. We have much to discuss.'

'Brother, there is no lovelier woman in Heaven and Earth than this woman; no more beautiful children than yours and hers.' Without waiting for his brother's response he gathered his men and swept from the hall, Gyrth following in his wake.

Elditha felt heartened by this open support for her cause. She would always love Leofwine. When she called for another horn of wine, she was smiling.

Later, after a course of sweet pastries served with custard, the Archbishop laid down his spoon and coughed politely. 'My lord king, I must speak to you, about a matter that has come to my attention. I would speak of it in private. And since it concerns the Lady Elditha, she should hear it too.'

Harold's brow creased with puzzlement. 'Then perhaps we can speak in my lady's antechamber.'

Elditha called Ursula to her. 'Fetch me a jug of hippocras and my crystal palm glasses.' If this talk was connected to Brother Francis, she must defend her villagers.

They climbed the staircase to Elditha's private chamber. The Archbishop stood by the window while Ursula filled his crystal cup. He held the precious glass up to the candle glow, turning it so that its honeyed contents were transformed by moonlight into a pool of liquid gold.

'From Byzantium, a wedding gift from Godiva of Mercia,' Elditha said with emphasis on the word "wedding". It was obvious from the way he held his cup, sipped, opened his mouth to speak and closed it again, that the Archbishop had something difficult to broach. Elditha waited.

'Speak,' Harold said.

He wiped a crumb from his mouth. 'A matter at Reredfelle has come to my ears. I have heard disturbing stories from Brother Francis.' So that was it, and he still had not thanked her for her gift of pale linen to the monastery.

The King said, 'And, your grace?'

The Archbishop turned to Elditha. 'Lady Elditha,' he began, 'how do you find Brother Francis? I understand that the King's son progresses well under his tutorage?'

'Brother Francis has worked hard. He devotes himself to prayer and to the care of our son and the Lady Chapel – and to the precious and holy relic, of course.'

'The cotters, how do they progress under his care?'

'The villagers have their own monk-priest.'

'Perhaps this priest, Father …?'

'Egbert.'

'… is behind the times, my lady.'

'How do you mean, Stigand?' Harold interrupted.

'Perhaps, my lord king, it confuses the people of Reredfelle to have two priests. Father Egbert could be moved to Canterbury, where he can receive instruction and learn the humility befitting his calling.'

'Or we can introduce him to my College at Waltham.'

Elditha clutched her cup. 'Father Egbert has a wife and children and the villagers respect him. He knows the scriptures well; he can read and write and he recites by heart many stories from the Old Testament.' She turned from Archbishop Stigand to Harold. 'I wish to keep him with us.'

'Then you shall do so,' Harold said gently. He stroked his moustaches. 'But we must persuade him to visit Waltham after the harvest is in.' He plucked a small strawberry from a fruit dish and nibbled it. 'These have ripened early, my dear. They are delicious.' He turned to Stigand. 'Now, my lord archbishop, permit me to walk you down to the hall.'

Archbishop Stigand was dismissed before he could extend his cup to Ursula for refilling.

'Ursula,' Elditha said with a mischievous smile, when Harold had gone. 'The loving cup?' Ursula nodded and crumbled a herbal mixture from her belt pouch into the jug. 'Godspeed, my lady. May heaven's angels lie with you both tonight.'

'I hope for human comfort, not angels.'

Her ladies turned down the bed in her chamber and dressed Elditha in a robe of embroidered linen so fine it was translucent. They placed a mantle of silk around her, the same sea-coloured silk which had been her Easter gift from the King. Ursula unbound her hair and allowed it to tumble over her shoulders. Elditha could smell her own scent mingling with her perfumes of chamomile and musk.

When Harold returned to the chamber, he drew her to him, buried his head in her hair and whispered into her ear the words, 'Elditha, how I have missed you. We parted badly. It has made me so sorrowful to hurt you in this way.' He held her away from him. 'But, first, take me to my son. I want to see him sleeping.' It was what she had hoped to hear.

Ulf never stirred as his father looked down on his face. It was serene, like that of a seraph.

'Ulf may, one day, become a churchman.'

'Not like Brother Francis and never like Archbishop Stigand,' she said.

'Neither of them!' He lifted Elditha's hand and folded it into his own. 'I will wake him in the morning. Come, my love, it has been too long.' He added softly, 'And I miss the sound of your breathing when you are sleeping next to me.'

She handed him the loving cup and they sipped the herb-sprinkled wine. That night they lay together as husband and wife, though his passion told her that the love potion had been unnecessary.

'How I wish we were back at Nazeing,' she said, when sated and rested they awoke to the sound of church bells ringing.

'I wish it too,' he said. 'But, Elditha, our wyrd has not

87

intended it so.' He cupped her chin and traced the curve of her cheek. 'Fate decreed that I had to marry her, but, my beautiful swan, remember that whatever happens I love you and our children, all of them.'

'I do know it,' she whispered back. He had hurt her deeply and, though she might forgive it, she could not forget. As she stroked his long hair and dozed in the familiar safety of his arms, she thought, but for how long will you stay?

8

Summer 1066

And when his fleet was gathered, Harold went to Wight and lay there all summer and a land army was kept everywhere by the sea, although in the end it was to no avail. Then when it was the Nativity of St Mary, the men's provisions were gone, and no one could hold them there any longer.

The Anglo-Saxon Chronicles, July 1066, Worcester Manuscript, edited and translated by Michael Swanton

Harold rode into Reredfelle from the south coast and they came together again as husband and wife. If it felt as if Christmas had not happened, it also felt as if this was like all the other reunions they had had before when Harold had been on campaign. It was as it had been after that dark year when he was in Normandy trying to free his nephew and brother. Ulf scurried about the estate, happy to be with his father. Harold took him riding in the deer hay and taught him to get Elf to jump. The three of them ate in the wood in the open air from baskets of food, breads, honey cakes, pies and fruit preserved in mead. Her ladies clucked and wove daisy chains but always gathered away from the little family.

One evening Harold gave Ulf a rare chess set of carved ivory figures and taught him how to play. Ulf loved the expressions on their faces and was quick to learn their moves. Elditha stitched as she watched them play. Ulf's face was stern with concentration. 'This is Duke William and this is me,' Harold said pushing the kings across the wooden chequered board.

Ulf lifted a queen. 'And this is my mother,' he said. 'She will win the game.'

Elditha glanced up from her embroidery. She did as she usually did when there was nothing more to say. She raised her very mobile eyebrow.

'Indeed, she will.' Harold smiled at her as he said it.

Harold promised that on his return to London he would have documents drawn up making Reredfelle Elditha's own property. He was impressed by her rescue of the decaying estate. In July he returned with copies of these and stayed for several weeks, riding out to the coast to supervise his fleet. Earl Tostig had occupied the Isle of Wight.

A week later, Harold's messenger rode in. 'There is no sign of them,' he said. 'They are dislodged. Earl Leofwine says to tell you that Tostig may have a plan. His ships are sailing north.'

'Tell Leofwine to pursue our treacherous brother. He must not raid the eastern coast, either.'

'Earl Leofwine has already set sail.'

'Good,' Harold said. 'Go and find food in the hall, man. You look exhausted.'

'Hopefully, then, that is an end to it. He could not land around Bosham so off he goes and good riddance,' Harold said to Elditha after the messenger was gone, but there was tension in his shoulders as he spoke.

She said that she had oils that might relieve this and sought them out from a cupboard in their bedchamber. Massaging his aching limbs with sandalwood oil, she thought sadly, he will return to Westminster soon, and to that woman. Aloud she said softly, 'Harold, I hope that we can retrieve what we had together before last Christmastide, for our children's sake and for us …'

'Elditha, it will not always be so.' He turned over and grasped her hand and, pulling himself up, kissed her.

'You have wed with her and you have bedded her. Her children must not be raised above our own boys.'

He gathered her into his arms. 'I swore to you once that Godwin will be king after I die. I meant it then and I still mean it. He will return from Ireland a prince and a warrior fit to inherit this land. That will not change.' Harold lay back and watched her pour a little oil into the palm of her hand. When she turned back to him his arms were folded behind his head. 'Elditha, England may be attacked at any time. I still need them, Morcar and Edwin.'

She said, 'Bring our boys home.'

'Elditha, we are beset by enemies. Harald Finehair watches England with greed in his eyes. William watches for his best chance to invade us. Tostig will look to both for opportunity. Our boys must remain in Ireland until danger is past.'

'And I, Harold, have now but one child left to me.' She paused.

'And?' he said.

'And I am not too old to conceive again.' With her finger she traced a birthmark shaped like a swan's feather, which lay where his right thigh joined his groin. Her finger dropped to a dragon tattoo that circled the thigh below the birthmark. She kissed the swan's feather. This birthmark was hers, she'd said, after she had discovered it. She, he had said, was his swan.

'A last child would make me happy.'

'Then, let us hope.' He turned to kiss her, gently parting her hair and finding her mouth. She felt the old, old desire rise again, and she knew that she would always love him with a great passion.

That night it was as if the world beyond Earl Godwin's chamber had forgotten them. Afterwards they whispered words of love until morning filtered in through the window glass and captured them in its sea-green glow.

After prime, a few days later, she watched from the palisade as Harold and his house-ceorls rode away to the Godwin estate at Bosham. A young warrior carried his standard, a fighting man outlined on a green-and-jewelled background which went flying before them, the replica of which now hung in her hall beside her own swan.

A week later, Padar rode into Reredfelle, not on the handsome mount he had used in Canterbury but on his usual horse, the smaller, friendlier Otter. She greeted him in the yard as stable boys rushed to take charge of the sweating beast.

'You have returned to us at last, Padar?'

'For a few nights; I bring news, both good and bad.'

He handed her a small roll of parchment. She turned it over. The seal tag was Harold's but the letter came from Leofwine. She cut the letter open with her belt knife and slowly read its content.

'Tostig has not returned south. The King has disbanded the fleet and has allowed his men to return to their families to help with the harvest.' She glanced up. 'Is this wise?'

Padar said calmly, 'We need the harvest, but, my lady, I have heard from our merchants that the Duke of Normandy is building an invasion fleet. He is making alliances with Boulogne and with Brittany. He has sent a mission to Rome requesting the Pope's support for an invasion. It will take time and it may not be this year. After the harvest is in, the King will recall the fyrd.'

The scare died down. There was no evidence that William was about to sail a great fleet across the Narrow Sea. Elditha was busy making mead, supervising the churning of cream into butter. Hours flew by in her bower hall where the women passed their afternoons embroidering golden borders on their new linen shifts.

On Lammas Day, Brother Francis led a limping Ulf up the stairs and into her antechamber. 'I found him lying on the ground by the bee skeps. He should have been at study,' the monk said crossly. 'He climbed the tree above the skeps. Look at the stings!'

She peered at Ulf's leg. He whimpered when she touched him. 'Ulf, I can make it better. It will take only a moment.' She leaned down and kissed her child's soft head. These swellings needed more than lavender oil. She turned to the monk. 'Stay with him.' She hurried into her bedchamber, reached into a basket in her cupboard where she kept salves and medicines. In it she found a mandrake tuber she had placed in a linen bag. She had purchased all these medicinal herbs and healing salves in Canterbury. She opened the cloth and stared at the root. It looked like nothing, a wizened apple. The wise woman who had sold it had told her to use it sparingly and with good will. 'Rare, it is, my lady. Keep it with you for it owns you as much as you own it,' she had warned. 'The root has travelled here from Jerusalem, from the lands of our Lord.' Elditha understood its power. She would rarely awaken it. She scraped a little into a balm. If she used it with a prayer chant, she knew she could heal Ulf's stings before they caused him a fever. Yes, mandrake could be used for good or evil but she was using its power for good.

She returned to Ulf and began to gently prise out the stings with a needle. As she removed them one by one, she whispered the chant.

'Ouch,' Ulf yelped.

'It will soothe. Look, Ulf, the stings are out.' She pointed to her needle but even Ulf, with his sharp sight, said he could not see the stings his mother had just removed.

Brother Francis looked on, growling his disapproval. 'What are you saying? Are you praying?'

She ignored him. Ulf was settling. 'I believe so,' she said carefully, as she rubbed the oil of lavender with a scraping of the mandrake root into the swellings on Ulf's hands and legs.

'Will that ointment help? I could bleed him.' He whipped out a scrap of parchment from his small Gospel Book and scanned it. She peered over his shoulder, at a figure of a man with pins protruding from every section of his body. She shuddered. 'Not for your eyes, my lady.' He glanced angrily at her but she had already seen a maze of symbols, including astrological signs.

'His birth sign is the fish, I believe. I can bleed him from the ankle today,' the monk said folding the paper back into his Gospel.

'No, you will do no such thing. That would weaken him.'

'What is this?' the priest demanded, lifting the root from the bench between his long finger and his thumb. He dropped it again as if it were poison. 'Mandrake root! Is this what you mixed with that oil? It is forbidden by the Church, my lady. You must rid yourself of its evil influence. It is the Devil's root.'

'Mandrake is only used here for salves like this one.' She showed him the clay pot. The innocent whiff of lavender filled the air.

He frowned. 'I fear for your soul and for the child's. This is the Devil's doing.'

She shook her head and placed a wax seal on the lavender salve again and pushed the root back into its linen bag. She would keep it safe under her mattress where it could not be found. 'Ulf, go and play with your friends and keep out of mischief.' She patted his back and pushed him towards the door. The monk spoke again as she wiped the table with a dampened rag, saying he had business in a remote abbey on the Romney marshes. He would be gone for only a few days.

She looked suspiciously at Brother Francis. 'So when will you return, Brother Francis, and what is this business?'

'The monks from Féchamps have a prayer book for the Lady Chapel. I go to fetch it.'

'I see,' said Elditha. 'As long as that is all; then we expect you back before the month is out.'

The monk inclined his head and said smoothly, 'Indeed.' But as he turned to leave she was sure she heard him mutter the dreaded word "witch". It hovered in the air like a malevolent odour long after Brother Francis had left her chamber.

After the Lammas feast day everyone who was able-bodied helped to gather in the harvest. Padar departed, then came home to Reredfelle again a week later with news of Thea and Gytha. This time he carried a correspondence for her: two scrolls. She took them to read in the privacy of her chamber. There she sank back into the soft cushions in her sewing chair. She set aside Harold's letter and examined the other. It came from the Earl of Meath. She leaned forward, flattened the small scroll on her knees and scanned its contents. She read that Earl Connor thought that she might wish to hear news of her sons. The three princes had improved their skills with shield and sword. They rode stallions with ease and they were popular at court. They sent their greetings to their lady mother and to their father, the King. Elditha read it over and over. She laid it down on the small table beside her chair.

Harold's message was a roll of parchment tied with gold thread and his seal. She broke the seal, untied the thread, unrolled it and flattened it out with her palm. It must have news. She clapped her hand to her mouth at what she read. Harold could not come before September. Instead he reported that Aldgyth was with child, saying that he would rather Elditha had this news from him than from others. He wrote that he did not intend to disinherit their sons. Her hand flew to her belly. She had not herself conceived as she had hoped.

She clattered down the staircase and stamped out of the back door to the kitchens. Furiously, she seized a bowl of cherries and snatched a jar from the shelf. Using a spoon abandoned by one of the cook's servants she packed fruit into jars. No one spoke to her. They quietly went about their own tasks. Later Padar tiptoed in, looking for her.

'My lady, may I have a word?'

'The Irish court is full of barbarians and the sons of Thor,' she said angrily. 'My sons will not learn the skills of courtiers there.' She emptied a dish of gooseberries into a sticky liquid of wine and honey.

'My lady, they must be kept safe.'

'Harold has sent our boys into that barbarous land so that they are out of his way.'

'No, he has sent your sons to be taught the skills princes must have. Many scholars attend the King of the Irish. You lived there for a summer once, yourself. The King wants to keep the boys safe. These are difficult times.'

'She is pregnant and I am not.'

'But he loves you, my lady; that is what matters.'

'He is gone. Is he with her?'

'Lady Aldgyth is in Chester with her mother.'

'Where is he?'

'This is what I have come to tell you. The King is marching north; Earl Tostig has been in Norway.'

'What do you mean, Padar?'

'Harald Finehair has sent a fleet into the Northern Sea.'

'But Tostig has recognised that the King's army is more powerful than he. That must be an end to it.' She dropped her spoon. 'Oh, he can't. Oh no, not Tostig and Harald Harthrada!'

'Yes, Tostig seeks allies.'

'What will happen if …?'

'If the Finehair attempts invasion the King will win the battle.'

She called for the kitchen serfs to finish her tasks. England would soon be at war, but Harold had been born into a family of warriors. She had seen him win victories in Wales. He would call out the fyrd again, and she must make sure the harvest was pulled in before all her menfolk left her for the north. She must talk to Edwin.

A few days later, Harold called out the men of Sussex and Kent. Osgod came to her. 'I must follow the King, my lady.'

'Go then, and God go with you, Osgod,' she said. 'God go with the King, my love,' she murmured under her breath.

Osgod began a trickle that became a stream. Soon she was left with a small garrison, her villagers and the last of the harvest to get in.

Brother Francis returned with the Psalter, but after his return he made short visits about the countryside, claiming that he wished to visit shrines to pray for the King's victory. No one noticed or even cared about his absence except Ulf, who trailed after his mother around the estate. Elditha sent him to Padar until Padar too rode away.

Elditha carried on as before, spinning, preserving fruit and directing her people herself as they worked hard in the fields. In the late afternoons, she embroidered the hem of a new cloak. She worked slowly and carefully, creating a border of chains and tendrils of leaves, making the small depressions in the centre of flowers particular to English embroidery. Into these she stitched seed pearls. It gave her pleasure to lose herself in the final touches to this mantle, the borders where she imagined a future as rich as her embroidery. She prepared for the coming winter, seeking out distraction, hoping and praying that catastrophe would be avoided.

9

Then Earl William came from Normandy into Pevensey, on the
eve of the feast of St Michael, and as soon as they were fit,
made a castle at Hastings market town.
The Anglo-Saxon Chronicles, 28 September 1066, Worcester
Manuscript, edited and translated by Michael Swanton

September days held fast on to harvest sunshine as the villagers
safely brought in the last of the grain. Elditha and her ladies
worked in the fields too. Then news of another threat, not
entirely unexpected, seeped into her hall. The Normans were
gathering on their coast and everyone knew that soon they
would cross the Narrow Sea. She persuaded herself that
Reredfelle was safe, on the way to nowhere, hidden, surrounded
by woods and drovers' tracks. Just to be sure, however, she put
guards on her gates and warned her villagers to make new bows
and practise with them in the deer hay. But those men who were
left to her were either old or very young boys and only a few of
them joined her remaining house-ceorls for evening target
practice.

Today was Sunday. Not all Sundays were set aside as rest
days and they often forgot the day unless Brother Francis
reminded them. Although everyone else would be in the great
field, today she insisted that her ladies must rest. Slowly waking
late, she opened her eyes, propped herself up against pillows
and still in a state of half-sleep she lay on, only partly hearing
sounds of activity in the hall below. She watched the light seep
through the glass windows. Its quality varied depending on the
weather and this morning a great pool of green light filtered
through them. She glanced away and upwards, but the
crossbeams along the roof felt too close, as if they were

pressing her concerns down on her. She was wide awake. There was something she ought to do, something half-forgotten and now remembered, an irritant that was entangled in her memory. She tossed the covers off, knelt on top of her high mattress, craned her neck, and looked up into the rafters, straining to see her casket of bone and silver – the box that she had hidden months before behind her shoes, and which until a moment ago she had forgotten. She pulled her shoes and boots down and tossed all five pairs in a heap beside her clothing coffer. Peering up deep into the roof space again she could hardly see the box. As time had passed she had pushed it back until she could only glimpse the edge of it. Standing on tiptoe, she reached up into the space, caught the casket with her fingers, edged it carefully along the beam and pulled it down.

Sinking down onto the bed again, she leaned back against her pillows and for a moment stroked her thick golden plait. These were precious possessions. There was, of course, Harold's Christmas gift of sapphires but the other things it contained had sentimental value. She opened the lid to look at and smell again the tiny christening robe embroidered with gold thread and recalled its heritage – all the children for whom it had been used. God willing, perhaps there could still be another child. The sapphires nestled in their soft purse and her little figurines of St Cecilia and St Brigit, the Lady Mary and St Margaret gleamed in the soft light. She lovingly lifted them out one by one and fingered their delicate and smooth contours. Then she slipped her hand under the mattress and removed the mandrake root, and placed it inside the box. Carefully, she laid the fragile garment back into the casket and closed its lid. Now she needed to climb into the roof and hide it properly.

She dragged her bolster into position below the beam and stood on it. This time she leaned her arms on the broad rafter, slowly levered herself up and threw her legs over it. She sat on it, her legs dangling, and shuffled along clutching the box. The roof was dirty and damp and smelled of rotting thatch. She held her breath as she ducked under another crossbeam, her face brushing against cobwebs, felt deep into the corner, and pushed her treasure into the stench. She clung to the beam again, swung back over and dropped her legs back down and fell back into the bed – just in time, for as she did, the tapestry shifted. Panting, she swept cobwebs from her hair, gathered her pillows and pushed the bolster back behind her, lay against it and pulled the embroidered coverlet up to her chin.

It was only Ulf. He ran across the floor and leapt onto her bed, pulling a pillow away and, as he tugged, a flurry of feathers escaped. Immediately, he blew at them until they floated up in a miniature storm.

'Catch them, Ulf. They are much too precious to lose. You mischief, I should make you sew them back in.'

Ulf laughed and cupped his hands. He caught some of them as they floated down and gave them to her. 'Mama, *you* can sew them back in now.'

'Away with you off to chapel,' she said, stuffing the tiny feathers back into the rent. 'There, just a stitch.' She ruffled his hair. 'Brother Francis will be waiting.'

'Padar's back, Mama. He wants to speak with you.'

'Oh, is he? He will have news. Quick, go and tell him to come up and I'll see him next door. Then, tell Ursula that I shall come below to break my fast.'

Ulf obediently dropped from the bed and padded across the wooden floor to slide back out through the curtain. She heard him open the door at the top of the staircase and the thud as he closed it.

Elditha lifted the heavy lid of her clothes chest and dug her arms deep into it, scattering linen and woollen garments onto the floor, ransacking the coffer until she drew out a gown of green linen with tight sleeves. She slid her hand along the fine fabric. It would be another warm day and for now the linen felt cool against her skin. He must come south again soon. She hastily bound her hair under her veil, fixed her fillet in place, and finally, sliding a gold ring onto her middle finger, she stepped through the curtain into her great antechamber.

Padar was on the stairs shouting at servants. He knocked, but before she could answer he'd pushed past the guard and thrust himself unannounced into her presence. His red cloak was filthy, its dirty hood draped from his shoulders. His beard, usually so neatly trimmed, looked unkempt and he smelled of sweat and horse.

'They tried to make me wait until your women came. The King hurries south.'

She clasped her hands together. 'Please tell me that he has had a victory.'

'A great victory, but hard-earned; Harthrada and Tostig are dead. The Norsemen have sailed home to their fjords.'

'Give thanks to St Augustine.' She crossed herself. She tried not to wrinkle her nose as he stepped closer. 'Where have you been to smell so rankly of the ditch?'

'South, the coast by the old fort at Pevensey, concealed in a stinking river as Norman soldiers marched over me.'

'They have sailed already?'

'I rode through the night to bring you a warning.' She saw how his eyes looked strained. He caught his breath and continued, 'Norman soldiers are raiding our barns, burning our villages. They have ranged along the whole coast near Pevensey.'

'Exactly what have you seen, Padar?'

He pushed aside his cloak. His tunic was blood-stained, muddy and torn; his hands were covered with scratches. He held them open. 'Look at these. I've crawled into briars to avoid the Norman Bastard's scouts. I've slept in a pig pen at night.' He paused. 'I saw the soldiers come, steal a peasant's sow, all in the time it takes to saddle a horse and ...'

'What happened to the peasant?'

'They kicked in his door, wrecked his home, cut his throat and raped his wife.'

'And slaughtered her too?'

'Yes.'

He waited as Elditha crossed herself again. She said quietly, 'Continue.'

'Everywhere I went, I saw death and destruction following in their wake; villages burned and men slaughtered. They came

102

with great ships, piles of weapons, and thousands and thousands of men. I've watched their horses thunder over the land. I have learned that the Bastard's fighters have carried planks off the ships.'

'Planks – what for?'

'They are throwing up a motte-and-bailey near the market town of Hastings. My lady, take the boy and go to Canterbury.'

Outside a blackbird sang and she could hear a cart trundle across the yard. She went to the window and threw open the shutters. Below she saw two of her women chattering with the keeper of her hounds. The distant murmur of voices blew in from the fields. She turned back to Padar and shook her head. 'Padar, how can I? I have my ladies to think of and villagers to protect.'

He shook his head. 'The enemy will descend on us like wolves into a sheep pen.'

'The watch by the gate have seen nothing strange.'

'My lady, they are no good.'

It was true. Her best house-ceorls had gone to fight in the north for the King. She thought for a moment. She could not ride away leaving everyone to be slaughtered. 'Padar, can you ride again today?'

'With a fresh horse.'

'Then ride to Canterbury. Bring us a garrison.'

'My lady, if you will not leave, then you must set whomever you can spare on the palisade and keep a watch on them.'

'The women and children will come into the protection of my hall. Those who cannot must stay in the village church with Father Egbert tonight.' She left the window, crossed the room to him and took his hands in her own. 'May St Cecilia watch over you.'

'And you, my lady.'

He shook his head, pushed out, back through the heavy tapestry, and was gone.

She was left with the noise of the morning's usual activity: the rattling of plates, the calling servants, the slam of coffer lids, laundry maids shouting for dirty linen, the thud of logs and yard boys laughing as they stacked them beside the hearth.

Later that morning she climbed up onto the stockade and shaded her forehead with one hand. She gazed out at the deep blue sky, over trees that were turning to gold, over her villagers gathering fruit along the hedges and others who were helping in the big field. She wondered if, after all, she had been unduly concerned for their safety. After all, Reredfelle was not on the way to or from anywhere.

Below, in the field, Guthlac was directing villagers and ceorls to load the very last stokes of wheat from the harvest onto a cart. This year the barley had been late. The women and children were collecting dried stalks left behind, filling up huge reed baskets, nothing wasted. When she looked out to the west along the river and towards the mill, she could see a cart pulled by a donkey on the path. A villein sat on top of the sacks flicking at the creature with a stick. The miller was coming out to greet them. To the east a group of swineherds were collecting pigs into two pens on the edge of the woods. When she came to the top of the ladder, she turned and glanced back again towards the forest. Jet-black rooks rose up from the trees into the sky, careered for a moment above the canopy, set up a cawing, and then swooped down again. She shuddered and climbed onto the ladder to descend. She looked back and counted the guard: 12 men stood at intervals, armed with shields, bows and spears. It was not enough and she thought about her women and her son. For a moment Elditha closed her eyes and prayed to the Holy Mother, 'Dear Lady Mary, help us. Help us all to survive this. Guide us to safety.'

As Elditha walked towards the hall, she saw Brother Francis ambling with Ulf along the path from the chapel. She hurried to greet them. In the hall the trestles were laid for dinner. Not wanting to frighten her women she sat in Earl Godwin's oak chair under her swan pennant and, beside it, Harold's banner. As dinner passed everyone's conversation was a jerky dance jumping from subject to subject. It was a relief when the meal ended.

After dinner, Elditha gathered her ladies around her. They

sat in the antechamber sewing and talking in low tones. Ulf bent over a wax tablet struggling to make his letters with a stick. From time to time he glanced over at his mother.

Hands fumbled with the cloth, stitches unpicked and redone, scissors dropped, threads split. She thrust a taper into the smouldering charcoal, lit a candle and lifted her little book of riddles from the table. 'Come, Ulf,' she said. 'You will guess these easily.' Ulf left his wax tablet and sat cross-legged on a cushion by her sewing chair. Slowly and carefully, she began to read. The sentences created tiny mysteries. Her ladies liked to hear them told over and over again. When they had guessed a few, she turned the page and said, smiling, 'This is the last one for this evening. It is time for supper. Listen, Ulf. Let's see if you remember this one: "I am a lonely being, scarred by swords, wounded by iron, sated with battle deeds" ...' She paused. '... But cuts from swords ever increase on me ...'

Ulf leapt to his feet and called out, 'Shield!' But she didn't hear it. She heard shouting out on the palisade, muffled at first then clearer, then jeers and yells, a swish in the air followed by the twang of arrows released from bows. Weapons were clashing. She dropped her book and ran to the half-opened window shutters.

Pushing the shutters back as far as they would go, Elditha stared over the yard to the palisade. She thrust her head out. Smoke drifted towards the hall from the west. The stockade was on fire. The yells of men rose above the crackling of burning timber. Geese and hens were squawking. Dogs began barking. There were more shouts, the plunk of bow strings and the hiss of arrows again as they flew through the air.

The flames engulfed the three-barred gate, spitting sparks and blazing debris. Clouds of thick smoke rose up, blotting out what was left of the sunset. Now, not a man could be seen on the palisade. The guards had vanished with the sun. Riders appeared through the smoke, spurring their steeds forward through gaps in the estate's great ringed fence. Pennants unfurled behind them, glowed red as dark horses galloped towards the hall. Hooves pounded. Servants and villagers

105

poured from the barns. Others raced from the stores. A villein came running at a horse with a pitchfork, another horseman sliced at him from behind. He toppled forward onto his crude weapon. Men fell and others ran. Women were kicked aside. An anvil went flying through the air but missed its mark. Although the horse reared up, the rider remained seated. He pulled an axe from behind his saddle and swung it at the man who had thrown the anvil and missed. A woman shrieked as her toddler was trampled. Children ran for cover.

The riders surged forward. Dust flew up in dense clouds. More figures appeared on the path. Her fighting men, those left to her, now helmeted and heavily armed with axes and shields, yelling curses and battle cries, ran from the hall. They stood firm in front of the grassy swath and attempted to lock shields. A hedge of spears angled outwards. For a moment the horses backed off whinnying and snorting, kicking dirt, on the brink of panic.

Their riders yelled, '*Glemure, merde!*'

Someone yelled back, 'Filth and shit, you spawn of Hell. You bastard sons of bastard mothers!'

Waving their weapons and shouting insults, the riders urged their horses back towards the shield wall. One sliced his battle-axe through an overlap and forced an entry. They pushed and pressed and shoved at the wall of men until it broke into two sections. A hall servant ran out, stabbed at a horse's leg with a short sword, missed and stumbled. Its rider leaned over and sliced at the sprawling man. Horses pushed, rose up, whinnied and stamped but the foreigners held firm and lashed out furiously. Swords cut and shield clashed against shield. All at once each side of the shield wall disintegrated. The ghost of courage remained before the survivors fell back. The well-armed Normans trampled over broken shields and swords and the bodies of fallen men.

A second wave of ceorls and villagers surged out of the hall. They beat at the Normans with axes. The dark fiends moved quickly, manoeuvring in circles around them, catching the angry villagers inside a tight ring. Trapped, a few of the hall ceorls dropped their weapons at the feet of the victors. Others broke away by stabbing at the horses' legs, forging a way out through the circle. Two riders pursued them. One struck a young ceorl with his long sword. He fell forward slowly, his blood pouring from the wound. The horsemen chased his companions towards the barns. Others fled back into the hall through the small gap between door and doorpost. Those inside pulled the door fast and bolted it. Elditha heard it whine closed and came away from the window.

Her women clutched each other, weeping. They could hear people dragging trestles across the flagstones in the hall. Soldiers began banging on the great front door.

Ulf clung to his mother's hand.

Elditha said, 'I'm going down.'

He snatched at her skirt with his other small hand. For a moment she froze, afraid for them all. Determination crept back into her voice, 'Margaret, hold on to Ulf.' She handed him to the nurse and pulled her cloak about her shoulders.

The calls continued. *'Putain, putain!'* And in English, they bellowed, 'Harold's whore, come out.' Holding her head high, she walked down the staircase into the crowd of servants, men, women and children who had already sought the shelter of the hall.

Children huddled behind pillars. Others clung to their mothers. Everyone turned to watch her pass. She saw her linen table covers in a heap among rushes on the flagstones. Wooden bowls had toppled from trestles which had been dragged away to make barricades. Dogs whimpered and cowered in corners.

Again and again, their chant penetrated the great door, 'Concubine, concubine, come out.' Guthlac ordered the men to pull more trestles against the door. Brother Francis sank against a pillar crying, shaking and sweating and holding aloft a great wooden cross that hung around his neck. There wasn't a fighting man left in the hall.

'Are they all out there?' she said.

'There's none of them in here!' Guthlac exclaimed. 'Go back up to your women, my lady.'

She pushed him aside. 'Let me through, Guthlac, and Brother Francis too.'

Guthlac glanced past her to the priest. 'Some luck that one will bring!'

A firebrand of rushes was shot into an opening; another and another and another. Hangings caught fire. Everyone began running. They tried to beat out the fire with linen cloths. More and more burning torches flew through window openings. The villagers ran along the wall beating at flames but to no avail. The flames took hold and snatched at banners, devouring them in a red-and-gold blaze.

'Look out for the shields!' Guthlac yelled and pulled Elditha towards him.

A shield with a great dragon painted on it came crashing down. The fire raced, eating into tapestries and hangings as it flew. Children were pulled from chests and clasped close to their mothers. Hounds went mad, barking and growling, snapping, wildly shaking the bells on their collars. Everyone coughed and spluttered as smoke rose in the hall. Those who could lay their hands on a ladle or a pitcher ran back and forth from the vat that stood by the central hearth. They hurled water at the flames. It was hopeless.

Flames grasped at Elditha's swan pennant and Harold's warrior, swallowing feathered bird and fighting man. Small fires began to flare up, catching at the straw strewn over the flagstones. Smoke thickened in dark, suffocating plumes.

Elditha's ladies hurried down the stairway clutching veils over their faces. They ran with the crowd to the entrance. Elditha screamed at Guthlac. 'Let my ladies out.' Then she cried, 'Where is my son?'

She began searching frantically through the smoke for Ulf, pushing into the crowd that surged towards the entrance.

'Margaret, where is he?' She clutched at a woman she thought was her. Then, 'Have you seen Margaret?' The woman shook her head. Her ladies began to pull the burning timber away from the door themselves. Elditha shouted louder but no one heard her above the yelling from outside, the crashing of

108

shields and the roaring flames. At last a pathway was cleared. With a whining and groaning and the pressure of men pushing and the enemy pulling from the other side, the door opened.

Men, women and children and barking dogs clambered over each other in their panic to escape. The pressing human river closed behind her. Elditha sped in the opposite direction, back towards the stairway, screaming, 'Ulf! Margaret! Where are you?' As she reached the bottom step the child's nurse came stumbling through a cloud of smoke and ash towards her, spluttering and calling for help.

'Ulf!' Elditha shouted.

Margaret waved towards the roof and began running back up.

Elditha followed. She pushed the nurse through the doorway.

Margaret pointed above the table. 'He's in there,' she choked. 'I can't get up.'

Elditha lifted the candle, held it high and looked into the dim roof, searching along the beams. She couldn't see him. There was the splitting of burning wood. The smoke in the chamber thickened. A shriek came from high above them.

She climbed onto the table and, for the second time that day, pulled herself up into the rafters. 'Wait!' she called down coughing. She could see him now, above her head, crouched over behind the crossbeams and vertical struts that supported the highest point in the building. He was frozen like a wooden effigy. She reached upwards with one hand, steadying herself with her other. Gasping for breath, she gathered her strength and called up, 'Ulf, climb down to me.' She heard the rush of flames on the thatch of the roof. The roof space was filling up with a dense, pungent smoke. 'Ulf, you must move now. I can't get up,' she shouted.

Ulf began to inch towards her. He climbed through the cage of wooden struts and down and down until she was able to pull him to her. Grasping Ulf tight, she swung her legs round and dropped onto the table.

They propelled themselves down the stairs and behind the

pillars that led to the rooms beyond the hall. Armed men rushed in, racing through people who still surged out. They mercilessly lashed out at the hall's inhabitants, tore veils from women, pushed them aside and shouted, 'Where is she?' Soldiers ran for the stairway. Fed by the draught from the opened doorway, the fire was gaining in strength. Elditha held Ulf tight and ran into the chambers behind the hall. Margaret followed. They could hear feet thundering above them. Soldiers had already reached the upper floor. She heard them come back down again, shouting, 'The roof is burning. Nobody's up there!'

'Run, Margaret, run!'

She held on to Ulf, shocked and numbed. Dragging him with her, Margaret pushing him on from behind, she raced through the gathering smoke and out through the side doorway onto the pathway that led to the bower hall. Timbers were falling. A whirlwind of debris blew between the cook house and the store huts. There was a hot rushing draught, followed by the thumps of falling wood. Sparks flew in the smoke. Leaping yellow flames engulfed the back of the hall. The wails and screams of women, cries of children and soldiers' shouts penetrated the roar of the fire.

They hurried through blazing timbers and around burning bodies, bent low until they reached the bower hall. Inside, soldiers were shouting. Women were crying and screaming. Doubled over, they ran along the building's side towards the end gable. Halfway there, her foot caught on a broken body and she was staring down at a dead-eyed corpse. Elditha pulled her cloak tighter around Ulf and sidestepped the body. She lifted her head at the next window opening and glanced in. Soldiers were prodding the terrified women with swords. One shouted in English, 'Out, you whores. Or burn alive!' Tasting bile in her mouth, Elditha dragged herself along the last few feet of the wall. Margaret followed, still coughing into her veil. They paused. It was a short run to the garden.

'Now!' Elditha shouted above the noise of falling timber. They ran.

It was clearer by the chapel and garden and more dangerous too. Smoke rose above them in shapeless clouds. They could see Brother Francis's silhouette by the chapel door. Shadowy figures held up torches and appeared to be searching all around. They pushed past the monk and disappeared inside. At that moment, seeing her chance, Elditha set Ulf down but he clung onto her cloak. She clutched Margaret's arm. 'Get into the orchard. Go through the door behind the apple trees. You take Ulf.'

Margaret pulled Ulf from Elditha's cloak.

'Listen well. Padar will come with a garrison along the river path. Cut him off. Take the riverbed. Give Ulf into his care.' She kissed the top of her son's head, breathed the smoky but still lingering little-boy smell of him. 'Go!'

Elditha watched Margaret crouch low with Ulf clinging to her neck as she raced forward. She waited until she saw her circle the sundial and stumble into the shelter of the trees in the orchard. Elditha glanced back at the hall. With a sudden gust of wind the smoke blew upwards and she could see the spectral-like lumps of bodies scattered around the swath. Body parts were scattered everywhere she looked, guts spilling into slimy piles; all that was left of her servants and many of her villagers. The wind dropped as suddenly as it rose and all was smoke again.

Soldiers had finished herding women and children out of the bower hall. A band of them had separated a small group of noble ladies and were pushing them onto the wide path, towards a row of waiting, already harnessed, carts, yelling at them to hurry. Elditha turned and moved slowly onto the path, into the firelight, hearing their shouts rise into the night. As she came through a patch of smoke, a sentry by the chapel wall alerted a mounted knight who rode from the shadows onto the pathway. He was helmetless and she could see his monk-like tonsured red head. She had seen that knight once before at King Edward's court. Her head held erect, Elditha walked forward to meet him. And when she reached him, she looked at him fearlessly and said, 'I am Elditha, she whom you dare to call concubine.'

'Harold's concubine and Normandy's hostage, my lady.'

'Hostage I may be, but whore I am none. And by Christus, Count Alain, you will regret this day.'

He did not meet her gaze.

A driving rain began to fall as the procession of carts and wagons reached the smouldering gate. Elditha sat in the foremost covered cart with the priest, Ursula and her two other ladies, Freya and Maud, both of whom quietly wept. She looked back through the falling rain at her burning house. Only part of the hall's roof and a section of the west wall remained. The crashing of collapsing timbers, the sound of Reredfelle's destruction, echoed into the night.

Ursula whispered, 'Ulf?'

'Shush, he will be safe.' She squeezed her friend's hand and glanced over at Brother Francis. She laid a finger on her lips and Ursula nodded.

The heavily armed convoy skirted the forest edge and followed the road south towards William's lair, through silent villages with doors shut tight. Rain seeped in under the cover. The women cupped their hands to collect the water. They sipped thirstily, and as hour chased hour Brother Francis murmured prayer.

10

The wild hawk must sit on glove; the wolf must live in wood wretched and lonely; boar must dwell in grove strong with his mighty tusks; the good on Earth must work for glory.

Gnomic Verses, in *A Choice of Anglo-Saxon Verse,* edited and translated by Richard Hamer

Margaret gathered Ulf into the folds of her cloak and held him close. Rain was seeping from the sky, and now that the heat of the fire was behind them he was shivering with cold. The noise of falling timbers filled the emptiness of night, but she did not dare look back. She hurried on, clutching Ulf's hand, following the riverbed, all the time keeping close to the sheltering trees.

For a while she wondered if this was what Hell was like: a dark smoky territory where terrible creatures lurked around every corner. For a long time smoke stung her throat and the air they breathed held its pungent smell. The midnight hour must have passed. The mistress had told her to follow the stream and Padar would find them, yet there was no sign of a garrison moving through the woods. She stopped, raised Ulf onto her back, moved forward for a while and set him down again. As they moved deeper into the forest's rustlings and shadows he stumbled beside her as mute as a wooden puppet. She realised that he was in shock. In one terrible day his whole world had been destroyed and his mother separated from him. It was concern for the little boy's safety that numbed her fear as they struggled through the darkness.

Later the riverbed became a narrow trail following an incline that looped around a wide stand of ash and vanished. To Margaret's relief, a trickle of water emerged farther on as they descended. She followed it and her common sense was rewarded when the stream became a river, eventually widening into an elongated pool. 'Ulf, you must drink. Here, sweeting.' She helped him to scoop up water into his hands and encouraged him to drink. She sank into a hollow on the bank, leaned her back against a tree trunk and pulled Ulf into her arms. He fell asleep instantly and moments later she felt her own chin drop as she too drifted into sleep.

Ulf was still snuggled against her breast when she woke up. Margaret undid her cloak, covered Ulf with it and eased him into the hollow. She stood, stretched her cramped limbs and then wandered a little way along the river bank. On the far edge of the pool, wraiths of morning mist rose up around a cottage so that it looked as if the small house had floated out onto the water, as if it could shift and slide away again. She could make out a squat jetty thrusting into the river and a cloaked figure emerging from the building. It paused, lifted a pail and moved through the thin tendrils of vapour towards a squawking noise that rose up from the rushes.

As the figure walked into the reeds and closer to where she stood, it looked up and over the pool, as if sensing Margaret's presence hovering there. Then the woman, for a woman it was, she decided, beckoned to her. Margaret raised her hand in greeting and hurried back to the sleeping child. 'Come, Ulf,' she said softly, wakening him. 'We can have shelter now.'

Ulf began to whimper but Margaret hugged him. 'Hush, hush, child, it will be safe.' She took his hand and hurried him through the mist. What she could not see was the gleam of mail caught by the rising sun glinting beyond the trees. She never heard horses nosing through the foliage behind the hut until soldiers emerged out of the wood and into the clearing. She stopped walking and pulled Ulf closer. The silent woman gestured at Margaret to come forward.

Margaret wanted to lift Ulf up into her arms and run back along the track, but she was too frightened to move. The soldiers' leader, a helmeted man of small stature, dismounted and began to walk forwards, leading his horse. Even clad in armour, a chain-mail tunic, his gait was familiar and that grey stallion was surely from Reredfelle's stables. It was Thunder, the horse Padar had taken.

He stopped, removed his helmet and called to her, 'By Christ's holy bones, Margaret and Ulf! Where is my lady?'

'Padar! Padar; sweet Lady Mary, St Augustine, St Christopher and thank the holy angels of Heaven for you. But, Padar, you are too late. Reredfelle is destroyed, burnt to the ground!'

Ulf began to wail.

Padar shook his head and leaned down. 'You are safe, Ulf. We thought as much. We could see smoke from the high ground. Where is she?'

Margaret choked back a sob and shrugged her shoulders. 'I don't know. She gave Ulf to me at the garden gate and told me to find you. My lady turned back. Her ladies, you see …'

'They have taken her.' He gave the reins of his horse to one of his men and took Ulf from Margaret, lifted him up, looked at the child's frightened face and said, 'Ulf, we will find your mother. But first you will break your fast. The woman here will care for you until I return.' He set Ulf down and turned to the man who held his horse. 'And Hamlet will stay with you. After that we'll decide what to do about all this.'

He knelt and chucked Ulf under the chin. 'Trust me, it will be all right.'

Padar drew Hamlet a little way off into the trees and, after a short discussion, Hamlet nodded. Padar returned, handed a few coins to the woman. Then he introduced her to them as Hilde. She smiled toothlessly but never spoke. Her silence was as eerie as the early mist.

Padar said to Hilde, 'You will care for these people. This soldier will protect you. If you betray them to anyone who passes this way, he will kill you. I shall return by nightfall.' Padar's face was grim and Ulf began to cry again. The skald patted Ulf's head, mounted his horse and led his armed troop on along the river bed.

Margaret and Ulf rested with Hilde for two nights waiting for Padar to return. When Ulf cried for Elditha, Hilde gave him infusions of chamomile in mead to help him sleep; she fed them on barley cakes, fish and eggs and gave them pallets to lie upon. Ulf grew calmer. Margaret discovered that although Hilde could hear, she could only grunt in response, and though she knew that Hamlet was watching over them, and observed Hilde disappearing into the forest with bowls of fish stew and loaves of barley bread, she never discovered his whereabouts.

On the third day Padar returned without his troop. He led Elditha's mare, Eglantine. Ulf buried his head into Eglantine's flanks and rubbed her nose. The mare had miraculously survived the blaze and had not been taken.

Margaret said, 'How did Eglantine survive? Did they not steal the horses?'

'Some, but not all; a couple of them were tethered out in the deer hay.' He reached up and patted the mare's neck. 'They missed this one.' He was rewarded with a whinny.

Ulf asked, 'Where is Elf, Padar?'

'Your pony is with my men, Ulf, gone to be a warrior pony in a great battle.' It was a lie. Ulf's pony was gone.

Hamlet shimmied down from his lookout in the tall sycamores nearby and called to them that he had sighted soldiers south of the woods. 'Normans are scouting manors close by. They'll be occupied out there for a while but we need to move by nightfall in case they come closer.'

'No, they won't come here. They will have been to Crowhurst. They'll take what they can from the King's estate and return to their camps around the old Roman fort down near Hastings.'

'Where are the others?'

'They've gone to find the King. There will be a battle. Go, Hamlet; if you hurry you'll find them. The fyrd is gathering near Bidborough.'

'And you, Padar?'

'I must take the little lad to safety. There are soldiers on the routes south and east of here so we shall ride west along the drovers' tracks and deliver him to Queen Edith in Winchester.'

Margaret asked, 'What about my lady?'

Padar touched her arm. 'Come with me, Margaret.' He left Ulf with Hamlet and guided her into the trees. He said in a quiet tone, 'They took them away in carts. A Breton led them. He carried a standard with a wolf emblem. Those who have survived say that after that there was no mercy towards those who had fought them. And the fortunate who remain living are still burying their dead. There is little left of Reredfelle. Wait here.' He went back to his horse, dug his hands into his saddle-bag and lifted out a small casket. 'Except this, I was given it by Father Egbert. He survived in the village church with the villagers who never came to the hall and he found this near a section of the roof which had collapsed. Do you recognise it?'

Margaret traced over the scorched bone plating and the tarnished silver below, where pieces of bone had torn away. She smiled. 'This belongs to my lady. She keeps a key for it on a chain that hangs around her neck.'

'We'll keep it for her, shall we?'

Margaret nodded but there were tears in her eyes. 'What is to become of us all?'

'For a start we cannot waste any more time here,' Padar said, as he tucked the box back into his saddle-bag. 'We will leave when night falls. It will be slow and dangerous. If we move through the woods and avoid the roads, it will take us, maybe, three nights.' He patted the pack strapped to his horse. 'And by day we will camp out of sight, snug among the trees.'

As they parted, Hamlet said, 'If I meet the King, I shall tell him that his son is safe.'

'Tell him.' He felt tears gather in his eyes and stared at his feet for a moment. He managed to smile through them. Looking up he said, 'May a circle of God's holy angels watch over you, Hamlet.' Then he helped Margaret climb onto Eglantine, lifted Ulf up onto Thunder's saddle and sprang up behind him. With Ulf leaning into his chest, he lifted his right hand in his customary backward wave and rode into the trees.

118

11

There at Waltham he [Harold] received a message about the landing of the Normans, news that was only too true, and straightway he decided to go and meet them, allowing nobody to stop him. […] he was too headstrong and trusting too much in his own courage, he believed he would be attacking a weak and unprepared force of Normans before reinforcements came from Normandy to increase their strength.

The Waltham Chronicle, circa 1177, edited and translated
by Marjorie Chibnall

Countess Gytha hobbled into the candlelit chapel at Waltham. Her bones ached and she could hardly make it onto the cushion. She felt Thea's anxious eyes follow her as she arranged her hands on the rail. *There, that was better; on her knees now.* She settled at last and bowed her head, murmuring whatever came into her thoughts. 'Queen of Heaven, intercede for him. He was my boy, my Tostig. Bathe him in Heaven's light. You were once a mother too … Holy Mother, wash away his sins …'

As Gytha prayed, the plainsong chanted by monks echoed through the Church of the Holy Cross, dispersing beauty through the chancel and the aisles. It brought little comfort. Tostig had begun the destruction of everything the family had strived for. Tostig had been cut down by Harold's fyrd during the battle in the north and Harold had marched south again to Waltham. The Norman horde had landed and was harrying his lands in Sussex. He would destroy William the Bastard as he had Harald Finehair. Shakily Gytha rose to her feet. She was tired – so tired – and must rest.

The following morning dawned with a brilliant blue sky.

Harold, Gyrth and Leofwine rode out after they broke their fast, early. Later that morning, the Provost of Waltham came to Countess Gytha. He recounted a tale that made her shudder with foreboding. At dawn, when Harold had prayed for God's blessing on his campaign, Christ had bowed His carved head and looked down on him from the cross with an expression of sorrow on His usually peaceful face.

He shook his head. 'Countess, it is an ill omen.'

Gytha said, 'It cannot be. Provost, the spinners do not make his end yet.'

He shrugged, 'Spinners weaving his end! What talk is this, Countess? I have sent two of our monks with the King.'

She laughed hoarsely. 'With maces and sticks! Much good will they do.'

'Not to fight, but if the King is killed they will bring his body to Waltham.' Seeing the look on her face, he added, 'It is unlikely, of course, Countess, but in case God ...' he faltered.

'Get out of my sight, Lord Provost.'

After that, Gytha marched through the palace, tapping her stick before her, creating an icy wind, looking darkly at any who dared oppose her. She scattered her servants before her as she moved through the hall, back and forth, banging at tapestries as if beating the provost's words from them. Then, she called her servants to pack her baggage.

Summoning her steward, she ordered, 'Have a chest filled with gold coin.'

'In such terrible times, Countess Gytha, that would be madness? What do you intend?'

'We may have to buy ourselves out of this.'

'The countryside is dangerous ...'

She dismissed him with a wave of her hand.

After breaking her fast with a small meal of hot broth and bread, she changed into her travelling dress: a voluminous skirt, cleverly created to allow her movement when riding, and a loose tunic. She demanded that her horse be saddled and she ordered a wagon to be packed with items necessary for her journey, including her gold and silver hoard. If the house of

Godwin fell, she would be there to gather up the pieces.

She called Thea to her chamber and looked at the girl more sternly than she had ever done before. 'Thea, wear your warmest garments. I'm not leaving you here to be raped should our enemies reach Waltham.'

Gytha watched the delighted Thea hurry off. Not every girl was permitted to follow her father to battle. Her mouth twitched with a thin shadow of a smile. Not for nothing was Thea her father's daughter.

After breaking away from the route south, Thea close by her, Gytha rode towards Canterbury. A monk battalion led by their abbot passed their retinue as they entered the town. These monks wore chainmail over their brown habits and all of them carried weapons.

Thea stared at the small swords tucked into their belts and the shields and arrow quills hung on straps slung over their shoulders. She remarked, 'Monks are not permitted to draw blood.'

'But they will,' Gytha replied.

The fluttering Wessex dragon brought the group of monks to a sharp halt. Recognising the Countess, they knelt. When she asked after the Archbishop, their abbot shrugged, said he had no knowledge of him and that they were off to join the King's army at Bidborough.

'Stigand won't draw blood; he cares too much for his own skin,' muttered Gytha under her breath.

Now the Countess had to make a decision. They could become camp followers and ride after Harold south and west to wherever he chose to strike camp, or they could rest in Canterbury and await news.

'We could go to my mother's hall at Reredfelle,' said Thea.

'No,' Gytha replied. 'We ride on. Elditha will have gone to Canterbury already, you can be sure.' Gytha sat erect on her horse, her loose garments falling down each side of the animal's flanks.

The captain of her guard pleaded with her. 'Countess, you

121

have already slept one night in a wagon. Another will not do.'

'Grandmother, please allow us to wait here for news. My back aches and at your age you must have even more pain. How can you sit a horse for so long when you walk with the help of a stick?'

'You are not often wise, Thea, but this time you show a wisdom beyond your, what is it now, 14 years. We will lodge in the Archbishop's palace. My child, the horse is doing the work, not my legs.'

'Riding is tiring on the legs. You'll never admit that, will you?'

'Theodora Gytha, my legs lost their feeling miles back.'

Thea began to fret again. 'If my mother is not in Canterbury, then she is in grave danger.'

'Never fear, Thea, you will see your mother soon,' Gytha said reassuringly, but in her heart she was not convinced that Elditha would have the sense to flee her estate. They could only pray to the Queen of Heaven that she was safe.

An hour later they rode into the precinct of St Augustine's monastery. The yard was empty, apart from a motley collection of stable boys. A monk, plump as a pigeon, scurried out of the monastery building. Her first question was, 'Is the Lady Elditha here?' He shook his head. 'We have sent her a guard. That was two days ago. The lady is to return with them. She has not arrived and they have not returned either.'

'They may have gone to meet the King,' said another who had come running, his dark habit threatening to trip him up.

'Show us to our chambers. Then send us food and wine. Where is Archbishop Stigand?'

'In London,' the monk said.

'And never available when our lives are in grave danger; come, Thea, we must rest.' She watched as her guard carefully unloaded her coffers and then she made sure that they preceded her to her chambers within the abbey.

Duke William was making ready for battle. There had been comings and goings all night and now, as morning dawned,

Elditha hovered by the opening of their tent and watched men form up in columns ready to leave. Thousands sat on war horses, but an even greater number, armed with swords, bows and quills of arrows, marched in lines out of the town of tents, through gates set into a stockade. The bailey at Hastings swarmed with soldiers, thousands of them, yelling to each other in many languages: French, Breton, Italian and others that she did not recognise. Archers were collecting arrow sacks from store tents; the clanging of weapons rang out and horses snorted. Like silver insects, their leaders climbed up and down the ladder to the tower at the top of the motte.

Brother Francis had departed from the women on the day after they had been brought to the camp and they had not seen him since. They whispered prayers without the monk's guidance, but they never missed him.

'Do you think he was a spy?' Freya whispered, with an eye on the guard outside.

Ursula said, 'When I fetched our water, I overheard a priest say that Brother Francis is with Bishop Odo now.'

'That tells us where his loyalties lie,' Elditha said dryly. She turned to them and added, 'Don't say that monk's name again in my presence.'

The Normans had treated the women courteously. Alain of Brittany came daily to enquire after Elditha's wellbeing. Though she could speak French, she chose to communicate with him in English. She sat by the tent opening where the air was cooler, watching and thinking. There must be deeper motives for his solicitations; maybe he hoped for financial gain. His men had called her concubine and whore, but she was often known as Edith the Rich. They would know that too. Her lands in Cambridgeshire and in Essex were many. She also owned houses in Canterbury. By English law this all still belonged to her, despite her marriage. If the Normans won she would lose it all, and if they did not she would remain their hostage and they could demand a ransom. But, for now, she was the enemy's captive and soon England could be too. She worried for Harold, for herself, for their children, and for what would become of England if William, with his great army of disciplined mercenaries and with so many fighting knights on horses, won the battle.

Duke William refused her an interview and his aloofness infuriated her. Yet she considered her lot better than those poor peasants Padar had spoken of in her antechamber. We are all of us nobility, the Count, William and our earls, she thought to herself, and us women singled out for special favour because of it. The Count of Brittany sent them feather mattresses, clean linen and old but dry mantles. He had set a protective guard on their tents. Two local women attended them. He even asked his own Breton priest to say mass for the women on Saint Calixtus' Eve. When the waiting became unbearable, Elditha requested needles and thread and mending to keep their hands busy and he sent them baskets of torn leg-bindings.

From a distance she watched Duke William walk the ramparts of the wooden watchtower on the top of the mound that his men had laboured for several weeks to build. His body was still long and lean, his hair tonsured like a monk's, his cloak was richly coloured and he was flanked by a group of elaborately clad bishops. The Pope's banner, a great red crusading cross on a white background, flew beside his own. Elditha turned away from that sight and entered her tent.

'Perhaps I should have kept Ulf with me,' she said to Ursula, who was sewing a rent in a soldier's garment. 'Who knows if they met with Padar? There are perils in the woods too.'

'Our Lady will protect him from evil. If they are in the woods, we can pray that God keeps them safe from our enemies.'

Elditha touched Ursula's hand. 'By St Cecilia, I hope it is so. Come, Ursula.' She turned to the others. 'Maud, Freya, leave those leg-bindings; let us pray together for our King's success in battle, for the safe-keeping of my child and our deliverance from this foul place, though why they have taken us four women as their captives, I cannot really fathom. It may be ransom.'

'Better than dead,' Ursula said dryly.

There was shouting outside. Elditha hurried through the entrance, elbowing their guard aside, and accosted one of the soldiers who had ridden in. He was a scout, she quickly discovered. 'What news?' she asked as she ran alongside him.

'The King's army is marching towards us. There is to be a battle.' The scout wheeled round on his horse and she watched him follow the last group of archers out of the camp.

'Go back inside and pray, lady. Pray for mercy,' one of her guards said. Elditha said back, 'It will be you who begs mercy before this day is finished.' She turned on her heel and marched back into the shelter to pray.

12

Edith, surnamed Swanneshalls, knew secret marks on the king's body better than others as she had been admitted to a great intimacy of his person.

The Waltham Chronicle, circa 1177, edited and translated
by Marjorie Chibnall

It was past midnight when a monk rode in from the battle. He fell to his knees. 'Countess Gytha. It is all over. The King and his brothers are dead. The battle raged all day …'

She raised her hand to stop what she suspected would be a long and painful account. 'Just tell me this. How did my sons die?'

'Lord Gyrth and Earl Leofwine fell when they came off Senlac Ridge. That is all I know of them. They lie there murdered somewhere in the valley below. It was a massacre. After that there were more assaults on what was left of us, over and over until the sun fell in the sky. Many, many, died. I was with our horses behind the King. I saw it all.'

'How did the King die?'

'The Duke's army came up at us where the King was fighting beside his standard. Our great shield wall had broken, chipped away every time a group of our warriors ran the Normans down that slope. The horsemen fought their way up the hill where they smote and pierced the King's ranks. They shot arrows up into the air over our shields. The King fell … a chance arrow but it struck his face under his nose-plate. His house-ceorls tried to protect him, Countess, they tried but they failed and they died beside the King – all, as was he, hacked brutally to death.'

The monk hung his head. He swallowed and tried to speak,

then covered his face with his hands. Stiff backed, Countess Gytha tapped her stick. 'It's not all, is it? Find your voice, monk.'

He looked up, his eyes shot with blood. 'Countess, they came in among the dying. One knight hacked at the King when he was down. Another decapitated him and struck at his legs, parting leg from body.' His tears flowed. He swept a dusty sleeve across his face.

'And?'

He cleared his throat. 'That was when I turned my horse and came from the ridge. I outrode the pursuit. I gained woodland and lost myself in there until I found the route out farther on. It was ignoble. And, God knows, I should have died there too.'

Gytha sat still in her chair.

'God will avenge my sons, all of them,' she said. 'There will be time to weep tomorrow. Today we must claim our dead before the crows pick them over.' She sent the monk away. 'Go and find food and rest. It is as well you lived. The Greatest of Lords wished it. Enough blood is spilt already.'

She called for her guard. For two hours she impatiently tapped her stick on the floor as they deliberated and hesitated, fearful of the roads. At last, she took decisive action. She ordered her wagon to be readied and her horse saddled. With Thea beside her, she rode out through the south gate with the silken and jewelled Wessex dragon flying before them and her hoard concealed in the wagon.

'My mother?' Thea said.

'The Normans will not find Reredfelle. That estate is on the way to nowhere, my dear. Be assured, they will not find her or care about her either.'

The soldiers brought Elditha to the battlefield shortly after Matins. They brought her to where Duke William had remained all night in his bivouac encampment. She could see Harold's captured standards flying alongside the Duke's own by the entrance to his tent. Desperately looking around she saw a horrific sight. Everywhere bodies were already stripped of mail, hauberks and weapons. Even boots and hose had been taken from them. The Duke's soldiers had been at their grisly plunder during the night. Torches burned over it, lighting up the grim sight. She sat on her horse, her long neck erect and with Ursula by her side. They were accompanied by the two monks who had come with the King from Waltham. They had said that they could not identify the King's fallen body, only his head. The rest was mutilated, in pieces. They told the Norman leader that only Elditha Swanneck would be able to recognise her husband and reunite the King's severed head with his body. So here she was, unceremoniously lifted onto a horse, escorted from the camp and marched north to the boundary of Harold's estate of Crowhurst that was marked by a grey apple tree, and into the meadows of death that lay around the ridge.

Her very sense of herself was frozen. She searched for him through the piles of the dead, pointing for this body or this limb to be turned over. Her fine boots were slippery with blood and she had to clutch her veil close against the metallic smell of it; not only that, but also the stench of shit and spilt guts. Duke William, his brothers Bishop Odo and Robert of Mortain, and a group of knights were watching her as she moved among the corpses of departed Danish house-ceorls and Saxon aristocrats. A great gathering of priests was permitted to take away the corpses of fallen noblemen for burial. Another quarter hour passed and still she had not found Harold.

'You have done what you can, Lady,' said William Mallet, half a Norman and half Englishman, a knight who had lived at Edward's court. She had known him then. 'Would you rest?' he added.

'This place will too soon become a Golgotha of skeletons, a vast field of bones,' she cried out. 'What evil have you done here? You will rot in Hell for this, Mallet. I shall find my husband.'

He turned away from her. She refused to be consoled or stop searching, but frantically carried on asking for bodies to be lifted, peering closely at any torso that resembled her husband's. It was as she made a second tour of the dead up on the ridge that she found him. She identified his long body by marks on his shoulder. There were battle scars too, which she now recognised on his torso and bracelet tattoos on his other arm. When she found his severed leg close by she could see the swan's feather and the blood-stained, green-eyed dragon that encircled it and, by these marks, she knew the limb was his. It was then that she sank into the mire and wept for her loss.

'May my lord's soul rest in peace.' She took a cloth from her belt and carefully wiped away the blood from around the marks.

Elditha and Ursula left the place of death as they had come, on horseback. The monks remained with the dead King. The sun was up and it promised to be another hot day. As she rode away she saw other women moving among the bodies just as she had done, searching for any marks that identified the men they had loved, looking for any tokens left to them.

As the sun began to disappear that day, Elditha heard that Gytha had reached the battlefield. They brought the Countess to the camp. Sobbing, she hugged Gytha, whose face was as white as dried bones. Elditha pulled Thea close and clung to her weeping child, weeping herself and between her sobs trying to comfort her daughter, promising that soon they could all go home. She wondered at the truth of her hopeless empty words. Where was home? The Normans had destroyed everything: her home and her heart, and her child was wandering lost in the woods. Gytha told her that on the field of bones, as far as the eye could see, there were many more sobbing women and chanting priests than she imagined the county ever held. William had taken no prisoners. Thea had been sick with the horror of it and had leaned over her mount and had vomited. Gytha had demanded to see Duke William, saying that she had come to claim her own. The Norman knights who remained on the ridge had looked upon her haughtily, until finally William Mallet came to speak to her. It was Mallet who had guided her to the camp at Hastings, and here they were.

Elditha sobbed, 'They burned Reredfelle.'

Gytha looked around and then let out a cry. 'Elditha, where is Ulf? What has happened to my grandson?'

'When they fired my hall, I sent him away from Reredfelle into the woods with the nurse to find Padar, who was bringing us a garrison from Canterbury. It was a mistake. I should not have let him go.' She bit her lip hard, drawing blood. It tasted bitter on her tongue.

'Then let us pray that they have found him.' Gytha reached out and took Elditha's hand. 'Have faith; Padar will discover him. I feel it.'

Darkness fell and the camp was once again lit up with torches. The women sat in a circle inside the tent praying, wondering what would happen next. Sometimes they reached out for each other's hands, trying to find a desperate, fragile comfort in simple touch. William summoned the family of women. As Alain of Brittany escorted them through the camp to the Duke's pavilion, they could hear the racketing sounds of a jubilant and celebrating victorious army.

The Duke was seated in a winged chair. He never spoke but gestured to them to follow him. He led them to the tent where Gytha's three sons lay on trestles, each under linen cloth. Shields and swords were placed by their sides. Candles flickered by their remains. Numbed by shock, Elditha listened to the rhythmic sound of chanting and smelled the pungent smell of incense.

On seeing the Countess, the monks of Waltham ceased their prayer and bowed their heads to her. Gytha lifted away the cloth coverings and looked for the last time on her sons.

'This is God's will, Countess,' the Duke said coldly. 'Many men's lives were wasted who, if right had been honoured when it ought to have been, would be living now.'

Elditha only saw hatred in Duke William's cold stare. His eyes were as deep as an open grave. When the Countess finally spoke her voice rang clear. 'My Lord Duke, I will take my sons' bodies for burial at Waltham.'

'Earl Gyrth and Earl Leofwine you may have, Countess, but

I claim Earl Harold's body. He will be buried in a place of my choosing, a place that will be known only to myself and those who are close to me.'

'Then, I offer you the King's weight in gold for his corpse.'

'No, I keep his body. And I claim your gold for the Church. By Christus, I will build an abbey here as a monument to our dead.' He paused. 'All of our dead, English and Norman.' He looked at the women in a haughty manner. 'Tomorrow you may leave my camp.'

'Then I ask that Leofwine and Gyrth are laid beside him. As they were in life, so they will be in death, warriors and brothers together.'

'If that is your wish, Countess. My priests will pray for their souls.'

Duke William turned away from them to speak with his two brothers, Bishop Odo of Bayeux and Robert of Mortain. It was as if they were of no importance, dismissed and forgotten. Count Alain escorted them back to their tents. He touched Elditha's arm and said in a quiet voice, 'Lady, I am sorry for your loss and that of the Countess. I will see that tonight she has a comfortable couch. Tomorrow, you are to travel to Winchester with a guard to protect you.'

Elditha took Thea by the hand. 'It is too late to be sorry, Alain. You have murdered the father of my children.' She turned her back on him, lifted the tent flap, pushed Thea in first with the flat of her hand, and then helped the silent Countess to enter. She turned back to the knight. 'Winchester? We want to return to Canterbury.' Count Alain only shrugged.

Later, the Duke charged William Mallet with the King's burial. When night fell, Mallet spirited the corpses from the camp and travelled with them west along the coast towards Pevensey. There King Harold was quietly laid to rest on a cliff with his brothers by his side, overlooking an angry sea that swirled onto the shores of the kingdom he had lost.

PART TWO

A Journey

And Earl William went back again to Hastings, and waited there to see if he would be submitted to; but when he realised that no one was willing to come to him, he went inland with all of his raiding party which was left to him.

The Anglo-Saxon Chronicles, September 1066, Worcester Manuscript, edited and translated by Michael Swanton

When the great Duke William first arrived in this land, many of his men, pluming themselves on so great a victory and considering that everything ought to yield and submit to their wishes and lusts, began to do violence not only to the possessions of the conquered but also where the opportunity offered to their women, married and unmarried alike, with shameful licentiousness. Thereupon a number of women anticipating this and fearing for their own virtue betook themselves to convents of sisters and taking the veil protected themselves from such infamy.

Eadmer's History of Recent Events in England, Books I-IV, written in the last decade of the 11th century, translated by G Bosanquet

13

Once out of the woodlands Padar clutched Ulf tightly before him on the saddle. With Margaret on Eglantine, they galloped furiously across the weald towards the Queen's town of Winchester. When they reached the gates, they mingled with refugees, grim-faced country folk who lamented that Duke William's army had ridden like devils through their villages, had fed his soldiers with food from their barns and destroyed their homes with fire. His men had violated their wives and daughters. Padar called to Margaret, 'Do not be frightened by their talk.' But she was very afraid; terrified for the boy and for herself.

They parted from the column of the dispossessed near the two minsters, old and new, and rode on slowly towards the royal palace. Although the Queen's Gate was usually wide open, guards were stopping refugees from seeking shelter there. One of them prodded Padar's horse with a spear, and told them to move off. Margaret reined back as she watched Padar turning his horse from side to side, clutching hold of Ulf, rising up in his saddle to peer into the palace courtyard. An angry soldier reached through the partially opened gate and touched the soft leather of Margaret's boots. She recoiled and pulled Eglantine back another pace.

Padar shouted over Ulf's head. 'I'm Padar ... the King's skald. The boy is Harold's son.'

'We have no king! Where were you on Saturday when our warriors were cut down?'

'Saving the King's boy from harm.'

137

'Turn around, skald. Go and write songs about our defeat!'

Margaret murmured a prayer as Padar bawled at them, 'You sons of whores, let us through now.'

A dark column of canons filed out from the palace and across the yard, walking in a procession to the gate. The Provost leading them stopped. They were on their way to the Old Minster and he demanded that the sentries move aside and allow his canons through.

'Take these people with you, my Lord Provost. They think they have King Harold's boy.'

The Provost stared at them. Margaret saw him look from Padar to her and back to Ulf, who was wide-eyed watching the fracas. The Provost raised his hand. 'No, hold your tongues. I know this man. He is the King's skald. Allow them in.' He called out to Padar, 'There was a fire on the Lady Elditha's estate. Her hall burned to the ground. Is the boy her son?'

Padar shouted back, 'He is Ulf Haroldson.' At last the guard stood aside for them to pass. As they rode through the great gate and into the palace yard, Margaret kicked away the soldier who had fondled her boots and now had dared to touch them again.

The Provost turned to one of his canons and ordered, 'Find the Queen's steward.' Seeing the monk hesitate, he bellowed, 'Go at once!' He waved his hand at the others. 'And the rest of you to the minster. I shall follow.'

The guards drew back to let the choir file out through the palace gate. The bystanders, mostly women and children, stood aside to let them pass. One woman cried out, 'Tell them to have pity on us. Our sons died at Hastings.' When the last canon was through, the guards all raised their spears and shouted at the crowd, 'Go on to the Nuns' Minster.' The women stubbornly stood where they were until one of the guards repeated, 'Go on. There's nothing more here for you today.'

Inside the palace courtyard everyone seemed to have a purpose – fetching wood, carrying milk pails, exercising horses. A pack of hounds barked as they squabbled over a bone. The keeper of the Queen's falcons paraded about with a hooded bird perched on his leather glove and attached to his wrist by a chain. At last the Queen's tall steward, Fitz-Wimach, came bustling through monks, servants, soldiers, horses and stable boys that thronged the yard.

'Little Ulf.' He laid a hand on Ulf's head and turned to Padar. 'So it really is you, Padar, teller of tales, and with King Harold's son, and his nurse too, I see. At last something good has happened today. Come, come on into the hall.' Shaking back his long white locks, he called two stable lads over to take charge of the steaming horses. He turned to Margaret, 'You are courageous to bring the child to us in such terrible times. The Queen will be relieved to see the boy.'

They waited in the hall close to a raised dais on which stood a great throne-like chair. A time candle placed on a table burned a quarter hour slowly away. Padar never spoke. Ulf clung to Margaret's skirt and sucked his thumb. At last, Queen Edith glided into the hall, her voluminous veil floating around her and her dark clothes rustling as she walked. She stopped in front of the great throne-like chair. They fell to their knees. Margaret pushed Ulf forward.

'God has spared this child from fire and sword,' she whispered, awed by Queen Edith.

'Rise,' the stern-faced Queen said, 'we have lost his father and his uncles. It is with thanks to the Queen of Heaven that this child is safe.' She stretched out a jewelled hand. 'Ulf, come here.'

Ulf clung to Margaret's cloak.

'He is tired and frightened, Your Grace,' Margaret said timidly, not daring to look into the Queen's eyes. Instead, she focused on the enormous onyx pendant that hung on a gold chain below her dark-clad breast.

'Why was the boy not with his mother?'

'His mother is the Duke's prisoner,' Padar said.

'Nonsense, she is no prisoner. A messenger rode to us from Duke William yesterday. The Countess Gytha and the Lady Elditha will ride to Winchester today.'

'Will the Countess Gytha not accompany her sons' funeral journey to Waltham, Your Grace?' Padar asked boldly.

'There will be no journey to Waltham, Padar. The journey is too dangerous, the roads thronged with fleeing people, brigands and thieves. The Duke has laid the King to rest on the seashore and our brothers also. The Duke has won the battle and I have no doubt that he will bring us many desired Christian and civilising ways. Crops will grow; the sun will rise each day and set in the evening. People will recover. You are a Godwin skald, so sing to them of godly ways and of the joys of the fields.' She lifted her hand, summoned her ladies and addressed Margaret, 'Come with me, my dear, and bring the child.'

Ulf touched the Queen's heavily ringed hand. 'Aunt Edith?' he said so quietly he could hardly be heard. She inclined her head towards him, and he asked, 'Aunt Edith, why did the Duke bury my father's body on the seashore?'

She leaned down and said, 'When times are more settled, your father will rest in his own abbey – your uncles also.' Taking Ulf by the hand she hurried through the curtains to her chamber beyond the dais. Margaret began to follow. She stopped. *What about Padar, would he find a sleeping space in this vast palace building?* She turned back to speak, but Padar was hurrying off towards the great door they had just entered.

14

And joyless is this place. Full often the absence of my Lord comes sharply to me.

The Wife's Lament, in *A Choice of Anglo-Saxon Verse*, edited and translated by Richard Hamer

A few days later Elditha rode into Winchester at the head of a small procession of two wagons and Gytha's guard. As they had tried to circle around burned and smoking villages she had sat on her horse, never smiling or weeping. Her concern was now for Ulf. It was too easy to lose a small child in a countryside turned upside down and inside out by war and, as they travelled to Winchester, she was haunted by images of wild beasts and marauding soldiers, each as dangerous as the other. Once inside the palace courtyard she slid from her horse, leaned against it and closed her eyes.

Thea could not speak as she descended from her wagon. The horrors she had witnessed on the battlefield had struck her silent. Elditha opened her eyes again, reached out and wearily grasped her daughter's hand. Gytha tossed her sheepskin covering aside and climbed down after Thea, refusing help, just using her stick to steady herself. When she reached the straw below, Elditha took her arm and guided her into the palace.

Queen Edith came hurrying through the hall to embrace them. 'Thank the Queen of Heaven that you are all of you safe. Come and sit close to the hearth.'

When they had cups of spiced wine and bread to dip in it, Gytha shook her head. 'We gave the Bastard the perfect opportunity. We were a divided family. Tostig was a traitor to this family. He encouraged the Norwegians to attack us in the north and that weakened our defences down here.'

Edith placed a hand on her mother's arm. 'It was God's will. Tostig should never have been sent into exile. That was our undoing.' Edith looked over at the three ladies who sat quietly across the hearth, and again back to Elditha. 'You abandoned your son for those women,' she accused. 'But I have news for you. Ulf is here with me. You are fortunate that he has lived to tell the tale. You should not have sent him into the woods with only a nurse to protect him.'

Elditha's breath caught in her throat. 'I had little choice, Edith. He could yet be their prisoner. The Normans may not want a band of women now they have won the battle, but a boy hostage is another story. They would keep my son, just as they have kept your own brother, Edith. Do not question my decisions. And it clearly was the right choice since Margaret has brought Ulf safely to Winchester.'

'By our Lady's mercy, she did. The Godwin skald was with her.'

Elditha felt her anger rise into a fury at Edith's criticism at what she, herself, considered her wisdom in sending her son away from a raiding army. Surely the Dowager Queen was being unreasonably naïve? As the King's son, Ulf would be a prize captive for the Norman Duke. Edith was being difficult. She jumped to her feet, allowing her emptied wine cup to crash onto the tiles where it broke into pieces. 'I must see him.'

'Your rooms are above the hall. I shall send him to you. He has been very afraid.' The Queen's voice was icy. She turned from Elditha to Thea to her mother and laid her slender jewelled hand on Gytha's shoulder. 'Mother, rest in my own apartment. We shall hold a vigil in the new minster for my brothers' souls. Prayers will commence as darkness begins to fall.' She snapped her fingers towards a corner of the vast hall where the servants hovered. One rushed across the hall with a torch flame streaming behind him. Others followed, floating over the gleaming tiled floor as if skating on ice. She said, 'Elditha, take your daughter and maids and go.'

Elditha said not another word. She couldn't. Anger choked in her throat. She turned on her heel. It would be a relief to take refuge in her own rooms, away from the domineering Edith; a place where she could be alone with Thea and Ulf and her ladies. She reached out her hand and drew Thea to her side. 'Come with me,' she managed. She signalled to her ladies to follow her. Holding on to Thea's hand she pulled her daughter along with her and followed one of Edith's silent, grey-clad servants through shards of broken pottery towards stairs that climbed up the wall of the huge hall. As she reached the stairway she heard Edith shouting at her servants, 'One of you, fetch a broom and clear up that mess.'

Edith sent her chests of clothing, gifts of combs and jewels. Her servants hung tapestries on the walls of Elditha's chambers, tended the charcoal braziers and struggled up the stairway with enormous tubs, buckets of hot water and soap, blankets, pallets, clean linen and strewing herbs, chamomile and rosemary, to throw among the floor rushes. It was a kindness and Elditha was grateful for it, although she pointed out to Edith, when the Queen bustled into her chamber with a new cloak for her, that it was a luxury to have such comforts when so many others were desperate and hungry.

'My dear, we must show the invader that we are neither impoverished nor are we waiting for his charity!' was Edith's supercilious response. 'We must survive and survive well.' Then she swept away from Elditha's chamber, followed by her dark-cloaked women.

Thea began to speak again. She told Ulf stories and amused him by teaching him how to use a needle and thread, and to embroider. With nimble fingers he created a small tapestry depicting a dove. A tutor came to her palace rooms and Ulf resumed his learning of Latin grammar. Reluctant to allow him out of her sight, Elditha kept him close. She managed to get through the day by devoting herself to Thea and Ulf, walking with them in the palace garden, collecting acorns and showing them how to make them into little figures, but night after night she grieved for the warrior husband who had been twice taken so cruelly from her. She wept at the horrific memories of his naked body that had been broken and separated from his head. She tried to revisit the days of their youth, but the memory of his death was too raw and too bloody and too recent to recollect his image as it had once been.

Margaret returned her casket to her. It was a small comfort. Wondering at how a small box could survive a fire, she placed it by her bed where she could see it as she moved around the chamber, as she fell asleep at night and as she awakened each morning. Occasionally she unlocked it and removed the contents one by one, the ivory figures of saints, the sapphires which had been her Christmas gift from Harold, the tiny christening garment and below that the mandrake root which she wrapped in tightly knotted linen.

She remembered the months at Reredfelle until it was too painful to remember. One by one, she slowly returned each small possession to the casket again. She had lost everything else in the fire that had consumed her hall. They were only possessions, she told herself. Yet it was a small miracle that this casket had survived, a reminder of what she had lost and the man she had loved, the father of her children. Gradually an idea formed in her mind. As soon as it was possible to travel, she would take Ulf into safe-keeping to Ireland, to his brothers, to where he would grow up with them to avenge his father's murder. Gunnhild was safe in Wilton, but Gytha spoke of Exeter. That was it. Gytha must take Thea south to safety in her dower town.

15

He [William] sent to Winchester and ordered the chief men of the city to pay tribute to him as others were doing... she [Queen Edith] yielding, ordered them to take what was demanded. And in this way she and they lived in peace.

The Carmen de Hastingae Proelio, attributed to Guy, Bishop of Amiens, 1068, edited and translated by Catherine Morton and Hope Muntz

Elditha never spoke of her plan. It was too dangerous to leave Winchester yet. The roads were full of fleeing people and dangerous, and to execute such a plan she needed help. She did not trust Edith to give it to her. Edith surrounded herself with Norman priests and even some of her women were of Norman origin. As the month passed Elditha determined to be of use to others less fortunate than she and also to find out a way to quietly leave the town. Since there was no help within the palace she would see what help there was to be found outside it. The Nuns' Minster close by had an infirmary where those who had been wounded or were ill were permitted rest. When Ulf was with his tutor and Thea was attending Gytha, she took her three ladies to the infirmary, where they mixed salves to soothe wounds, and potions to send those who were disturbed to sleep. They made powder from the precious mandrake root, shaving off tiny pieces, using just a little at a time and only in extreme cases. Elditha returned it, wrapped protectively in soft linen cloth, to her casket every evening. While listening to others who had suffered loss, she grew stronger.

More and more refugees trailed into the town, to where bakers still baked, to where there were vegetables to buy and pigs and sheep were slaughtered. The townspeople lived in fear, daily expecting an invasion of Norman troops. News crept in. Kent fell, Sussex and Hampshire; and Duke William was riding south again towards Winchester. That did not surprise Elditha as the town was England's second royal stronghold and here Queen Edith possessed a vast treasury.

'Margaret,' Elditha said after the nurse had put Ulf to bed one evening, and Thea was ensconced with her grandmother in Edith's private apartments. 'It is time to search for Padar.' Margaret had told her how he had found them in the woods after the fire and brought them safely into the town, then disappeared. But that was not unusual.

'My lady, he may be in the woods again by now, but I'll try to find out.'

Margaret's search took her to both the minsters, to bake-houses and taverns and eventually to workshops belonging to the goldsmiths, because she had heard a rumour that the Godwin skald had been seen with a master coiner. She found the coiner but the skald had disappeared.

'Just as we suspected, the coiner says that Padar the skald is with the men of the wood.'

Elditha had heard that a resistance movement had grown up in woods around the town – outlaws who lived in camps hidden among the trees. People called them silvatii. One of their warriors, who had been injured by a Norman raiding party, was brought into the Nuns' Minster with a fever. Elditha suggested to the abbess that she tend the man's injuries. There was salve of rue boiled in old wine she could try. She busied herself around the man, set his broken arm in a splint and, when his fever lessened, she lost no time trying to find out more about Padar. Yes, the skald came and went from the camps.

'Tell Queen Edith that we can hold out if Duke William tries to take this town,' he told her.

She repeated his message to Edith, but the Queen did not want to know. She banned the rebels from entering the town and condemned any who helped their resistance. After the edict, the abbess sent the warrior out of the Nuns' Minster. Then, Duke William himself arrived at the East Gate of Winchester demanding the keys to the town. Now there was no opportunity to look for Padar. To Elditha's horror, Edith handed her town over as if she intended co-operation all along. In one short November day, Duke William's soldiers occupied the palace and took control of the treasury.

No one felt safe with Norman troops patrolling the streets. Townspeople predicted that soon the Normans would build a castle within the town walls and that their homes would be knocked down to make room for it. Soldiers marched about the town in a threatening manner, carrying long shields with fierce beasts and chevrons painted on them and bearing great swords. The Royal Mint was closed. Goldsmiths hid their gold by slipping away with it at night, taking to the rivers. Townsmen disappeared after dark to join the resistance, as Padar had done. Women feared for their honour. Husbands feared for their lives.

Elditha kept away from the hall and ordered servants to carry up their meals, using the outside staircase that led down into a garden. Her fear was for Thea and Ulf. She was frightened to allow either of them out of her sight and she never left her rooms. Finally, the day Elditha had feared all that week came with a knock on the door. She tentatively opened it and peeped around to see one of Edith's messengers behind it. He looked scared as a startled hare. 'My lady, the Queen requests your presence. I am to wait.' He waited on after she shut the door in his face. She pulled it open again to see him still shuddering behind it. This time she said she was coming. Even Edith's servants were afraid.

She ordered Margaret, Maud, Ursula and Freya to watch over Thea and Ulf, to bolt the door and not allow anyone in after she left. She pulled her mantle from its peg and followed the messenger down the stairs into the hall and then back through a long passage to Edith's antechamber.

The room was lit with expensive candles. Edith sat on a stiff, upright chair by a shuttered window, wearing a plain linen wimple that made her face look pinched, her voluminous sleeves trailing the ground. Duke William occupied her comfortable two-armed, throne-like chair, reclining with his long legs sprawled in front of him. He did not even rise as Elditha entered. Instead, waving towards a bench opposite, he grunted, 'Sit.' If she refused her legs might give way so she sank uncomfortably onto it. What did he want from her? He had taken everything already; her house and her people, and he had murdered the father of her children. He turned to Queen Edith and broke the silence by announcing that he would leave one of his knights, William Fitz-Osbern to organise the garrison in Winchester. In return for her loyalty to him, he added, she could keep her personal possessions, her lands and her treasure. He studied Elditha for a moment. 'I shall need a hostage, of course.'

She started. She was worthless as a hostage. But her children were royal; surely not her children! Her hands shook.

She heard Edith say in a glacial tone, 'Which of us do you intend to take, my Lord Duke? We are a household of women. Our men are slaughtered, and the rest may perish when you attack London.'

He leaned towards Edith. 'A monk tells us that King Harold's son is among you. I have not seen the child.' He drew back and stared at Elditha. 'Nonetheless, others confirm the monk's story, so the boy will travel with my army. He has a brave nurse, I hear it said. She may travel with him, and there is that loyal monk.'

There was silence. Outside rain fell steadily. She could hear it pouring off the wooden troughs in the yard. Would Edith deny that Ulf was here with them? If she did, would the Bastard tear the palace apart until Ulf was discovered?

'A harsh price for our loyalty,' Edith finally replied.

Elditha leapt to her feet. 'No, you cannot have him. My son is a small boy.'

When he looked at her, his face betrayed nothing: no emotion, no kindness or unkindness as he said in a brisk, factual manner, 'My lady, I will care for him as I would my own son. Six years old and in a year he would be of an age to go into another noble household anyway.'

'There are other Englishmen, older and stronger than my

child.'

The wind and rain rattled the shutters, and because the wood was damp the hearth fire belched an acrid, bitter smoke. Edith reached over and gently touched Elditha's hand. 'Be sensible, my dear. Sit down. This battle you cannot win.' She looked at the Duke and said, 'Take him. But remember, Duke William, if you harm a hair on his head you will lose my support. We want him back when you are king.'

William muttered, 'When I am king, I shall find one of my knights to wed the mother, a loyal knight, to raise the boy and educate him as a good Norman.' He looked again at Elditha, who had sunk despairing back onto the bench. This time there was the hint of a smile on his lips. Then it vanished again. He was hard, she thought. And he will get his way.

'You might find that the Lady Elditha would prefer a convent to marriage,' Edith said.

'She will be glad of our protection for the sake of her children.'

'Then, my Lord Duke, you must choose that knight carefully. For now, she is in my protection.'

He stood. 'We shall be leaving this afternoon, so the boy and his nurse must be ready to travel.'

Elditha clattered up the stairs in a fury to her chamber. There was nothing she could do other than hope that Brother Francis would care for her son. She called Margaret and instructed her how to watch over Ulf. Margaret wept as she packed a small coffer with clothes and some new wooden chess men that Ulf loved to play with. He had begged his Aunt Edith for these to replace those his father had given him and which were now lost for ever, burned to ashes in the fire at Reredfelle. She hugged Ulf to her breast and said that they were going to see his cousins in Westminster and that his mother would follow soon. Elditha tried to control her emotions as she agreed with the lie. She promised herself that she had not found Ulf only to lose him again. She would get him back.

Later that day Ulf and Margaret left the palace. Brother Francis rode with them. He hardly gave Elditha a passing glance, but he made a great fuss of Ulf. Elditha wept. In a final plea to Duke William, she requested that she travel with them but the cold Duke refused. Gytha consoled her, saying that Ulf would be with relatives in London. It could not help, because her heart was broken into shards.

On St Cecilia's Day, the 22nd day of November, Elditha attained her 32nd year. Her ladies gave her small gifts: silk threads and needles. The Queen presented her with jewelled hairpins and Gytha's gifts were a silver cloak-pin with runic inscriptions and a ring with an opal set into the gold band, which had once belonged to old Queen Emma. Thea stitched Ulf's little dove tapestry into a purse which Elditha hung from her belt. She blinked away tears and said that she would treasure it always.

A few days later the Countess Gytha, Thea and a group of noble ladies, including Maud and Freya, departed for Exeter, Gytha's Wessex stronghold.

'The Duke has not forbidden our journey. I think he sees us as mere women and no threat,' Gytha said. 'I am going before he changes his mind. He trusts Edith.'

'Take Thea too,' Elditha begged. 'I want her to be safe. I cannot go. He must release Ulf to me.'

Now, only Ursula remained behind with Elditha. They would pass Christmas in Winchester alone with Queen Edith.

16

January 1067

For a wolf shall carry to the woods our wretched welp.
Wulf and Eadwacer, in *A Choice of Anglo-Saxon Verse,* edited
and translated by Richard Hamer

Edith announced after Christmas that London had fallen
without a siege. Archbishop Stigand and the young Edgar
Atheling accompanied by Earls Morcar and Edwin had ridden
out to greet Duke William and his half-brothers Odo and
Robert. Duke William was crowned king on Christmas Day in
Westminster. Perhaps now he will return Ulf, Elditha thought as
Edith said how they must remain positive. No promise of
freedom followed from London.

Elditha's days were short and dreary. She listened to the
daily noise in the yard below. She could hear how women's
anxious voices bounced around the stone walls as soldiers
swore, banged weapons and thumped around the yard, their
leaders yelling at their men in French, a constant reminder that
Winchester was occupied by foreigners. She thought of Harold
every day, her heart breaking until she thought there was
nothing left of it but instead an empty space where once there
had been a heart. When Ursula accompanied her to the Nuns'
Minster there was a brief distraction as they cared for the sick.
She thought of setting out for Exeter, but she knew that Edith
would never permit it. It was evident that Ulf was not coming
back soon.

On a chill January day Edith came to the bower hall where
Elditha was stitching a shirt to send to Ulf in London. Edith

showed her a letter that had arrived from King William, which Elditha seized as if she was starving of hunger and it was bread. She slowly and painstakingly read the Latin script. At first the Duke assured the Queen that her nephew Ulf was in good health and was content. He had joined a group of young English noblemen with whom he was familiar. Ulf sent his greetings to his lady mother. Then she read, 'The Saxon Lady, Eadgyth Swanneshalls, is expected to wed the Breton Lord, Count Alain of Brittany. The Count of Brittany will visit her in Winchester as soon as we can spare him from our service.' King William's own red wax seal dangled from a yellow ribbon. Elditha furiously threw the script down, cracking the seal on Edith's tiled floor. 'I am not a mare to be bargained off to a rapine horse-dealer.'

Edith said smoothly, 'It may be for the best. How else can you survive?'

'You sold my son, but you will not sell me.'

'They would have taken the town and slaughtered us all.' She tapped the scroll angrily. 'This marriage will help us to ensure the family's survival here in England.'

'Edith, my answer is still no.'

'Then you had best hide in a convent, and if you do, I cannot guarantee the safety of your children – Ulf, or Thea; not even Gunnhild will be safe.' Edith swept out of the bower, having first ordered her cringing servant to gather up the damaged wax seal.

Edith sent Elditha messages every day. The Bishop wished to see her. The abbess of the Nuns' Minster wished to discuss Elditha's duty as a mother. Finally, Edith climbed the stairway to Elditha's chamber, sat in her chair, accepted a cup of hippocras and announced, 'Count Alain is expected for the Feast of St Benedict on Saturday. You must appear.'

'He is nearly ten years my junior. He burned my hall, terrified my people. He allowed his men to call me a whore. And how will that Norman save my lands, since they will soon be his own in any case?'

'He is not Norman. He is Breton and it is a good match. Think of Ulf's future.'

'Ulf is Harold's son. He will always be a threat to the Bastard.'

'Elditha, he is your overlord now and by Norman rules he owns us all. He has kept the boy safely at his own court with the Atheling Edgar and the young earls Edwin, Morcar and Waltheof of Northumbria.'

'All of them hostages. When William returns to Normandy, the hostages will accompany him. He can never release Ulf.'

'How do you know that, Elditha?'

'That man will trust no one, not even a count from Brittany. He will not trust Countess Gytha, nor will he trust me. We are Godwins. And he will suspect my older sons of rebellion.'

'I am a Godwin,' Edith reminded her.

'You were wed to King Edward, whom Duke William claims promised him a throne. He will want others to think that he trusts you, who gave him the keys of your town. And he wants to be sure that you, Edith, trust him, which, perhaps, you do.'

'Elditha, you go too far.' Edith left, shaking her head.

Elditha lay awake that night, thinking of ways to avoid her fate. There was a pond in the garden, but it was not deep enough. She had a seax, a sharp knife, but she could not bring herself to use it. She looked up at the high rafters and over to her chair, to her long twisted belt cord, and finally exhausted, she ran her hand over her sheets. She was still awake when the bell for Prime began to ring out. An idea had come to her at last, and it could work. She did not have to die yet. She could survive and avoid this marriage and get away to Ireland.

Once again the minster bells began to ring furiously, this time for the blessed saint. The door flew open. Ursula called to her, 'My lady, Queen Edith requests that you attend the service for St Benedict.'

She pushed away her coverlet and sat up cross-legged with her hair falling loose. Smiling, she pushed its heavy weight back. 'Ursula, I have thought of a plan, but I need your help.'

'How?

She opened her palms. 'Simple, find Padar and he will help us to disappear. We had thought it possible before William came to Winchester.'

'But, my lady, I have no idea now where to look for Padar.'

'He is in the woods. Go to the goldsmiths' quarter and talk to the goldsmith called Alfric. Margaret mentioned him. You will ask Alfric to tell Padar that we need his help.'

'If I am caught, you know it will be the end of us.'

'There is always the convent.' She jumped off the bed and began pacing. 'But, Ursula, try. You must. Please try to, or I shall have to myself.'

Ursula said, 'Everywhere will be busy today. I can mingle with the crowds.'

Elditha stood before her clothes coffer. 'Good. Now, let us see what garments would be suitable. I have a feast to attend.' Not wasting a moment she lifted the lid of the chest and drew out a wine-red dress of soft wool. 'It may be her cast-offs, but it will do very well.' Then she pulled out a brown woollen mantle with a hood. 'Ursula, take this cloak. It will protect you.'

Elditha dressed quickly, wore a heavy veil and circlet, lifted her own mantle, slipped it about her shoulders and fastened it with a brooch, changed her slippers for warm boots and took her friend's arm. They climbed down into the hall and out into the yard. 'Now, Ursula, listen as we walk, this is what you must say.'

They arrived in the minster just as the plainsong was commencing. The Queen knelt apart from the onlookers, with her hands folded in prayer. Near the front of the long nave the group of Normans stood, some vigilant, others with bowed heads. One of them was Count Alain of Brittany. She would recognise that head anywhere. Elditha pulled her hood over her veil, around her face and withdrew behind a large pillar. She spoke into Ursula's ear. 'Slip away as soon as you can. If you are stopped, say that you have to visit the infirmary at the Nuns' Minster.' Ursula glanced around at the pilgrims who thronged into the church. 'Godspeed,' Elditha said softly so that only Ursula heard. 'And take this. He will remember it.' She drew a small gold ring seal from her finger.

Ursula slipped it into her belt purse. As the choir sang the Latin masses, she drifted into the crowds of pilgrims. Elditha watched her disappearing back until she had melted into the press of worshippers. Then she moved forward closer to Queen Edith, determined now to be seen, praying that Ursula would have success, hoping that she was making a decision that would not threaten Ulf's safety. It was the only decision she felt she could make. Never would she wed with the enemy.

17

February 1067

He has as many knights as there are fish in the sea, and you could number his ranks as the stars of Heaven. He is seizing boys and girls, and the widows also; and at the same time, all the beasts.

The Carmen de Hastingae Proelio, attributed to Guy of
Amiens, 1068, edited and translated by Catherine Morton and
Hope Muntz

The sound of many languages, Norman-French, Latin, English and even Norse circled Edith's table in Winchester's Hall that afternoon. Elditha leaned towards Count Alain as he attempted to engage her in conversation. Throughout the many courses that accompanied the feast of St Benedict, she could not forget that this knight had been responsible for the destruction of Reredfelle. She never forgot, either, that his army had called her concubine or that Duke William had stolen her child or that Ursula was risking her life for her in the streets as she, herself, dined with the enemy.

'My lord I am a king's widow,' Elditha said to Count Alain. 'I need time to pass before contracting a new marriage.'

'It is in question as to whether your marriage to Earl Harold was a true marriage, Lady Elditha. Although I have no doubt your handfasted contract was blessed by God and his saints, it was not sanctified.'

She felt her face heat with fury. Bad enough that she should dine with this monster who had burned down her hall, mistreated her villagers, murdered her thanes – but this old insult! She rose and then, seeing others looking her way, she said loudly for all to hear, 'How dare you challenge it? I am sure that God does not care whether a priest sanctions a handfasted wedding.' The Normans seated nearby hushed. Then, as he glared at them, they lifted their eating knives again and continued their own conversations. A warning look from Edith and she sat down again.

He solemnly shook his head. 'It was not, I understand, conducted according to the laws of the Church.' He lowered his voice since the other eaters were only pretending involvement in their own conversations. 'Madam, our contract must be one that will be seen throughout Christendom as honourable. We shall wed in the new abbey. It will please King William and it will please the people and ...' She felt his hazel-shaded eyes appraising her. 'And, my lady, I would wed you within the six month.'

'And I shall consider the pressing nature of your suit, my lord.'

Elditha glanced along the table. Ursula was now in her place beside Queen Edith's ladies. Edith, busy speaking with a captain's Norman wife, smiled at her, obviously pleased that she was now apparently co-operating. Elditha rose. She looked at Edith. 'May I have permission to leave? The service today, the standing and this long feast has tired me. I discover my appetite to be gone.' Edith studied her, looked curiously at her for a moment, then nodded and waved her away. Relieved to be let off so lightly she rose and curtsied, 'Goodnight, my lord.' She caught Ursula's eye and then fled from the hall. When she reached her chambers she lit fresh tapers, poured a cup of hippocras and nibbled a honey cake that she had deftly filched from the hall's sideboard on her way past. She waited patiently for Ursula to follow her, thinking, never, ever, could she wed that man.

A few days later, Alfric took Ursula to Padar. On her return to the palace, Ursula told her Padar's plan. She must find an excuse to get away from Winchester. The best plan was to travel to Wilton on the pretext of visiting Gunnhild. They must then stay overnight in St Swithun's Priory, which was the usual Godwin stopover between the two places. When she was decided on the day, then Ursula would tell Alfric. Padar would abduct them both from the priory and help them to travel in secret to Dublinia. It was a simple plan. She knew that it could work. But Padar had stressed it had to appear that she was abducted, so that her child could not be blamed for the mother's broken faith. From Ireland she could work to free her son from King William.

Distasteful though the deception was, Elditha permitted Alain of Brittany to woo her, attending meals and sitting beside him. He accompanied her to services in the minster. He showed understanding and sympathy for her loss. She tolerated it, knowing that she was a convenience. Any financial penance that the Pope might inflict on those who had so brutally taken part in the killing of the English King, her own husband, might be avoided if he took the King's widow to wife.

At last Alain of Brittany departed for London, saying that he would return to Winchester in a month's space. She would sign a contract and their marriage would follow. The day after his departure Elditha sat sewing in the Queen's antechamber and quietly announced to Queen Edith that she must travel to Wilton to see Gunnhild.

She was canny about it all. Gesturing towards the window she said, 'Let me go now. The weather is fine, Edith. It might not be so, later in the month.'

'My dear, if I permit you to visit Gunnhild, I expect you back before Count Alain returns. We have a wedding to plan, linens to purchase and silks and tapestry no doubt. As the wife of King William's friend, you will be a great lady and you must look like one.'

She nodded, and then asked Queen Edith for Eglantine as her own mount and another gentle horse for Lady Ursula.

'And I can spare you three guards. They are from the Norman garrison, trained fighters. You can break the journey at St Swithun's Priory, a desolate place in winter but very welcoming. They keep a good table. And, Elditha, do not fail to

159

remind me to the Prior of St Swithun's. He was always such a good friend to the Godwins.'

The following day Ursula visited the goldsmith. They would set out for Wilton on Thursday. Elditha clasped Ursula's hands in her own. She heard the relief in her own voice as she spoke the words, 'At last.'

On Thursday, Elditha, Ursula and their guard rode into St Swithun's Priory. The sun was fading and the weather looked as if it might turn. The sky was heavy with dark clouds and the temperature had suddenly dropped. As they trotted into the yard, Elditha noticed a small, grey-clad monk sweeping the pavement outside the refectory. She knew him by his small height and his movements. He glanced up at her and boldly winked as she passed, jingling her bridle bells loudly. The guards were shouting for the stable boys. They hauled themselves off their horses, their armour clanking, and started looking around. Two boys came running from the stables. She quickly glanced back at Padar. His hood had fallen back. He had lost his pigtail, his beard had disappeared and his head was tonsured like the other monks.

'Heave in that sack of strewing herbs, Brother Matthew, then we are done,' a monk shouted from the refectory. 'Sounds like the company have arrived.' He came out and stepped in front of Padar. 'God bless our King's lady.' Using his sleeve edge, he wiped away a rheumy tear from his eye.

She called down to him, 'God bless you.'

Their guards helped them to dismount. Elditha handed Eglantine's bridle to the stable lad and took charge of her saddlebag. Ursula carried a larger travelling bag that was fashioned from sheep skins. A guard took it from her and, as cold rain began to spit from the heavens, glancing up at it, he led them towards the prior's house. Hurrying out of his doorway, the prior ushered the women inside his hall and sent their guards off to sleep in the stable.

A little later, the priory's six monks were rounded up to meet the Lady Elditha. Servants rushed from the kitchen to the refectory with great steaming pots of barley and pease pottage, roasted carp and baskets of bread. The fire was built high. Logs crackled. The ride had given Elditha an appetite. Comfortable but nervous, she ate well. As the meal reached its end, the prior leaned over and said, 'My companions and I will be dead to the world this night between Angelus and Matins, my lady, so Godspeed. Your guide will meet you on the stairway after the bell sounds the Angelus. You must hurry when you hear it. There is but a short time between that and Matins.'

She inclined her head and thanked him. He looked away but she could see that his kindly eyes had filled with tears.

When the Angelus bell began to ring, slow, loud and heavy, she signalled to Ursula. They must be ready after the monks returned to their dormitory. For an hour's space they waited. Then there was silence. No one was about. Silently they lifted their bags and slipped out into the freezing rain that lashed against the outer stairway. Not daring to speak, they stood shivering in their mantles, huddled in the shadowed darkness of the building's walls.

Elditha saw him first. He was moving slowly across the yard. She touched Ursula's arm and pointed. 'Are you ready?' she whispered. She took a step onto the stone stairway, set her bag down and raised a hand in greeting as Padar climbed up towards them. 'Make haste,' were the only words he spoke to them as he reached for her bag. He gave her his free hand and silently guided them both down the outer staircase and around the back of the church, keeping close to the walls until they reached the stable entrance.

A boy led three horses out of the stable. He had muffled their footsteps by tying cloths around their feet. There was a snort and then another. She started and looked back at the priory, but after that – apart from the occasional rustling of creatures in the hedging – the quiet was absolute. The boy helped Elditha up onto Eglantine and secured her bundle behind. After Ursula had mounted her mare, Padar led them back round behind the barn, past the kitchen, down a dark lane and out of the gates. He held the reins of his own stallion. The creature moved as quiet as the night itself.

'Our bodyguards?' she whispered.

'Are now at the bottom of the ditch. To the Devil with the bastards. And before you complain, there was no other way. My boy here will be on his way to Exeter first thing in the morning.'

'You have a way with the horses,' the lad murmured from his other side. 'They came with me quietly.'

'I think it is you who has that,' Padar said and reached for the saddle. With the lad's help, he hauled himself up onto the stallion's back, allowing his long robes to fall to either side of his legs. 'This gear is an accursed hindrance.'

The youth parted from them among the poplars. Elditha reached into her cloak pocket and drew out one of her cloak pins. It had a silver head carved with runic letters. She reached it down to him. The silver gleamed in his opened hand. 'When you reach Exeter, show this pin to the Countess Gytha. She knows it well and she will protect you.' She added so softly it was a whisper, 'May St Cecilia watch over you.'

'Keep that hidden,' Padar warned. 'When we have gone don't hang about these parts. There'll be uproar when they find Lady Elditha has disappeared and those bodies in the midden back there. The priory's cook will get you into the woods.'

With his backward wave, Padar led the women through the trees and onto the heath beyond. Sleet turned to snow. It drifted onto their cloaks and, as they travelled through the night, Elditha prayed that the snow did not worsen and swallow them up.

18

The English groaned aloud for their lost liberty.
The Ecclesiastical History of Orderic Vitalis, 12th century,
edited and translated by Marjorie Chibnall

By dawn the snow had become a wetting rain that fell in a sleeting, windy downpour. The downland was exposed. Padar peered ahead into the corners of fields looking for landmarks, confirming where they were, occasionally calling out to them to turn left or right until, before long, they rode into an abandoned hamlet. Huts had been fired, fences destroyed and wild dogs slunk about the lanes, growling and barking at them as they rode through. The church was deserted, its cross leaning forlornly, pointing towards the ruined houses.

They crossed a low hedge into another large field. 'We should reach the abbey at Abingdon soon,' Padar said, slowing his horse and shouting above the rain. 'Most of the monks there are loyal to us and the abbot should be in London with the Bastard.' He stopped and caught his breath. 'The countryside nearer to Oxford will be occupied by soldiers. We can wait at the abbey until we work out how to move west into the hills.' He pointed back at the destruction they had just left. 'You can see, the villages are not safe.'

Elditha looked down and, through the sleet, saw several twisted and naked bodies lying in the ditch. She pulled her hood close and drew her mare closer to Padar. 'They'll search west for us.'

'I threw two of your guard into a midden. They'll look everywhere for me. Still, they'll have to call out a troop first.'

Elditha looked at him, alarmed.

He laughed. 'Never fear, the prior hates the Norman bastards too. My lady, the river's not far from here. The abbey lies on the opposite bank.'

It was still raining when they left the downs for the flat of the valley. The bell of Abingdon's church rang out its slow, deep tolls. They could hear the river crashing and tumbling through a water mill. For a while they could hardly hear anything else, just water gushing and the bell's clanging.

'They're ringing it for early morning services,' said Elditha, as she pulled her horse up short beyond the mill.

'Padar,' Ursula called, her words blowing away from her. 'Is this abbey safe?'

'Yes, the abbey's infirmary monk will conceal us until the hue and cry has died down.'

'How do you know him?' Elditha shouted.

Padar called back, 'I have played my harp here on feast days. We two became friends.'

The abbey appeared across the river. Built of stone, it rose up above a high, stout outer wall. Padar rode ahead to the gatehouse. He spoke to the gatekeeper, who waved them through. They crossed a bridge and passed through another gateway into the abbey courtyard. Dismounting, they handed the reins of their horses to stable boys, who appeared through the rain as if from nowhere. Shivering with cold and with sleet stinging their faces, they trudged up the hill to the abbey building.

Though there was no one out in the abbey's precinct, echoes of plainsong issued from the great church. A long, two-storey stone building with a huge chimney leaning into its side now faced them, its imposing door looming out of the sleet as they crossed the swath. A bell hung on the outside wall. Padar reached up and pulled the sodden cord that hung from it and its ringing reverberated loudly. They waited. At last the door opened. A tall monk, who looked like a flowing grey line against the bare abbey walls, stood in the doorway. He never spoke but indicated that they should enter into the porch. Padar introduced himself as Brother Matthew from Durham. He asked for Brother Thomas from the infirmary and the monk nodded.

The door creaked noisily as he pushed it closed behind them. He lifted a rush light from a sconce on the wall, and gestured to them to follow him across the hall.

He led them to an antechamber situated at the farthest end of the smoke-filled hall, and then glided off again.

Elditha said, 'Where has he gone?'

'To find Brother Thomas,' Padar replied, and pointed her towards a glowing brazier that stood in the centre of the tiny room.

Elditha and Ursula removed their cloaks, letting them fall onto a crude bench, and stretched their hands towards the glowing charcoal. Moments later, Brother Thomas pushed through the arras. 'By Christ's holy bones, what has the wind and rain blown in tonight?' His small, round presence emanated kindness.

'Thomas,' Padar said, drawing back his cowl so Brother Thomas would recognise him.

'Mary's sainted shawl, you! Miracles. God bless us all. The poet is become monk!' Brother Thomas let out a guffaw.

Padar embraced his old friend, two little men caught up in a cub-like hug. 'Thomas, you look well. I haven't seen you since last spring. We talked much about the world then.'

'The world is changing.' A frown creased his round face. 'You make an odd monk, Padar,' he said. He surveyed the women. 'And you come with companions?'

'The Lady Elditha, Thomas.'

The monk scrutinised Elditha. 'You are the King's lady?'

She nodded. 'And I seek sanctuary here.'

He looked thoughtful. 'My lady, surely the Abbey of Wilton is best for your purposes and …'

'Not Wilton, it is too dangerous, Brother Thomas. We intend to ride north-west.' She hesitated. 'I do not wish to endanger your abbey but …'

He opened his arms in a welcoming gesture. 'Sanctuary is granted, Lady Elditha, but be aware that our abbot has followed Archbishop Stigand's lead. He has given King William his blessing, though I suspect with reluctance.' He turned to Padar.

'Does anyone know you are here?'

'Only those who saw us ride through the gates and the monk who greeted us.'

'It will soon be common knowledge that we have guests. Ah, well, they don't know who.' He chuckled and looked at the women's garments, which were dripping puddles of water onto the tiles. 'Let me think of how to manage things. You must have dry garments and food.' Brother Thomas bustled over to a chest in the corner, opened the heavy lid and pulled out a linen drying cloth which he handed to Padar. 'You wait here. Dry yourself with this.' He lifted a candle holder that held three dripping candles and opened a low door opposite the arras. 'My lady, follow me.'

He led Elditha and Ursula along a hushed corridor, past low, bow-shaped doors to a large archway that was situated at what Elditha suspected was the gable end of the building. Through this opening lay a greater oak door studded with ironwork tracery. It was decorated with a carving of the tree of life, in which many differing birds nested and around the bottom of which many beasts appeared to prowl. But there was no time to look more closely. Brother Thomas lifted an iron key from the bunch which hung from his belt, turned it in the lock and pushed open the door. He revealed a magnificent chamber containing a high bed, a table, four winged chairs with cushions, several carved chests and a wall hung with tapestry. He ushered them in. 'Come,' he said, pointing to a coffer. He lit a candle from his own candles, handed it to Elditha and opened the chest, allowing the familiar whiff of fennel to escape from it, mingled with a pungent smell she recognised as myrrh.

The monk dragged out two habits woven in white wool. 'God will forgive me, I am sure, if you were to accept these.'

'Canons' robes!' Ursula exclaimed, touching one.

'The robes are indeed for our canons and this chamber is the abbot's own. No one will enter here when he is not in residence.' He chuckled as if he was enjoying a jest. 'It is one of two which have a chimney, so I'll light the fire after I return. Change into these.'

166

Elditha placed her candle on a chest and laid the garments on the bed. They were clean, the wool was soft and they were dry.

By the time Thomas returned, shouldering a basket of wood shavings and logs, they had changed into the habits and were draping their own damp gowns over chairs. He built up a fire, struck a flint and held the spark close to the wood shavings. Once the kindling caught and the logs began to blaze, he said, 'There, it's drawing up and out of its tunnel.' He drew a bench to the hearth and collapsed onto it. 'The infirmary is full to overflowing with those who have suffered since the battle. Our guesthouse is full. I shall explain that two women of noble birth have come in the storm.' He chuckled again. 'And that there was nowhere else for them other than the abbot's own chamber. Abbot Ealdred would wish it, though no doubt if he ever finds out, I shall do penance for that lie.'

Elditha sat beside him. 'Thank you, Brother Thomas. And if I could, I would do your penance for you.'

The monk shook his head. 'God will forgive, lady. It is a little lie.'

'And so, where is Padar?'

'Seeing to your horses, and I had better stir myself and find you something hot to eat.'

He hurried off again and returned with a pail of pottage and a basket with soft white bread, meat and cheese. 'There are bowls in the cupboard. God bless you both.'

With those words, the little monk disappeared and, for several days after that, they never saw him. Padar slept in an empty cell and it became his task to bring them food and drink. Abingdon, he told them, was a large abbey with a scriptorium, a stone church, cloisters, a refectory and farm buildings.

'The abbot is pragmatic and, like Queen Edith, he has acquiesced,' she said sadly.

'As well he has for now, since, my lady, it is easier to disappear by remaining here until we know that the Normans are searching for you elsewhere. Even if they suspect who you are, the monks will not betray you,' he said. He stroked his shaven chin. 'But we should be away before their abbot returns.'

Days passed slowly. The abbot's bedroom led on to a garden. When the sleeting rain stopped and the sun reappeared they walked there. The abbey bell rang regularly for service, allowing them a sense of time's passage, and although monks shuffled along the corridor beyond their room with regularity, no one disturbed Elditha and Ursula. Other than monks' footpads, distant murmurings of prayer and the bell's regular ringing, the abbey was a place of solitude and quiet. They listened to the cockerel that crowed every morning, a robin chirruping as it stalked the garden and magpies chattering on the top of a wall. They listened to the weather, the rain when it came and to the wind's keening in the trees. As darkness fell, they slept peacefully, cocooned from the tumultuous world beyond the cloister.

A week after their arrival, they were seated on a stone bench by a sundial. The white cowls of the habits, which they continued to wear over their gowns for warmth as much as concealment, were drawn close around their faces. Padar appeared through a garden door.

Ursula moved along and he sat on the bench between them.

'Are we leaving?' Elditha asked.

'I had hoped that we might travel within the week, though a horse dealer near the abbey advises me that there are soldiers marching through every village between Winchester and Oxford.'

'What must we do?'

'I can enter Oxford tonight by river and find my friends. I must send a messenger ahead of us to Deerhurst in Gloucestershire and see what can be arranged by way of a crossing into Ireland. The Godwins still have friends. The Normans have not taken the south-west, though all riders west of Oxford need to be alert. And, since the battle, there are bands of brigands on the roads.'

'Would they dare attack a dead king's wife?'

Padar snorted. 'There are Mercian folk loyal to the Godwins, but there are also those who seek profit and do not hesitate to take hostages from either side. We must use the river. Eglantine, I fear, will remain here in the abbey. I will return soon. If not, then you must ask Brother Thomas for help.' Ursula looked startled. He repeated, 'I promise you, I'll return by Saturday.'

'What if Duke William's soldiers come here?' Ursula asked.

'Brother Thomas will hide you.'

Padar left that night, rowing a small craft upriver to Oxford.

Later, as they prepared for sleep, Ursula said to Elditha, 'Do you think that Alain of Brittany will send out troops to find us?'

Elditha climbed into the abbot's bed. 'Ursula, Count Alain will search every abbey and nunnery west of Winchester, so let us pray that they think we have been abducted for someone else's gain. They will have found the bodies in the midden. Sleep, Ursula, worry cannot help us.' She blew out the candle. Soon Ursula was snoring softly beside her. As she drifted into sleep, she thought, *and Edith too will be furious by now*.

19

Winchester
Late February 1067

Edith watched the sunrise burst over the palace garden in hues of yellows and pinks as she waited for Count Alain. She did not relish the interview ahead. It was she who had permitted Elditha to leave for Wilton. Her *Vita Edwardii*,– her book, her great work – had been on her mind when Elditha had made her request. Had she not been thinking of that, she might have accompanied Elditha to Wilton herself. She shuddered. Had she travelled that day, she too might have been abducted.

Watching over Elditha had been too easy after she had agreed to wed Alain of Brittany. The prior of St Swithun's himself had ridden to her in terrible weather with his tale of murder, bodies in a midden and the abduction of the Lady Elditha and her maid when all his five monks, his cook and a young guest were asleep. They had heard nothing. A new monk had come to them recently from a monastery in the east. They had taken him in, given him charity, and he too had vanished that night. The enemy had stolen my lady and her maid away.

Edith should have never allowed her sister-in-law to travel abroad in such terrible times. She sighed. Elditha was so beautiful and she had once been so very wealthy. She and Harold had been a beautiful couple. The marriage would give Alain of Brittany all that under the cloak of legality rather than simply by conquest. In one move – that of marriage – he would have her beauty and her wealth and the legal tenure of lands in Norfolk, Essex and Kent, lands where Harold had appointed diligent stewards to guard the wealth and on which substantial halls stood. What if Alain of Brittany looked elsewhere for an heiress and Duke William seized Elditha's lands anyway?

Fitz-Wimach slid into her presence and announced that Count Alain had arrived. Edith sat with her hands neatly folded in her lap and, when the angry Count pushed through the curtain, determined to remain in control she calmly indicated a winged chair opposite her own.

'So the swan has flown?' he opened in good Latin. 'And you have no idea where she roosts?'

Edith replied, 'I do not.' As she made an impatient gesture, her wide sleeve fell back from her hand. She let it fall again and drew herself tall. She sat very still and spoke again, this time in perfect Norman-French. 'Count Alain, I am not part of any scheme to aid Lady Elditha's disappearance nor, I am sure, is my mother, the Countess Gytha. A monk was responsible, a Benedictine monk. No one can say who he really is. He calls himself Brother Matthew, an apostle's name.' She paused and emphasised, her tongue rolling over his name as she thought for a moment. 'Brother Matthew, an interesting choice, don't you think, since St Matthew's symbol is that of a human angel? I am quite sure it was against her will.'

'Angel, my belt and boot; this Brother Matthew, whoever he is, is now an outlaw.'

'Perhaps he always was. I have sent word to Wilton and to Exeter.'

'My soldiers will question the monks of St Swithun's Priory. Then they will descend upon every abbey and priory north, south, east and west of Winchester until she is found.' He clasped his hands into one fist. 'I have duty and honour to consider. My marriage was to be a gesture of recognition from your family of the King's rightful kingship. I am a second cousin to the King through my mother.' He glanced towards a small altar, a statuette of the Virgin and two comfortable prayer cushions in the corner of the antechamber.

Queen Edith watched the knight. 'Elditha has not broken faith, I assure you,' she said. 'Let us pray that Lady Elditha is returned to us. We shall find her.' But the idea niggled. Had Elditha, in fact, absconded without a thought for how it could endanger her son? How could she have been so careless?

20

The falling tempest binds in winter's vice
the earth, and darkness comes with shades of night.
The Wanderer, A Choice of Anglo-*Saxon Verse*, edited and
translated by Richard Hamer

Brother Thomas knocked on the door of the abbot's chamber
and entered, carrying a pot of stew and the usual basket of bread
and cheese. When Elditha lifted the lid of the pot to peep inside,
meat and herbs filled the room with a delicious aroma. Usually
Brother Thomas rushed back to the infirmary. But as she turned
from the cupboard with their bowls she saw that the monk was
hovering by the bench. His face was creased with anxious lines.

'We are a burden to you, Brother Thomas.' Elditha said, as
she slowly filled their bowls with the stew.

'It is a pleasure to serve you, my lady. But a delegation of
monks is expected from Westminster tomorrow. We have
known of it for weeks but we had thought that they would wait
until after Lent. They intend to investigate our abbey's
treasures, our relics but, most importantly, our library before
they return to Normandy.'

'Does Abbot Ealdred come with them?'

'I fear it may be so.'

'He will know my face.'

'My lady, I hope that he would grant you anonymity but I
cannot be sure. And it would be strange if he does not use his
own chamber, so I must move you to another – my own in the
infirmary. It is a plain cell, but it is only for a few days.'

'You are placing yourself in great danger. Is there any way
in which I can repay your kindness?' she asked.

The monk closed the basket. He began to look animated, as

173

if something had just occurred to him. 'There is something,' he said, now hardly containing his excitement. 'I wonder, I wonder if it would be safe if ... later tonight, when the abbey sleeps ... then I must show you a great treasure. My lady, you may be able to take it into safety.' He gestured to the table where the stew was already cooling in the bowls. 'Eat your dinner. I will reveal all later,' he said and scuttled off, pulling the chamber's great door shut behind him.

That evening, in the grey quiet that fell between Vespers and Compline, Elditha and Ursula slipped away from the abbot's bedchamber and followed Brother Thomas to his cell. He left them to settle in, saying that he would return before midnight.

'I wonder what he wants to show you, my lady,' Ursula said, after he had closed the door.

'I cannot imagine, though a treasure could be a relic or a book.'

Elditha looked around the small, chill room. It contained a bed, a pallet, a chair and a desk. She breathed in the scent of herbs slowly, trying to place smells of the earth, the sea, lichen and rocks and a hint of faraway places that existed beyond the monastery walls – places from beyond the oceans and distant mountains. A simple wooden cross was nailed on the narrow wall opposite her. Beside that there was a small shuttered window onto which rain splashed in a low, monotonous tone. 'I think his treasure rests in the library,' Elditha guessed as she surveyed his desk.

Vellum sheets, roughly sewn together and without covers, were laid out neatly. She lifted a candle and peered closely at them. They contained unadorned writing with plain stroke after stroke. Letters merged into other letters, making translation difficult and the margins contained recent insertions. She examined these closely, wondering if they were Brother Thomas's own additions. These leathery pages smelled of a life hidden away from daylight, musty and old, and as her candle burned down, Elditha turned them over, peering at them, trying to decipher the ancient script. Eventually, she was able to make sense of them. They were recipes for salves with descriptions of the attributes of various herbs. She already knew the usual remedies, such as those for coughs and aches, but here she found new suggestions. There were cures for headache, boils and toothache using unusual ingredients such as powder of onyx, tusk of unicorn and ground shells from the beach. She glanced at a shelf above the desk which held pots and boxes. Labels, written in the same script as the notes in the margins of the book, pasted onto the jars, indicated their contents.

'Ursula, look at this – myrrh and frankincense, powder of sapphire, so good for ulcers if dissolved in milk,' she said, taking two of them down. 'Sapphire to cure disease of the eye. And these …' She read the labels slowly. 'Good St Cecilia, balsam, possibly from Jerusalem, ammoniacum, tragacanth and galbanum! These are rare. They come from places east of our Lord's own lands.'

Ursula reached along the shelf and lifted down a small wicker basket that held a collection of twisted and knotted roots. She dug her finger in, feeling around until she found one that was different to the others. She lifted it out. It was a plump root. She smelled its pungent scent and puzzled at its familiarity as she turned it over. Elditha leaned over Ursula's hand and touched it with the tips of her fingers. She knew this one too, because she still possessed it, hidden deep within her casket. Murmuring sleepily as if its magic overpowered her, she said, 'Mandrake – the Devil's root.'

Ursula returned it to the basket, pushing it deep inside among the others.

As she replaced the basket on its shelf, Brother Thomas bustled in. 'Our visitors will arrive before noon. We were just in time.' He glanced at the papers on his desk. 'Ah, I see that you have discovered my recipes,' he said closing the cell door softly. 'These ones are simple salves for use in our infirmary – old and well-known remedies, but what I have is much more interesting.' He came closer. 'And if it were to be taken from this abbey into Normandy, a part of the medical knowledge held on our island would disappear. I have a book to show you and,

175

if the Norman monks discover its presence in our library, they will remove it. Some fear the things spoken of within its pages. Come with me, and you will need your cloaks. Then, my lady, you must decide if you can help us.'

They covered themselves with monks' mantles and followed Brother Thomas through the abbey to the internal stairway at the end of the building. In single file they climbed up to an arched narrow door decorated, as had been the abbot's chamber's, with acanthus leaf carvings. The carvings inside the decorative leaves depicted the four saints of the Gospels with their symbols: a human angel hovered above St Matthew; a lion reclined by St Mark's feet; behind Luke an ox appeared; and above John hung an eagle. Elditha traced the lion of St Mark with a finger. 'The abbey has beautiful carvings,' she remarked.

'And as you will discover we have more wonders hidden here than ancient carved doors, great statues which line the abbey's church or the magnificent black cross which stands in the chancel.'

'There are so many of these crosses throughout England that I cannot imagine which one is the real cross.'

'I often think about that. We have a relic collection below in the ossuary. One cannot help but wonder how many fingers St Benedict had, there are so many of them in our abbeys; and toenails, and teeth, portions of the crown of thorns, shreds of the apostles' shrouds, nails from the true cross, a snip of the Virgin's veil, the purse belonging to St Benet, St Catherine's shoe, a rib of St Uncer, a bone from St Helena's arm. So it continues, bones of this saint and that apostle; oh yes, we have bits of them too.' He caught his breath and said, 'But the abbey's collection of books is our greatest pride. Come now and see the library and observe how we use our window glass here.'

Brother Thomas shook a great key ring from his belt and, lifting it up to the light, chose one and then unlocked the door. Holding the sconce high, he leaned against the door and swung it open. He led them into a long room and, with a gesture of his free hand, he indicated tall windows of plain clear glass. These were divided with lead into sections and were deeply set into the abbey's walls. The rain had ceased and stars and the moon shone through breaks in the cloud, breaking into the great chamber to illuminate it with a silver light. Along the length of the room ranged desks on which lay the tools of copiers: their inks and quills, vellum sheets, many already faintly ruled, others with beautifully decorated pages and books set above them, all opened at the pages the monks had been copying.

'There must be so much light here by day,' Ursula said. 'Such a beautiful room; books everywhere.'

They were stored on shelves which reached toward the rafters, hundreds of them piled beside each other from one end of the hall to the other. At the far end of the scriptorium was the partner fireplace to the one which was to the abbot's bedchamber and, although the hour was late, a glow still lay within it. The room was cool, but not yet cold.

'It is a wonderful place,' Elditha said. 'Busy with scholarship, so much learning contained within this one room.'

Brother Thomas led them to the shelves, and walked along them saying, 'Here are the Gospels, here the codices of the Apocalypse, here Psalters; here are books of poetry, riddles and fables and here the works of the Venerable Bede.'

'Bede?' repeated Ursula.

Elditha provided the answer. 'Bede was a great scholar, Ursula. I learned about him when I learned to read, after I had married Harold. Since Queen Edith and Countess Gytha could read, I learned to as well.'

'Yes,' echoed Brother Thomas, 'Bede's *Historia Anglorum* and his *De Aedificatione Temple*. Next, we have collected King Alfred's Colloquies and here we have Annals that reach back from our own time to the time of Cedric. And look on that desk beside you, Ursula, where one of our brothers is copying our own *Chronicle*, the story of our abbey from the time of Hean, who founded it, until the present day.' He moved on, holding his torch high so that they could see the great collection more clearly. 'And here the teachings of Aristotle and Plato, Apuleius, Virgil and Horace. The Moorish copyists from Iberia have made many copies of books of mathematics and medicine from at least the time of Plato, and they have set down in Latin many of their own medical treatises.' Brother Thomas lowered his voice. 'We have a copy of their Koran here, the Bible of the Infidels, a perverse book too, and I expect the Norman monks will disapprove.' He sighed, moved farther along and waved his hand at a large collection in a new case of shelves. 'Look at these very old scrolls dedicated to the study of herbs and plants, and of course the encyclopaedias of animals. Beside them, see, we have collected three great bestiaries of fantastic animals living in distant lands, unicorns and so on, though I believe few have ever been so privileged to have seen these creatures, and we have five work calendars. There is no time to examine all these works. My Lady Elditha, come and look at our treasure.'

Brother Thomas drew one book out from the last shelf. Like many of the other volumes it had a leather cover, but unlike many books where the cover had been embellished, this one was plain. Its only ornamentation was a gold clasp with a small gold key. Brother Francis turned the little key in its miniature lock, then carried the book to a table by the dying firelight and laid it open there. 'It is a lapidary, the only one, I believe, on our island,' he said.

It was not a great volume. In fact, it was only the same size as a Psalter carried by a travelling monk; indeed similar to the Psalter that had belonged to Brother Francis. However, when it lay open on the table Elditha caught her breath as she bent over it and examined the miniature drawings contained on every page. It was a book of stones and jewels and every jewel and every stone was described in detail, as were their medicinal properties. Tiny mythical creatures journeyed through jewelled magical landscapes from page to page: basilisks, lions, unicorns, the phoenix, birds with men's heads and angel wings, mermaids and sirens and even more wondrous creatures of the seas, whales and urchins, sea hydras with arms and twisting eels with men's features. Every initial letter was delicately decorated with fantastic designs of intricate knot work in gold leaf, so tiny that it was almost impossible to see them. However, as they looked even more closely, the letters turned into odd, sometimes studious, little creatures, occasionally mischievous, their tails studded with gems. It was indeed a great treasure.

'This is the most beautiful book I have seen.'

'And you say that you can read, my lady?'

'Yes, but I cannot write, and now I wish I had paid attention to writing when I was a girl. This work is so beautiful that I envy the scribe whose work it is.'

'Not envy, but admire, my lady,' Brother Thomas admonished in a gentle tone. 'You can still learn to write. If you can read, then the art of writing is simple. My lady, now for my question: can you protect the lapidary?'

'Yes, if you wish me to take the book into safekeeping. But where to; where will it be safe? Is it wise to trust it into my keeping?'

'It would be safe in Ireland. Padar tells me that you will go there as soon as he arranges your travel. You will succeed in your journey, my lady. I feel it. I shall pray for it, for your safety, for the book's safety. Take it to the Abbey of Bangor and hopefully, one day, in more peaceful times, it may be returned to our own abbey, where it belongs.' Brother Thomas closed the book, locked it and gave the key to Elditha. 'Keep the key safe too.'

Elditha added it to the chain on her neck. It nestled against the key to her casket. One key was silver and the other gold, but both were now as precious to her as the air she breathed. Brother Thomas then took a sealskin bag from his cloak, placed the book inside it and gave the package to Elditha. 'I will keep it close to my own person,' she promised.

'My lady, come here,' called Ursula. She had crossed over to a window and was staring down from it. 'A boat filled with monks is landing on the wharf. There are torches on the river bank.'

'Abbot Ealdred already?' exclaimed Brother Thomas. 'Stand back from the window. If you can see them, they may see you. It is unusual for the scriptorium to be occupied at night.' He doused the flame of his torch and hurried with Elditha to a second window and looked out over the river. Moonlight illuminated the figures on the water. 'Yes, it could be the abbot's party,' he said. 'Look, the abbot's staff is gleaming in their torchlight.'

Elditha peered down. From below came shouts and a stir and the noise of boats splashing and knocking up against the jetty. When the arrivals disembarked they were immediately surrounded by stable boys, novices and monks. They began to snake their way along the bank from the jetty, a band of dark-cloaked and silent monks. The abbot strode at their head and led them onwards up the slope, holding his silver staff before him. One monk just behind the abbot glanced up at the abbey building. A rush light, held before him, illuminated his features. Elditha immediately drew back from the sill. 'Abbot Ealdred must never know of our presence in his abbey.' The monk shook his head and placed a finger on his lips. He wouldn't reveal them. She added quietly, 'Because, Brother Thomas, there is one down there in the abbot's party who means us harm.' She sent a prayer up to Heaven. 'St Cecilia, bring Padar back to us soon.'

21

> Master: What fish do you catch?
> Fisherman: Eels and pike, minnows and burbot,
> trout and lampreys.
> *Ælfric's Colloquies,* in *A Choice of Anglo-Saxon Verse,* edited
> and translated by Richard Hamer

Footsteps outside their cell were followed by an urgent rap on the door. 'My lady, are you awake?'

Elditha threw the coverlet over her shoulders, hurried to the door and opened it a crack. 'Padar?'

'Who is there?' Ursula sat up on her pallet.

'Hush, Ursula. It's only Padar.'

'My lady, we must leave or you will be discovered.'

'You know, then, that the abbot returned last night.'

'I rowed in on his heels. Guards by the boats challenged me.'

'What did you say?'

'That I was fishing.'

'In February!'

'Not unusual. I said that a cook wanted a fish for the abbot's breakfast. I told them that there had been a rumour that pike lay upstream, though I never caught any …'

'How do we avoid the guards?'

'Cover yourselves with those monks' robes and walk out. If challenged, I'll say I am rowing novices to Oxford. Hurry, Brother Thomas is waiting for us by the orchard door.'

Elditha pulled the loose novice habit over her head, snatched the sealskin bag from the table and packed the lapidary underneath her treasure box, pushing it deep inside her pack. Then she threw the monk's cloak over her gown and cloak. 'Thank Mary, this garb is wide enough to cover all of me and more. In any case these robes will keep us warm. The river will be freezing. Hurry, Ursula.'

Ursula nodded, but, as was usual, she took time to fold the covers from her pallet. She tidied Elditha's bed and only then did she pull the voluminous garments over her slim frame. The monks were still singing as they hurried out of the cell.

Padar lifted the pack from Elditha and led them along the corridor, past closed doors, to where the monk waited with a lantern. Brother Thomas lifted his bundle of keys and unlocked the orchard door. As she slipped by him, he whispered, 'You have it safe, my lady?'

Elditha pointed to the pack.

'Blessings, my lady. May St Christopher guide you to safety.'

'Thank you, Brother Thomas. Thank you a thousand times. And may your kindness to us be rewarded in Heaven.'

Padar lifted the lantern, hurried them through the door and along an avenue of apple trees. Their twisted trunks appeared bare and menacing, reminding Elditha of the danger ahead of them. They continued down the slope to the river, where a large rowing boat was waiting. Elditha looked over at the wharf and saw why Padar was worried. The guards by the moorings opposite were awake and alert and a familiar voice was shouting.

'You haven't seen it. There it is.' Brother Francis pushed past the guards and lifted a silver censer from a boat. 'You will do penance for your neglect ... If it is ruined ...' He trailed off and he stroked the object as if it were a prized hawk.

Padar lifted a warning finger to his lips as they climbed into their boat, but the priest spun around. He stroked the censer again with one hand, moved a few steps closer to their mooring and peered across the wharf at them.

The guards laughed and one called over, 'Out again,

fisherman?'

'It's never ending,' Padar grumbled to them, pulling his cowl up, concealing his face. 'Now I am to ferry these tardy novices to St Frideswide's.'

The priest clutched the censer tightly as he came along the planks and closer to their boat.

'Do I know you?' he asked.

Elditha and Ursula bowed their heads beneath cavernous hoods. Elditha felt they were trapped like sparrows caught in a net.

Padar mumbled, 'You are mistaken, Brother ...'

'Brother Francis,' the monk said. 'But, yes, I have seen you before.'

'You are mistaken, Brother,' Padar repeated, and using his staff, carefully pushed the craft away from the bank. In an unhurried manner, he sat in front of the women, took up the oars and began to row the boat through the narrow cut that lay between the abbey and an island, just as the abbey cook was crossing from the island with a boat full of fish. He shouted over the water, 'Catch us a pike today. Abbot likes his fish.'

'I'll see what I can find,' Padar called back. 'I'm off to St Frideswide's.'

'Godspeed, then.'

Padar rowed furiously out into the river and guards and the monk were swallowed by mist. Elditha glanced back expecting pursuit, but there was none. They glided on through the water, not speaking. Squalls of icy rain blew. Patches of mist clung to the dripping willows. Occasionally other boats passed them and there was the odd greeting, but none took particular notice of a boatman ferrying novice monks upriver.

A few more hours passed and a distant bell rang for Sext as Padar manoeuvred the craft into a fast-flowing tributary towards a mill on the left bank. As he pointed to it and called out that they could rest, a current caught the boat and spun it around in a whirlpool. For a moment it seemed that they would either be tipped into the swirl of the river or tossed about until they crashed into a bank. Elditha clutched the side and hung on

183

and called to Ursula to do likewise.

'My lady, take the oars,' Padar yelled. He reached over and placed the oars one by one into her hands. She managed to grasp them and, by leaning first right and then left, she helped to keep the boat afloat. 'Row harder,' Padar called to her. His pole was in his hands and he was standing feet apart in the boat's stern. He reached for an overhanging tree to give them leverage. Elditha threw her weight into rowing, finding a strength she had not realised she possessed.

'Well done, almost in,' he shouted, letting the branch go and pushing the pole into the stream. He threw the pole out, caught an elder trunk that leaned from the bank and pulled them alongside the entrance to a mill house. Wobbling precariously, he jumped onto the floating jetty, and secured the craft to an iron ring that hung from it.

'Here is where we'll break our fast.'

Elditha steadied herself on the shaky platform. Ursula's foot became entangled in her robe but Padar caught her as she fell forward.

'Careful, the current here is fierce,' he said, above the crashing sounds from mill and water. 'It's dangerous, don't fall in.'

The miller was ambling towards them.

'Keep those hoods pulled over your faces. Today Benedictine silence will serve us well.' He waved to the miller. 'I said I'd be bringing monks for breakfast,' he called.

The miller nodded. 'Simple fare it is, but good enough for monks. Welcome, brothers.'

He showed them into a large room stacked with sacks of flour. On the table a meal was laid out – a hunk of cheese, ham shanks, bread and a jug of buttermilk. The miller waved them to a bench. 'Eat as much as you want. I know you young men have a hunger on you.' He held out a hairy hand and Padar pressed coins into it.

The miller pushed them into his belt purse. 'If you need anything else, shout. I'll be loading my boat.' He grabbed a bag of flour, heaved it over his shoulder and disappeared outside.

They ate in silence until Elditha spoke. 'Padar, what will happen when we reach Oxford?'

Padar gnawed at his ham bone for a moment, laid it on the table and said, 'We will stop there for a night. There is a small nunnery upriver, a priory dedicated to St Margaret. It's close to the water, before Lechlade. It was endowed by Godiva of Mercia. The nuns will shelter us. Once we are in Gloucestershire, there'll be fewer Normans and it'll be possible to ride on towards the Severn.'

'Godiva of Mercia, Padar, she who was wed to Leofric?'

He nodded.

Godiva of Mercia had witnessed her handfasted marriage to Harold. The Countess had been widowed by Leofric, one of the great triumvirate of Saxon earls who had watched over King Edward so carefully, who had kept England safe from invasion and who were ever worried about the Norman knights whom Edward had invited into the kingdom, and the Norman priests whom he had introduced into the Church. The three great earls were all dead now, all of them – Leofric, Siward and Godwine. And now, Harold, Gyrth and Leofwine too, all gone, the end of their world, the end of their best and greatest warriors. She wiped a tear away with the back of her hand.

'Yes, my lady, the same. She has survived,' Padar said in a gentle tone. 'Even though she is older than Countess Gytha, she lives on her manor near Coventry, quietly enough, I'm told.'

'I'm glad of it. Who is at Deerhurst on the Severn now?'

'The manor house is owned by Edward's doctor but he never took up residence. He is always in London, I'm told. The manor has a reeve to see to things, and he is one of us. There is a group of thanes who wish to meet you there, my lady. Lord Beorhtric leads them.'

'You have worked hard on my behalf.' It was more than she had hoped for.

'When we reach Deerhurst, there will be an escort waiting to take us to Ireland, but the bad news is that we need to wait for Easter.'

'Not before?'

'These are the arrangements.'

'And until then?'

'You will be safe at St Margaret's Priory.'

'So then, we must remain novices, Padar?'

'No. After Oxford you can become dispossessed women, travelling west to seek sanctuary in St Margaret's. Lady Ursula there would make a devout nun.' He winked at Ursula and, seeing her bite back a retort, said more seriously, 'These are dangerous times. Where safer than a nunnery? I doubt that even Brother Francis will show up there, never mind Count Alain of Brittany.'

'I'm not so sure, Padar. Will the miller reveal us if either come here?'

'The miller lost sons at Hastings. There are many who want to see the back of the Bastard.' Padar wiped his hands on his robe. 'And, now, are you done eating? If we are to reach Oxford by nightfall, we must get on.' Padar rose and led them back to their craft. The miller was loading his boat. He waved as they rowed away and on out to the main river. 'Lady Mary protect and watch over you,' he called after them.

Dusk fell as Oxford came into view and Padar rowed them under a bridge. He moored the craft by a church close by to the burgh's stone wall and they entered through an open gate into the town. They hurried along streets that swarmed with women carrying purchases. The open spaces near the churches were filled with people of all kinds, rich and poor, and children. Since it was just before Vespers, hawkers of meat pies and pastries were trying to rid themselves of their produce before the church bells rang for service.

Here in Mercia even ragged children looked fed. 'But hunger may yet come,' said Padar when, remembering the desolate villages they had passed through on the way to Abingdon, she remarked that no one was starving here.

Soon Oxford's fortress rose up ahead of them, a solid tower, like those the Normans were building all over Wessex. It was set on a mound with a bailey before it, so that it easily dominated the town. It was one of King Edward's wooden castles. Soldiers swarmed around the motte, so Padar guided them away from it, along lanes that stretched like a spider's web out from the castle mound. He took them through a narrow passageway to a church door.

Bells began to ring out all over the town for evening service, drowning Padar's speech.

'My lady, if you wish to pray, there is a little time,' Padar said, as they entered through the low door. 'Our protector here has not arrived yet.'

Closely followed by Ursula, Elditha walked along the tiled nave, until, noticing a statue of the Virgin Mary that was set in a niche in a shallow side chapel, she paused before it. It had been weeks since she had prayed inside a church. Even in the Abbey of Abingdon, where there was one of the most beautiful churches in the land, they had not ventured into the nave for fear of discovery. She fell to her knees and, looking up at the statue, she thanked the Virgin Mary for bringing them safely from Abingdon. She prayed for Ulf, for her older sons, for her girls and finally for Harold's soul. 'What have we done to bring such displeasure on the House of Godwin?' she whispered, but there was no answer. If God's silence had convinced Queen Edith that the lax ways of the English clergy had displeased Him, she was misled. It seemed to her that God had left the world to fight its own battles.

Padar remained in the shadows near the entrance door. Every time Elditha glanced back through the pillars she saw him watching them and waiting. Soon, a thin man in a rich, fur-trimmed cloak entered the church and touched Padar's shoulder. Padar nodded, stepped along the nave, touched Elditha's arm and in a hushed voice asked the women to follow him. As they walked along the nave, he introduced Alfred the Coiner.

'My lady,' said the stranger, in a voice so low none but she heard his words, 'I knew your husband, the King. I minted his coin. My manor house lies by the old church near to the North Gate, not so far off. There I can promise you hospitality.'

Passing the gathering crowd and the priests who were chanting and swinging censers, they hurried out of the building and into the narrow lanes.

'Stay close now,' Padar warned.

They stumbled through alleys, avoiding offal and steaming lumps of animal shit, then over a humped bridge and into a wider street. They picked their way through until they came to another stone church. Elditha could hear snatches of plainsong as they passed. There was one voice only and it was simple and pure as a thrush singing on a summer morning. She paused to listen.

'My lady, I'm not far from here,' Alfred chivvied them on. 'Just behind the church.'

Moments later they were standing by the gate that led into Alfred's yard. The houses here seemed too huddled together, despite being separated by fences, yards and cross-gated lanes, but Alfred's was behind a solid, wooden, door-like gate that was set into a stout palisade.

Alfred called out and a gatekeeper slid open a small window set in the gate. Seeing his master, he nodded, closed the window and called to yard boys to unbar the door. Alfred lost no time ushering them through the door and across a cobbled yard. His house had been built on to, so that instead of being low like a normal hall it reached up several storeys high. Alfred hurried them to a wooden side staircase that climbed to the second storey of his house, saying, 'The staircase here goes down into my cellar and climbs up the side of the house to a second floor and a loft. Follow me and mind your step.'

Lifting a lantern hanging on a wall and holding it high, he led them up the steep, narrow staircase. Two doors opened out on to a small platform above. He rapped on one of these and immediately a woman opened it and gestured for them to come inside. 'My wife, Gertrude,' he said.

Gertrude was a smiling, handsome, brown-haired and rosy-faced woman of middling height. Elditha warmed to her immediately. She stood smiling in the doorway. Ushering them in, she said, 'My lady, you are welcome here. This will be your chamber and Alfred will take Padar to the hall.'

The room they entered contained a curtained box-bed, chests

and a lattice-work cupboard that leaned into the opposite wall. Gertrude pointed to a saffron-coloured, finely woven bed-covering where she had laid out two gowns. They were plain, but of soft good wool, one brown and the other blue and both with cross-stitched patterns embroidered on the hems. She touched Elditha's white robe. 'You won't need these now. I think the blue will suit you, my lady.' She went over and lifted a veil and plaited linen fillet and held them up. 'The veils were embroidered by my own hand last summer and they have never been worn.'

Elditha wistfully fingered the delicate silver embroidery, 'Too much kindness, Gertrude, such exquisite work.'

'Thank you, my lady. My maids will bring you hot water for the wash bowl, and we have soap here too. I make it myself and add rose petals to mask the smell of ash and fat. When you are ready we can take supper together in the antechamber below.' Her dark eyes were laughing. 'It is private and apart from the world of men. Come down when you are ready.' She pushed a heavy curtain by the cupboard to one side and revealed the gallery and the interior staircase. Gertrude pointed towards the back of the hall below and, bending over the rail, Elditha could see that below them another room was curtained off from the main hall. 'That is where we shall sup tonight. The servants think that you are widows of the old court; that you are travelling into Mercia where you will take the veil. I have told them that you are Torfida and her companion, Ailith. Now, come back into the chamber and remove those robes.'

Elditha hurried, glad to remove the monk's scratchy habit. 'Thank you,' she said, after they were standing in their old gowns.

'Give those to me also. I will brush them and fold them with lavender and send them to the boat tomorrow, along with food and drink for your journey.' She bustled off, leaving Elditha and Ursula to the task of cleansing their tick-ridden skin.

Later, bathed, smelling faintly of rose-scented water and dressed in fresh gowns, Elditha and Ursula descended to Gertrude's antechamber.

'You are transformed,' Gertrude exclaimed, obviously pleased to see them looking like women. 'Come and eat, for you must be hungry.'

They sat down to a table covered with an embroidered cloth and with fine linen napkins to cover their laps. Gertrude signalled to a girl to serve portions of a meat pie, a barley pottage and winter greens. The servant daintily placed a little of each dish onto their wooden plates and left the food platters on the table. Gertrude turned to the girl and said politely, 'Thank you, Drusilda, you may leave us.'

Elditha praised everything: the fine cloth; decorated plates; the Eastern rug that covered the planks instead of rushes; the posy of snowdrops on the coffer by the small, high, shuttered window; the beer; the meat. She ate as if she had not eaten for days, her appetite heightened by the river journey from Abingdon.

Ursula picked at the pie and put down her spoon. Gertrude looked concerned and asked her if she was unwell.

'Oh, my lady, do not be offended. Everything is delicious.'

'It will be the Lenten time tomorrow, my dear. Where you are going there will be no meat for weeks.'

'I have lost my appetite, but I am not ill. I am confused. You see, today, in the church, I had an idea that just grew and grew. It is in possession of my whole being.'

Elditha reached out and took Ursula's hand and quietly said, 'A vision? What happened? Can you tell us?'

Ursula took a deep breath and said, 'It was so strange, very peaceful.' She looked shyly from Elditha to Gertrude and hesitated.

'I am a stranger, my dear. You do not have to speak now if it is difficult,' Gertrude said quietly.

'No, I want to speak. As I prayed to the Holy Lady, I was bathed in her heavenly light. That is all, but I felt as if she was calling me to her.' She looked at Elditha. 'My lady, when we reach Ireland, if you permit it, I would enter a convent.'

'Ursula, life may yet settle. One day you may long for a husband and children,' Elditha said. 'You must be sure.'

'Women can never have a happy life and men are cruel,' Ursula said bitterly. 'They war and they cause wars. They dominate our lives or try to.' She smiled at Elditha through tearful eyes.

'Men are men, Ursula, no matter whose tune they dance to, and yet they are not all unkind. I would be sad to lose you. We have been close since your grandmother sent you to me. However, if you wish to become a novice, the abbess of the Convent of St Edmund at Bury is my old friend. I could make endowments on your behalf.' She looked away. 'But it may be long before I can make any more endowments.'

'Thank you, my lady, and I can wait until it is time. It is a relief to speak my mind.'

Gertrude reached out and wiped Ursula's tears away with her napkin. 'My sweet girl, no more sad talk tonight; what will be, must be. I pray that you will find your vocation. These are the worst of times. And now, I have cakes to tempt you.' Gertrude bustled to the sideboard, and returned with a plate of almond cakes and a dish of dried figs.

'Figs in winter,' Elditha said, delighted at the sight of them.

Ursula, now that she had spoken her mind, accepted the fruit. For a time they nibbled figs in comfortable companionship as Gertrude spoke to them of her embroidery. She was working on napkins which would have borders of intricate spirals. She had seen the design in a book of patterns that had been kept in a nearby monastery. It was a monastery, she confided, to which her husband had made generous donations and, in return, they had permitted her to copy the designs.

She crossed the room to a chest, pulled open the lid and lifted out a napkin she had already completed and brought it to show Elditha.

Elditha turned it over. The pattern was intricate, reminding her of the embroidery design that she knew existed in Irish workshops. She ran her finger over the geometric shapes. 'Even Queen Edith, the greatest embroiderer at the old court, is not capable of such exquisite intricate work, though she prides herself on her fine stitching.'

'I have a niece who can better my embroidery, my lady,' Gertrude said. 'The girl is in Wilton, training to become highly skilled with tapestry. I shall be making a journey there during Lent to see her. Her parents died of flux and I am her only remaining kin.' For a moment she hesitated, before saying, 'My lady, your youngest daughter dwells in Wilton. I could carry a message to her.'

Elditha studied Gertrude's face. There was no deceit there. She remembered the figurines she kept in her little chest. 'Gertrude, it is her name day soon and she will be ten years old. I have something she would like. Give my gift to the abbess for her, and if you may speak with Gunnhild, tell her that her mother thinks of her every day.' Elditha stood up. 'The Normans killed my husband and stole my youngest child and I cannot forgive them. When my home was burned to the ground, I was taken prisoner and carried in a cart to William's camp. I walked through a battlefield of the dead, where I found my husband's mutilated body. I cannot and will not forget it. I want her to know that I live. I want her to remember her father.' Gertrude opened her mouth to speak, but Elditha added, 'Let me fetch that gift for my daughter.'

She lifted a sconce and left the chamber. Moments later she returned with a linen bag. She placed the effigies of four female saints on the table. Gertrude examined first St Brigit, then St Margaret, St Cecilia and finally the Lady Mary, the Holy Mother herself, clad in blue, and smiling serenely. Each figure was unusually individual of feature and each was as real as any that stood in a church chapel. Gertrude traced her finger over the ivory and sighed at the beauty of the figurines. 'I think your daughter will understand that the love you have for her flows through these effigies,' she said.

Elditha returned the figurines to the linen bag and with a quick gesture placed it in Gertrude's hands. Gertrude selected one of her household keys, unlocked the doors of her sideboard and pushed the bag into the back of it, behind tableware, knives and boxes of spices. 'For now they are safe from prying eyes.

When I leave for Wilton, I shall conceal this gift among my possessions.'

From the hall beyond the chamber, the strains of Padar's harp had paused. Benches were scraping over tiles as people began to claim sleeping places. From the many churches of Oxford, bells began to ring out the midnight Angelus. It was time for them to retire as well.

'There will be no opportunity to talk tomorrow, so let us part now. I shall pray for you and for you too, Lady Ursula.' She touched Ursula's hand. 'I shall pray, my dear, that you find your true vocation,' she said as they parted. 'May the Queen of Heaven grant all of us courage,' she added, holding Elditha's hands in her own. Her warm-hearted clasp filled Elditha with hope.

22

Lent

We strew ashes upon our heads to signify that we ought to repent of our sins.

Ælfric's Lives of Saints in *A Choice of Anglo-Saxon Verse*
edited and translated by Richard Hamer

They marked their foreheads with ash since they were travelling on Ash Wednesday, the first day of Lent. Padar led them down to the bridge where the boat was moored and dismissed Alfred's guard with a few coins from his own purse. A linen bag with their clothing, a small sack with food and a bow and sheaf of arrows were already stowed on the boat. Thick, purple-hued clouds hung on the margins of the sky. There was snow on the way. Elditha and Ursula huddled deeper under their skins and Padar put all his effort into guiding them into the middle of the river.

The water was quiet, apart from a sluggish lapping against the skiff. At first, nearer the town, a few coracle ferrymen were conveying a number of godly inhabitants from hamlets upstream into the town. A large craft passed them, packed with monks on their way to services. After that they were alone on the river.

Elditha pulled a mittened hand from beneath the furs and pointed. 'Look, Ursula.'

Two swans were floating past close to the bank, one long neck looped around the other, entwined. Padar stopped rowing, and as he allowed the boat to drift towards the bank, they watched the swans glide back down towards Oxford. They did not immediately see a craft with a dragon figurehead appear from the cut to the left. It moved in front of them into the midstream. Padar looked away from the swans and took a sharp intake of breath. He began to row, increasing his pace. Elditha saw why. Five soldiers wearing leather hauberks sat silently watching them pass. Although their heads were bare, unlike Normans they were not shaven. All five had long locks and untrimmed beards. Padar nodded to them and called, 'God bless you.' One said something back to him in a language she did not understand.

'Not French or Norman,' she remarked.

'Mercenaries,' Padar said through his teeth. 'Russ, maybe, and vicious-looking bastards too.'

Elditha could feel the mercenaries speculatively sizing them up. Padar rowed steadily towards the next turn in the river, then slowed to steer their small craft around the bend and then another and another, ploughing upstream against the current. He pushed all his strength into his rowing until they had covered a half-dozen miles in the space of an hour. There was no church, mill or home within sight on this stretch of river. Thick woodland straddled the banks, and exposed tree roots reached their frosty beards down into the water, their straggled treetops appearing as sinister watchers guarding the woods beyond. Waterfowl swam past with the current. A flock of geese flew overhead in a strict formation. At times heavy reeds edged out into the river, concealing dark and secret pools. Far off in the trees a hawk screeched and an unseen bird rustled among the bare branches that scratched the skyline.

Then, as ominously as it had first appeared, the dragon boat was behind them. Its rowers shouted with gleeful whoops on seeing their prey. Their small boat shook as the undertow from the larger craft caught it. Padar tried to row farther on, but the mercenaries rammed their long craft into them, pushing them into the reeds. Two of the mercenaries pulled out knives while the others worked the oars. Padar steadied their skiff, drawing it close to the river bank. He shouted at Elditha and Ursula, 'Get up onto the bank.'

Elditha clambered over the side and grasped tall reeds. She

pulled at tree roots and managed to scramble to the top of the bank's incline. She reached down to help Ursula up, but Ursula couldn't catch hold of the bearded roots to get leverage and slipped. Elditha watched with horror as she slid down into the river, clinging onto rushes as she went.

The dragon-prowed craft moved alongside the skiff. Two of the mercenaries climbed aboard. The first one came at Padar with his knife raised. Padar lurched forward and pushed an oar up against both assailants. They fell backwards, the one in front knocking into the other who was just behind him. Padar lifted up the oar for a second time and, putting all his strength behind it, shoved it towards them again. He caught the first mercenary, a stocky creature who was even smaller than he, in the chest. As the man doubled over, gasping for breath, Padar rammed the oar at him again and tipped him over the river side of the craft out into the current. He sank below the water. Despite the craft's rocking motion Padar immediately pushed the oar with such renewed force that the second man caught its thrust in his groin and doubled over, cursing. Before he could rise, Padar lifted the oar high and slammed it onto his head. As the foreigner fell back into the boat's cradle, Padar seized the knife from him, turned it into the man's chest and drove it home. He turned towards the others who had manoeuvred their boat into a position in front of the smaller craft, blocking any forward drift.

One of the men plunged into the reeds. He tried to catch hold of Ursula, who was desperately scrambling up the bank again. He could not quite reach her. She reached out and clung to the roots. Elditha slid down the bank a little way. Now she caught Ursula's hand and held on to it. She was still half in water. 'Try to hold on. Try to pull yourself up,' she shouted above the noise of the water and the echoing shouts of men.

Padar climbed out into the river, waded forward and plunged his knife into the soldier's neck, but now two more soldiers had clambered out of their craft, dropped into the reeds and were wading towards him. Padar was so quick, Elditha hardly saw it happen. He pulled himself back into the boat, dragged the bow and arrows from the prow of the craft, withdrew an arrow and

197

set it. Taking aim he released it. With a loud hissing sound his first arrow caught the mercenary who was tying up the boat. The other two soldiers had almost reached Elditha and Ursula. Although the boat was rocking Padar spun round like a dancer and repeated his performance. One after the other his arrows flew home. Both men went down into the river, screaming and cursing. Neither of them struggled back up.

Padar threw himself into the water again. He half-swam and half-waded back to the women. Ursula was gasping for air. Elditha caught her fingers but they were slipping from her. Padar called, 'Let her go now. The mud drags and she will pull you in. I have her.' He pulled Ursula away from the bank and struggled with her, as he waded the few yards back to lift her into the boat. Then, he leaned her over the side and pounded her back until she retched. Clambering over the body lying in the cradle of their craft, he gently laid her in the stern.

Elditha slid back down into the river and waded towards their skiff. She grasped hold of the boat. Padar shouted, 'Hold us firm.' Elditha steadied the craft as Padar dragged the mercenary's body up to the boat's rim and tipped it over into the water. He climbed back into the river beside Elditha. 'Now, push.' Together, half-swimming and half-wading, they pushed the boat upriver, out into midstream and away from the mercenaries. With a joint burst of strength they lodged it farther upstream among tree roots and reeds. She leaned back gasping.

Padar called out, 'Get in.' He helped her back into the boat and threw her a blanket. He pointed at Ursula. 'Cover her and yourself.' Elditha sat shivering in the prow, with her arms about Ursula, who had paled to the shade of bleached linen. Padar glanced back. 'They may all not be dead.'

He half-treaded water back down to the dragon boat. A body was still slumped over the boat's rim, tilting the craft into the bank. Padar's arrow was protruding from his back but he was breathing. Padar reached round and sliced his throat. A pale red mess gathered and swirled among the reeds. When he tried to put the body into the water it was so heavy that he could not get it out of the boat. Instead, he pulled it back in and threw a wolf-skin mantle cover it. There was a stock of weapons in the dragon boat too: axes, swords, knives, but no bows or arrows. He would have to send somebody for these. He pushed the boat among the willows and left it only partially concealed.

Anxious minutes passed as he waded about checking bodies, his knife poised in his hand. There was no time to do any more here.

Ursula's skin was green as the algae that floated between the reeds. She was shaking with shock. 'Try to vomit, my love,' Elditha said. 'You swallowed the river. It will make you feel better.'

Ursula moaned, leaning over the rim of the boat, heaving and choking. Elditha tried to pull off her outer garments and dry her with what was not drenched. She wrapped her in the blanket, but she was still shuddering. At last Padar was beside them. 'How is she?' He handed her a water skin. 'Here, it was in their boat.'

She held the water skin to Ursula's mouth. 'Drink and spit. It will help.' She looked up at Padar. 'What about their boat? Will no one come looking for them?'

'I've pushed it into the willows and tightened its mooring. Tomorrow I'll arrange for monks who dwell near St Margaret's to come down river with coracles and clean up. Monks from Mercia fought at Hastings and lost many of their own.' Padar laughed. 'They can strip the craft and then pray for the bastards' souls.'

Elditha took an oar and began to help Padar row. A cold damp seeped through her drenched clothing but she ignored it. She rowed, knowing that their lives depended on every stroke they made. Flakes of snow fluttered out of a darkening sky. The weather was turning.

The large stone nunnery of St Margaret stood out white against the tall, dark poplars surrounding it. Padar pulled the craft into the landing, as snow floated above the river, melting when it touched the water.

'Just in time to avoid another drenching,' said Padar, and

helped them from the boat. 'Wait here on the jetty.'

Padar scrambled up a pathway, through a wicker gate set into a wattle fence and vanished. Elditha sat patiently holding Ursula until a group of nuns carrying torches appeared down the pathway leading to the bank. Their prioress, her great black mantle flapping behind her, hurried forward to the boat. Padar held up a lantern. She cast her eyes sharply over Elditha and then Ursula. 'You need food, warmth and bed-rest. The sisters will carry your belongings for you.' She looked closely at Ursula again and placed a long, pale-fingered hand on the girl's forehead. 'It's the infirmary for you, my child.'

The prioress reached for Elditha's pack. 'No, I can carry this one,' Elditha said quietly and held it close under her cloak, praying that the precious book had come to no harm. She remembered her promise to Brother Thomas to protect it.

'As you wish,' the prioress said, turning to two large, strong-looking women. 'Winflaed, Ann, see that the lady is made comfortable in the infirmary.' The women gently helped Ursula from the boat.

Following the prioress they made their way up the path and into the sanctuary of the priory, Ursula helped by the sisters and Elditha wearily following with Padar. The skald left them when they reached the buildings, muttering that he had business to attend to, and the nuns would care for them now. He disappeared into the cookhouse.

The prioress said, 'He will sleep by the bread oven; it's the best sleeping place in the priory.' Her smile was amused. 'Sustenance and sleep, both are there.' She led Elditha to a small guest chamber. She showed Elditha how to open the narrow and ancient window shutters and ordered her to rest. With a flurry of cloak and skirt she abruptly announced that she had to hurry to prayer with her novices. Elditha watched from the narrow window of her chamber until the prioress vanished into the snowy cloisters below.

She drank the posset the prioress's servant brought her. It smelled of honey and poppy and she drank it all. As her head began to nod, she tumbled onto her cot and fell into a deep and dreamless sleep.

The bell for Lauds was ringing. Mysteriously, the gown she had left lying by the bed had been aired and brushed. She dressed hurriedly and pushed through the heavy fleece door curtain. It was a short step into the prioress's hall. A nun standing by an alcove pointed to a leather curtain that hung to the back of the hall and whispered, 'She is there.' Elditha hurried on, pushed the hanging aside and found herself standing in the prioress's private chamber.

The prioress glanced up from her tall desk. 'Ah, there you are, Lady Elditha.' She studied Elditha for a moment and raised a very mobile eyebrow. 'Your countenance is improved this morning. Let us hope it is so with your companion. Come with me and we'll find out.'

She led Elditha outside and through the slippery cloisters to the infirmary. She could barely keep up with the prioress. Pushing its wooden doorway open, she ushered Elditha into a wide hall with a central hearth and many alcoves off it. Sisters criss-crossed the floor, lightly treading on rushes, carrying pots covered with linen, bed sheets and bowls of food. On each pillar, before every alcove, small bunches of dried lavender were tucked in below the candle brackets. It was an organised and spotlessly clean infirmary.

The prioress paused at the last set of pillars on the left side and lifted a hanging aside. A slither of amber light entered the chamber through a narrow rectangular window covered with oiled parchment. As they stood on the threshold, the two nuns of the previous night rose from stools by a cot and slipped past them like silent, moving shadows. Fragile, pale and still, Ursula lay against her pillow. Elditha leaned over her. She was cool and dry to Elditha's touch, but when she opened her eyes and tried to smile, she began to cough.

'We must pray and hope.' The prioress turned to Elditha. 'She is young and strong and she will recover,' she added.

If Ursula did not survive, Elditha knew that she could never forgive herself for bringing a girl with her on this journey, far from Edith's protection. After the prioress left, she held

Ursula's hand until her friend fell into a deep sleep again. Later, as Ursula's breathing eased, Elditha ventured out. Dragging her hood over her dirty, unveiled hair she hurried through drifting snow towards a long, low building with a tiled roof.

She pushed opened the door and entered a hall that was lit with lanterns. As her eyes adjusted to the dimness after the bright outside world, she discerned a wall painting of St Margaret of Antioch, the convent's patron saint. She was painted in beautiful colours standing beside a gorgeous dragon that was touched with gold. As she studied the painting and thought of Gunnhild's pleasure on receiving the little statue of the Eastern saint, she became aware of the hum of voices. Dragging her eyes from the wall picture and peering deep into the room, she realised that they came from a long row of embroidery frames. Nuns were sitting before them in pairs along the length of the room working on tapestry. Sensing her presence, seeing her standing there on the threshold watching them, they glanced up. She backed out again.

A nun rose and came towards her. 'Wait. Don't go. We are working on a tapestry of the Wedding at Cana for our prioress's chamber. Would you care to join us?' Elditha hesitated, mindful that she was intruding, but the same nun indicated the stool she had vacated.

Elditha removed her cloak and mittens, took up a proffered needle and worked at a flower in her corner of the tapestry. The work was comforting and the tension she had not realised she was carrying in her began to ease. As she worked, she found that her shoulders and her back had relaxed. Rowing had caused them to ache and worry had made her feel tense. The nuns did not chatter like magpies as the women often did in the bower. Their serenity was soothing. Later, as a bell rang and the nuns tidied away their work, saying they must hurry to midday prayer, Elditha returned to the priory's main building and saw the prioress approaching from the direction of the church.

The prioress walked with her. 'It is a cold day and we can drink a little warmed wine together,' she said. 'After Nonce let us eat dinner together in my chamber and then talk seated by the hall's hearth.'

As they settled on stools by the hearth with cups of spiced wine in their hands, the prioress said, 'Now, first I must tell you that early this morning Padar took monks back along the river. He will not come back here yet. He is arranging the next part of your journey.' Elditha slowly sipped the wine. 'This is, we pray, the last snowfall of the year,' the prioress continued. 'For a few days the track-ways into the hills will be difficult and, if it freezes, riding over them can be too, and Lady Ursula still needs to rest.' She set her cup on a small table and smiled. 'But I hear that you are a fine embroiderer, and perhaps here you will work alongside us. Otherwise these six weeks of Lent will feel heavy.' She leaned forward and took Elditha's hands in her own. 'Would it be comforting for you who have lost so much to create something new, a personal piece? Your own tapestry – perhaps, a pillow covering or a small hanging?'

She looked at the lovely embroidered cushions on the bench, in the chairs, the hangings on the white-washed walls. There was colour everywhere in this parlour. 'It would be a pleasurable task,' she said. 'You are kind to protect us.'

'The Godwins were kind to us too.'

They discussed tapestry for much of what remained of the afternoon and later that evening as she sat in the hall under a sconce she began drawing with charcoal on linen. She delighted as her hands and imagination worked hard together and she felt pleased as her idea began to take shape.

23

March 1067

Elditha sketched a house with flames pouring from its windows
and roof and a woman and child in flight. Skeins of fine,
brightly coloured tapestry wool nestled in a wide basket, from
which she selected colours, carefully choosing crimson, ochre,
green, an indigo blue, brown and black. Next she placed stools
on either side of her frame, and moved from one to the other as
she slipped her needle in and out of the panel.

As Elditha concentrated, small, fat clouds of her own
exhaled breath ghosted before her in the cold air. When she
tried to stretch her fingers they were numb. She blew on them
before continuing to work her needle. Noticing her discomfort,
the nun closest to her rummaged in a basket and found a pair of
woollen mittens with the fingers cut away. She tapped Elditha's
shoulder, 'Wear these,' she said. 'They help.'

Later, as the room warmed up and movement was easier, the
nuns wandered over to admire her work. They asked her why
her small embroidery depicted a house that was burning. She
explained, 'The prioress suggested that I re-create my
husband's coronation. A coronation tells the story of great men,
but this is the story of a woman's suffering.'

The nuns made approving noises and persuaded her to tell
them her story. In the closeness of this company of women,
Elditha felt a healing spirit envelop her. She understood the
attractions presented by a cloistered life and that she must help
Ursula to it. She would speak with the prioress.

As had been predicted the weather began to improve. Elditha
realised that Ursula was recovering. She had visited Ursula
every day and although no nursing was necessary – just rest and

the quiet of the cloisters where Ursula sat if the sun shone – as the days passed she could see that as Ursula grew stronger she wanted to stay secluded within the nunnery. She was not surprised when Ursula confided in her as they sat sewing together by the hearth in the infirmary.

'I wish to remain,' she said to Elditha. 'Can you allow me to stay here?' Elditha held her close and said, 'I have already spoken to the prioress. I shall miss you, but of course you must remain here – at least until I can return.'

As the last week of Lent approached, Padar rode into the courtyard, saying that they should be on their way. He led Elditha into the yard. 'I hear that Ursula will stop here and in time take her vows. You will miss her. I shall miss her. I loved her, my lady.' There were tears in his dark eyes.

'I thought you did, Padar.' Elditha reached out a hand and touched his arm in sympathy, but did not dwell on his declaration. 'Good to see you wearing that red cloak again. And your hair has grown too.'

'Ah well, our horses are ready and stabled,' he said brightly. 'Yours is Homer, a black midnight stallion. Can you ride such a beast? I mean, are you able to handle a stallion?'

'I think I can handle this Homer. I like his name. And yours is?' she said.

He laughed and said breezily, 'Hercules. It took me a week to find a horse merchant. I had to go far to the north, but the horse dealer was away. I waited. It was worth it. When he returned, he arrived with these creatures.'

'So, where did they come from?'

'The horses had been in the great battle and had bolted. They were christened by the men who stole them. They drove them out of Norman reach. And they answer to their names.' He ushered Elditha into the stable. She exclaimed at the magnificent mounts. Homer nuzzled at her hand when she gave him a stumpy yellow carrot. When they were leaving the barn, Padar said, 'They must guard Ursula well. She must never be discovered. We must completely disappear. There can be no

206

trail.'

After Vespers, as the setting sun filled the infirmary's high windows with rosy light, Elditha and the prioress visited Ursula. She was still delicate and slept in the infirmary. When she was totally recovered she wanted to work there.

When Elditha explained that Padar had returned and it was time to leave, Ursula simply said to the prioress, 'My lady Prioress, will you permit me to make my vows soon?'

The prioress smiled. 'Permission is granted, Ursula. You are welcome here. We have a great need of embroiderers and healers, as you can see.'

Elditha leaned over and kissed her friend's forehead. 'Dear Ursula, I shall include you in my prayers, every day until we meet again.' She held Ursula's hand longer. As the night gathered she said it was time to part. 'Ursula,' Elditha said, 'I have left the tapestry panel for you to finish.'

'I shall complete it,' Ursula said after a moment of silence.

Elditha decided to make a gift to St Margaret's Priory. Miraculously, she still possessed the sapphires that Harold had given her. Then, she thought of something else. 'Ursula, I wonder if my gift has reached Gunnhild. I worry that I should not have sent it.'

'Why?'

'Something Padar said. He does not know about it – that I sent that gift, I mean. I just pray that Gunnhild never reveals how she came by it.'

'Oh?'

'There must be no trail, Ursula. The nuns here must keep you hidden if our enemies ever come here.'

'I pray they will not.' Ursula shuddered.

'I suspect that I may have been foolish to send a gift to my daughter. It was just that I did not want her to think that her mother had forgotten her.'

208

24

Wilton Abbey
March 1067

In the spring William went across the sea to Normandy and took with him Archbishop Stigand, and Aethelnoth, abbot in Glastonbury, and Prince Edgar, and Earl Edwin, and Earl Morcar, and Earl Waltheof and many good men of England. And Bishop Odo and Earl William were left behind here and they built castles widely throughout this nation, and oppressed the wretched people.

The Anglo-Saxon Chronicles, 1067, Worcester Manuscript,
edited and translated by Michael Swanton

Edith could not understand how Elditha could disappear so completely, despite her thorough search between Winchester and Exeter. Count Alain was in the west, in Gloucester, where he was settling strife in the outlands that bordered the Severn and Wales. He had not discovered Elditha's whereabouts either.

On a snowy day during Lent, Queen Edith packed everything of personal value, her jewels and her many linen chests. She set out for Wilton with her ladies, five Norman scribes, the faithful Fitz-Wimach and a small guard. Secluded behind Wilton's walls she could forget Norman soldiers with their distasteful habits and bullying manners. In Wilton Abbey she could continue her great work in peace; scholars would come to consult with her and, under her guidance, the embroidery workshops would thrive.

By the third week of March she was settled. She attended service twice a day and for the rest of the time she directed her scribes and supervised her embroiderers. The peaceful murmur of prayer hummed soothingly through Wilton Abbey's church. After the paternosters ended, the girls from the embroiderers' school looked up simultaneously with serenity on their countenances. Their voices had rung out, beautifully and clearly as the new crystal box in the chancel that contained St Edith's relics. At the abbess's nod, the nuns began to file from the church, followed by the novices, and finally, the girls. The abbey had given an education to many daughters of the English nobility; girls sent here to learn the skills they needed in order to equip them for their lives as wives, mothers and as embroiderers. Naturally, before the great battle, the abbess had hoped that a small number of the chosen would remain devoted to God's service, bringing valuable gifts to the abbey rather than to husbands. This was changing. Now they came as refugees escaping marriages.

Edith let her sharp eye glide over them. The girls appeared neat and tidy. Their plaits peeped below simple linen veils; their gowns were sober in colour with plain twisted belts, from which hung simple work purses holding needles and scissors. Not a speck of mud was to be seen on their mantles, and their silver cloak pins were like the girls themselves, beautiful in their simplicity.

A new girl walked alongside her niece Gunnhild, a girl who seemed poorer than the others. Her cloak was spotless but, as Edith observed, it was well-worn and her cloak pin contained no embellishment – no enamelled bird or beast. Edith's eye paused. Although the fillet the girl wore today conformed to sober colours, the embroidery on it displayed an unusual pattern of intricate spirals. This charity case, Eleanor of Oxford, was an embroiderer of great talent, much spoken of by the abbess. The girl could work with intricate knot designs and even draw those difficult patterns. Of course, that explained the interesting embroidery on her fillet.

Edith hurried away from them through the cloisters, ignoring the slippery snow that lay on the pathways. As they followed their mistress, her dark-cloaked women could barely keep up.

Letters from Gytha awaited her attention. She wondered how these could come from Exeter with seals unopened by Norman spies. One was intended for Gunnhild. If Gytha had sent yet another request for Gunnhild to depart from Wilton for Exeter, she had already decided that Gunnhild would refuse to go.

She sent her women off to the embroidery workshop where they were stitching a new tapestry to adorn her receiving chamber. When the last of her ladies had lifted a box of silver thread and had disappeared through the door into the cloisters, Edith unlocked her scroll chest, withdrew the letters and examined them. She separated the scrolls and broke open the seal on the letter to Gunnhild. She glanced through her mother's writing. Gytha had always used an exquisite older script, where the letter "w" was written as a "p", and though this was a fine script, Gytha's writing was unclear, as if written in haste. Edith peered closer at it and read:

Many of our noblewomen have gathered in my burgh of Exeter, in particular, your aunts and your cousins, therefore, Gunnhild, I shall send an escort to carry you south.

Edith read the final sentence aloud. 'I want to ensure that you will remain protected from any who might wish you harm.' Edith sniffed haughtily and laid the letter aside. Where could be safer than an abbey? She broke the seal on her own letter. Here, she discovered a further explanation:

Alain of Brittany, on the authority of Duke William, came into my burgh last week, terrifying the townspeople and causing my ladies anxiety. He demanded that I give up the Lady Elditha. This knight claims that he is betrothed to her. And, there is worse. I discover that my grandson, Ulf, has been taken into Normandy. You will send me Gunnhild at once, and then you must treat with the usurper for my grandson's immediate release. He is a child. Moreover, where is Lady Elditha since she is not in my keeping?

211

Edith set the letter aside. Had Elditha married as she had promised, Ulf would be released, Gunnhild would have a father and Thea would be assured of an opportunity to marry well. And, had Thea remained in Winchester, *she* might have married Count Alain to protect her mother's holdings and lands, keeping all that they would lose safe.

Edith sighed and locked the scrolls in her chest. Today there would be drawing lessons for the girls in the design workshop. Gunnhild would be there. She pulled her cloak down from a peg, wrapped herself in it and exchanged her shoes for boots.

When she entered the workshop, two craftsmen – both monks – were busy creating patterns at a long bench close to the window, their shoulders bent forwards so that the light slipped over them and onto the parchment. One was designing a border pattern. He had begun to erase a part of the drawing with a piece of bread. She paused by the bench as he lifted his charcoal stick and began to redo the image.

'Brother, what are you drawing?'

'A ship, my lady. Alas, it refuses to conform, since I need enough space above it for a pair of doves, and on either side two angels. The ship's size is not right.'

'Ah, Brother Martin, you are a perfectionist.' Edith leaned closer. Her eye was drawn to the central design. Here, the Queen of Heaven was seated on a throne; on one side of her a church entrance, not unlike the entrance to the church at Wilton, but on her other the cartoonist had drawn an arch with steps leading up towards the ship. With ease, Queen Edith's eye was now pulled in through the entrance to the central figure and then out through the archway and up the steps. She glanced below it. The lower border was already completed. There three devils were tugging two humans through tangled acanthus leaves. She looked more closely and nodded her approval.

'The border is overly repetitive, my lady,' the monk said. 'The lower borders of all three sections are similar – too many devils, too many acanthus leaves.'

'Truth is stressed through familiarity, Brother Martin,' she replied, and edged her way along the bench to where the second

212

monk had just completed his section. As Edith gained his workplace, he leaned down and swatted away the workshop cat that was attempting to crawl about her boots.

She moved on past the monk, and, barely touching the parchment cartoon with her long pointing finger, she approved here, suggested a change there, another leaf or flower or an additional horned creature that was waiting to prey on man. She crossed the room to where the drawing for the central panel was now being transferred to linen. The fabric had been stretched taut on a wooden frame and a third monk was blowing pounce through the hundreds of tiny holes pricked in the parchment, transferring the design onto the material.

The craftsman stopped working when he saw her and said, 'If you seek out Gunnhild she is drawing. We are proud of her accomplishment.' He waved towards a table at the end of the barn-like room.

'Is that so?' Edith asked frowning. She observed that Gunnhild and Eleanor were working by sconce light, absorbed by an object on the table. Unaware that Edith was watching, Gunnhild slid it into a new position and bent her head over her work.

Edith nodded a greeting to a group of nuns who sat sorting wool nearby. When she reached them she saw that the girls were using a selection of precious miniver brush heads set into quills, and a jar of ink. The object of her niece's interest was clearly visible now. It was a small statue carved out of ivory. Edith lifted it from the table and turned it round in her hand. St Cecilia; was not St Cecilia Elditha's name-day saint?

Gunnhild slipped from her stool and fell to her knees before Edith. 'Aunt, this is ...' She never finished her sentence. Following Gunnhild's lead, Eleanor leapt to her feet to kneel. Her sudden, quick movement caused an elbow to knock over the ink pot. It crashed violently to the floor, splattering dark dye onto Edith's boots, spotting the hem of her gown and staining her cloak. Charcoal sticks paused in mid-air. The embroiderers looked up. A nun rushed forward with a rag and began to mop the Queen's boots. She began to dab at the hem of Edith's gown but Edith impatiently waved her away. 'Clumsy girl,' she said through her teeth and glared at the quivering Eleanor.

Gunnhild scrambled off her knees, picked up the shards of shattered ink pot and placed them on the bench. 'Lady Aunt, it is my fault. I begged Brother Alfgar for old ink, ink that was no good for him to work with.'

'Silence, Gunnhild. You have used expensive brushes with old ink.' Edith turned to Eleanor. 'As for you, go and change that filthy cloak. It was a disgrace before in church, and now it is more so. You will miss the dinner hour. Instead you will go to the chapel and remain on your knees until Compline. You will never use ink again, certainly not before you have mastered your impulsiveness and your tears. Go!' Eleanor scurried off through the workshop, all eyes following her as she passed. Edith turned to the nun who hovered close by. 'Sister Hegga, you are at fault. You have allowed these girls licence. What are you thinking of – miniver brushes! I shall speak to the abbess about this lapse.' She stabbed her finger at the nun. 'And it must never happen again.' She turned to Gunnhild. 'As for you, Gunnhild, wipe your hands on the rag there and follow me, and bring that statuette with you.'

Gunnhild obeyed and tried to rub the black ink away but it stained. She grasped the small statuette tightly and crept after her aunt.

When they reached her receiving chamber, Edith examined the child's drenched boots, much too thin for such cold weather. She made a mental note to have them replaced.

'On the table,' she said indicating the figurine. 'Then sit.'

Gunnhild perched on the edge of a stool. 'Will you send Eleanor away, Aunt?'

'I am undecided. She was given a place here by the abbess herself.' Edith knew that in truth they could not afford to lose such a talented embroiderer.

'I wanted to draw in ink and with the finest brush. It is not her fault.'

'I see, Gunnhild. There is much to learn in this abbey. Many young noblewomen leave their father's hall for their husband's hall, ignorant. Here, they learn to become great ladies, and, my dear, you also, if you are permitted to remain, will become a great lady.'

'My lady Aunt, are you sending me away?'

Edith softened. 'Not I, my child, but your grandmother thinks it suitable that you live with her.'

'But I do not wish to go to Exeter,' Gunnhild said. 'I like the abbey here. I am learning to write and to read and to design. And I have companions here.' She looked at her feet.

'That is as well, Gunnhild. Permit me to read you the letter my mother sends you.'

'I can read it for myself, Aunt.'

'Today I shall read it and you must listen closely.' Edith leaned down and, unlocking her scroll chest, removed Gytha's parchment and read it to her. Gunnhild never spoke. 'You see, Gunnhild, I am concerned for your well-being. This is not a good idea because it interrupts your education.'

Gunnhild said, almost in a whisper, 'Aunt Edith, I do wish to stay with you.'

'Then, I shall keep this safe for you in my chest. But I have a question to ask.' Edith laid the scroll down and lifted the statue of St Cecilia. 'How did this come into your possession?'

The girl hung her head and said without looking up, 'Eleanor's aunt brought four carvings when she visited me.'

'Does the abbess know of this? Are they all carvings of St Cecilia?'

'No, she brought me St Mary, St Bridget and St Margaret as well.'

'Why would Eleanor's aunt bring you such a valuable present?'

'My mother sent them as a gift for my name-day.'

'Your mother, Gunnhild? How?'

'My mother was in Oxford with Eleanor's aunt.'

This was an unexpected turn, thought Edith. She remained calm. She had shielded Gunnhild. The girl knew nothing of the abduction. 'And where is she now?'

'I do not know, Aunt Edith.'

'A beautiful gift, but I fear that your mother may be ill-advised.'

'Oh! But, Aunt Edith, may I keep them?'

'You may, but for now leave St Cecilia with me. You will have her back when you have done penance for your concealment. You will pray all of this afternoon to St Edith that she continues to lend you her kindness and the protection of her abbey.'

Could Elditha have been responsible for her own disappearance? Edith sat pondering, unable to pick up a needle, call for her scribes or even join the midday meal in the refectory, as was her habit. She lifted her mantle from its peg and slipped in through a private and secluded entrance to her personal chapel. She prayed for guidance as to what to do about Elditha. Should she say anything? She could be held responsible.

That afternoon, Brother Francis and a man called Wadard, Bishop Odo's man, rode into Wilton. As they trotted into the abbey precinct, a magpie flew past and knocked the cowl from Brother Francis's head. Brother Francis righted it and remarked to Wadard as he spotted another magpie settled on a snow-filled ledge above, 'Two magpies are a good omen, Master Wadard. Perhaps the abbess will agree to a gift of two tapestries for the Bishop.'

'Ugly creatures! I never took you for one who paid heed to old superstitions.'

'Of course not,' Brother Francis said quickly. 'Let us stable the nags and call on Queen Edith.'

Edith had her back to the brazier when they arrived in her receiving chamber.

'Brother Francis, this is indeed a surprise,' she began, after the bowing and scraping and shallow smiles were done with and she had told them to sit on low stools by her hearth. 'Why are you here and not with my nephew?'

216

'Your nephew, Ulf, is with the King in Normandy, Your Grace.'

'Ah, I see. Then, where is the nurse, Margaret?'

'She remains with the boy. She is content and the boy thrives. He is spoiled by King William's son Robert.'

'In that case, why are you here?' She studied him. Brother Francis's hands began to shake. She saw him clasp his hands under his habit. He gave Wadard a shifty look.

Wadard said, 'We have come with greetings from Bishop Odo. His Grace the Bishop rules the realm whilst his brother, King William, is in the Duchy. The King is introducing the great thanes of this land to his own people.'

Edith raised an eyebrow. 'To the point, Wadard.'

He went on, galloping now with his words, 'My lady, we come with a request. Bishop Odo wishes to commission a tapestry from your workshops; a great tapestry to hang in his new church at Bayeux.'

'The completion of the church at Bayeux is still years off.'

'Then there are years left with which to design such a work and execute it.' Edith glared at the weasel man. He had once been a loyal thane, a Godwin man. 'Wadard, what exactly is your business here?'

'The Bishop is concerned for you and those girls you have in your care,' he began. 'We have discovered camps nearby. Queen Edith, do you suspect anyone in this abbey of wrongdoing against our sovereign King?'

There were many who wished King William ill. There were also those who wished her misfortune, ever since she had given over the keys to Winchester's treasury last November. She considered for a moment. This man might be of use to her and after that she might be rid of him.

She tapped her side table with a long, bejewelled, middle finger. 'There is indeed a service you can do to our mutual benefit.' She lifted the statuette of St Cecilia from her desk and held it out to Wadard. 'Fine craftsmanship, don't you think, ivory and valuable.' She looked at Brother Francis. 'You do remember Gunnhild, Brother Francis?'

'Lady Elditha's daughter; an intelligent girl.'

Edith lowered her voice. 'Gunnhild received this gift only a few weeks ago from her mother, a gift for her name-day. Yes, I see your surprise. You are aware, of course, that we seek the Lady Elditha. We think she has been abducted. But now I believe that she may be travelling west.' She turned to Wadard again. 'Gertrude, wife of Alfred of Oxford, brought this gift to my niece. Elditha was in Oxford.'

Brother Francis drew a quick intake of breath. 'I saw him. I knew it was odd. I saw the Godwin skald ferrying novices from Abingdon Abbey up-river. Perhaps the Lady Elditha was with him.'

'Yes, maybe she was. And she will be with her lady-in-waiting.' She grasped her hands together. 'But this important fact you may not know, monk. Lady Elditha is betrothed to Alain of Brittany. So, if you seek her out and bring us news of her, I shall reward you.'

'And the skald?' said Brother Francis.

'The skald is a nithing, a murderer, and he must be brought to justice.' Edith turned to Wadard. 'Seek your information at the house of Alfred the Coiner in Oxford. Find proof of Lady Elditha's movements. I want her returned to us.'

Wadard bowed low. 'We can be inside the town walls tomorrow.' Turning to Brother Francis, he said, 'Come, we have work to do.'

Herne, Queen Edith's charcoal carrier, slid from behind the curtain, where he had concealed himself as the visitors arrived. He too hurried out into the night.

25

Here is Wadard
Embroidered on the Bayeux Tapestry

Herne took a horse from the abbey stables and cantered to Oxford over shortcut tracks, riding all night through thaw-dripping woodland. His banging on Alfred's great gate awakened the doorkeeper, Athelstan, and his yard boys. Herne could hear them grumbling as the peephole window slid back.

The aged gatekeeper's toothless face appeared lit up from the side by the moon. 'It's only the fifth hour,' he squawked.

'I must speak with your master.'

'Come back in the morning.'

'No, I must see him now.'

'Can't it wait? It's still starlight.'

'Your master is in danger; messenger from Wilton; let me through.'

Athelstan banged the window shut and Herne heard wooden bolts being pulled back. Two yard boys dragged the gate open and he led his snorting horse forward. The gatekeeper ordered the boys to push the gate closed again, bolt it and to answer to no one else. 'Here you,' he said to one. 'Stable the nag. Be quick.' He indicated to Herne to follow him. 'Master Alfred rises early.'

Herne climbed after him up to the first landing, where Athelstan pulled at a bell and shouted, 'Master. There's someone come from Wilton.'

Herne heard a key rattling in the lock and Alfred saying, 'Wilton?'

'Aye, it's Herne,' Herne called into the door.

The gatekeeper waited on the staircase until Alfred waved

him off.

'By St Frideswide's sainted veil,' Alfred lifted a lantern up to Herne's face, 'you look done in, man. What's wrong?'

'Can I have a drink first?' Herne leaned against the wall, catching his breath.

Alfred ushered him in and offered him a cup of wine and a loaf of bread. Between bites, Herne told him about the monk Brother Francis and Bishop Odo's servant, an ugly man named Wadard. 'They are travelling around the country poking their noses into monasteries and convents, checking up on us all. They know Lady Elditha was here.' He told Alfred what he had overheard.

Alfred frowned. 'I knew Gertrude was taking a risk. I should have stopped her taking that gift to Wilton. Who is after the Lady Elditha?'

'It's Queen Edith who's looking. Wadard and the priest are her agents in that, though their own business is rooting out resistance and plundering convents and abbeys. You had best disappear, Master Coiner. They work for Odo and they'll mark those who help her as part of the resistance. You'll be up in that keep on the hill and you won't be seeing daylight again.'

Alfred scratched his head as the enormity of this sank in. At last he said, 'Herne, Lady Elditha's trail will jeopardise our cause. I'll leave Oxford now. I know where to go. Gertrude must come with me.'

Herne nodded. 'Hurry, Alfred. I'll wait.'

Alfred and Gertrude packed one saddle-bag each, a change of clothing and a pouch with Gertrude's jewels.

'No questions and no maids, Gertrude. We'll be back soon.' Alfred swallowed as he spoke the lie.

'Why ...'

'Not now, I'll explain all when we are on the road.'

Alfred hurried to workshops at the back of his hall where his three apprentices were snoring by the fire. He selected a key from the chain that hung from his waist and unlocked the door leading into his store-room and softly closed it, lifted two saddle-bags off the wall and opened a chest. Digging his hands in, he lifted out handfuls of gold coin, and filled the bags almost to the top before stuffing leather cloths over the hoard to conceal it from prying eyes. After locking his storeroom, he awakened the sleeping lads and sent them off to the kitchen to break their fast.

Herne met him in the stable. Pointing to a large piebald pony, Herne said, 'I'll take a fresh horse and I'll saddle up two for Gertrude and yourself. Then, I'm making for the woods. Where do you intend to go?'

'We're riding south and west. Herne, can you help Gertrude? She is on her way. I have something else to do first.' Then he rushed off again.

Godfrey, the foreman, a cousin of a cousin, arrived just as church bells began ringing for morning service. Alfred explained that he was off to London. 'I have to forge new coin and the old lot not a year old.' He unhooked his keys from his belt, muttering, 'Ah well, best to obey a summons. Keep an eye on the house and the servants whilst I am gone.' Godfrey scratched his head and looked confused.

'Be careful whom you trust. Set a guard on the building at night. I'll send word when I'm returning.'

'Gertrude?'

'Gertrude will accompany me, Godfrey. She needs new silks for her embroideries.'

Godfrey nodded. 'Be careful then, and Godspeed.'

Alfred hurried down the wooden stairway to the barn where Gertrude was waiting with Herne and the horses. By the time the bells rang again for Terce, they were on the road to Exeter.

Later that day Brother Francis and Wadard rode into the castle bailey. Wadard demanded food and drink and asked for a guard of ten to twenty men, saying that they were on the Bishop's business. Brother Francis was beginning to understand his companion to be determined. The quaking warden did not dare refuse after seeing Odo's seal. By Vespers, Wadard's recruits were hammering on Alfred's gate. Athelstan refused them entry. 'Master's gone away for a week to London – on King's business.'

'Open up or we'll break down the gate. *This* is the King's business.'

The old man reluctantly ordered his boys to draw back the gate.

'At last.' Wadard spat the words. He barged through the yard, with the troop of soldiers following and shouting threats at Alfred's terrified servants.

They found the mint at the back of Alfred's yard where Godfrey was firing up the oven. Startled Godfrey looked up, wiped his hands on a rag and slowly came forward. A boy was setting out coin dies and two others were working the bellows. Wadard looked at the dies, lifted one up and turned it over.

'What treason is this? There's a new King now.'

'We don't do the face image. We do the other side only. One side is blank. These are temporary coins, tokens. All we've done is melt down the old ones and give these tokens in exchange. We need new moulds. Master is gone to London for them. The finished coins have to have a consistent weight.' Godfrey pointed to the scales on a corner table.

Wadard reached out and grabbed Godfrey's tunic. 'I have questions for you.' He dragged him from his work and shoved him onto the earth floor, where he held him at the end of a short sword. Wadard's band of soldiers stood behind their new commander with their swords pointing at Godfrey.

Wadard said, 'Where is Alfred the Coiner?'

'I told you. My master has gone to London.'

'When?'

'Today. He's gone to fetch the new dies.' Godfrey looked up at the bench, where an apprentice's hands were shaking so badly that a mould dropped, crashing to the floor.

'He's a liar,' said Wadard, kicking Godfrey in the belly. 'Has Alfred the Coiner entertained a lady and her servant lately, a storyteller like you?' He laughed at his own joke and twisted the point of his sword, drawing blood from Godfrey's throat.

'I don't know,' Godfrey gasped. 'I come in the morning and

leave by nightfall.'

'Name?'

'Godfrey, son of Robert the Merchant,' Godfrey said.

'French, Breton, Norman?'

'Father, Norman. My mother is English.'

'You had best be loyal then,' Wadard said as he kicked Godfrey again. 'Get up and return to your work. No image of the dead King or his kin is to be imprinted on coins.' Wadard put away his sword and, with his men following, left the mint. Terrified, Godfrey shook and wobbled like his mother's sloe jellies as he hurried back to the great fire in the forge.

'Get on with your work,' he said to the quaking apprentices. 'Your loyalty is to the master. Say nothing. Get the heat up.' They obediently worked the bellows.

'The gatekeeper is the one we want,' Wadard shouted at the soldiers. 'Bring him with us.'

Brother Francis meekly followed as Wadard hauled Athelstan up to the castle. He had seen violence before but this Wadard was brutal. Brother Francis tried to protest as Wadard ordered two soldiers to hang the old man upside down in the castle bailey. Wadard hissed at him, 'Say your prayers for his soul, priest.' When old Athelstan passed out they threw icy water in his face. Wadard prodded him with the point of a knife until he croaked for mercy and cried out the name of the servant who had made ready a boat for a skald called Padar only a few weeks earlier. The servant was in the woods, the old man cried out, and it didn't matter any more since they would never discover his whereabouts.

Brother Francis returned to the mint with Wadard and his pack. The soldiers bound Godfrey with rope and dragged the apprentices and servants out into the yard. The monk looked away as they intimidated them, prodding them with swords, threatening them with captivity and worse, but Alfred's servants knew nothing that Wadard didn't already know. One soldier smashed his fist into a kitchen boy who smirked at him. Another pushed a maid up against the wall and kicked her in the belly because she spat at them. Brother Francis felt sick to his stomach. The Norman soldiers from the castle were taking their cruelty beyond what was reasonable.

They began to work on Godfrey. They bound his hands and began circling him, punching him and cutting his arms and legs with their long swords. Godfrey shrieked at Wadard, 'If you kill me, there will be none to keep order here. I know nothing.'

'Get him to talk,' Wadard ordered the captain of his guard. 'He knows.'

'Stop! Let me ask him,' Brother Francis intervened.

'You? What will he tell you?' He threw his sword down in a fury. 'Go on, try.'

Brother Francis leaned down. 'Tell us where your master is and all will be well, my son.'

Godfrey choked on his own blood and sobbed, 'I have told you. The master has gone to London to get new dies for the coin.'

Wadard shouted at Brother Francis that his ways were not working. He signalled to his soldiers. But no amount of punching and threatening revealed further secrets. Godfrey said that he just came every morning to work in the mint. He slept at home, not here. Wadard stood in front of the battered, bleeding Godfrey and said icily, 'You, not Alfred of Oxford, are in charge here now. You will live in his house and you will take your orders directly from the castle. The hall and the mint here belong to us. You bastards are under the castle guard.' Wadard turned to Brother Francis. 'You see, Brother Francis, this is how we deal with rebels. We prick them until they die; but this one we'll save for later.' He clicked his fingers at the torturers. 'Unbind him. He knows nothing.'

Brother Francis pushed through the crowd of shocked servants and out of Alfred's yard. Wadard yelled at his men to follow. One tugged at a girl's plaits, grabbed her breasts and said he'd be back. Another deliberately knocked over one of the yard boys and stepped on his hand, crushing it, as the boy sprawled in the muck, howling with pain. That was enough. Brother Francis made an excuse to return to the castle while Wadard and the rest of his soldiers set out to harass their way into houses and inns, to threaten the men, to terrify their women and prod at their children with their sharpened swords.

Later, Wadard returned to the castle in a buoyant mood. He had met with success. He had continued to the river, where they questioned as many boatmen as they could find. Finally, they had discovered that Alfred's servant had joined the camps in the woods and had not been seen for weeks, but they knew the direction the skald and the women had set off towards; it was up to the source of the river.

By sunset Wadard had set guards on Alfred's house. His soldiers ransacked the hall. They turned coffers out and confiscated goods. Alfred's cousin would work under guard. They would watch all who came through his gate. The coiner would return and then they would destroy him. Wadard returned to the castle to finish off the gatekeeper.

Soldiers dragged Athelstan into the castle yard. The old man found courage to stand straight. He pointed his shackled arm and named Wadard the Saxon as a traitor to King Harold. He spat and blasphemed and shouted prophesy, 'The bastard King William will meet an evil end.' Another thwack from the back of a sword knocked him down again but he managed to rise onto his knees to groan out the strangled words, 'He will die hated even by those he calls his own kin.' Then, he cried, 'May the House of Normandy be cursed.'

This was the end for the gatekeeper. Wadard drew his own weapon, ordered two men to hold Athelstan. He cut out the man's eyes and, as he worked himself into a furious frenzy, he shouted, 'Silvatii' and 'Liar'. Still the gatekeeper screamed obscenities at his torturer. The soldiers then beat Athelstan until he was torn flesh and broken bone, and had fallen into a crumpled heap of guts and blood, his shrieks finally silenced. Brother Francis knelt at what was left of the gatekeeper, praying over him, while Wadard shouted, 'He is not worth your prayers, brother.'

After sunset, Wadard ordered the soldiers to throw Athelstan's bloody remains through the gate to the dogs. Brother Francis hurried away through the town streets and sought out a place to pray. *This was all Harold Godwin's fault. He was responsible for this destruction when he had broken his faith with William of Normandy.*

A few days later a fisherman seeking reward came into the castle, claiming that he had discovered a sunken boat far upriver and several decomposing bodies. The boat was stripped of weapons, he said. The dead men were soldiers from the Slav lands. He had met them once, near Godstow, one morning before Lent. Wadard pieced one and two together and said to Brother Francis, 'That skald will hang for this.'

The castle warden sent a troop upriver to examine the sunken boat and collect the remains. He reported back to Wadard, 'The boat was stolen from the castle fleet before Lent. The Slavs were probably looking for slaves to sell in the East. They had it coming.'

'They were mercenary trash,' Wadard said to Brother Francis over dinner in the castle hall. 'Tomorrow we ride upriver and into the hills. We will visit every nunnery and monastery between here and Bristol until we find them.'

'That will be a multitude of monasteries,' Brother Francis said. He had been sickened by Wadard's cruelty and now he remembered the cruelty with which the Normans had treated the women and children at Reredfelle, his own flock, when they fired the hall. For this, he blamed Elditha. She had put all their lives in danger on that day. She was the Devil's own concubine; a curse on the House of Godwin.

Then Wadard was saying, 'And there's a heap of treasure for Normandy in the monasteries. Think of the favour you will earn from that shrew, Queen Edith, when we find the Lady Elditha and her skald.'

Without a moment's hesitation, Brother Francis agreed to accompany Wadard.

'So we set out tomorrow?' he said, gladdened at the thought of escaping the infernal town that was Oxford.

26

Forth I go, may I meet with friends.
An Old English Journey Charm

Padar and Elditha rode through the hills west of St Margaret's Priory, following an ancient track that crossed the escarpment. Whenever Homer slowed, a light flick of the whip drew a quick response. The sky was a pale blue, the air clear and Elditha was relieved to be on horseback again and moving.

Farther along the escarpment, near a place that Padar called Barton Wood, Padar told her they should rest. He slid down from his own horse and then slipped his hand under her stirrup and helped her down. Elditha unstrapped her saddle-bag and produced griddle cakes, cheese and a flask of ale. They sat on their mantles by a stand of chestnut trees and shared the food, looking over the grey ploughed land where bright green crops were pushing through the soil. A pair of magpies strutted across a field, like wooden puppets at a Christmas feast, their heads jerking up and down as they foraged. A blackbird sang in a tree. Sheep grazed on the springy grass by the wood's edge. It was so peaceful, she thought, as if there hadn't been a new king set on the throne and towns and villages attacked, different to the ruined countryside south of Oxford.

As if he were reading her thoughts, Padar said, 'We can avoid the Normans if we stay north of Gloucester. Tomorrow, we must follow the salt road to Tewkesbury.' When, later, they rode into the monastery at Hailes he looked back at the unguarded opened gate and remarked, 'The way it was and how it should be. No bolts on doors, no closed gates. I wonder how long this will last here.'

That night they shared a communal hall, empty of guests

excepting a pair of wool merchants from Gloucester. They wore their hair long in the English manner and their beards plaited. Elditha observed that neither was young nor old. The pair talked of King William, of the new coin forged with his image, and they discussed the price of wool. They expected a good return for their merchandise in the Flanders markets, but only if they could drive their wagon of bales north-east of Lincoln and only if they were able to avoid the Norman patrols.

'Have you no guard?' Padar said.

'It draws attention, brings us into trouble, lucky to get our wool out.' The merchant then drew his hand across his throat. 'There are weapons in that wagon and we'll kill to protect what is ours.' He went on to say that the new King's henchmen were already in and out of the old palace of Gloucester. 'There will be a castle there soon instead of a palace; the bloody bastards.'

Elditha shuddered, thinking of Gytha and Thea in Exeter. As the merchants exchanged news and talked of changes to come to the borders – castles, soldiers, taxes – she busied herself separating barley from the vegetables in her bowl of pottage.

She complained in a low voice, 'The barley is full of grit. I can't swallow it.'

The merchants stared at her. The taller of the two remarked, 'Your woman doesn't say much, and look at her grumbling and picking; should be glad of food when many an Englishwoman is starving.'

'Not my woman, my friends. She was my thane's wife. Poor lady lost her husband in the great Battle. Then she lost everything else: her hall, her land, everything. She wouldn't marry a Norman so they burned her house. We're travelling to her brother's farm near Worcester and then I'm off to Wales to fight for the Welsh prince.'

'Good man. Keep the bastards out,' said one, spitting into the straw.

'I don't blame her not marrying a Norman. Who wants children raised to speak in a foreign tongue?' said the other. 'By St Oswald's bones, she is right, this is a rotten stew.' The wool merchant stirred it with his finger, lifted out a gritty lump and threw it on the fire. 'She's well rid of the Normans.' He grunted. 'Worcester is safe.' He spat again. 'That farm, sheep or cattle?'

Padar chewed a piece of stewed turnip. 'Her brother sells hawks to noblemen.'

'Hope he finds her a good English husband. She's got fine green eyes and a lovely head too on that long neck; a beauty, I'd say. I'm looking for a wife,' the man's companion remarked. Elditha watched as Padar's hand automatically strayed to his seax.

'She won't be looking for a merchant,' the other said. 'I'd say that creature is too good for the likes of us.'

At that, Elditha withdrew to a pallet behind a shabby moth-eaten curtain. She wrapped herself in her cloak and listened to Padar laughing with the merchants. He began to strum his harp. She slept fitfully and was relieved when he whispered that they must be on their way before the sun rose. 'They'll suspect us if they see the horses,' he said, taking her pack and his own. As they rode out, the wool merchants were still snoring and only a couple of monks were crossing the yard. Padar waved and they rode out through the gate.

Late in the afternoon, Padar guided their horses onto a hill from which they could see the monastery complex of St Mary's at Deerhurst. Behind the monastery the Severn flowed lazily through a flood plain. This river would take them to the coast.

'My lady, we can lodge in the old hall. There's only the reeve there. Lord Beorhtric has arranged for a ship from Ireland to come up the river to meet us. We settled on Holy Saturday and by my reckoning there are only three days to wait.'

'And Beorhtric?'

'He should be at Leckhampton. I will ride down to the old hall and find out his whereabouts. There are no Normans around these parts, but we must be cautious. The monastery of St Mary is connected to France.'

'I'll ride down with you, Padar.'

'No, stay out of sight in the trees.' And he cantered off.

She watched until he was swallowed into the landscape, then

turned the stallion into the beech trees and dismounted. Homer grazed and she sat on a log. Every now and then he nuzzled her hand and she stroked his great damp nose. Bells rang for Nones. She waited and dozed for a bit, and soon her head was drooping into her arms. The bell for Vespers sounded and she started, wide awake. Padar had not returned. Hours had passed as she slept and now it was chill. She looked towards the west. There a liquid sun was dropping behind the distant monastery. Leading Homer she came out of the trees and peered down the valley. She could just see a helmeted and armed patrol climbing the hill towards her, carrying the Mercian standard, another dragon. This must be Beorhtric and Padar at last.

As they rode closer she knew all was not right. There were no smiling faces returning her greeting. Moments later the soldiers ringed her in and their commander dismounted and removed his helmet. She stared unbelieving. He had not changed in the half year since they had last encountered each other. His hair gleamed red and he wore it in Norman style, shaved close up the back of his head.

'Not you,' she managed to say.

'So, Lady Elditha, perhaps you are relieved to see me.' He smiled. 'You will come with us.'

Somehow she found her voice. 'You order me?'

'As my affianced wife, it is no less than my duty.' He reached over and touched her arm.

She moved away. 'I am never that.'

'My lady, I think so.'

'Where is my servant?' she said evenly.

He pointed along the valley towards the monastery. 'I left him under guard. He murdered two soldiers from our garrison at St Swithun's Priory. And,' he added, 'there may yet be other charges, such as abduction of a royal noblewoman.'

'Not so, Count Alain, not so. I have chosen to travel west and he travels with me. I ordered him to ride with me,' she said, keeping her tone firm.

'Mount.' He glared at her, took the reins of her horse. Homer snorted at him and danced a few paces. She tugged the reins back. 'Homer come here, closer,' she said.

Now, she realised with horror that Beorhtric himself had ridden up beside Alain of Brittany, his piebald horse prancing and circling. 'My lord,' he said without looking at her, 'take as many of my men as you need, but I must return to my manor.'

'I have enough of my own, Beorhtric. Odo's man, Wadard, has brought us reinforcements from Oxford. Your loyalty will be rewarded. Return and enquire exactly what arrangements the skald was making.'

'That we know already,' said Beorhtric.

'Ah, of course, Saxon, you made the arrangements for him yourself. Well, he travels to London with all his body parts, and make sure that the Norse ship does not land or you could lose yours.'

'You have the lady, Count Alain. Send for the skald when you want.' Beorhtric of Tewkesbury whipped his horse around and, accompanied by a dozen fighting men, cantered off with his Mercian banner flying before him. Elditha swallowed the outrage she felt at Beorhtric's betrayal.

The remaining soldiers gathered closer to their commander. Count Alain offered to help Elditha mount but she declined, preferring to climb up into the saddle from a log where Homer stood still for her. He shrugged. 'As you will. That horse looks like one of ours, a stallion. Did the bastard skald steal him? We can hang that skald three times over now.' With that remark, Alain of Brittany turned around and sprang onto his mount and then manoeuvred the beast closer to her. With soldiers surrounding them, they rode along the track to a crossroads which she had passed with Padar several miles back. There, they turned south on the route to Gloucester.

The palace at Kingsholm, near Gloucester, had not changed since Elditha had been there several years before. The palace exterior looked as tired and as weathered as ever. It loomed up eerily in the moonlight, a large and rambling place with other halls joining the main hall, creating the impression of a series of crosses. A maze of outer buildings, stables and bowers lay scattered around it, as at the Palace of Westminster. Large groups of soldiers paced the yard, and as they went to and fro, fierce-looking hounds leapt and followed, barking and snapping at their heels. An underfed yard boy took Homer's reins from Elditha and helped her dismount. She clutched her saddle-bag, half-concealed it under her cloak, and watched the boy struggle with the horse. Homer rose up and nearly overpowered him. Waifs carrying torches came running to help. She felt despair for them and especially for the stallion, as, pulling and dragging, the team of them managed to force her great horse across to a stable block close to the old orchard.

Count Alain led her into the hall. As they walked towards the long raised hearth, Elditha half-recognised the servants who were setting up trestles; the same people who had worked there in King Edward's reign. Glancing at her, they quickly turned away again. They had new masters now, she thought sadly. A severe-looking woman – tall, slim and dressed in an elegant long-sleeved gown – came walking from the shadows, holding a candle. She greeted Alain of Brittany and for a moment they conversed in French. Elditha understood the language and gathered that this long-faced person was to be her companion, or her gaoler, though for the moment that remained unsaid.

Count Alain said, 'This woman is Alice of Gloucester. She will see to your needs.' He stooped and wiped mud off his boots with a rag that was lying on the bench and added dismissively, 'Give Lady Elditha food and drink and see that she is comfortable. Her chamber has a door. Bolt it on the outside.' He glanced up at Elditha. 'I would keep you safe.' Without another word to her he stretched, and began to walk away. She could not work out how he intended to deal with her, other than possibly insist on the marriage.

Alice said to his departing back, 'It will be done, lord.' She studied Elditha with a quizzical look. 'My lady, I have a chamber where you can rest,' she said in perfect English.

As they walked into a second hall, she saw people, shades in a thin light, moving about a central hearth. She thought she could make out a cooking pot swinging over a fire. As her eyes grew accustomed to the dark she saw a group of soldiers eating from a trestle. Of a sudden, strangulated whimpers pierced the dim chill, cries that sounded like those of a creature caught in a woodland trap. She stopped walking, her eyes searching about, peering into the dim shadowy light, looking for the source. She followed the sound, which had faded into low moans. They seemed to come from an open alcove at the next cross where the hall led into the newer west hall. Elditha drew closer to the alcove pillar and stared down. A bundle of rags was curled in a foetal position on a pallet, writhing to and fro, gasping and keening. She reached out to touch the creature, who appeared little more than a child. This was no child. It was an undersized, but grown, woman, heavily pregnant. Elditha almost gagged as she leaned over, towards a fetid smell that emanated from her.

'Lady Elditha, you have no business here. Come away quickly.'

'Alice of Gloucester; that girl is in labour.'

Alice caught Elditha's arm. 'My lady, come now, this is no place for you. There are others to see to her.'

'Others? Where are they? Why is she not in the bower hall?'

'There is no bower now. It is full of soldiers.'

'She won't survive without help. Nor will her child.'

'Leave her. You will make Count Alain angry.' Alice pulled Elditha away. 'I will send a slave to her. She is a soldier's whore. I promise that she won't be abandoned. Come.' She turned to a shapeless girl hovering close by, snapped her fingers and pointed back. 'See to that woman.'

Elditha was helpless. How could these people be so unfeeling? Alice hurried her along yet another walkway into the west hall. She stopped at the back of it, lifted a curtain, unhinged a key from a collection that fell from her belt, and opened the lock on a low wooden door.

Elditha stared around the chamber. They could not know, because if they had they would never have allowed her to take possession of the very apartment which she had occupied with Harold when they had come to this hall at Gloucester. It was a spacious room. The bed was covered with its usual tapestry depicting a Wessex dragon, its colours still brightly touched with gold thread. They could not have discovered the secret under this bed. She would not be here if they had.

The trapdoor in this chamber was an unusual feature. Godwin himself had had it cut into the floor planks as a convenient way in and out of his apartment. It blended into the run of the beams and at a glance was insignificant, because the ringed handle was created of the same beech wood and the bed was kept in place over it as an additional concealment. Elditha remembered the door set into the orchard wall at Reredfelle. Lucky for her that Earl Godwin had always liked secret entrances and exits. Alice thrust her hands out from the trailing sleeves of her gown and pointed at Elditha's belt. 'My lady, I fear I must take it.' Elditha unstrapped her seax and, without speaking, held it out. Alice's long hands reached forward and took it from her. Elditha noticed that Alice wore rings on her fingers that were of English design, patterned with English enamel work.

Alice reached for the saddle-bag which lay on the bed. Immediately Elditha thought of the precious book, her gems and the christening robe hidden beneath her linen. She did not want this woman rummaging through her treasure. 'I have concealed no weapon,' she said sharply and reached out to stop the woman. She had not needed to. There was a rush of skirts. Alice whirled round. Servants came running in shouting, 'Lady Alice, we need the wise woman now.'

To Elditha's surprise Alice looked desperate. 'But we have none. You must do what you can for her. I shall come in a moment.'

'But …' The girl hovered in the entrance.

'Find the priest. I shall come.'

Elditha said with determination, 'I have had seven children of my own. I know the art of midwifery. I may be able to save her.'

'It may be too late.'

'I can try.' Elditha reached deep into her bag and withdrew

234

the small package that lay nestled in the corner, under the book. She concealed it in the purse that hung from her belt. Then, she lifted the saddle-bag from the bed and, using her heel, kicked it underneath and out of sight.

They hurried back through the west hall to the alcove at the crossway, where the girl was now screaming in pain. Elditha knelt by the pallet. 'It helps to walk. Could you, do you think?'

'I cannot,' the girl said. 'My leg ...'

Elditha gently lifted the dirty cover and said, 'Ah, I see. Your leg ...'

'She is crippled,' Alice said.

Elditha knew what she had to do if she was to save the girl. 'I need water heated to boiling, and clean rags. And for the Virgin's sake, hang a curtain here. Hurry, if you care about her life, and that which she bears.'

'Fetch a curtain and hang it,' Alice said to one servant. To the other, she said, 'Bring us help.' When the servant asked whom, Alice replied, 'Choose two who have children of their own.'

'She will bear fruit,' Elditha said, touching the girl's swollen belly. She moved her hands gently over the stomach and said, 'Bring me herbs – fennel and mint. Her womb will follow their sweet smells and the baby will have an easier release. When I have warm water, I can bathe the passage.'

Alice lowered her voice to a whisper. 'This girl told her Norman lover where to look for her cousin, a Saxon, who stole weapons from them.'

'From whom?'

'The Normans, my lady.'

Why did Lady Alice care if a Saxon was betrayed?

Alice went on in a low voice, 'They speared him with one of the swords he had stolen and strung him up as an example to others.'

Elditha studied the woman. She looked worn and sad. There was no time to fathom this now. 'Send for a cup of warm wine for her to drink. And I will have my seax back.'

Elditha held out her hand and Alice returned it, saying, 'That girl was foolish, but I should have sent slaves to care for her sooner.'

'God will forgive you,' Elditha said. 'Hush, the servants come. I think we can save her.'

Two servants hung a curtain from the garment hooks protruding from the pillars of the alcove. A woman brought a kettle of boiling water, another brought a sponge and strips of linen and placed them on the alcove bench. One of the torch holders returned with a flask of wine and a cup. 'And bring me the herbs,' Elditha said. She pulled the package from her purse, opened it and took a pinch of the powder and dropped it into the wine. This she held to the girl's lips. 'Sip slowly,' she said. 'It will ease the baby's passage.'

'Do not look on my face. I have no husband. It will bring you misfortune.' The girl gasped. 'Lady Alice despises me ...'

'Do not speak nonsense,' said Elditha. 'You have no need to be ashamed. And I do not believe in bad luck. We make our own. Drink slowly.' And when she looked up again, she noticed, for the first time, a smile hovering about Alice's pursed lips. Her face looked less pinched for it.

They eased a linen sheet over the stinking straw and beneath the girl. She untied the strap that had held her knife and gave it to her. When a great pain grasped the girl, she bit hard on the strip of leather and grasped Elditha's hand so hard that Elditha wondered how such a small creature could cling so strongly. Then her grasp eased. 'It is like being in a boat riding on a wave,' Elditha said, and at last the curtain moved aside. The servant had returned with a small basket of herbs.

'Let the curtain fall,' Elditha ordered, as she took the basket from the servant. She dropped mint and fennel into the water and dipped a rag into it.

She asked the servant to help Alice to lift the girl's skirt, gently wiped the girl and felt inside her. 'I can feel your baby's head.' She glanced up and said, 'What is your name?'

'Greta.'

'Greta, push now because I have the head. Your baby will be born in the sign of the ram, Aries, and that is a good strong sign.' She spoke to Alice. 'Make her sneeze. A feather from her pillow will do it.'

Alice drew out a feather, peered down at Greta and tickled her nose. 'Push,' Elditha said. Alice tickled the inside of the girl's nostrils again. Greta's nose wriggled. With a great sneeze and a final push her baby was born.

'Well done,' Elditha said, as she caught the baby and stared at it. 'A girl, Greta, you have a girl.'

Elditha slapped the baby into life and felt joy at her healthy cry. She wiped away the blood from the baby's face with a clean wet linen cloth, wrung it out and carefully wiped away mucous from her delicate nose and mouth. She pressed back the baby girl's tiny ears and laid her on Greta's breast. 'She is healthy. Have you a name?'

Greta shook her head.

'The Queen who once lived in this palace was called Ethelfreda. She was King Alfred's daughter. I think it would be a good name for her.'

'Ethelfreda is a princess?' Greta said.

Alice smiled, 'My lady, you fill this girl's head with nonsense.'

Nonsense yourself, Alice of Gloucester, thought Elditha, but she said, 'Thank the Mother of Heaven, Greta, that I was here this night, because you will live to have grandchildren.' She measured three fingers from the baby's belly, cut the cord and tied it. She looked down. No afterbirth. 'Can you push again, just once?' Greta pushed. The afterbirth was safely expelled.

Alice cleaned it away into a basin. She frowned. 'My lady, it is not good.'

Elditha looked at the sheet. Greta was bleeding copiously.

'Alice of Gloucester,' Elditha said, giving Alice the powdered mugwort root, 'we can stop this too. She will need a combination of herbs to drink regularly now. Put a little of this powder into a mixture of sage, pennyroyal, willow weed. Bathe her with the rest.'

But before Alice could reply, the curtain was sharply dragged away and a black-clad figure bent down to enter. 'You

237

asked for a priest ...' he said, then stopped and stared at Elditha. 'So, the Lady Elditha is in charge here.' Brother Francis drew himself up to his full height and folded his hands under the sleeves of his habit.

The servant who followed said to Alice, 'My lord has sent him.'

He looked like some tall, brooding crow. Why was he here? Elditha glared at him and then spoke with authority in her voice, 'The child is healthy. You may thank God for a new life.'

Brother Francis looked aghast. He turned from Elditha to Alice, and reached out and snatched the purse she held from her. He turned it over. 'I recognise this purse. Our church forbids the Devil's root.' He shifted his cold gaze to Elditha again. 'It is witchcraft,' he said.

'Brother Francis, it is no such thing. Prayer is the business of monks. Do not meddle in the affairs of women.' She turned to Alice. 'It has been a long night. Leave two of your women here and send the meddling monk away.' She held out her hand towards the priest. 'Give it back to me or I shall speak with my lord Alain.' Brother Francis grudgingly placed the purse in Elditha's opened hand. 'We shall see what Count Alain has to say.'

'Tell the servants to use this sparingly,' she said to Alice, ignoring the monk. 'A little in the washing water,' she said. 'Keep her clean. Bathe her and change the sheet.'

'Witch,' Brother Francis muttered and drew the sign of the cross before lifting the curtain and disappearing into the hall.

The chapel bell rang for Matins. In a few hours the cocks would crow. Elditha was tired.

Alice said as she set a candle on a stool, 'My lady, I will see that they are cared for, but Count Alain will hear of this. The monk will complain.'

Elditha shrugged, turned her back and plunged her hands into the basin of water sat on a stand. The water became streaked with brown. She didn't care what Count Alain thought. Nor, right now, did she care how Brother Francis had come to

Gloucester or what revenge he was intending.

'My lady,' Alice said as she handed Elditha a napkin. 'Lady Elditha, I am not as I seem.'

Elditha said, turning to face the woman, 'I have wondered what or who you are. How are you then?'

Alice said, 'My father is English. He is with the rebels in the woods.' She placed a finger on her lips. 'This will be difficult, dangerous beyond belief. I had not intended to save you, but I shall try to help you and the skald.'

Elditha gasped. 'What?'

'Shush, the guards are beyond the door. I shall return in the morning.' She crossed to the door and turned to add in a low tone that was almost a whisper, 'You supported the girl. I won't forget that kindness. I had turned my back to her.' Alice quietly opened the door, bolted it and was gone without explanation.

Elditha did not know if she could trust this woman. On her own it might be possible to escape from the hall itself, but the palace yard, through the stockade, the woods and out into the darkness beyond? And she needed help to save Padar. She fell onto the bed exhausted. To her surprise, the next morning, she discovered that she had fallen into a deep and dreamless sleep.

27

Easter 1067

'My lady, are you awake?' The voice came from close to her pillow. Wide awake, Elditha sat up. 'You will be hungry, so break your fast.' Alice indicated the table below a high, shuttered window. 'There is bread, butter and small beer, but hurry. Count Alain asks that you join him for prayer. Later, he says, you must dine in the hall.'

'What if I decline?'

'You won't save the skald that way. If you agree to dine with Count Alain, I can help you flee.' Alice sank onto the stool by the table. 'But you must do as he says and arouse no suspicion. I do this every day, dine at his table, look after his household and deceive.' She glanced down, then up again at Elditha with a profound sadness on her countenance. 'Lady Elditha, let me explain. I lost my husband at Hastings fighting with Count Alain's Bretons. Alain of Brittany was his cousin. Yet I am born English. Since Senlac, I have seen for myself English lands pillaged, crops stolen and women used and abused. When war comes to the countryside, the poor suffer. My father has sworn loyalty to the silvatii. They will free your skald.' She hurried to the door, opened it, looked out, closed it again, returned to Elditha's side and lowered her voice. 'Tonight is Holy Friday. The soldiers will be at prayer and Count Alain too. Your door will be unbolted and unguarded. Slip out, keep your mantle close. You will have to get through this hall and out of the back of the first hall. You must get down to the river before they start searching for you. Take the track behind the hall into the woods. On the pathway a boy will be waiting for you. He will guide you. I know that a ship is expected on the Severn.'

'And Padar?'

'We will rescue him, and this I promise, but he may not be able to go with you on the ship. You must go without him.'

Elditha pulled the blanket around her shoulders. 'In that case there is no choice, but promise me you will help him.'

The woman nodded her reply and left Elditha to break her fast.

A little later, Elditha pushed the unlocked door ajar and peered out of the curtain that separated the chamber from the hall. The west hall was full of soldiers and women were stirring pots on the great central fire. Alice was directing them. Closing the door softly, she went to peer under the bed. Yes, the old chest was still there. She pulled it towards her and opened the lid. It contained a broken saddle. This part of the hall was near to the stables. When the west hall was constructed the hatchway had been set into the floor planking, designed so that old Earl Godwin could slip in and out and reach his horses secretly by night.

She made herself as flat as she could, crawled under the bed and traced the outline with her fingers. She felt around, moving her hands over the rough planks of the floor. The wooden ring lay flat against the floor. If she moved the low bed it would be easier. She could pull up the trapdoor and drop down into the undergrowth below, close to the stable doors. As she pushed the box back over the trapdoor she felt something caught on the chest and pulled it away.

'My lady? What are you doing?'

Elditha wriggled out, straightened up and brushed one hand along her dress. A maid had followed Alice inside. She would tell Alice to lock the chamber door, for her own sake, and she would explain about the trapdoor, but not while the maid hovered close. 'I dropped my pendant, Alice,' she said and held up the trinket she had dragged from under the box, a tiny garnet that dangled from a gold chain. She slipped it over her head, praying silently that the pendant she had lost many years before would bring her good fortune. The chapel bells began to ring as Alice handed Elditha her cloak. They were just in time for Sext. There was no time to explain the door below.

Conversation, the spitting of the fire and the clanking of pewter spoons on the table: this was no different to other feasts held at Kingsholm, except that Harold was dead and she was sitting next to Count Alain at the top table. She observed the faces of minor thanes, faces that were lit by firelight into familiarity. Sitting with Count Alain were those who had, like Beorhtric, thrown their lot in with the conquerors, hoping to hold on to their lands. At least their wives had the grace not to meet her cold stare. Farther down the board she picked out a face that she had never seen before: a man with his head shaved in Norman fashion. She watched him turn to speak with Brother Francis. The two men were familiar with each other.

'Wadard, Bishop Odo's man,' said Count Alain in French, seeing her look at the man. 'He is with Brother Francis, whom I hear you displeased only yesterday. It is as well that I am not of Normandy. We Bretons do not pander to priests.' She contemplated the plate, gold and probably stolen from the English, and did not reply. Count Alain lifted the choicest pieces of fish and offered them to her saying, in French, 'Fish and lentils test a man.'

'And a woman,' she responded in English. After a while, she said, 'My lord, we must talk. My skald is a prisoner. I do not want him hurt. I want him back.'

'We negotiated before. Norman soldiers dead. Your escort murdered and you were abducted by this creature and his accomplices.'

'I was not abducted ...'

'*N'est pas vrai*, my lady. No more of it. We are to be espoused in London in May when La Reine Mathilde is come. You will meet our new Queen.'

'Count Alain.' Elditha looked down at the gleaming plate and pushed it away. 'I find I am tired.' She began to rise. 'I wish to retire.'

243

'But first, a glass of sweet wine and, well,' he played with his eating knife for a few moments, slowly turning it over in his hand, 'shall I tell you about your son?'

She nodded. As a slingshot catches a hedge sparrow, his words had found their mark. He clicked his fingers at a servant, called for hippocras, lifted the curtain behind his chair aside and ushered her through into what had been once, a long time before, King Edward's antechamber.

He indicated the chair that once had been Edith Godwin's. Alice served wine and sweet cakes before retiring into the shadows. Elditha gathered her courage and waited for Count Alain to speak, her hands folded neatly in her lap and her gaze steady. 'Tell me about my son,' she said at last.

'The child is with his nurse and with other royal children. The news from Normandy is that Ulf is happy. We can allow my stepson to live on in Normandy. They will make a priest of him.'

Elditha felt tears well up behind her eyes. 'Ulf is too little to know his future.'

'It is not for him to decide. Who knows?' he said. 'Perhaps you can give me a son.'

'My eldest son is not much younger than you.'

'Godwin is seven years my junior. Besides, Queen Emma gave Canute a son when she was 36. We shall better that and have two.'

She sat silently sipping the wine. He spoke of wedding plans. Candles burned, wax melted. At last he rose, saying that he must attend the midnight service with his soldiers. 'Tonight the Angelus will be for my soldiers. Tomorrow we shall observe all the services together, and then we shall set out for London. If there is anything you need, Alice will see to it.'

As he swept through the curtain, Elditha prayed to St Cecilia that this was to be their final encounter.

'My lady,' Alice said softly from the shadows, 'there is no time to lose. It is best that you slip away when they are at chapel.'

In a low voice Elditha explained how she would leave

through the trapdoor.

'I shall lock the outer door to your chamber, but I shall leave before dawn also. I intend to join my father and the men and women who live in the woods. I have had enough of Count Alain. He was my husband's cousin, not mine. God go with you.' Alice clasped Elditha's hands. 'We will save the skald, I promise you. But tonight, Elditha, you must travel alone, and may God go with you.'

'Send him to Exeter. He will be safe there,' Elditha whispered.

When the church bell sounded, Elditha climbed off the bed and drew on her mantle. Pulling with her whole weight she dragged the bed back from the wall. The bell continued to toll, and monotonous as the sound was, she was glad of it as it hid her noise. She moved the chest until it was possible to pull on the ring and haul up the trapdoor. She threw her saddle-bag down first and then she dropped through the hole onto the earth below after it. Bending low, she crept forward, but just as she was almost ready to break her cover, she stopped. She could see the hem of a black gown moving slowly beyond her. It paused and she caught a whiff of incense. A pair of woollen-clad, heavy-booted legs stopped beside the gown. Brother Francis and another, the man Wadard, but if she kept very still, hardly daring to breathe, she would not be discovered. She was able to snatch at slices of their conversation. Brother Francis asked Wadard where he was going at so late an hour. Wadard replied, 'Deerhurst, and after that I ride to London.'

'Do not fail to speak of my part in it to the Bishop. And now, Wadard, we part company. Count Alain is waiting ...' They moved off towards the chapel, their words became indistinct. Then they were gone and there was quiet, except for the bell's impatient toll.

She lay on the damp earth and wriggled forward, pushing her satchel before her. She peered out into darkness and drizzle. If she hurried through the stamping, the coughs and the swishing of tails and kept close to the stable, the horses would

245

cover her footfalls. A groom called to another from inside the barn to get horses ready for Wadard. She must be quick. She watched the stable door and listened. The clip of horses beyond, and voices, many voices; Wadard was leaving by the front yard. Clutching her bag she hurtled towards the path into the woodland, lightly sliding through trees to the river, hearing every breath she took, every rustle in the undergrowth. Ghosts flitted past her, imaginary things closed in on her, and water dripped from overhead branches. She hurried forward through cracking twigs and under shadowy trees. At last, she could hear the river's lapping.

She waited and, when no one came, she wondered if she should continue along the path. The moonlight slid along the branches, dark and bruised, blue-white like thinning ancient skin. Cloud obscured the moon, and then she could see nothing.

'My lady.' The soft whisper brushed past her ear, making her start. A hand clutched her arm and she dropped the saddlebag. A figure emerged out of the gloom leading a horse and a cart, a slight youth, no older than her son Magnus. The boy stopped momentarily and pointed, indicating that she must climb up and crawl under the sacking in the wagon.

'Try to sleep, my lady,' he whispered and then he carefully and slowly turned the cart around and they were off. He had hardly stopped.

The cart jolted gently through the trees and, eventually, wrapped in the warmth of sacking, she began to doze.

246

28

There was a clash of shields. The Vikings came, enraged by
battle. Many a spear passed through the life-house of the
doomed.

The Battle of Maldon, in *A Choice of Anglo-Saxon Verse,* edited
and translated by Richard Hamer

Water sloshed through the long grasses beyond the cart.
Confused for a moment, Elditha threw off the sacks and
climbed down and came around to the front of the wagon. The
drizzle had stopped and the pallid, veined moon was visible
above. They were beside a wide river. Their cart was under a
dripping tree. The boy had slumped over. He was wrapped in a
cloak, asleep, the reins loose in his hands, and the horse was
patiently grazing among the tall grasses. At her movement, the
boy awakened and jumped down.

'My lady, we are on the Severn, at a place where the river is
at its widest and deepest. Across there,' he pointed, 'a half mile
off, the kingdom of the Welsh. The ship should have come by
now.' He walked forward into the reeds and stood absolutely
still. In the distance, she could hear voices calling into the night
and hooves thudding on bracken. She pulled her seax from her
belt.

He hurried back, saw her seax and said, 'You hear them too.
Beorhtric's men are coming through the woods, maybe two
furlongs off.' He looked about them. 'There is tree cover
between us and the jetty up there.'

'How far is the jetty?' Elditha asked, putting back her knife.

'Not far. Wait here.' He pushed through grasses to the shore
and returned saying, 'The ship is here. See for yourself. It is
opposite the jetty up there, anchored in mid-river. We must pull

the cart back into the trees and let the horse graze.'

They led the horse back and looped the nag's rope over a branch. Elditha lifted her saddle-bag from the cart and, bending low, they made their way to the river bank. Beyond the tall grass, where the wide grey, heaving river threatened to open and swallow them, she could see a large vessel at rest around two furlongs out, silhouetted against the sky with its sails down, a mighty bird with tired wings. Some distance off, to their right, a wooden jetty thrust out into the water. Already riders were gathering in a large group and were silently watching the ship.

The youth pulled her into the tall reeds.

'They are dropping currachs from the big ship.'

'How long will they be?'

'They need to find us, but remember, they will still think that Lord Beorhtric is your man.'

She parted the grasses and peered upstream. She could hear voices echoing over the stretch of water that separated shore from ship. Beorhtric's men had cut off access to the jetty and were sitting rigidly in their saddles, watching the water. She counted half a dozen riders, maybe more. Looking towards the big ship she could see men climbing into currachs. Moments later three currachs were rowing towards the jetty and the sailors were lowering a fourth into the water.

'Stay here,' the youth whispered, 'Beorhtric's riders must not see us, so I'll swim out.' He pulled off his boots and shirt and crawled to the river. He slid into the water and glided off, keeping below the surface, occasionally coming up for air. She stuffed his grubby shirt into her saddle-bag and held on to his precious boots. As he glided below the water, she tracked his progress by the air bubbles as he came up to breathe. Time was punctuated by shouts upstream, the snorting of horses, taunts and the sound of weapons clanking against shields.

The first two boats reached the jetty. A third and fourth were still around a furlong out in the river. The boy rose up for air again, halfway to them. She laid her head on the sheepskin bag with her arms forward, protectively encircling it, and turned sideways again. The long-haired Norsemen, with swords that

248

glinted through the moonlight, were climbing onto the jetty. They faced the helmeted horsemen who had gathered on the stony crescent by the jetty's platform. Words were exchanged. She thought that she heard her name called out. Then she saw a rider trot forward. It could be Beorhtric himself. Something was shouted back to the currachs still on the water and, in a synchronised movement, the men on the currachs out in the water raised their bows and began to shoot. Beorhtric, if it was him, backed off. Another horse, a dark stallion caught by an arrow, reared up. Its agonised whinny reverberated downriver towards her as it threw its rider to the ground. One of the Norsemen raced forward and cut the soldier down, and as he did, the horse thundered off through the trees. Beorhtric's men fell to and lashed out with their swords, their horses leaping and careering. Elditha could see that their numbers were evenly matched. Those on horseback had the advantage of height as long as they were not caught by arrow fire. The Norsemen on the landing stage fought back. She closed her eyes and prayed for help and, when she opened them again, weapons were flashing through the grey dawn. The noise was deafening, the air full of shouts and the ringing of swords. The battle was coming towards her.

The horsemen drove the Norsemen before them into the trees behind her, between the cart and shoreline. The arrows-men rowed their currachs closer to the shore, closer to her hiding place. As arrows flew overhead, Elditha wriggled forward into taller grasses. She whispered her prayers, not daring to raise her head to look behind again. Then, glancing over the water, she saw her rescue. One currach glided close to where she lay, but she did not dare stand up and reveal herself. Then she saw the trail of bubbles. The youth was swimming alongside it. St Cecilia had answered her prayer.

The oarsmen stopped rowing a little way from the shore. The boy raised his head and called out, 'Jump for it!' She stood up, tossed her bag forward into the currach, then the boots. She gathered up her skirt and tried to jump forward, but her foot caught in the folds of her mantle and she flew forward into the river. For a moment the cloak dragged her down. Arms reached down to catch her. She tried to swim but could not. Something caught at her legs. For a moment she thought that she would die here, within the grasp of a river snake. But then she was being lifted up from below. The snake was spitting her out. Her vision cleared and she saw the boy's face beside her own. As they hauled her on board, she choked and spat out river water. She was alive. The boy swam alongside the craft until he too was pulled aboard. With the two extra bodies on board, the currach was riding dangerously low in the river, but it moved slowly away from the shore.

Elditha looked back where the horsemen were fighting close to her hiding place. She heard the nag whinny from the trees and she could just see its bulky shape as it bolted into the woods, dragging the cart behind. The Norsemen yelled and slashed at horses' forelegs, causing them to throw riders. Elditha gripped the side of the currach, her teeth chattering. She watched the boy watching the shore. His eyes were round and staring. No wonder. He would not be going home. She reached out and took his hand.

At last their currach had reached the mother ship. Seamen were calling down to her, 'Hold on to the rope.' She clutched it. Hands lifted her up from behind and hauled her to safety on board. The oarsmen drew up their skin boat after them. She sank against the walls of the Viking craft. The tide began to turn and they were already manoeuvring the great ship round.

She heard the call of a horn echo across the river and looked back toward the shore. Warriors hurtled through the grass. As the horsemen pursued, swiping with swords, they leapt into the river and struggled through reeds holding shields aloft, slashing a way clear with swords, staying close to the shoreline and steadily moving back along it to the jetty. The arrows-men provided cover as the warriors reached their currachs. They untied them, climbed into them and rowed back out into the river. But three did not make it. They remained trapped on the river bank where the horsemen had caged them in.

Beorhtric's men easily destroyed these last warriors. Elditha looked away as their dying screams reached out into the night, bouncing off the water. It was for her that these men had fought so courageously. Someone threw a blanket over her shoulders and said. 'It's over. We're headed for the Irish Ocean.'

'What do they call this ship?' she asked.

'The *Sea Serpent*.'

She turned to see who was speaking. 'You!' she said.

'Why so surprised? I have long been of service to the Godwin family. Your sons will be pleased to see you, Elditha.' Earl Connor looked down towards the small crafts that had reached them. The great ship was now moving forward with the turned tide. He yelled, 'Hurry, get them up.' The sailors threw a rope down and hauled the fighters on board. The ship heaved as the last skin boat was thrust along a tunnel of warriors and into the stern.

'Row hard, we've caught our tide, men.' Connor pointed up at the boat's two sails, directing his seamen to raise them. She was dripping river water but she did not care. 'We are not clear until we are in the Channel,' he warned. 'They will ride along the bank and summon ships to cut us off.'

'Beorhtric's men,' she said pointing to the bank. 'That bastard traitor.'

'Outrun them,' Connor shouted at his crew. He glanced at the youth who clung to the walls of the boat and tossed a leather flask to the boy. 'Here, drink, lad, and take an oar. It will warm you up. Three of my best oarsmen are murdered on that jetty.' He returned to the front of the craft.

The youth drank and spluttered and passed the flask to Elditha. 'My lady, you must go inside beneath the covers. It will be a long cold night.'

As she drank, the liquid filled her belly with fire and warmed her. The boy clambered back through the stern and took up a rowing place beside the Norsemen.

She did not go under the shelter yet but leaned against the side of the ship. A wind blew from the north, helping to push the craft onward. Even though she was shivering she waited. Out of the corner of her eye she noticed how Earl Connor's dark mantle flapped in the wind and his hair streamed behind him. The oarsmen grunted as they pulled back and forward. Elditha watched the horsemen galloping along the bank. Curses flew over the water to merge with the splashing of oars, rowers' grunts and the wind's keening. The horsemen tried to keep pace with the boat. Eventually the pursuit slowed and shouts faded into the distance. Beorhtric's soldiers lined up on the riverbank, watched for a moment, and then turned into the trees.

Beorhtric's family had once been their people. If thanes who kept halls by the Severn joined with the invaders, what hope had her sons of recovering a kingdom? She stared into the widening channel that would lead them to the sea and into Ireland and felt ashamed for Beorhtric. She silently prayed to St Cecilia that Padar would escape his captors and that he would soon be making his way to Exeter.

'Padar,' she whispered into the night, 'You have been my help and protector. God save you and bring you to safety.'

When the stars shone like candle points above a heaving sea she retreated at last under the awning on the deck of the enormous bird-like vessel, seeking shelter from the wind and the bitter cold.

PART THREE

Rebellion

Meanwhile the English were groaning under the Norman yoke, the petty lords guarding castles oppressed all the native inhabitants of high and low degree and heaped shameful burdens on them. The English groaned aloud for their lost liberty and plotted ceaselessly to find some way of shaking off the yoke that was so intolerable and unaccustomed.

At this time, the force of citizens held Exeter, young and old seething with anger against every inhabitant of Gaul.

The Ecclesiastical History of Orderic Vitalis, 12th century, edited and translated by Marjorie Chibnall

29

Exeter
April 1067

Within months of her arrival, the Countess Gytha had created a kingdom of women in her palace at Exeter, a collection of one-storied buildings surrounded by orchards that was situated close to the town's northern wall. Hilda, Gytha's youngest daughter, set out to Exeter from her estate near Wallingford. She travelled west with a small train and three wagons containing chests of silver and gold, one filled with church paraphernalia, and a fifth wagon just for her tapestries. Soon, other noblewomen who dwelled in the west sought Gytha's protection. They came carrying their children and their treasures; all that was left to them after their husbands were killed in the great Battle.

Every day Gytha's bower hall reverberated with the bird-like lightness of their voices. Women dropped spindles and spun thread; they busied themselves in the brewery; they made cheese and butter in the large dairy; they baked bread and competed to invent new puddings for Lent. The women of Exeter worked hard to bring a renewed rhythm into their broken lives.

As spring emerged, the Countess walked in the garden with her granddaughter, inspecting plants and poking her stick into the soil looking for new growth. Thea ran ahead, climbed up on the wall and walked a little way along it. After a few moments, she shouted down, 'There are travellers by the North Gate. I can see a man riding a large black horse and a woman on a brown mare ... and churchmen crossing the moor. I think that must be Bishop Leofric with one, two, three, six monks, all riding horses. Do you think that the Bishop will bring news from my mother?'

Gytha glanced up at the wall and leaned her leather-gloved hands on her stick. 'How would the Bishop have news of Elditha, child? The boy Padar sent us said she was travelling away from trouble, not into it. Hopefully, she's safe with your brothers by now.'

Thea shouted back down, 'Grandmother, please write and find out.'

'Maybe soon; now come down off that wall. We are going to find a gift for the good Bishop Leofric.' She grunted. The Bishop of Exeter might be turning his mantle. Leofric would need a special gift this Easter to keep him sweet. She snapped her fingers at two women who were gathering primroses. 'Go inside and find jars for the posies. Put them in my chamber.' She pointed her stick at Thea, who had just jumped off the bottom step. 'And Thea, you follow me.'

She led the girl to stone stairs that descended the outside wall of the palace. A small door below opened into cellars below her main hall. 'You go first,' she told Thea. Following, staying close to the wall, Gytha felt each step with her stick, before placing her foot on the next, until they reached the bottom. She selected the larger of two keys from her belt ring, pushed it into the barrel lock and creakingly turned it. She pushed the door. It didn't shift. 'The wood has swollen with the rain. No one has fetched anything up for a week,' she grumbled.

'I can do it.' Thea put her weight against it. It was still sticking. She pushed harder until, with a groan, it gave way.

'Wait, Grandmother, there are lamps.' Thea leaned down and lifted a tinder box kept ready by the entrance. She struck a spark, lit a spindle, and with it three lamps which she placed carefully along the length of the cellar. The lamps lit up the undercroft's shadows. Shapes became objects as gradually Gytha's eyes adjusted to the dimness.

A sequence of spaces lay underneath the hall paralleling the alcoves above, containing stored tableware, large bowls carved of oak and metal pans. 'The women rescued all they could from their halls before coming here,' Gytha remarked. 'Come, I need to show you something else.'

Herbs hung from the rafters to dry. Along the walls, flasks of mead and barrels of wine stood neatly stacked in rows. Her cellars contained sacks of dried lavender; fat sacks of goose feathers and several packs overflowing with duck feathers. In one corner of the undercroft, two chairs awaited the attention of their new carpenter from Hampshire. Sacks filled with oily fleece waited for Gytha's ladies to spin it into wool. She led Thea past them all. At the back of the cellar, just below the Countess's sleeping chamber, there was another room. 'In this cellar we shall find a gift for Bishop Leofric.' She unlocked the door and pushed it, expecting it to stick, but it gave way without difficulty. Once they were inside she lifted the lids of several chests.

Thea gasped. She had never seen so much gold and silver. 'It must be greater than the treasury in Winchester, Grandmother.'

'Indeed, and some of it will provide your dowry.'

Thea went from coffer to coffer as Gytha opened lids. There was one filled with expensive cloth, then one with a hoard of glittering jewels, amber and garnets set into silver. Next to it stood another chest filled with books on hawking, scriptures, psalms and poetry.

'These, my dear, belonged to your father.' Gytha explained. 'He collected books and I have saved these ones. The Bastard stole my sons. He will not have Harold's books.'

'How did you get them here?'

'I sent for them in December. When the sea was emptied of shipping, my messengers sailed to Bosham. They raided the hall and brought them out.'

'I never knew.'

'You don't know everything, Thea. God help us if you did.'

'I can keep secrets, Grandmother.'

'Secrets are dangerous.' She knew that only too well. In her time she had kept many.

There were other chests in the hidden chamber, beautiful painted wooden boxes containing gold and silver cups and plates, large and small gem-studded ornaments. One cedar-scented coffer held valuable tapestries. 'Smell it, Thea.' Thea inhaled its exotic, musty smell. 'And there,' said the Countess, pointing with her stick. 'There, you see, my dear, how I have protected my ladies' futures. Wouldn't the Bastard like to get his wolf paws on all of this?' She pointed to a row of chests neatly placed at the far end of the room. Thea held up the lamp and peered at them. These were the treasures carried to Exeter by the noblewomen who had fled into Gytha's care that winter; these were their most precious possessions: jewel boxes, small panels of wood painted with biblical scenes and touched with gold paint, rolls of valuable silk cloth and great tapestries. Gytha released a sigh and leaned on Thea's arm. 'Never speak of what we have in our care outside this cellar.'

'No, Grandmother, I promise.' Thea looked at Gytha with her dark, solemn eyes. 'Never,' she whispered.

'That chest over there is locked.' Gytha removed a small brass key from her belt ring and pointed to a chest which had a lid that was painted with a blue-robed pregnant Madonna. 'Take this key and open it,' she said.

Thea twisted the key and the lock opened. She cautiously lifted the chest's painted lid. Gytha hobbled closer. Peering in and probing with her stick, she daintily poked about a collection of ornate boxes. 'Ah, there it is, that casket,' she said with one final tap of the tip of her stick. 'Just look at the garnet in that crystal lid. There's a slither of the holy cross inside, brought to England by St Helena herself – if you believe it. It is our most valuable relic. Carry the casket upstairs for me.' She tut-tutted to herself as she slammed down all the lids that remained opened. This was a present that the greedy Bishop would surely covet.

They dressed in their richest overgowns to visit the Bishop of Exeter and Gytha, looking approvingly at Thea's neat fillet and veil, remarked as they came into the courtyard, 'Your grandfather always said, intimidate the clergy with your own power, dress proudly and travel in elegance. Our power may be reduced, but the Bishop must not see it.' Their litter, usually used to descend the hill from the palace and attend Vespers in the cathedral, was draped with heavy wool curtains decorated with Grecian figures that were spinning threads, and was pulled by two white horses, their silver harnesses studded with amber decorations. Gytha sat imperiously within it determined to do business with the Bishop, steeling herself to take no nonsense from him concerning the Bastard's tax.

Bishop Leofric received them in his hall. He led Gytha to a comfortable padded chair by the hearth. Servants placed wine and cakes on the small carved table close to the Countess's elbow and, for a while, they exchanged pleasantries, drank a cup of wine and nibbled hazelnut cakes. Gytha asked about his journey to Winchester.

He told them that Norman troops were busy guarding the roads south of Gloucester. He then remarked, 'Bishop Odo will be collecting the King's taxes here soon.'

'Really?' said Gytha dryly. 'There's no coin for tax here.'

Bishop Leofric went on, 'Well, you know that the King ...' She frowned and then noticed how he quickly shifted tack, 'I mean, Duke William, is in Normandy.'

'And he has my grandson with him.'

The Bishop coughed. 'Countess, here there is nothing we can do about that. The child is motherless since Lady Elditha disappeared ...'

'Nonsense, he has a grandmother, aunts, sisters. I want you to work for his return. Ulf belongs here with his family.'

'The child is a guarantee that there will not be rebellion in Wessex.'

'If they leave us alone, we'll leave them alone.' She knew that was a lie but said it anyway. Her grandsons would plot revenge, and so would she. Aloud, she said, 'Continue, Leofric, you were speaking of Bishop Odo.'

'The Bishop has taxed Winchester and Oxford too, so we must expect the same here. Of course, in return we get a new castle for our town's protection.' Bishop Leofric shifted his plump feet on his cushioned footstool.

'Let him try that here, Leofric, and he will see how we resist. Just watch tax collectors come to my towns. They will be seen off back to London. Do you think I shall allow the Bastard to tax us or let him get a castle built in my town?' She tapped the tiles impatiently with her stick. 'So, Leofric, I hear that you visited Wilton on your travels. What news do you bring of my granddaughter?'

Leofric bowed his head. 'She is with her aunt, Countess. Gunnhild draws designs for lettering. She is talented, an unusual child, and she appears happy there. Edith has sent an answer to your letter of last month.' He waved to a monk who hovered close to him. The monk ducked behind an arras, and returned moments later with Edith's letter.

The Countess passed it to Thea. 'My dear, put it away for now.'

'Don't you wish me to read it to you?' the Bishop offered.

'No need. But before we leave, my Lord Bishop, we have an Easter gift for you.' She looked at her granddaughter and reached out her hands. 'Thea, the gift.'

Thea handed Gytha a linen sack. Gytha took it and held on to it, amused, watching the Bishop's eyes goggle with anticipation. At last she passed it over into his podgy jewelled hands.

The Bishop lost no time unwinding the silk cord that tied the neck of it. He drew out the gift, and gasped, turning the box around and around, examining it. 'Countess, what a marvellous thing and well, well, this is a truly magnificent garnet.' He held it up to the sconce light. It seemed to glow. 'It is a crystal box!' he exclaimed. His rubicund face creased with smiles. He delicately tapped the side. 'What treasure lies inside this casket? A finger, a bone, a fragment of the Madonna's veil?'

'A slither of the cross.'

'How unusual!'

Determined to remind him of where his loyalty ought to lie, she said quickly, 'In return for this Easter gift to the cathedral, masses must be sung for my sons' souls.'

'Countess, it is done.' He passed the crystal casket to a

hovering monk. 'Place this in my chamber, Brother Paul.' He reached out and touched Gytha's gloved hand with his plump fingers. 'Now, Countess, before you leave us, I have something to ask of you too.'

'Do.' Gytha wondered what the Bishop could possibly want of her now.

'I met with travellers on the road west, a thane and his wife who request speech with you. These are wealthy travellers. They have already made a generous donation to my church of St Mary's. May I send them to you?'

'Very well, Bishop. Send them to me tomorrow.' She gathered up her mantle, took her leave and, linking her arm in Thea's, hurried back to her waiting litter. She grimaced as the litter jolted and rattled her bones as they climbed up the steep, rutted path to the palace. Yet, all told, the interview had had a satisfactory outcome. She had made it very clear to the Bishop who was the power in this town.

Later, in the privacy of her chamber, she read that Gunnhild would remain in Wilton. She sighed and put the letter away. The girl was probably safer in Wilton Abbey than in a town that the Bastard had marked out for his attention. On the following evening, though, Gytha received more news when Alfred and Gertrude entered her palace. When Alfred had told her all, she said, 'I am glad you did not reveal your true story to Bishop Leofric. You have suffered on our account.' She reached out and patted Gertrude's knee. 'My home is yours for as long as is necessary.' Gertrude wiped tears from her eyes. Gytha found them sleeping space in an alcove at the back of the main hall, almost a room, since it contained a curtained box bed made of beech wood and carved with Wessex dragons. 'We used that bed ourselves when Godwin first built this hall. I was keeping this space for Gunnhild, but I fear she will never return to us.'

Gertrude said she was sorry that Gunnhild could not come to Exeter. She told Gytha about the gift. 'Countess, it was a terrible mistake, a dreadful, careless thing to do. It has brought about this disaster and I fear to think what revenge my action may be wreaking even now.'

Gytha said, 'Elditha did not use her wits either. Now it is in the past. You were not to know what could evolve.' She took Gertrude's hand. 'And, my dear, you will be welcomed by the ladies in my bower.' She turned to Alfred. 'I almost forgot to ask. What tale did you tell the Bishop?'

'That the Normans took my estate.'

'Ah, then, we must think of something suitable for you to do here. In the meantime, you can join my guard.'

That night, as she lay awake, Gytha wondered how Alfred could use his skills to their benefit. Gradually an idea formed itself in her mind. She shifted her aching bones in her feathered bed and folded her ancient hands under her chin as her idea grew like a ball of tapestry wool weaving webs of intrigue. If Alfred could forge coin of silver, then perhaps he could work with other metals too. They may need to defend Exeter. At length she snuffed out her candle. Satisfied with her plan she turned on her side, curled up like a younger woman and drifted into a pleasant sleep.

A new pattern of living emerged for Gertrude. She embroidered a linen table covering with her exquisite stitching and told stories of the queen of the fairies and her husband who lived on the heaths, moving as royalty does move, from invisible winter halls to summer bowers. Her collection of stories included tales of elves with their mischief and accounts of fat, evil trolls who dwelled in the summer-lit northlands but by winter moonlight travelled in sleighs over tundra of hard-packed snow. Gytha smiled to watch Thea become animated. Her granddaughter was entranced by Gertrude. Perhaps she was a tenuous link to Thea's mother, or more likely to the world of her imagination, where she believed she would wed a prince.

On a soft April day Gytha collected her ladies together in the palace yard and suggested that they ride out to the small Priory of Our Lady. It was attached to the Abbey of St Ronan's vast estate and conveniently secreted among trees close to the river. It was time to call on her old friend the prioress, since she planned to involve both Alfred and Prioress Mildryth in her plans for Exeter's protection.

Grooms led mares out from the stable and helped the women mount. A small guard followed on foot to protect them. Town wives and traders fell to their knees as they trotted through the morning market. They made slow progress down the rutted path from the palace and through the narrow streets because Gytha would stop and ask her men to distribute purses of pennies to the poor.

'God bless the House of Godwin,' a woman cried out as she caught a miniscule linen purse.

'St Osyth watch over you,' the Countess called graciously back.

'May the Holy Virgin bless you, Countess.'

She bowed her head and acknowledged them all. She was gladdened in her heart that here in this Godwin outpost, her house had always been much loved by the people. Chattering, with their bridle bells jingling, the women proceeded through the River Gate towards St Osyth's cross and past the wharfs. They crossed a bridge to continue along a sunken track close to the river. A watermill creaked. Birds sang in trees. Spring flowers released their scent as horses trod on them. Gytha felt stronger – much younger than her 65 years – as she rode through the sunshine. Her troubles, for a while, could be hidden away behind Exeter's stout walls.

Shortly after noon they rode into the priory's courtyard. Alfred dismounted first, cupped his hand for the Countess's small, booted foot and lifted her carefully off her mare. Hilda and Thea slid from their side saddles unaided and hurried to Gytha's side. They offered her their arms for support, but Gytha shook them away, leaned on the stick and walked forward with a determined step. Her old friend the Prioress Mildryth was already hurrying towards her from the chapel.

'My, my, Countess Gytha, you are so welcome. It is good to see you again.' The prioress looked at Thea. 'What a lovely girl your granddaughter is, ripe for spoiling. Welcome, welcome. We have much to talk about.'

'Ah, good to see you too, Mildryth, though I'd say we have all enjoyed better times.' She sighed. 'It has been a bitter grieving winter; my four handsome sons cut down in their prime. But let us think of happier times. This visit has been long in the coming. Tell me, how is the priory doing?' She took Mildryth's arm as they entered the priory's guest hall.

They sat on cushioned benches in the hall. Novices served buttermilk and honey cakes. After a little conversation and refreshment and seeing her ladies contentedly talking to the nuns, exchanging chatter concerning recipes, the Countess rose and signalled to Alfred. She asked him to accompany Prioress Mildryth and herself into the garden. Tapping her stick along the pathway, she walked through new growth, pointing out the herbs she needed for the palace garden. 'I will have the gardener cut slips for you, my dear friend,' Mildryth said. By the time they reached the orchard, Gytha was tiring. She sank onto a long, stone bench and caught her breath. Her two companions waited. She had no intention of going farther. She had important business with them. She began, 'Listen, this is what I want you to do, Mildryth, so sit beside me.' She lifted her hand. 'You too, Alfred.' She patted the cool stone. 'And not a word from either of you until I have spoken.' The prioress folded her hands neatly in her lap. Gytha looked from her to Alfred and back and continued, 'Alfred, here, is a coiner. He knows the working of metal. You remember how we discussed setting up a foundry close to those tin workings on the priory land? Alfred could build our foundry, but not for the forging of coin.' She laughed. 'Not at all, because we can import metals from Ireland to mix with the tin we have here and we can make weapons. Swords, axes, arrow heads – weapons of every kind that we need for our own protection. Our boats will easily slip past Norman patrols into the inlets on the north coast. Are you agreeable?'

'I will help however I can,' the prioress replied solemnly.

'But can you grant Alfred somewhere on the estate to live and work?'

The prioress raised a pair of delicate eyebrows. A smile

hovered on the edges of her elegant mouth. 'There is the old forge. We can make the cottage comfortable.'

Gytha turned to Alfred. 'At least we can try to save our corner of Wessex. Can you help us, Alfred?'

Alfred made a steeple of his hands below his chin, closed his eyes, opened them and said, 'My life is yours, Countess.'

Gytha rose from the bench. 'Good. This is where we begin, here with a forge. Prioress Mildryth will shelter you and Gertrude.' She felt a smile play about her mouth. 'We shall tell Bishop Leofric that Gertrude is teaching the novices embroidery and that you are helping the prioress manage her estate.'

As they walked back to the building, she wondered if she was creating great danger for them all. Perhaps for the sake of her town, their trade, their future, she should not be planning armed resistance to that bastard William of Normandy. Yet, she could not allow him to take control of the south-west. She thought of her grandsons. For their sake, she would challenge the enemy when they banged on her gates demanding the keys to her town.

30

Late April 1067

The *Sea Serpent*'s bright sails caught the wind, and the ship sailed unimpeded through the channel at Bristol into the open sea. Once out on the Irish Ocean, as Elditha had requested, they set the ship northwards towards Bangor in Ulster. The abbey had been destroyed 50 years before and its monks and treasures were housed in an old and weathered wooden building the local people amusingly called the New Monastery. One day, Earl Connor said to her, a great new stone abbey would be raised from the old ruins.

He wanted to send the *Sea Serpent* to trade for seal skins in Iceland and they would have only been dropped off in Dublinia, anyway. 'It can be done,' he said granting her request, and grinning at her. He flashed his white teeth and added that her very wish was his command. The thought occurred then that he had more than a simple feeling of friendship for her as the mother of the Godwin boys. His black, laughing eyes constantly followed her and he was extremely solicitous for her comfort on the sea journey. He sat with her under the awning and placed his own heavy mantle about her shoulders, pointed out seabirds to her as they sailed close to the coast, ate with her and slept, wrapped in a blanket, at her feet. He made her feel safe, and now relieved that, after guarding it for several months, she would deliver the lapidary to the New Monastery as she had promised Brother Thomas. The Earl would ride with her from the New Monastery back down to Dublinia. Afterwards the *Sea Serpent* would sail on and into the Northern Ocean under Connor's sea captain, a man called Ulich, but he, himself, would not make the journey. He would see her safely to her sons and send a messenger before them to announce their impending arrival.

After a day and a night on the sea, a landscape of greens and woody browns revealed the coast of Ireland. As the tide began to race towards the shore the *Sea Serpent* lifted on the waves. Moments later the green hills of Ulster were rolling inland from the coast. Through trees that hugged the coast she could see how a tall, thatched, roofed building scraped the sky. It belonged to the monastery church.

'Into the currachs,' called Earl Connor. Once in, they were among the call of seagulls and the slap of water and, with oars moving them through a flooding tide, they sped to shore. The landing was an easy one as the water was calm. They trailed up through the trees to the monastery. She was bedraggled, her gown torn and her cloak muddy. She looked more like a fishwife than a lady of England and she knew she smelled like one too. Yet, at that moment, nothing mattered more than Brother Thomas's precious book.

The abbot welcomed her with food and drink. He declared that he was overjoyed to see the woman who had been Earl Harold's wife. When Elditha brought him news that Thomas of Abingdon, the renowned scholar and herbalist, was safe, he clasped her hands and tears rolled down his lined face.

'The news from England has been terrible. The old Norse raids of all those years gone by are as nothing in comparison.' He wiped away his tears with his cassock sleeve. 'I have heard that the Normans will take many valuable treasures from the great English houses into Normandy.'

'They don't destroy churches, but they are taking them over. It is all part of their great plan. But here is good news for you.' Elditha opened her battered leather saddle-bag and gently lifted out the leather sack containing the book. 'Brother Thomas charged me with this. We have saved a precious treasure and brought it to you. It has survived water and sword. It is a miracle that I still carry it.'

The abbot carefully lifted it from her hands and, leaning down, sniffed the leather covers. He slowly placed the lapidary on his table, with reluctance, she noticed. 'My lady, how marvellous of Thomas to rescue this and ...' He looked up at her with tears in his eyes. He leaned down and kissed the cover. He raised his head and then his arms, stretching them up and cried out, 'Be praised. Thank you, Lord.' He turned to her. 'God bless you, my lady.'

She slipped the fine silver chain from her neck and handed over the tiny key. He opened the book and, as he turned its stiff pages, he made little gasping sounds of delight, remarking on the book's physical beauty and at the important knowledge it held among the beautiful illustrations. 'It is no surprise that our Holy Mother has protected its journey while rendering it invisible to others,' he said, with astonishment in his voice. 'Here in Bangor it will be seen again by all who seek its wisdom.'

After he turned its pages, the abbot wept again and dabbed at his eyes with his sleeve. 'My lady, I am old and in my time I have seen many beautiful works, but I have never seen the like: the pure colours, the golden leaves, skies so blue that it is always summer and the precious gems so magnificently rendered. It will be one of our library's greatest treasures. May the good Lord bring you many blessings.'

As they rested in the New Monastery at Bangor, Elditha prayed and gave thanks for their safe delivery to Ireland. There, in the airy wooden church, she prayed for Harold, Leofwine and Gyrth, and for her son, Ulf. She prayed that soon he would be returned to her.

The boy who had helped her to safety on the Severn stayed close to her. He knelt behind her, guarding her as she prayed, and when Earl Connor was not around he walked with her between the abbey and the lough shore. They stood by the shoreline where they watched the Norse sailors load barrels of food and water onto currachs and row them out to the *Sea Serpent*.

She discovered that the youth was an orphan of Hastings. He said that he wanted to be an oarsman on Earl Connor's ship. She repeated this to the Earl and it was done. The boy would sail with Ulich and the crew north on their trading mission to Iceland. Soon, towards the end of the week, the best sailing day arrived. When the wind had turned, the large, striped-sailed ship set its sea-serpent prow northwards into choppy seas and sailed towards the midnight sun.

A few days later, Earl Connor and Elditha set out for Dublinia. The abbot provided them with horses, and Elditha, in a spontaneous gesture – one she never regretted – gave him two precious blue gems.

'You have lost your kingdom, my child. You will need your jewels.'

'I have no need of these. If you have them set in gold they will be a suitable page marker for the book of gems. Take them.'

'Every day we shall pray for you,' he said as they parted, and Elditha took pleasure at his joy.

News of their arrival flew before them. When they trotted into Dublinia and up the hill to King Dairmaid's house, her three sons were waiting in the palace yard to greet her. She called out their names. She could not wait to be off her horse. She saw no one else in the gathering crowd in the courtyard, just Godwin, Edmund and Magnus. And they had grown into handsome, strong youths. She thanked the Lord that they had been here last year and not with their father and uncles.

'How we have prayed for you,' Edmund, her middle son, shouted back to her. He was still her elegant, laughing boy, the one so like her, his pale hair flowing onto his shoulders, his cloak flapping gracefully in the spring breeze. His eyes were the same green, and his neck rose above his gem-studded brooch pin, long and graceful as was her own. At 16, he was a young warrior, well able to take up arms to fight for a kingdom.

Godwin's muscles bulged under his tunic as he lifted her down off the mare. He held her aloft as if she were goose-down. She saw Harold in him. Curling locks framed his face and his mouth was generous, like Harold's; his eyes the same deep blue. At 17, he wore a moustache in the fashion of an English nobleman. Elditha saw before her a king's son full-grown, and one who would be thoughtful, thorough and brave in battle.

Dark-haired, slim Magnus hugged her as if he were still a young child. She held him close and smelled the young sweat of her boy. Yet, in 18 months, all three of her sons had grown older, even Magnus who all too soon moved a step backwards, letting go the embrace. Anticipation and pleasure, the like she had not felt in months, caused her heart to burst open like a fat peach filled with the warmth of summer. 'I love you all,' she whispered, trying hard not to weep for joy in the presence of Dublinia's great men.

The King of Dublinia came to join them. He received her before his small court that had gathered by the grand, carved bog-oak porch door into his palace. After he had embraced her, he led her by the hand into his feasting hall. Inside, a score of servants scurried about a great raised hearth; warriors bowed as she passed and their ladies, dressed in richly decorated gowns, gathered to greet her, wearing kind, welcoming smiles.

It had been 16 years since Elditha had last met Dairmaid, King of Dublinia, and he had aged. His beard, once black, was now white as a winter fox's fur, though his eyes had remained the startling blue of the Icelanders. A statuesque woman, wearing a gold fillet, with dark plaits that swung against her slim waist hurried out of the group of noblewomen. Two wolfhounds followed her and rubbed against the King's leg bindings.

'Sinead will care for you,' said King Dairmaid, introducing his wife and pushing the hounds away. 'Elsa died in childbirth,' he said by way of explanation, and then grunted, 'They both died. The Lord willed it.' Elditha did not enquire further. It was heart-breaking to lose a wife and a child.

The young Queen embraced Elditha. 'Your sons are as dear to me as my stepsons, and you, Lady Elditha, are welcome as a sister to me.'

The King looked fawningly at his young wife. 'And later you can talk, but now, my dear Sinead, find food and drink for Earl Connor. I must speak to Elditha alone.' He took her arm and nodded to her sons. 'You also,' he added. Turning to the

Earl he said, 'My wife will give you the ale cup.' He winked. 'Her women have missed you.' Elditha now noticed that the Queen's ladies were looking boldly at the handsome Earl, and that he smiled back at them. So he is a woman's man, she thought to herself. Off to your ale cup then.

In contrast to the great hall, which was filled with the smell of firewood, human sweat and the wolfhounds' damp coats, the private room she found herself in was scented with spices and wine. A carpet covered the length and width of its planked floor. Tapestries touched with gold threads covered the walls. Carved side tables held gaming boards, ivory counters, dice and boxes inlaid with silver. On one table, higher than the others, amber chess pieces were strategically placed, waiting for an interrupted game to resume.

'Sit, my dear.' King Dairmaid indicated an enormous winged chair close to the brazier. Accepting the imperial-looking chair, she sank gracefully into its woollen cushions. He indicated stools for her sons.

He poured wine into exquisite gold-and-glass drinking vessels and handed them around, but he did not sit. Instead, he hovered over her. 'Now, how many years has it been? You were but a girl then with a small child.' He waved his glass at Godwin and Edmund. 'And that one there,' he jabbed his large pointing finger towards Edmund, 'was in the belly. Fifty-two, was it? Young Magnus was not even a thought. You are still a beautiful woman, Elditha.' His stare was penetrating. 'Let us drink to your health.' He paused and raised his cup to her, drank back the wine and poured again. 'My home is your home. Tell me of your travels. Later, my wife will give you fresh linen and a chamber in my hall and she will find servants for you.'

Elditha thanked him in Norse, the language he had spoken to her and one that she had known from childhood. It was not greatly different to the English tongue. She sipped the sweet wine and told him of how she had escaped marriage with the Norman earl and how she had crossed the sea to Bangor.

When she had finished he laughed. 'So, I had best not find you a husband after all, though, believe me, many will try for your hand.' The word "husband" hung irritatingly in the air.

'An empty house close by my hall will be made ready for you, my dear. You must have your own house, for you will be here some time.'

'A sleeping place in the bower would suffice, Your Grace,' she said.

'Not so. I expected that you might consider yourself an obligation, my dear. Not so, Elditha. Your husband was my good friend and his father Earl Godwin was my father's friend. The trade the Earl brought us was the best trade we ever had. Godwin made me rich. I have amassed a fortune. He traded me slaves to sell on, wine, spices, you name it. Earl Godwin had his elegant, long fingers in many sweet pies. But you could not know that, I suppose.' She caught a whiff of the sweet wine as he leaned closer to her. 'Harold sent me gold – a great part of your sons' inheritance. They are my warriors. I am as their father. My home is your home. My town is your town. You must have your own household. It is courtesy to the mother of princes.' He looked at her shabby dress. 'There will be an allowance from the inheritance for you, of course. A small chest of coin should be sufficient for your immediate needs. King Harold was generous.'

Later that night, as she lay on a pallet in a curtained alcove in the bower, Elditha wondered what this King would demand of them in return for his generosity. He could not invade England on their behalf. He was not the High King of Ireland with a great army of warriors able to wage war on a foreign territory. The Normans were invincible as warriors, terrifying foes with clever strategy, as their conquest of England was already proving. They were moving so quickly through England's towns, building castles, marrying into their old nobility and destroying their peasants. If her sons fought against Normandy's horse-mounted knights to regain their kingdom, could this Irish King give them a ship army? He would not help unless they were sure of victory. And if he intended to set her up as a great lady in Dublinia, then he must have a motive, but other than alliance she could not fathom what it might be.

31

In the course of the tenth century a recognisable town developed at the point where the River Poddle entered the Liffy. This town had an enclosing wall, Christ Church Cathedral and a number of other churches.

Dublinia: The Story of Medieval Dublin, edited by Howard Clarke, Sarah Dent and Ruth Johnson 2002

Elditha wandered around the palace buildings, the garden and orchards. She rode into the town. Dublinia had grown in wealth since she had visited it as Harold's young wife. It had always been a town of merchants and a slave-trading town but it had expanded in 16 years. The town's rich merchants and nobles wore jewels and richly embroidered garments and lived in large halls. They kept slaves, a tradition that deeply perturbed her. Long ago she had released her own slaves and, though there were still slaves in England, the Church frowned on the practice.

She moved into the empty hall. It had been cleaned out of someone else's belongings and made sweet for her. She wondered who had owned it. King Dairmaid had simply said that for as long as she remained in Dublinia, it was useful to have her occupying it. The building stood on a high spot near the King's palace, staring down on the harbour with an outlook as far as the grazing land across the River Liffy. The Queen sent her two ladies, who would learn English ways from her. Olga, the elder, was a distant relative of the King. Sinead confided that the girl had little hope of a husband on account of a large birthmark on her left cheek and a limp. Anya, the Queen's own youngest sister, was a small, pretty girl with red hair and pale skin. She would have no difficulty finding a suitor, and Elditha saw her watching Earl Connor when he entered the hall. Elditha liked them both well enough, but her heart went out to Olga most. The girl tried so hard to please. She kept Olga close by her and determined to teach her all she could about English embroidery. Olga responded to her kindness and learned quickly.

She also found herself passing many hours in the stone building of Christ's Church. During the summer she would enter the cool nave, sit on a bog-oak bench and remember Harold. Amid the scent of candles and incense she recollected their youth together and their love. She remembered how they had moved around their estates, the long feasts they had in winter, the May days, the harvest celebrations. She remembered how she had loved Reredfelle too. Her heart became heavy as her thoughts turned to Padar, Harold's greatest gift to her, there in her greatest hour of need, now in the hands of enemies. How would he survive? Where was he now? She hoped desperately that by now the silvatii of Gloucester had hidden him from Beorhtric and Count Alain. She prayed for him and sent messengers to the harbour to watch for vessels sailing from England so that they could enquire if anyone knew about the Godwin skald's fate. She often had an overwhelming feeling that she had abandoned him, and when no news arrived she prayed even more regularly that God would keep him safe.

Connor of Meath took her out riding along the sands south of Dublinia, arriving with grooms to tend his horse and servants to accompany them. He brought her small gifts: jars of honey, candles scented with wild roses from the hedgerow. She wondered if the Earl was wooing her, though he never pushed his suit upon her. She hoped that they were friends and she looked forward to their rides. Was Connor of Meath the suitor King Dairmaid intended for her? Because, if so, he was mistaken. She would not marry Earl Connor.

One day Earl Connor found her alone in the church. He leaned down behind her and softly touched the fabric where her veil fell onto her shoulder. She knew that touch. He had often lifted her onto her horse. But when he whispered, 'My lady,' he made her jump. 'My lady, a fleet of ships have docked at Wood Quay. I thought you might need things for your hall. We can look, if you care to.'

Elditha pretended to continue her contemplation for a moment. Really, she was wondering whether she would go into the market with him. And then she looked up at him, smiling. 'A moment, my lord, I shall fetch a purse.' She scrambled to her feet. 'Wait in the yard for me.' It occurred to her that it was in similar circumstances that she had encountered him in Canterbury just over a year ago. Who could have foreseen this day then?

When she came into her courtyard, Earl Connor was making himself useful, directing the boy who chopped wood to stack it. Two dairy maids passed close to the Earl, carrying jugs of cream, simpering with blushes on their faces. He had not noticed them, nor had he heard them giggling, but the girls were her servants and they were bold. She glared at them and they hurried on. She would speak to them later about being demure. He looked up. 'Ah, are you ready? I was helping the boy here. Go on, give it a crack.' The boy split the wood perfectly.

She said, pointing to the lads who followed her, 'They will carry for me today. I hope the merchants down on the quays sell quality wool. We need wool for the weaving shed I have set up here.'

He laughed at her. 'Ah, so you are not in need of me now. I had better split wood then.'

'I do need ...' Was she blushing? And he was laughing at her as if she were a girl of 15 and not a woman of past 30. She added primly, 'I need the wool, and more help than those two can give if I am to find stuff of quality.'

'Aye? And you think I can tell the quality of fleece better than the bower women?'

'Earl Connor, I would appreciate your help.'

'Then I give it gladly.'

As they picked their way through the squawking geese and snorting pigs that were crowding the muddy lanes, her boys swung large reed baskets that smelled of the river and dashed ahead, calling out at people to clear their beasts because Lady Elditha needed space to walk. Soon they had passed through Fishshamble Alley, the last of the narrow thoroughfares, but one that reeked of fish barrels. Finally, they reached the quays. Here traders had set up temporary stalls and Elditha forgot her quest for wool when she discovered that they sold saffron, cinnamon and cardamom, all of which she purchased for her kitchen.

As she wandered about with the Earl and her two boys, she took a child-like pleasure in the cages of pet birds, larks and blackbirds. There was even a nightingale which could sing. She parted with a precious gold coin and asked its keeper to bring it to the hall. Followed by the boys and protected by Earl Connor she moved easily from stall to stall, filling her baskets with distaffs and spindles, carding combs, bone needles so fine that she knew they would slide through the most delicate linen. She examined cloth smoothers of good glass and bought two of them. She discovered a trader with spatulas and cups decorated with intricate animal carvings. Tempted by a long spoon with owl decorations on the handle, she bought it.

As they walked, she felt Connor moving close behind her, ready to drop her purchases into her baskets, stopping by her side to watch her turn objects over and examine them. He found wool for her and she ordered a sack of it for her looms. It was of good quality. He knew the value of domestic things, which made her speculate if he had ever had a wife. She discovered combs intricately carved from antler bone alongside a tray of amber pendants. Then he left her to look through them saying that he must seek a gift, and she wondered who for.

When she caught up with him later, he reached into a tray of silver and lifted out a finger-ring, set with a small amber stone. To her amazement, he slipped his arm around her waist. 'You have lost everything, Elditha, and yet you never complain of it. This ring is for you. It will only fit the tiniest of fingers.' Before she could move his arm, he had already removed it and had lifted her hand and slid the ring on her little finger. It fitted perfectly.

As she held her hand out she felt the comfortable warmth of his arm about her waist again. Flustering about for words, she said, 'But I may lose everything again, all these things, combs, spatulas, my spices. Do not give me this gift. It is much too valuable.'

'Yes, you may lose all again, and if it is so, that is your wyrd, your fate, Elditha, but today you must have the pleasure of them, even if only for a while. For the moment, I too am fortunate. I have the pleasure of your company.' His voice was quiet. 'Yet, if you do lose all other things, please do remember to keep my ring safe.'

She held her hand out again to admire it, silver engraved with tiny leaves. It would be unkind to refuse his gift, but how could she explain if others noticed it?

Sensing her thoughts, he removed his arm saying, 'My Lady Elditha, it is not unusual for us to give gifts. No one will think anything of it, not even of a finger-ring, for we are a generous people.'

'But a ring has significance.'

'A finger-ring is not uncommon between friends here in Dublinia,' he said smiling. He lifted her hand and kissed her fingers. 'You are my friend, though I must admit that I have wished ever since I first saw you in Canterbury that we could be more to each other.'

'But that is …'

'Not possible. Yet I wanted to tell you anyway. If ever you need my help send for me and I promise that I shall come to you.'

She thought, I am admired and befriended. Maybe, even, I am loved and I am glad of it too, but I must never, never give this man any false hope.

'Come, not so thoughtful. Let us enjoy the day,' he said quickly and guided her away from the crowd that had gathered about the stalls.

'How can I ever thank you for your care of me?'

'Your smile is enough,' he replied. 'Now, I believe that there

281

is a magician on the quay who can escape from rope bindings and a Spaniard juggler who plays with pigs' bladders.' The mood had changed again. Once again simply good friends, they stood and watched and laughed together. The boys hovered close. She bought them sweetmeats, which they devoured greedily as they watched the juggler perform his tricks. When it was over, Earl Connor gave him a penny as a reward for his act. 'Elditha,' Earl Connor was saying, 'come and look at the snake charmer.' And so the day continued until, exhausted, they climbed the hill again and he climbed on his horse and rode back past Christ's Church and through the apple orchards to the King's palace.

Some evenings later Connor and her sons sat with her at supper. He noticed that she had removed his ring and said, 'What has happened to that ring?'

'My lord, I should not wear it.'

He lifted her hand, turned it over and kissed her palm. His kiss was light and quick, but it left an imprint on her hand. 'It is a ring of friendship. That is all.'

'Earl Connor,' she said, 'why are you not wed?'

'I had a wife for whom I cared very much. She died in childbirth. Now, I have a memory of my wife, an eight-year-old girl who is cast in her image and whose name is Aisling, a small song.'

'Where is she now?'

'She is in the west with my mother.' He accepted the horn beaker of beer from Olga. The girl poured a small glass of honey wine for Elditha and continued on down the table. Elditha thought that the girl's limp was hardly noticeable now. She seemed happier too.

'I am sorry for the mother's death,' Elditha said aloud.

'She is with God's angels.' He was flushed from the strong beer he had drunk, but his voice was steady and, as he spoke, she could feel his breath touch her cheek. It was not an unpleasant sensation.

She busied herself with her spoon and chopped at the fish on her plate. 'I will keep your token safe always,' she heard herself say to him so quietly none could overhear. 'Earl Connor, you honour me and mine.' She hesitated, and then broached a difficult subject of ship armies. 'I have a request.'

He looked at her with concern, as if he had guessed what she might say to him.

'My sons seek help from their uncle in Denmark. They need ships so that they can reclaim their kingdom.'

'I thought that would be so, and who can fault them. It will be a difficult task. King Swegne will have his own reasons, if he gives them to you. If an invasion were successful he would want part of the kingdom.'

'They all have greed in their hearts, but they are our kin, and of our own mind and Gytha is Swegne's aunt. We must try.'

'Then I shall advise the boys and help them in any way that is possible. I shall ask King Dairmaid for support. If the Danish King is willing to help, he will not refuse, but I think, Elditha, this will mean that Godwin must sail to Denmark himself. The *Sea Serpent* will return in a few weeks and we can sail on it before harvest.'

After supper Elditha retired to her chamber behind the hall. Before she lay down to sleep, she lifted her bone-plated box from the clothes chest. She laid her treasures out on the table. A midsummer moon slid through the opened shutters, casting a pool of light on the small, creamy christening robe. As she placed the silver ring into the box with her treasures, she touched the little garment and unfolded it. She thought again how it had once clothed a tiny child whose life had slipped away as effortlessly as the sand slides through an hour glass, and she thought sadly of how once she had lost another before it had quickened in her womb.

An owl hooted and farther off the tapping of a woodpecker echoed through the orchards. The Christ Church bells began to ring for Matins. She put the box away and climbed into her bed. Covered by a thin blanket she fell into a doze. Soon she was flying over a burning town on the back of a swan. As she looked down, she saw children and mothers crying. The swan swooped closer and she realised that the town she saw was Exeter, the palace and the cathedral and houses engulfed by flames. She awoke in a sweat and could not find sleep again. She lay brooding until the morning bells rang. No matter how she busied herself, instructing her servants with their daily tasks, a sense of terror remained with her. She could not dismiss the thought that Thea might face danger.

September 1067

When unable to rest at night Elditha finally confided her concern to Earl Connor after he remarked on the deep shadows below her eyes. 'It may have just been a nightmare brought on by anxiety for her. It may be nothing.'

'We shall put your fears to rest then,' he said, taking her hands in his own.

'I think about Padar too,' she said. 'I worry that he never escaped from Beorhtric's men or that Count Alain had him put to death.' She shuddered. 'He would have died for my sake.'

'Do not think that way. I shall try to find out.'

Earl Connor sent a messenger across the sea in a trading vessel that took silver to the forges in Cornwall. She began to sleep soundly again and the nightmare never returned, but she still worried. After a month the messenger returned. He told her that there was no immediate danger to the town. He said that he had asked after the skald called Padar, but there was no news of him; nothing. Summer passed and then it was harvest time again and, when winter came, the sailing season would be over. King Dairmaid promised that if the Godwin sons procured a Danish fleet from their uncle, he would contribute ships of his own – any he could spare. Almost a year to the day after the great Battle near Hastings, Earl Connor, Godwin and Edmund sailed off on the *Sea Serpent* for Denmark, leaving Magnus with Elditha, promising to return with a ship army.

Before they departed Connor sent Elditha another gift, one which he said had come to Ireland with his seal skins from Iceland. Elditha sighed, and glanced down at the ring that she was wearing again to please him. His gift was a harp. 'This is beyond kindness.' She fingered the wood and admired the carvings of leaf and berries on its burnished frame and then twiddled with the strings and coaxed them into tune. It became her solace as the evenings dropped earlier and earlier. Throughout the time of harvests and falling leaves, her hall was filled with the sound of her playing and singing.

In early December her prayers were answered and one of her deepest anxieties was removed. Padar sailed into Dublinia on a trading vessel. She embraced him and ushered him into the warmth of the hall. 'Thank God and all his Holy Saints. Padar, thank Heaven for you.' She hugged him. 'Thank God you are safe.' Immediately he seemed comfortable in her Viking house. It felt to her as if he had not even been gone.

He told her that the silvatii had attacked Beorhtric's guard as the traitors rode with him tied and bound on a sorry nag towards London. 'Unfortunately, Wadard managed to escape. More is the pity. He promised me a dire death when we reached London. Castration was mentioned.'

'But you have lived to tell the tale. I had faith that you would. So, where have you been since?'

He had returned to Winchester and after that had made his way west to Wales before crossing the sea. What he said next caused her to shudder despite her heavy, fur-lined winter mantle. 'I have heard that all is not well for Exeter. The Bastard is moving troops south and west. He is destroying any village or town that refuses to recognise his authority. Since there is a price on my neck anyway, here I am.' He supped his ale noisily. 'I missed the Great Battle but this one I shall fight. I want revenge on the scum.'

'My sons and Earl Connor are in Denmark raising a ship army.'

'I can wait.'

'Padar, how safe is my daughter?'

'William will not attack the town if they pay a tax. It is winter and in winter armies do not march unless they have to.'

'So for now we must wait and see.' She proffered a dish of

cakes. 'I baked them myself.'

He munched thoughtfully before saying, 'They taste good, my lady.' He ate each small cake in two bites and looked around. 'You have a fine hall. It's busy too.'

'The hall here is almost as pleasant as Reredfelle,' she said smiling.

He touched the cushions on the bench. 'Linen covers, interesting embroidery.' He relaxed back into them and stretched out his legs. 'And what does the King of Dublinia want of you in return?'

'I do not know if he wants anything, Padar. My sons are his sworn men. Harold sent a great inheritance here to Ireland with them. It keeps us here. But I worry that King Dairmaid may try to marry me off.'

'And?' he said, raising an eyebrow. 'There must be one earl you like.'

'I do not want another marriage.' She lifted the jug of honeyed drink and refilled his cup. 'But it is good to see you here. Like a cat, you have many lives. It will be Christmas soon; would you be our storyteller – at the feasts?'

He guffawed. 'I suppose I could be persuaded.'

'And by the by, Padar, do not quarrel with the King's servants here; do not compete with his skalds. Remember that we are the King's guests.'

'My lady, I see. But where can I keep my pack and rest my bones?'

'There's a free sleeping place over there.' She pointed to a corner opposite, tucked between two pillars. It contained a bench covered with sheepskin and a shuttered window behind. 'It has been waiting for you, Padar.' She smiled, reached out and touched his hand. 'And later, when you have rested, we must talk.' She called Olga from her distaff. 'This is Olga.' She lifted the plate and gave it to the girl. 'The cakes are all finished. See that my skald has bread and cheese and a pasty to eat.' To her amusement Padar winked at Olga and promised to sing for her later, a poem he would compose especially for her.

* * *

The next morning Elditha walked along Wood Quay with Padar, through groups of merchants and past warehouses that held bales of raw linen ready for dyeing, and barrels of French wine waiting for sale. The harbour teemed with river traffic. Bright banners flapped in the breeze. Colourful figureheads depicted a collection of strange beasts that belonged to bestiaries or in Padar's tales. They paused by a pile of fishing nets and watched the coracles navigate the busy waters and the loading and unloading of cargoes onto them. Padar caught sight of a new ship sailing into the harbour. It was bigger than the others. Dark figures were climbing into a coracle.

'Padar, where is it from?'

'Not from Denmark, unless they are sending us women,' he said, with his hand shading his forehead from the harsh sinking evening sun, 'bundles in dark cloaks.' He jumped up with a suddenness that made Elditha almost slip down the bank. 'Look, another ship and surely one that sails around the world's rim. See the sails. They bear a crescent; and look at the shape. It is more bulky than the other and squat.' He smiled up at her. 'There will be a goodly feast this Christmas. That vessel will carry a spice cargo.'

Later, the King sent a messenger for Elditha. She crossed the apple orchard accompanied by servants with torches to light her way. When she was seated comfortably by the hearth in the great hall, the King said, 'There are two letters for you from Exeter.'

The ship that she had seen in the harbour had sailed from Cornwall's south-western coast transporting a trinity of nuns who intended to pass the winter teaching English embroidery in the House of St Hilda in the hills. They had brought precious gold and silver threads from Countess Gytha for the convent and two letters for the Lady Elditha. One was from the Countess, the other from a novice who had recently joined their orders.

Elditha seized the small scrolls and broke the first seal. 'This,' she said, overjoyed, 'this is from Ursula.'

'Ursula?' asked the Queen, clearly puzzled.

'My waiting lady; we left her at St Margaret's Priory in Mercia.' She pulled open the parchment. Ursula had travelled to Exeter because the nunnery in Mercia was no longer safe. Wadard, the Bishop's servant, and Brother Francis had been sighted at the neighbouring monastery. When the prioress found out that they intended visiting St Margaret's, she had sent Ursula into the south-west to Exeter with a lock of St Margaret's hair held in an ancient golden casket. Ursula was sheltering in a convent patronised by the Countess Gytha.

Elditha set the parchment aside. 'Ursula is with the Countess.' She lifted the letter with Gytha's seal. 'Permit me to read my mother's words in the privacy of my own chamber.'

'Go, Elditha,' said Queen Sinead. 'And God bless you. The servants will light your way home. Oh, I have a gift for your hall. Another ship has arrived today from the East with spices and silk and ginger in its cargo. Tomorrow, I will send you some of the root.'

After calling a brief goodnight to Magnus and Padar, who were playing a game of chess near her hearth, she climbed the steep ladder to her small loft chamber. Pulling the heavy curtain behind her, she closed herself in, sat in her chair and broke open Gytha's seal. The Countess's letter confirmed much of what Elditha had heard and more that she suspected.

My daughter, my Council has decided that we challenge the King's taxation. I am preparing for our resistance. Thea will be safer with you in Dublinia. How can we live our lives in peace and dignity if he takes what is ours? I await your reply and for news of my grandsons ...

Gytha also wrote of how when he came to visit, Count Alain had been enchanted with Thea. Having lost the mother, he was wooing the daughter. No Norman was good enough for a Godwin, and certainly not the one who had burned down the mother's home and then offered her marriage.

As big a bastard as the one he serves, Elditha thought to herself; destroyers of kingdoms and violators of women; Normans, Bretons, Frenchmen – all bastards, the pack of them. She would bring her daughter to safety and Gytha too, if she could be prised from her dower lands.

33

This time there was no Earl Connor to help her. She stayed awake all night wondering what to do. By dawn she realised that she had no choice. She must ask King Dairmaid to send for Thea. If he refused then she would think of another way. She unlocked her box and looked at the three gems left to her. The following day, Elditha discussed her fears with the King. She said that she had need of a ship to retrieve her daughter before winter set in.

The King shook his head. 'Winter has already gripped the land. Elditha, it is not necessary. The women must seek sanctuary within abbey walls, safe there until the spring brings the sailing season. There will be no attack on Exeter. We must wait.'

Later that day, in the privacy of her waiting room behind the hall, Elditha spoke with Padar. 'And they will not go into sanctuary. The Countess will never leave her palace. We must fetch Thea here now.'

Padar pointed out to her, 'There will be the cost of a ship, horses, bribes. In winter, this journey will cost you too much.'

'I can raise coin.'

He tugged at his beard and set his cup of wine on the low table. In a quiet voice he said, 'When you do, then I can find a ship captain willing to sail in winter.'

Elditha summoned a jeweller to her hall. She showed him her remaining three pale sapphires, one of them a deeper blue than the others – the best of all, the one she had hoped to keep. She asked him for their worth in coin and, greedy for the beautiful gems, he gave her their value in silver. Next, she divided her hoard of silver into three purses. One purse was for Padar to hunt out a ship and a crew for her. Another purse she put aside for Magnus in case she never returned. The third she kept with her. She thanked God that Harold had had the foresight to give her this gift. It was a small miracle.

The next afternoon, Elditha rode with Padar beyond Dublinia's walls. She laid her plans as winter light played on the water and the wind bent the tall grasses that were growing thickly all along the shoreline. For a moment she huddled into her cloak and watched their graceful movement. She had come to a decision – one she knew carried great risk, but a risk which she felt compelled to take. 'If the wind holds like this,' she said aloud, 'we can cross the winter seas.'

Padar raised his black eyebrows. 'My lady, you would go yourself to rescue your daughter from the wolf's paws and get trapped by him once more? There is no sense there.'

'I was not trapped. I escaped.' She knew that he knew that she would not change her mind. 'Here, Padar, buy us whatever we need for such a journey.'

Padar scratched his beard and reminded her, not that she needed reminding, 'King Dairmaid will not allow this. You cannot disappear for long. This is no fishing trip.'

'My two women have returned to their families for Christmas. Magnus will be hunting birds with the King's sons and I shall say that I am visiting the Wicklow nuns.'

Padar said again that he had not rescued her from Wessex to have her recaptured by Count Alain. Elditha countered this with her best argument. 'Gytha has a great treasure. My sons need Wessex gold for a rebellion. They must not be dependent on the good-will of those who will seek rewards and alliances.'

'Or land,' agreed Padar. 'The north-men sought it once and they will want it again.'

'I intend to persuade the Countess to help us,' she said firmly.

Padar shook his head and looked over the water. 'If the sea

292

remains calm, we can cross in a fishing craft. We can slip into a port, travel upriver for miles and then ride to Exeter. The fishing vessel will wait for our return. They smuggle things: swords, knives, all sorts of things – even people in winter. That is, if you can seek the smugglers out.'

She nodded. The wind gusted about her cloak. If the wind rode high out at sea, or if a winter storm blew up, a winter sea journey would be hazardous. 'I know this will be difficult but we must try,' she said. She pulled the purse from her mantle. 'Take this. It is more than enough for our purpose.' Grumbling, Padar took the purse and concealed it inside his cloak. Elditha climbed back on her horse and galloped off with a lighter heart, leaving Padar to mount the scraggy mare he had acquired and plod back after her into the town.

She announced to anyone who might be interested that after Christmas she would seek instruction in Irish embroidery at the convent of St Brides. First, she organised a great entertainment in her own hall to be held on the eve of the Epiphany. It would be a distraction. Padar went down to the Wood Quay in the afternoon and completed his arrangements. He returned to find her supervising the laying of trestles. She left her work and walked with him to the back of the hall, where she gave him a small harp to tune. As he fiddled with the strings, he told her that the fishermen would sail up the coast and meet them at the Bay of Curlews. The wind was auspicious since it blew from the north-west. Once they were out on the open sea it would help them across, and no one would be looking for a ship from Ireland, not at Christmas.

As the Epiphany feast drew to an end, Padar told stories. Elditha grew restless, anxious for them to be on their way. She prayed to St Cecilia that her guests would not linger too long. They had complimented her cook on his meat pies, the saffron cakes, the goose and the partridge and especially the great confection of marzipan – a longship that was not unlike the *Sea Serpent*. The Queen broke off a sail, sucked at it and whispered to her, 'It is delicious. It is a pity its master was not here to see it.' Elditha looked down and blushed. 'He has been missed,' she whispered back.

King Dairmaid had laid his own plans for the following day. To her relief, as the Angelus bells rang out, the King and Queen, their sons and Magnus made ready to cross the orchard to their hall. Yet still Magnus lingered. It was as if he knew. The boys would leave early in the morning for their bird-netting trip, and that night Magnus said he would sleep by the King's hearth. Slipping him a small purse of silver, she said, 'Magnus, it is my New Year's gift to you. Use it well and I shall return soon.' Elditha held him close in an embrace and whispered her goodbye. He thanked her, kissed her and tucked the small purse in the folds of his mantle and then he was gone, her slim dark child, the gentlest of her brood.

Early in the morning and wrapped in a thick woollen cloak lined with fur, carrying only her saddle-bag, Elditha departed her hall. She had told her servants to sleep late, that Padar was the only escort she needed. They mounted their horses, walked them down the hill to Dublinia's eastern gate. The watchman recognised Padar and waved them through. Then they followed a track from the town wall to the Bay of Curlews, where they would board a fishing craft which would run across to the Devon coast, drop them off and continue farther south to unload a delivery of swords. They rowed a skiff to the sturdy fishing vessel that was at rest out in the bay. As the oars splashed, she scanned the heavens where a blue moon rode through the wintry dawn sky, haunting and pale. The water was still. Moments later they climbed up the rope ladder and safely onto the vessel that was to carry them over the swelling waves. As her oarsmen navigated their boat into the open sea, she gripped the saddle-bag that held a change of linen. At the last minute she had brought her bone-plated silver box with the Godwin christening gown and a slither of mugwort root. These were the only treasures left to her, apart from the box itself, though she found herself twisting a silver ring around on her tiny finger. As the boat moved into the open sea, she watched the coast of Ireland grow smaller and smaller, turned her ring and prayed to St Cecilia for a safe crossing.

34

Exeter
January 1068

Queen Edith sent the women of Exeter generous New Year gifts – spices from her store cupboards at Wilton, silk cloth, gold and silver thread. Her presents came with a warning that King William had returned from Normandy and he intended to quell resistance to his rule. So then, she mused as she set aside her goose feather, sprinkled sand on the ink, rolled and sealed a letter to her mother, if they were all to survive, Gytha must negotiate with King William as Edith, herself, had negotiated. She must pay his tax. Her lands no longer belonged to her.

On the first day of the New Year, Gytha visited Bishop Leofric. 'They will not steal my gold and silver, nor will they claim my lands.' After a moment during which the Bishop was clearly faltering, she growled at him, 'The Bastard will not marry off my granddaughter to one of his own.'

Bishop Leofric tried to soothe her. 'Thea cannot be forced into any marriage with a Norman.'

She snapped at him, 'Don't be naïve, Bishop. They tried to marry off the mother, a king's widow, whilst she was grieving for the husband they slew.' She paused before ramming her message home. 'The thieves are bedding and wedding our women, our daughters and their mothers wherever they discover them. And you priests are doing nothing to stop them.' She glanced around the cathedral's nave and her eye settled on the tall, golden candlesticks that graced the altar. She remembered the Bishop's collection of books and manuscripts, his gorgeous copes, the cathedral's richly embroidered altar cloths and the marvellous relics kept there. 'Just wait until they come and steal from this cathedral. You'll squawk like a wounded sparrow then, Leofric.'

Leofric's brow furrowed as he too glanced around his magnificent cathedral. He placed his plump ringed hand on Gytha's arm. 'Then, Countess, send the girl to a convent – the Abbey of our Lady and St Ronan, for instance. There is a delightful priory there. The prioress is your good friend, I believe.' Gytha leaned heavily on her stick. Surely Leofric, who smacked of Norman sympathy, could not have discovered the business she had with the prioress? The Bishop continued to smile in a honeyed manner. 'And, Countess, the good Lord will protect my cathedral. All is God's will.'

The moment had passed. She breathed again and rang her bell to summon her women. 'Come and dine with us tomorrow, Leofric,' she said pleasantly. 'And we shall have a roasted duck for supper.'

Gytha was not so sure that placing faith in a Lord who had permitted their defeat at Hastings was wise, but she took Leofric's advice anyway. On the day following the Feast of St Stephen, accompanied by her granddaughter and a small guard, she rode with Thea into the woods.

'I don't want to live away from the town,' Thea grumbled.

'The nuns will teach you Latin. You will learn how to be a useful wife.'

'I don't like the word "useful", Grandmother.'

'Too much freedom; times too unsettled; nothing in its right place any more,' Gytha muttered as she watched a robin flit from one frosty branch to another. 'You are to learn needlework from Gertrude and devotion from my lady prioress. You will not return to Exeter until I send for you …'

'Embroidery,' Thea interrupted, 'was never my talent.'

'Nonetheless, it is to prepare you for marriage.'

'I was to be married to the Earl of Northumbria once.'

'Not any longer. I hear he is to marry the Bastard's niece.'

'Then, Grandmother, I must do better and marry a prince. Perhaps my mother will find me one.'

They rode in silence ahead of their guard into the thick woods that surrounded the abbey. Then Thea said, 'What if he comes looking for me? That count who wanted my mother.'

'He won't dare.'

Before long they trotted through the opened wooden gate. Gytha waited a moment, caught her breath and, looking about her, remarked, 'How could he find you in this secret place? Now, get me down, Thea.'

Thea slipped from her mount and helped her grandmother off her horse. By the time their guard caught them up, Gytha was leaning on her stick and Thea was greeting the prioress.

Elditha's ship arrived on the north Devon coast on the eighth day of January. Disguised as a fisherman and his wife, Elditha and Padar travelled east. Two days later, just after Prime, Padar drove their cart, filled with sacks of dried cod, into the palace yard at Exeter. The cook came out to collect his fish and Elditha, every part of her seemingly a fishwife – apart from her ermine-trimmed mantle – announced that she had business with Countess Gytha.

'Where does a fishwife get herself a cloak trimmed with white fur?' the cook asked, scrutinising Elditha as she climbed down.

Padar stretched up and whispered into his ear. He opened his hand and gave him something. The cook nodded, looked at Elditha strangely and told her to come with him. She drew her hood over her head and walked close to him into the hall, past servants who were tending a cauldron and weaving through children who raced about chasing a scrawny puppy. Her eyes widened when they approached two ladies who were weaving on a large flat loom at the end of the hall. The cook spoke to an older woman and opened his hand. Elditha drew in her breath. In his palm lay the seal ring she had given Padar long ago. She had forgotten it. How, by the rood, had he kept it hidden when they held him captive on the Severn?

The woman looked at Elditha with utter surprise. 'Are you Elditha, King Harold's wife?'

'Indeed, I am Elditha, Lady Margaret. I am she whom you last saw at Westminster two years ago when my husband was crowned.'

'My dear Lady Edith, I remember that only too well.'

Other women were seated on benches beyond the weavers. One of them, younger than the others, dressed in coarse plain linen, jumped up from her stool and rushed forward, knocking it over in her haste.

'My lady, you have come?'

'Ursula!' Elditha took Ursula's hands and then embraced her.

Freeing herself, Ursula turned to Lady Margaret. 'Permit me to take Lady Elditha to the Countess.'

'My dear, of course. You will find her in her apartments.'

Murmuring wonder at Elditha's presence, the women returned to their weaving.

Ursula swept tapestries aside and led Elditha through chambers that lay behind the hall.

'My lady, I thought never to see you again,' she said, as they crossed through a large draughty antechamber.

'Ursula, I thought to seek you out in the convent,' Elditha said, as they moved into a narrow passageway.

'The Countess admires my needlework. I come to her house most days.' Ursula stopped walking. 'Will you remain with us here now?'

'I have come for Thea, with Padar. He will be filled with joy to see you.' She bent over laughing. Their arrival now seemed so amusing. 'Sorry, it is the relief of having arrived here without incident,' she said, as she recovered herself. 'And Padar is in possession of a cart of salted cod. I suspect the cook has him tucked away in the kitchen.'

'Padar and fish. Don't you remember Abingdon?'

'I do, and you will be pleased to hear that Brother Thomas's lapidary is safe.'

'Praise the Holy Mother for that,' Ursula said. She became thoughtful. 'The Countess will explain about Thea.'

What about Thea? But there was no time to seek an answer.

Ursula had pushed through yet another heavy tapestry into a room where the floor was covered with glazed green and blue tiles. Charcoal filled half-a-dozen braziers. The large chamber breathed warmth, and then Elditha saw Gytha, who was leaning against thick cushions in a winged chair, dozing.

Ursula melted back through a doorway, leaving her with Gytha. Elditha crossed the tiled floor, touched Gytha gently on the arm and murmured, 'It is Elditha come to see you.' Gytha sat straight up and peered straight at her from out of a great veiled wimple. 'Why, so it is; Elditha, you have come at last.' She sniffed. 'And you smell dreadful. Did you fall into a vat of fish?'

Elditha sank to her knees and took Gytha's frail hands in her own. 'Mother,' she said, 'I am come for Thea.'

'Thea is safely locked up in a priory.' It was said with determined amusement. 'For her own protection, and she is learning to embroider and read Latin too.' Gytha's formidable energy seeped into the chamber. 'You get up off those knees at once, girl, and sit by me.' She pulled her hands away and patted a little tapestry-covered stool by her side.

Gytha's voice was musical, like the blackbird's song on a spring morning, familiar and comforting. Elditha leaned over and touched her wrinkled cheek. She noticed the musty, elderly lady smell of Gytha, how it mingled with the scent of distilled lavender. Her eyes lit on the silver bell sitting on the table and Gytha's stick with its jewelled head. The passage of time was as momentary as the touch of a butterfly's wing. When at last Elditha began to speak, she poured out much of what had happened to her. It was a long story to shorten.

A servant came and lit candles as they talked, deep into the wintry afternoon. Elditha recounted her journey to Ireland and news of the King of Dublinia, and finally she confided her sons' plans. To regain the kingdom, they needed coin to pay armies, more than King Dairmaid had in his keeping from her sons' inheritance. The coin hoard that Harold had sent to him after he was crowned King of England was not enough. 'Gytha, can you help them pay for an army?'

At first, Elditha almost regretted asking. The fire crackled as a log split and the flames flared up and Gytha looked thoughtful. After a while, Gytha said, 'You remember the dowry coin, Elditha, Thea's and Gunnhild's money?' she said. 'I can release that to help buy ships and pay men. Most of the treasure here belongs to others. Perhaps they can contribute a little of that.'

Elditha raised Gytha's wrinkled hands to her lips and kissed them. 'And should I bring Thea back with me?'

Gytha smiled and when she did her face lines smoothed out and her countenance was beautiful. 'She is a few hours' ride from Exeter. Do you remember Alfred of Oxford and the young carpenter you sent me last year?' Elditha nodded remembering the youth she had sent to Exeter. She was surprised to hear that Alfred and Gertrude were with Gytha. 'Well, Alfred has exchanged the work of a mint for the manufacture of swords. We have a forge at the abbey and Thea is with them.'

'They risked all for me. And now they take risks again.'

Gytha waved her stick with impatience. 'Remember, Elditha, life is a journey. The knack of it all is to survive. Danger is everywhere, within and without, behind us and before us. They were destined to come to me. Alfred and the carpenter, Edgar, are fine metal-smiths now.' Gytha looked into her fire. 'Put another log on that, Elditha.'

Elditha lifted a log and tossed it into the embers. For a moment it hissed and sparked. She drew back and sat on her stool again.

'Gytha, come with us.'

'No, Elditha, my place is here. Now, we have talked enough. You must rest. The cook will see that the skald is housed and fed. As for you, there is the old sleigh bed in the chamber through the curtain there, close by me.' She lifted the little silver bell.

At its tinkling, servants came scurrying through the curtains. She sent some to the kitchen for food and drink, jugs of heated water, fresh linen and a clean gown.

When the servants bustled off again, Elditha said, 'As soon

as we collect Thea, we must return to the ship.' She paused. 'I wish you would come with us,' she said.

'No, no, my dear child, we are too many here for King Dairmaid. Send Exeter an army in the spring and they will be paid with silver. We shall collect Thea in a few days. Surely you can wait until Candlemas to leave us?'

'The ship's master is trading weapons into Cornwall. It could be a few weeks before he sails home.'

Gytha said, 'So, when the time comes, our thanes will be well armed. I think we shall be ready by summer.'

35

The king came back again to England on the Feast of St
Nicholas ... the Welsh became hostile ... and the king set a
great tax on the wretched. And then he travelled to Devonshire
and besieged Exeter stronghold for 18 days – and there a great
part of his raiding party perished.

   The Anglo-Saxon Chronicles, January 1068, Worcester
   Manuscript, edited and translated by Michael Swanton

A long column of men led by King William and Alain of
Brittany filed out through the gates of Wilton Abbey. As Queen
Edith watched them leave, her brow darkened. She glanced
back at Gunnhild who stood in the abbey entrance.

From the safe distance of the church porch Gunnhild,
flanked by the other noble girls, remarked to her companions,
'He's very handsome.'

'He's as ugly as an overgrown troll. And he's responsible for
your father's death.' Eleanor of Oxford wrinkled her pert nose.

Gunnhild said, 'No, no, Eleanor, not King William. I refer to
the knight.'

'Girls, be silent. Go in at once.' Edith swept them inside the
church. They would pray for the people of Exeter.

Edith reflected on her recent encounters with Alain of
Brittany: how, last year, furious at what she suspected now was
Elditha's deception, she had sent messengers out onto the road
to Exeter to help to find her. Returning messengers had assured
her that Elditha had fled south and west. Then she had appeared
in Oxford and was almost captured in Gloucester. Now she
could not help but admire Elditha's courage. The Normans were
proving a cruel race.

Her thoughts sped to the promised commission for Odo's

church in Bayeux; it was a small reward for her support for the new regime. Even though there were many other workshops in the land, Wilton surpassed them all. If Wilton's designs should be displayed in the new Cathedral of Bayeux, the Godwins would be remembered as the great nobility they truly were, and they would be immortalised on an English tapestry created for a Norman cathedral. Harold must always carry a hawk. His horse would be elegant. English halls would appear magnificent, with tiled roofs and two storeys and the pinnacles of the great Palace of Westminster would reach far into the sky.

Yet, during King William's brief visit she had met with a slight disappointment. Wadard had visited her on the previous afternoon to inform her that Bishop Odo was now considering Canterbury designers for the work, though, of course, Wilton might be asked to contribute a panel or two. She had told Wadard that she would consider a panel when the Bishop himself came to visit. Wadard was an unpleasant man and she had noticed today, as the Normans left Wilton, that he and the monk Brother Francis were riding among Count Alain's train. He must be travelling south-west with the Duke and the Count.

After the girls had departed from the church in their neat line of twos, Edith remained behind in a side chapel. She opened her liturgical book at the petition prayer to the Holy Mother and begged her intercession for the protection of her own mother's person. She prayed for her younger sister Hilda. Then she prayed that the Holy Mother's protection be extended to Thea, the niece who reminded her most of Elditha – wayward and determined. She remained on her knees until every muscle in her body ached and her women sought her out. As she rose, Edith wiped away a tear with her veil. What was a tapestry in comparison with a woman's safety? No amount of prayer would help Gytha who, she knew, would never allow the King to take Exeter without some kind of resistance.

Two days later Thea helped Alfred load the wagon's false bottom with weapons. They piled seaxes, short swords and arrows with deadly sharp metal tips into the cart. 'Careful with those and mind your hands,' Alfred called out. As daylight slid through the woods, the wagon was ready to leave for Exeter.

'Let me come with you,' Thea pleaded.

'You are safer here.'

'We need gold thread for St Olave's cope. I can fetch it for the nuns.'

'Is that so?' He looked anxiously up at the sky. It was filled with fat white clouds. 'If snow falls, we could be trapped inside the gates for days.' Alfred tossed the last sacks of flour into the wagon. He added a side of salt pork, two fat cheeses and a brace of partridge. 'Those are for the Countess, a gift from the prioress.' He studied the sky again, shook his head, threw a leather cover over everything, pulled off his hood and said, 'We'll see.' But Thea knew she had won when he ushered her into the cottage to consult Gertrude.

Gertrude confirmed the need of gold thread. She reminded Alfred that there had been no danger since November, called a maid from the dairy and sent her to the prioress with a message. Alfred and Thea broke their fast by the hearth and waited for a response.

The prioress asked them to fetch thread and two new spindles. Wasting no more time, Alfred hitched a horse to the cart and Thea, delighted at her freedom, climbed onto the crude wooden seat. It was a leisurely journey and for a while the sky cleared again, light blue patches swimming among the white clouds. But as they came out of the woods onto the river track, Alfred dropped his reins and let out a long, low whistle. Thea stared.

Beyond Exeter, to the north-east, a pall of smoke curled into the sky. Alfred shaded his brow and peered far into the distance. He saw a column of soldiers snaking across the moor land, approaching the town. 'St Olave's sacred shawl!' he exclaimed. 'They are coming.' He glanced back at the sacks and whipped up the horse, causing the cart to skate along the frozen ground.

He flicked his whip again and again, urging them faster along the river path. Thea prayed fervently that they reached the town gate first. Alfred cursed. Pillars of smoke were funnelling up from those villages that huddled closer to the town's eastern walls. 'Christ's holy bones.' He whipped again at the horse, hurrying them forward until they left the river where the track divided and took the fork along the walls up to the North Gate. 'It is the safest route in. Let us hope they open the gate to us.'

A host of fleeing villagers were crowding into the town through the gate. Those who had not made it in time would have to continue to the river or go west into the woods – anywhere away from the advancing army.

Perspiring profusely, Alfred pulled off his hood. 'Thea, the Countess will have my hide for this. You should not be with me.'

'King William won't dare do harm to us.'

'You think? Thank sweet Mary that you are safe for now.'

The gate behind them was dragged to and bolted. They were trapped inside the town.

36

January 1068

Elditha hurried from the dairy with a pail of milk for a posset for Gytha. The Countess had been brewing a chill ever since she had climbed onto the windy town walls that morning. Hearing a commotion around the gate, she stopped to see what caused it. Gytha's guard had allowed a cart through into the palace yard and the captain was remonstrating with a band of terrified refugees who were trying to follow it in.

From the top of the orchard wall that morning she had already seen fires to the east. She had watched the Normans march over the moor, at first a line of ants that later became armed infantry and later a cavalry riding huge war horses. She saw their banners of chevrons and animals unfurling in the wind. When she observed the baggage trains that followed, she knew for certain that they would camp outside Exeter's walls and wait for the town to surrender. The people now crowding inside the walls were disgruntled and frightened. She felt even sorrier for them than she felt for Gytha, who had ranted and raged when she saw the size of the Norman host approaching.

The carthorse that had arrived in the yard was stamping and snorting enormous belches of breath that billowed into the winter air. Still holding her pail she waited to see who had driven it so hard. When Alfred leapt down, she recognised him at once, even though his face was now red and raw; but why was Alfred here now with a Norman army circling the town?

She handed her pail to a servant and told him to take it to the Lady Hilda. Pushing through the crowd of grooms who were now gathering around the cart, she saw Alfred help a girl to jump down from the cart. The girl landed with a graceful spin into a dusting of snow. Elditha flew forward with her veil blowing back and shouting, 'Thea, oh Thea!' She stopped momentarily, lifted her hand and brushed away the snowflakes that were drifting onto her face. When she reached her child, she caught her in her arms and held her tight.

'Mother, by the Holy Virgin,' Thea said, when they let go the embrace. 'What are you doing here?'

'I have come to bring you to Ireland, though for that I may be too late.' Elditha took Thea's mittened hands in her own. She stared at her daughter's lovely features, then down at the simple woollen cloak and gown that hardly concealed her shape. At 15, Thea was a woman. She whispered, 'Thea, how you have grown up.'

She then grasped Alfred's hands. 'Why have you come into such danger?'

Shaking his head, Alfred handed his reins to a groom. 'We had no idea, but I bring weapons. The gates have closed. The peasants who followed us into the town are already destitute.'

'I watched them come over the moor.' Elditha felt her anger rise into fury. No one expected a winter campaign, not this, not now. She knew only too well what would follow. William would lay waste where he found resistance, as he had done when he had marched to Hastings. 'Alfred, where is Gertrude?'

'She is in the priory.'

'They will not attack a priory, Alfred.' She touched his arm with a reassuring gesture. Some men from Gytha's guard were already unloading a pile of short swords. They lay heaped up on top of sacking, the metal gleaming against the ground's frosted covering.

'Arrows too; be careful with them. Don't get them wet,' Alfred shouted at the men.

'We will talk when you are ready. There is a stew-pot on the hearth and bread and cheese on the trestle.' She hurried Thea towards the hall's entrance, then stopped and called over to the grooms who were helping Alfred with the cart. 'Send someone up onto the walls again. See how they are armed and count them. Look for their siege machines. Count them too.' She turned to Thea. 'Thea, you have disobeyed your grandmother. You should not have come here. Stay out of sight in the hall among the other women until I send for you. Entertain the children. Tell them stories, do anything to distract them.'

'I came to fetch threads for the prioress,' Thea said, her voice subdued. 'Are we safe, Mother?'

'That, Thea, is a question I cannot answer. We, at least, are not abandoned outside the town walls, nor are we escaping from a burning village. For that we must be thankful. Go in to the hearth and get warm.'

Thinking how quickly everything changes, she organised a sleeping place for Alfred. Then she hastened through the maze of inner rooms to Gytha's private apartment. The Countess was sipping her posset. After the initial shock she had felt at the approaching army, her normally high colour was now returning, but the set of her jaw was determined. 'They are at least 300 knights and there may be more. They saw William's own banner flying, that wolf. The Bastard himself has come.'

'What must we do, Gytha?'

'We sit tight. The skald sent out messengers the very moment he heard that the enemy was out on the moor. God willing King Dairmaid will send us aid.'

Elditha bit her lip and said, 'He does not know that I am here.'

'He soon will, my dear. He should have sent a ship of his own for Thea.'

'Gytha, I have to tell you that Thea is here. She came with Alfred. He has brought a consignment of swords and arrows into Exeter this morning.'

'I ordered her to stay in the priory.'

Elditha nodded. 'I know. She came for embroidery thread.'

Gytha grunted. 'Well, it may now be some time before you will take her to safety.'

Elditha leaned over and gently stroked Gytha's leathery cheek, wondering what King Dairmaid's response would be when he discovered where she was. And Magnus, her sweet Magnus, with whom she had left a purse. Now he could run her household. When would she see him again? She said aloud, 'I must bring Thea warm clothing. It is snowing. And, Gytha, we must keep busy. There will be extra mouths to feed. The homeless have descended on the town. They will need blankets and bread.'

Gytha sat erect. 'Elditha, send for Bishop Leofric. William will send representatives in to parley. Leofric must understand that I shall not yield my town.'

She is, Elditha thought, absolutely unbending. God help them, for they would soon need a miracle.

As the sun began to set, the Bishop hurried up the hill to Gytha's palace accompanied by his pale scribes. As he passed, his monks huddled in silent groups around the churches, watching and shuffling to and fro to keep warm, trying to be invisible.

William's messengers came into the town at Vespers, led by Alain of Brittany. They rode through the town, heavily armed, carrying a pennant with a wolf embroidered on dark fabric, its coat glittering with silver thread. The frightened townspeople ignored the bells for Vespers and kept to their houses. The armed strangers trotted past the minster, the Holy Trinity Chapel, the churches of St Stephen and St Lawrence, up the hill to the palace gates.

When their arrival was announced by Gytha's steward a hush seeped through those who had gathered to see the enemy close up. In the deepest shadows of the hall, out of the way of candlelight, hidden among a bevy of veiled women who sat on the padded bench behind Gytha, Elditha looked down at her hands and pretended to set stitches on a napkin border. Gytha sat in a great carved oak chair, coldly surveying the four knights and their boy pages, one of whom held aloft that sinister banner with the wolf's head. Elditha pulled her veil closer and bent over the piece of material that lay in her lap. Alain of Brittany spoke his master's case. They wanted the tax. Elditha thought: not just the tax; they want the town. Moving her lips in silent prayer she sent a plea to St Cecilia that the Count would not know her. Opening her eyes and lifting her head again Elditha saw that Gytha was now tense with anger, rigid like the jewel-headed stick she grasped in her hand. Her voice was ringing out, 'Tell your Norman paymaster, Count, that this dower land is my right. My town has never paid a tax and will not do so now. Always exempt. That is the law.' She glared at the prelate who stood by her side. 'So, it is an illegal tax. Bishop Leofric, is it not?'

The Bishop shook his head and gulped loudly. 'But, Countess, maybe just a little ... The law is changing ...'

'Nonsense. William of Normandy has no business here. We are a town of women and townsfolk who mind their own lives. None of us will pay his illegal tax. Go and tell him that, Count.'

Alain of Brittany's complexion reddened. 'You will regret this, Countess. The King carries the Pope's authority.' He addressed the Bishop. 'Talk to her, Bishop Leofric. We will expect sense by morning, by Sext.' He nodded to his companions. Ignoring the Countess, who was opening her mouth to protest, he turned on the heel of his leather boot and marched out, leading his clanking followers. The wolf pennant followed, fluttering as if trying to keep up with Count Alain's stride. Elditha could not suppress a shudder as he clattered from the hall and Gytha called after him again, 'Knight, tell him, no.'

Later, as they were seated at supper, the door into the hall burst open. The sergeant of Gytha's guard pushed the hall servants aside and marched straight up to where the Countess was seated. 'They are placing a boom across the river beyond the port gate. No one can leave by that route. No boat will enter our harbour.'

Gytha dropped her spoon. 'We had until Sext tomorrow.'

Of one accord the other women followed her lead and placed their spoons on the board. Elditha glanced down to where Thea sat at the end of the table fidgeting with her napkin. Her daughter's hand was shaking. They were all of them afraid.

The sergeant went on, 'The King is raising a siege. No provisions will enter the town. No person can leave.'

'How is he constructing it?'

'He has requisitioned our ships. It is a strategy designed to bring the merchants over. They fear the loss of their livelihoods. Countess, King William is a patient spider. He will watch and wait.'

'Then we shall stop that possibility. Has food from my stores gone to the monasteries yet?'

The sergeant explained that food, clothing and pallets had all been taken to the refugees. They would have full stomachs for some days.

'This may continue for longer than days. We must all eat less. Tomorrow I shall speak with the merchants whose ships the Normans are using. Let your men know that no one gives in to the Bastard. No one even considers surrender.'

When her man had gone to set a watch on the town walls, Countess Gytha lifted her spoon and began to sup. At this signal her ladies followed and started to eat also.

No sooner had Gytha commenced eating than she stopped. Again the women followed her example and placed their spoons on their napkins. She folded her hands and told her ladies in a clear voice that they must steel themselves for battle.

Gytha reminded them that William was an expert at siege warfare. He had conquered cities that way in Brittany and Normandy. 'No wonder London gave into him without resistance. Archbishop Stigand and the young Edgar saw siege weapons outside the town walls and rode out to meet the Duke. But if they had sat tight and outwaited William, help would have followed.' She leaned on the table. 'We are powerful and noble women. Ireland and Denmark will come to our aid. We can gamble for time. The thanes in the countryside will rise. Ladies, the outlaws of Mercia and Wessex will liberate us.'

Elditha thought that Gytha was admirable. She should have led their armies at Senlac, not Harold. As a quiet descended, the women supped the cooling broth, each keeping her own counsel. Salted cod seasoned and flavoured with precious herbs followed their soup. They ate slowly, chewing carefully, as if this were their last supper.

Gytha fiddled with her silver spoon. A smile hovered at the

corners of her mouth as she looked at Elditha and said, 'I suppose it is fortunate that you were not recognised by Count Alain. It just goes to show how we women become shadows in a corner.'

Elditha replied, 'Since I am a mere shadow, for now I remain safe.' But she thought of what the Bastard could do to a town. All of them had heard tales of rape, cruelty and destruction. She had been inside his camp, but with no threat of rape to her and her women. They were nobility, not so different to Norman noblewomen. There had been others who were not treated so kindly. The whole of Europe was aware that Duke William was an attacker of castles as well as a builder of them. As she supped, she wondered who would carry knowledge of her into the Norman encampment outside Exeter's eastern walls. Servants' eyes would follow her as she moved from the hearth to the loom. Only too soon, King William would know that she too dwelled among the ladies of Exeter.

As the meal drew to its quiet close, Hilda remarked, 'Mother, is it not best to negotiate this tax? Then they will ride away.'

'No, my dear, they are here to stay. Our lands will be gifted to knights who agreed to fight for the Duke's claim to England. They intend destroying our last sanctuary. Then it will be a castle. The Normans are as hungry for our land as their priests are for our souls.' Gytha held the women's attention with a hard look. 'I hear that the Pope will impose penance on knights for all the souls they sent to Heaven on the day they butchered my sons. It is not just Elditha they want to wed with. It is all of you who are young enough for them and even those who are past child-bearing age.' She waved her hand around the table. 'And, of course, your compliance would allow the thieves to cloak their theft with a semblance of legality and the Pope could reduce their penance.' Her eyes settled on Thea. 'You will leave Exeter with your mother as soon as we can arrange it.'

'No, Grandmother, I shall not leave without you.'

'Girl,' Gytha stood and raised her stick in a furious gesture, 'you will go as soon as we find a way for you to pass through that army.' With a jabbing gesture she pointed the stick towards the door, reminding everyone that there were four or five hundred soldiers encamped beyond the town gates. As if they needed reminding.

Ursula piped up in a small voice, 'We could ask the King for safe passage for Thea and Elditha.'

Elditha touched Ursula's arm. 'Do you really think he'll allow that?'

Gytha said, 'Of course not. Remember Winchester.'

'Queen Edith handed him the keys to her town,' Ursula said. 'But we could negotiate …'

'He won't have my keys.' Gytha speared a piece of cod and chewed it over and over at the back of her mouth since she was missing teeth from the front. She chewed as if she were chewing Ursula's words. She spat a small bone onto her plate and announced, 'Tonight we shall pray in the chapel. We must pray for deliverance.'

Elditha found appropriate words to rally all their spirits. 'Even as once he delivered David from Goliath, God will deliver us from the wolf at our door.'

For two days, the King's army waited for Countess Gytha's response. A tent village had sprung up on the flats close to Exeter's eastern walls. North of Exeter other villages were mercilessly burned to the ground, but not before the Conqueror requisitioned their grain stores and their salted meat to sustain his troops. Despite orders not to harm the women, many were raped. Elditha felt sickened by the stories that seeped into the town. Englishmen were killed in a variety of hideous ways – bludgeoned to death, strung up, stabbed. Every day smoke curled into the sky as hamlets smouldered, and the smell of burning thatch hung acrid in the sharp air. Any villeins who could escape did. Like hunted foxes they melted into the woods and hills west of the town. Still the women stood strong. They would not give in. And to Elditha's relief, the townspeople were of the same mind. They looked to Countess Gytha and Elditha, the mother of King Harold's children, for protection.

Later in the week, from high up on the town's ancient walls, Alfred and Elditha watched as a priest fell onto his knees. Elditha said, 'I recognise that monk. His name is Brother Francis. He betrayed us once and he will do so again.' The enemy camp seemed to stretch for miles. It encroached on woodland to the east. Trees that once grew tall were now stunted. For a week William's soldiers had been chopping them down, cutting back into the woods for fuel to feed their encampment fires. Their tents moved onto the moor north of the town. To the south, the Exe flowed and its mouth seemed leagues off. There was no way in or out through the boom that guarded access to the sea. Across the river Norman soldiers were using the meadow as a practice ground. If the siege continued, the only possible route out of Exeter was by the river. The river gate led out onto a long wharf with warehouses. The Normans had not occupied that area contained within a safe crescent, which was also protected by the deep Exe that flowed close to the walls on each side of the stretch of wharfs.

As she walked around the walls with Alfred, they checked that the men he now commanded had full quills of arrows. Approaching the north wall they saw Padar striding purposefully towards him.

Padar hailed them. 'What do they intend?'

'They may be waiting for their siege weapons,' Alfred replied.

'No sign of any yet?'

'Nothing.'

Padar said, 'Their patrols go out all the time. They are breaking down resistance. They did the same outside London after the Battle of Senlac Ridge. They harassed villages and waited for resistance to break. They did not need to wait long.'

'If they push into the woods west of the Exe they may find the forge …' Alfred began to say.

'They won't find aught but a blacksmith's forge,' Padar replied. 'We would know if the abbey had come to harm. There is as yet no smoke rising out of the trees to the west.'

'Not yet.' Alfred shrugged. 'But don't you think that it is all too calm?'

'Do not be deceived. The Norman bastards are waiting. They have food and patience. They'll attack when we are low.'

'We could run out of food within weeks.' Alfred's tone was bleak.

'Maybe so, but we can negotiate a better settlement if we wait.'

'It is not their way to settle kindly,' Elditha said. 'They take what they can.'

They climbed off the walls into Gytha's garden, where a robin hopped through the trees pecking at the cold empty earth. Elditha left them and continued back to the hall. Padar said, 'Alfred, if we can hold out for a short time our princes will sail into Exmouth with a great army.'

'They know already?' Alfred was surprised.

'I sent messengers out when they first appeared.'

'How do we know that they have reached the coast?'

'Trust me, Alfred, the ship we sailed into Hood Bay will be landing in Dublin's Wood Quay even as we speak.'

'It's no good. Gertrude is not safe.'

'God will keep her safe.'

They had walked in a circle and now they climbed to the wall again by the orchard steps. Alfred shrugged and glanced down past the hall to Gytha's chapel. 'Well then, let us pray that God protects us all.'

37

Afternoon and Evening

That afternoon, as Elditha helped Gytha across the icy yard towards the storehouse, Gytha told her that throughout the autumn she had weighed grain cautiously for her own use and her bakers had used barley mixed with wheat in their bread, but she had always allowed the poor generous gifts of food. She had regularly sent loaves to the monasteries inside the town walls to be redistributed to those who would otherwise starve. Elditha pointed out that if the siege held there would have to be an even more carefully managed distribution of alms.

'Aldric normally looks after the stores, but he is up on the walls,' Gytha said.

Elditha replied, 'Never mind, we can manage it.' When they reached the storehouse, she pushed the key into the lock and turned it. It was well greased and opened easily. She pulled the heavy door wider, saying, 'We can reduce the alms and our share too.' Inside she could not see anything at first. Eventually her eyes adjusted to the dimness and she was able to count sacks of grain. A little later she called out to Gytha, 'I think that there is enough to take us through until spring, but we must eat less bread if it is to last longer.'

Gytha considered. 'We can break our fast with a small cupful of buttermilk and half the portion of the bread we have been eating. We can have a pottage for dinner and for supper we can eat porridge.'

Elditha came out. 'But the children and old must have extra milk while the cows produce. And, Gytha, you also need to drink milk,' she protested.

'There are others frailer than I.' Gytha shook her head and

pointed her stick at the hay barn. 'I suppose when the hay runs out we must eat the cows.'

'I think that is still a while off. But we must each have a little cheese. There is enough cheese hung in the dairy for the household as well as the guard. There are dried apples, barrels of them in the orchard shed. I looked yesterday.'

'Good, tell the cooks that my ladies will have spiced apples this evening, a treat.'

Elditha closed the store door and locked it. 'That will cheer them,' she said, as she secured the key onto her belt. She helped Gytha cross back over the yard. 'The women could have a cup of wine or mead in the evenings. There is a good supply laid down in the kitchen cellar. Do you think that the Normans can poison our wells?'

'There is much they can do, but poisoning wells they cannot. The town wells are too deep. Nonetheless, if it rains we must collect the runoff in vats, just in case.'

'What if they tunnel under the walls?' Elditha said.

'It is possible, but if they try, we will be waiting for them.'

Elditha kept her fears to herself as she brought Gytha into the warmth of the hall. She settled Gytha by the hearth where a maid removed her boots and began to rub her cold feet with a towel. Elditha placed Gytha's work basket close to her chair and made her way out again, this time carrying a basket. She needed to be alone for a bit, to think, and more practically, to seek out mistletoe berries from the orchard for a salve.

On her way she stopped into the kitchen to tell the cook to collect apples for their supper from the store. As she looked around the yard outside, she noticed that the yard servants were pretending to do tasks they did not have. Two youths were replacing a wheel on a cart that might soon be chopped for firewood and a boy was grooming a horse that did not need grooming. It was the same with them all. The women all dropped spindles and embroidered as if with busy hands they could obliterate the looming threat beyond the walls.

As she pushed open the gate into the orchard, her thoughts turned to the daily alms they sent out to the poor. Every day they loaded a wagon with vats of porridge and salted cod. Protected by a guard Ursula travelled with it through icy lanes to the town's religious houses. The poor and ill survived reasonably well for now, but if the siege went on for months, what then? In a few weeks Lent would be upon them. They must brace themselves for the bleakness of the season of self-denial. This Lent Bishop Leofric must declare that everyone could eat what they had – even flesh, if fish, fruit, nuts or greens were not to be had. And when the winter cold spent itself out, they should plant every spare patch of soil in the town with wheat, cabbages and onions; every garden, orchard and all the common places where pigs and hens rooted, must be coaxed into production.

The days were quiet but once night fell, the shouting began. Arrow fire and screams followed as Gytha's men poured pitch on the enemy below. The previous night, when Elditha had opened her shutters and peered out, she had seen the glow of a fire in the north tower. She could smell the pitch now as she hurried through the orchard. She lifted her basket of mistletoe and opened the small gate into the garden. The soothing salve she intended to make from the fat translucent berries would soon be needed. William's patience would quickly run its course.

That evening, as the women sat around the bower hearth with wine and bowls of apple stew, Gytha remarked, 'At least we are warmer here than those bastards out beyond our walls are in their tents.'

'I hope they freeze,' Thea said, reaching her hands toward the fire.

'They will not suffer as the refugees in the woods are suffering,' Lady Margaret pointedly added.

Thea tossed plaits that shone red-gold in the firelight and said, 'The silvatii will care for the fleeing villagers. They have shelters, food hidden away and weapons. I know. I have seen them. Their men came to Alfred looking for arrow heads.'

'Then, niece, why do they not fight the enemy?' Hilda said.

Elditha laid down her cup. 'Sister, William has an army that is easily 300 mounted knights, and foot soldiers as well. We have fewer than 200 fighters, many of whom are youths with slings.' She folded her hands. 'The silvatii are outnumbered.' She paused and took a breath. 'But what do you think of this idea? I was wondering if they could bring us seeds to plant, if one or two of them could swim through the boom?'

'We must send messengers to parley with the silvatii,' Lady Margaret suggested.

Gytha banged her stick dismissively against the trestle leg. 'Parley, seed, what nonsense; they cannot defeat that army. The siege will be over by summer one way or another. Now, gather yourselves, ladies. It is time for prayer. Wrap warm.' She glanced at Thea's uncovered plaits. 'A veil, Thea; we may be captives but that is no reason to be careless.'

'Yes, Grandmother.' Thea lifted her veil from the bench and secured it over her plaits.

The women all collected their cloaks from pegs. Followed by their maids they walked into the night. Before she allowed Thea to go, Elditha tugged at Thea's cloak hood saying, 'Your grandmother is right. I want to see you wear a veil, even in the bower.'

'There is no one to see me here.'

'Even so, Thea, you should set an example to the other girls. Off you go. I want to look at Ella's puppies first.'

She sent Ursula for the bowl of scraps she had saved for the little dog that lay with her puppies in straw near the hearth.

Elditha stroked the hound's ears as it ate milk-soaked crusts. 'Scant fare for Ella too, I fear.'

'I have heard of burghs where during a siege the people were so hungry they ate their dogs and cats.'

'I hope it does not come to that.'

They left the puppies with the bitch. It was quiet outside. A sentry guarded a woodpile. Others stood by the grain store where only that morning Elditha had taken stock of the sacks inside. They crossed the yard, meaning to catch up with Gytha, but suddenly Elditha stopped. She noticed Alfred by the kitchen house.

'Ursula, go ahead. I must speak to Alfred.'

'My lady, do not stay out long. It is bitter.'

'Ursula, do not cosset me.' She had not meant to be dismissive of her friend but anxiety made her nerves sharp as needles.

The girl huddled into her cloak and scurried off. She waited until Ursula had reached the other women and called Alfred over.

'My lady?'

'Alfred, what are the enemy doing tonight?'

'They march around the north wall surveying our fortifications. We strengthened the towers and the walls over the autumn. They should hold strong.' He laughed the laugh of the nervous. 'As darkness gathers each night, we attack the bastards from the walls.'

'How long can we fight them off?'

'Boiling oil and the stones from our catapults will deter them for a while but they'll be back. They are taking many casualties already. They are looking for a place to tunnel into the town. To the east the river runs too close to the wall. We can access our harbour and the warehouses through the harbour gate. Yet we dare not because they will shoot across the river and pick us off. The Normans do not cross the river for fear of being trapped on the shore between river and walls. They have the bridge, of course. The boats are strung across the river and are guarded, blocking access to the sea.'

Editha considered. 'So when they attack, it will not be from the river?'

Alfred scratched his head. 'Nor the west, that is too hilly. But they can hammer our walls north and east of the town with ballista and their great catapults.'

'It surprises me that they have not brought those up already.'

'They have scaling ladders too, but they have not set them against the walls. Even so, they have caused us casualties, my lady. Their arrow fire is deadly. The monks' infirmary at St Lawrence is already full with our wounded. There are new

323

graves in the church cemeteries too.'

'I will send more salves and linen for bindings in the morning. How can we keep them out?'

'By remaining firm; maybe if the silvatii come from the woods to harass them. God knows I have armed the rebels.'

'So Thea tells us.'

'She notices everything.'

'As well she does. God go with you, Alfred.' Elditha reached out and took his hands. They felt cold.

'And you, my lady. Pray hard tonight for us all. Pray that Gertrude is safe inside the abbey. Too many fugitives out there in the woods, all keen to kill for a loaf of bread or a cloak.'

Dark shadows circled his eyes and there were deepening furrows lining his brow. She squeezed his hand quickly and pulled her cloak close, knitting its stitched edges together. 'Tonight I shall pray for Gertrude.'

'Pray for courage and for hope.'

'A curse on all Normans, Alfred. When next I meet one, I shall gladly send him to his maker.' She touched the seax that hung from her belt.

Alfred shook his head. 'I fear it will be long before we defeat them. Let us hope we can get an honourable settlement, that in fighting back we can at least stop our laws from becoming the stuff of legend. We are hurting them right now more than they are hurting us.'

She considered his words for a moment. 'You believe that rebellion will help us to this end?'

'We must hope. Where there is hope, there is life. Where there is life, there is a future.'

Later, as Elditha knelt before the altar in St Olave's chapel, she knew that unless her sons sailed south before the Normans built their castle fortresses in every town throughout Wessex, it would be too late. As Alfred said, in the end, the thanes, the merchants, all of the people of Exeter were fighting for the preservation of their old truths. As her tears began to flow, she wiped them away with the edge of her sleeve. She wept for those who had suffered, for the families who had lost everything, for the ill and injured who swelled Exeter's monasteries, for children without fathers and the women without husbands, for her daughters and sons and especially for Ulf, her beloved child, a small boy captive in a foreign place. That night, not noticing that her stiffening knees were being grazed by the chapel's bitterly cold tiles, she prayed that one day peace would return to what remained of their lives.

38

The king closely besieged the city attempting to storm it, and for many days he fought relentlessly to drive the citizens from the ramparts and undermine the walls. The citizens were compelled by the unremitting attacks of the enemy to take wiser counsel and humbly plead for pardon.

The Ecclesiastical History of Orderic Vitalis, 12th century, edited and translated by Marjorie Chibnall

More men died on the ramparts. The monks of St Lawrence were daily digging graves and tending the wounded. Elditha and Ursula delivered bread to the refugees sheltering in the monasteries, and helped in the infirmary making salves. They tore whatever linen they had into dressings. They gave comfort to the dying. Among the worst wounds were those inflicted by flaming arrows. Grown men cried in agony after their clothing had caught fire, causing terrible burns.

On their third day of helping in the infirmary Ursula came rushing into the cloisters. Elditha was wrapped in her cloak, resting her aching back against the monastery wall.

'My lady, we need your help. One of Leofric's monks was up on the wall. The arrow fire began again. One caught his ear. He fell down the steps, hit his head, and Heaven only knows what other injuries he has sustained. They are bringing him here. The prior says we must help him. Everyone else is too busy.'

'We can try,' Elditha said slowly getting up.

She was assembling her pestle and mortar and an assortment of jars on the table when they carried the monk in on a stretcher of tough linen. Hurriedly pushing a stray hair under her wimple, she directed the Bishop's men to a pallet in an alcove.

She followed them and leaned over the cot. One glance at the priest's face and she recognised him. Why was Brother Francis here? She had not seen him since she had looked down on the Norman camp. Now he was inside the walls. Calmly, she asked a servant to bathe the monk's torn ear and then to hold his head still while she examined his other injuries. His foot was badly twisted. He moaned and opened his eyes when she touched it. 'Witch!' he muttered, but, too weak for further protests, he closed his eyes again. She worked quickly, but when she asked the servants to lift his gown so they could examine his bruises, she gasped. Under his gown the monk had an array of seeping sores. There were lacerations all along his skinny legs. She ordered the Bishop's servants to turn him gently onto his side and ease the top of his habit back. He moaned again. She had thought as much. Brother Francis wore a shirt of goat hair under his habit. There would be more weeping sores, and with those the possibility of pestilence, and since that could not be permitted in the infirmary, they must burn the shirt.

She beckoned the Bishop's men away from the monk. 'Remove that, so I can treat him,' she ordered. 'If he protests, say it is God's will.'

When Ursula returned, Elditha drew her towards the pallet and said, 'This monk is no stranger to us. Look.'

Ursula peered at him. Turning back to Elditha, she said, 'It is a cruel fate that has brought the creature to us.'

'Or God has.'

'Or the Devil.'

'He has lesions on his back.' Elditha pointed at the hair shirt that now lay on the straw beyond the pallet, and added, 'And pustules running with pus. His body is badly bruised and scratched. His ankle twisted but, with care, he will live.'

'What thanks will he give us?'

'He shall live to thank us,' Elditha replied.

Ursula lifted the pestilent shirt and cast it into the fire. It blazed up and myriad tiny creatures rose to mingle with the smoke.

'Devils,' muttered Elditha, as she returned to the alcove. It still smelled foul despite the fresh herbs strewn on the packed earth floor – clearly Brother Francis had not bathed for weeks. He must have come in with Count Alain and remained with Bishop Leofric since, looking for preferment; and he was, no doubt, back to his old watching pursuits.

Elditha called for a candle to light the dim alcove. She filled a bowl with a sweet-smelling liquid, and waited in silence as the servants roughly raised the priest up. She lifted it to his lips. 'Drink, Brother Francis.'

He looked into her eyes said, 'Use none of your honeyed Devil cures on me.'

'There is no magic here, just poppy and honey to ease your pain. Open your mouth.'

She thought he would refuse again, but as she poured the sleeping draught into his open mouth, he swallowed. They gently eased him back onto the pillow. As he drifted into sleep Elditha began to rub a salve into the bruises on his legs. Finally, she eased his ankle back into position, placed a poultice on it to reduce the swelling and bound it.

She ordered the Bishop's men to clothe the priest in a clean shift, and take his filthy habit away from the infirmary. Then she dismissed them. 'Return in a few days. Tell Bishop Leofric that the priest's sores may take longer to heal than his ankle. Brother Francis can administer a salve for himself.' She added in a voice so low none heard, 'If he so desires.'

Brother Francis slept for two days and nights. When awake he set up an incessant prayer as Elditha changed his dressing and bathed his wounds, muttering, 'St Benedict, protect me from her.'

He suffered great pain but he refused to acknowledge it, as if he thought God was testing him, as He had tested His son in the wilderness. He refused to eat and was possessed by strange dreams. In one, he woke up screaming that the Devil was punishing England. 'He promised Duke William the kingdom', he cried out. 'Earl Harold promised.'

Elditha said then, 'No, that is a misinterpretation. My husband never swore an oath that the Duke should be king. He promised loyalty to our friend the Duke and it was the Duke, himself, who broke trust. Duke William attacked us. He took our lands and destroyed our nobility, and those he has not murdered at Senlac he is reducing to weaklings. Please eat.' Brother Francis stared at her and refused.

He claimed that he saw the Normans riding into Reredfelle and he seemed to relive the fear that he had felt that evening when they had carted them to the camp at Hastings. She discovered from his ramblings that it had been he who had informed the Normans of her presence at Reredfelle. He raved about the smoke, and woke in a sweat crying, 'Where is Ulf?'

Elditha shook her head sadly. 'At least on that we both agree. Remember how we all loved him so much, Brother Francis? You must eat, otherwise you will die. My son would want you to live.'

'God wishes it,' Prior Robert of St Lawrence said to Brother Francis. 'Lady Elditha prays for your recovery, as do we, every service.'

'I saw her cast spells to make corn grow. I saw her use mandrake ...'

'What of it? The field blessing happens everywhere in Wessex. It is a ceremony. The mandrake root is a cure. We all know that. The Church in Normandy may forbid it, but no one pays heed of that. It is your own imagination that poisons your thoughts. Enough of this; you will eat. Why, must we now send for Bishop Leofric?'

Fearful of the Bishop, he finally gave in and ate. For two days, the prior, Ursula and Elditha took turns to sit with him, spooning him broth. He accepted Elditha's ministrations and gradually began to change towards her. It was as if, with the healing of the body, the mind's torments eased.

Elditha heard him speak of angels in the candles' haloes. On occasion, as the choir of monks sang in the chapel, he claimed he heard Heaven's music. One morning when she was watching over him he suddenly raised himself up and looked out of the small window close to his bed. He gasped as he caught a glimpse of a cold blue sky outside and called out that he had been transported to the Kingdom of Heaven itself. Elditha felt pity for him. She helped him lie back against the pillow again and tried to get him to sip a cup of thin broth.

Later that afternoon she helped him to hop over to the hearth so that the servants could change the linen on his pallet. He sat morosely by the small fire but he appeared calmer. Not until the fourth day passed did she pronounce him well enough to return to the Bishop's service.

Only then did he speak to her. 'I came from the camp outside the wall and begged to speak with the Bishop. I attached myself to Bishop Leofric hoping for preferment.' His chin fell and he took a deep breath. 'I admit I have been self-seeking.' He looked away from her. It was a difficult admission for him to make.

Elditha stared for a long time at her old adversary, touched by this confession.

After a silence Brother Francis shook his head and added, 'My lady Elditha, I owe you my life. I have misjudged you.' He drew his shawl closer over his shoulders and lowered his voice so that she hardly heard what he said next. 'The child is safe in Caen, where he will receive an education. They will never harm him. I think he will return. I shall pray for that.'

She shook her head and murmured to herself, 'I must have him returned to me.' She looked sternly at the monk. 'And, Brother Francis, I need to know if you will stay or do you intend to go out to that camp beyond the walls.'

He shook his head. 'I shall stay with Bishop Leofric.'

'In that case I must ask Bishop Leofric to allow you to recover at St Lawrence and to find a permanent place for you.'

When she returned to Gytha's hall that evening she decided that on the following day Lady Margaret must take her place in the infirmary. Four nights in the infirmary had drained her strength and now she felt lightheaded and in need of sleep. She would remain at the palace with the Countess, unless her skills were urgently needed.

The following day merchants came to the palace. Falling onto their knees in an antechamber and appealing to Gytha, they begged her to end the standoff with the Normans. Elditha sat by Gytha's side as their spokesman said, 'The Normans have brought their siege weapons from Gloucester. If we do not negotiate, the siege will continue into the spring sailing season. Countess, you must pay the tax if we are to save our town.'

Gytha confronted them. 'Help will come by spring. Do not weaken before their threats. They dare not destroy the town.'

'But our trade will be ruined; our families will perish. With their ballista and ladders they can break down our walls without losing any more lives, Countess.'

'They want the town intact. They need our harbour. They will not destroy it. If it looks as if they are succeeding, then that is the time to negotiate, not now. I shall send you more grain from my stores to see you through, but, my friends, be resolute. Show them strength.'

The merchants were panicking. Either help would come by spring or they could bargain. They should wait. Yet she could see how disgruntled the merchants were as they rose from their knees. If Bishop Leofric listened to their complaints, they were lost. She prayed that the Bishop would not go against them, but did not voice an opinion. She could not. An opinion lay between a rock and a hard place. She had tended their injured and dying.

After the merchants departed she helped her mother-in-law up onto the walls. With Gytha's arm linked in hers, they walked through the north tower towards the eastern section of the town's high defences and watched the Normans construct their scaling ladders. Behind these, they saw for themselves the mangonels – tall, vicious throwing machines – now lined up menacingly close to the town's ditch. Gytha shook her head. Leaning on Elditha and deliberately measuring her steps, she returned along the wall. When they reached the steps to the orchard Elditha looked back over the moors. In the distance there was a plume of smoke. Another farm, village or barn was burning. They climbed down.

Sighing, the Countess stepped off the steep bottom step into the orchard. 'Those mangonels are up at the walls.' She sank onto a bench among the apple trees. 'All that treasure in the undercroft should be moved to the churches and hidden deep inside their crypts.'

'Is that wise? If Bishop Leofric gives support to King William, a royal treasure will not be safer there than here.'

'Let us look, Elditha, and then we can decide what is to be done.'

Elditha helped Gytha to her feet. She led her through the frozen garden to the hall's cellar steps. 'You cannot let the town fall to destruction. You may have to negotiate,' she said as they climbed into the undercroft.

'That would bring shame on our house. But if I have no choice, we must think of a way to save it all. I owe that, at least, to the women who have come to me for protection.'

Elditha lit the lantern. Stepping cautiously forward, they negotiated wine barrels and sacks of wool. Using Gytha's large key Elditha unlocked the door that led into the treasure chamber and lit two reed candles from her lantern. First she could only see shapes. They grew larger as her eyes adjusted to the thin candlelight and became chests. The chamber contained more treasure than she had imagined. She unlocked a chest and lifted the lid. It held silver coins. She let the coins slide through her fingers. 'It is worth much now we are robbed of our estates, and now we are about to lose our last Wessex stronghold, this may be all that is left to us.'

Gytha sank onto a stool. 'Yet this coin could pay for my grandsons' army if only we can find a way of taking it from Exeter. If only a ship could slip through.'

'And they have taken them all for their barricade,' Elditha said as she opened another coffer filled with jewels and pulled out a ruby pendant. She passed it to Gytha.

Gytha held it up to the torchlight. The ruby glowed. She straightened her back and dropped the pendant over her head. It lay against her chest, its red glow gleaming in the darkness. 'I wore this on my wedding day. Godwin gave it to me and I must save it.'

'And you, Gytha, were you handfasted or married in the church porch?'

'Our marriage was blessed by the Bishop in the cathedral. We were not cousins. I was related to Canute, not to Godwin.'

Elditha sighed. She lifted up an ornate silver-and-crystal box. 'And the relics?'

'That contains lace from St Mary's veil. Bishop Leofric can have that for his cathedral. He coveted it long before, when it was in our chapel. I had these relics removed here for safety. Now, we must return them to God's house, even though it seems that God has deserted our cause.'

From another chest, Elditha drew out two prayer books. She peered closely at the lettering worked into their leather covers. 'And these are surely precious.' She replaced them and lifted up another book. Opening it, she exclaimed, 'Gytha, one of Harold's books on falconry is here and, look, a book of riddles.' She lifted up the little book, opened it, shut it again and held it to her breast. 'It is the same as the one he gave me, after he married Aldgyth. It was lost in the fire at Reredfelle.'

'Take it, my dear. All these books belong to us.'

Elditha felt a great heaviness. Even now, Aldgyth remained on the edges of her vision, haunting her memories of her last day with Harold. Clutching the book tightly, she remarked, 'Aldgyth was with child.'

Gytha busied herself closing her chests again. She let the last coffer lid drop. 'Aldgyth's child was born in Chester last April, a boy. Do not dwell on it, Elditha. We have more things of importance to concern us than Aldgyth. I hear a bell. It is Nones already.' She smiled a wicked smile. Her eyes glowed like candles. They were those of a woman much younger than her great age. 'We shall leave all this here for now. I think it is time we spread a few home truths about the Normans among the women of Exeter.'

'What do you mean?'

'We need the town to continue to support us. Rumour is a

powerful weapon.'

When they came out of the cellar the town's church bells were ringing. Gytha's women were milling around outside the hall, waiting for her to return, their breath hanging about them like pale veils. Gytha tapped her way forward in front of Elditha, using her stick, picking her way steadily across the frosted earth. She pulled her little bell from her belt chain and, competing with the church bells, rang it insistently. She would lead them to prayer in her chapel.

Elditha excused herself and hurried inside the hall's opened doorway and past the hearth to the chamber in the far wing which she shared with Thea. She opened her saddle-bag and placed the little book there with her remaining treasures, the christening robe and a small purse filled with coins – the one lined with Ulf's dove which he embroidered a year ago. It was all the treasure that now remained to her; that and the amber ring on her little finger.

The following day, the palace women began whispers that the Normans would spare no one if the Countess opened the gates of Exeter. As Elditha moved around the bower and yard overseeing all, she heard their deliberate talk of terror as the women dropped their distaffs. They discussed how the Normans beat their wives and how they treated them badly. As they made samples and cut linen for bandages in preparation for an expected onslaught, they spoke of how the Normans ate stolen children in times of bad harvest and famine. As they talked, Elditha realised that Gytha's women had begun to believe their own stories.

Elditha went up onto the walls again. It was quiet. There was no arrow fire, no cries, screams or taunts. The Normans had moved their ladders closer, though they did not climb up them. Instead, down below, the ladders littered the frozen earth. They kept the mangonels back from the walls. At supper she learned that the women's tactics had been effective. The town absorbed their stories and there was no further talk of surrender.

*   *   *

To her relief, the townspeople had refused to support Bishop Leofric, who was lending his support to the merchants, and for now there was a reprieve.

39

Certain knights sent by him from Normandy had been driven by
a storm into their harbour.

The Ecclesiastical History of Orderic Vitalis, 12th century,
edited and translated by Marjorie Chibnall

As the siege slid into a third week the weather changed. A wind
rushed over the land from the western sea and a vicious storm
blew up. That evening Gytha's sergeant had sent a dozen or so
of her retainers out of the east gate to guard the quayside and
the harbour stretch between the river and the town ditches.
There was a score of her private army up on the fortifications
behind the palace. Beneath the driving wind and rain, Padar and
Alfred stood with Gytha's guard, pacing the walls as they
watched the Normans drag their mangonels farther back into a
stand of poplar trees taller than the machines themselves.

A number of ladders lay on the ground below, left there by
the Normans on the day before. Alfred suspected that when
morning came and the storm had blown out, the Normans
would attempt to scale the walls. The three weeks' lull granted
Gytha by the enemy showed signs of drawing to a close. The
enemy's patience must be worn thin by the freezing wet for
their tents were poor accommodation.

A boy came running through the rain, shouting for Alfred.

Alfred stepped forward to meet him. 'I am here, boy.'

'The Countess wants to know if the ship barricade is
breaking up.'

'Wait here, boy,' Alfred said.

After a final look at the Normans guarding the bridge, and
with Padar following, they wended their way around dripping
tar pots and close-knit groups of shivering soldiers, circling the

town below, until they came to the place in the east where the river started to hug the wall. From there they could see the shadowy outlines of boats crashing and banging against each other across the width of the river. They looked down. Gytha's guard was on the beach near the river gate.

Leaning against the wet stone, Alfred leaned over, peering down on the drenched quays and shadowy warehouses that lined the harbour. 'Come on,' he shouted and raced to the steps that led down to the river gate. Half-slipping, falling and fighting the wind, they came down. Padar called to the guard to unbolt the door. Struggling against the storm, they rushed out, down a steep track and onto the wharfs.

Padar reached the long, pillared jetty that thrust out into the river first. Pulling his cloak around him, he walked out onto it, scanning the river where it flowed to the sea, searching for the barricaded boats. Not far off, they loomed up. Looking back at the land, he could see no sign of Gytha's soldiers along the shore between the wall and where the river lapped up against it.

But Alfred's keen sight was able to make out the glint of spears on the shingle beach farther up the river near the bridge. He was not close enough to ascertain whether it was Normans or their own people. With the wind pushing behind him, he turned towards the bridge, and ran through the storm and along the quay.

Moments later, he could make out men wading across the river towards the town. Their hands were raised in surrender. Coming closer, he saw that it must be Gytha's guard who had surrounded them and were dragging them from the river, one by one, onto the muddy banks. They were cutting them down on the shore, deaf to their shrieks and pleas for mercy. Inches away from him, one of the surrendering men stumbled up onto the shingle. A spear flew past and caught the wretch in the neck. He fell against the wall ditch and slid down it into a bloodied heap. 'What are you doing?' Alfred yelled, rubbing his own neck. No one heard him. He recognised Gytha's captain. He was encouraging his men in a frenzy of killing. Alfred manoeuvred his way through fallen bodies and skewered victims closer to him. 'Who are these men?'

'English mercenaries who fight for the Normans. They are traitors.'

'But they are surrendering?'

'They are scum seeking shelter.'

'But they are surrendering scum, are they not?'

The captain shrugged. 'They would be mouths to feed. But if you don't like this, do you feel brave enough to stop them? The men would turn on me.'

Helpless, Alfred turned back towards the wharf. The rain was now beating into his face and pouring down his helmet in rivulets. His heavy, drenched cloak was slowing him down. He reached the jetty where Padar was standing above the swirling river, gazing from his hood towards the boom. As he came closer, he saw what Padar was watching: a small coracle. The craft was fighting its way through the churning water towards the quayside.

He reached him just as the craft rocked close to the jetty. It was pulled by an undertow between the jetty pillars, then disappeared from view, only to reappear on the other side. Padar raced across, leaned over and shouted down, but there was no reply. The figure in the boat stretched out to the pillar closest to him and caught hold of it. There was a sudden gust of wind. The boatman lost his grip and the coracle spun round. Again he reached out for the pillar, and grasped it. He raised his hand to the iron mooring hooks and hauled himself onto the dock. Then his boat was swept away by the force of the water. Collapsing at their feet, he bent double and spewed.

Padar pulled his sword from his belt and held it high, ready to strike.

The boatman was on his knees, yelling up, 'Stop, Padar. You know me!'

Padar dropped the sword. 'By Christus! What are you doing here?'

Alfred grabbed a handful of Padar's mantle and pulled him back. He reached for Padar's weapon. 'Are you crazy to unarm yourself outside the wall, man?' Padar blankly looked back at him. 'Here take it.' He thrust the weapon back into Padar's hands. 'Who is this bastard, Padar?'

'Connor of Meath, and he may be our deliverance.'

Connor struggled to his feet and began to speak.

Padar shouted at him, 'Don't try to explain now, just lean on my shoulder.'

Alfred said, 'Padar, listen to me. Gytha's guard are massacring mercenaries down there. They were seeking shelter here among the wharf buildings. The Normans will retaliate as soon as the storm blows out. I need the sergeant. He'll order Gytha's guard inside the gate again.'

'Help us behind the walls first.' Padar began to head off, dragging the Earl and fighting the wind. Alfred caught them up and grasped hold of the Earl's other arm. Pushing through the rain, they hauled Connor up the slope, through the wharf door and into the destruction the storm had wrought on the town. Alfred veered to the left and climbed the slippery steps to the wall towers. Padar was left with the Earl.

Pushing at Connor's sopping mantle, Padar guided him past the debris that came hurtling down the town's wider lanes with a loud banging and clashing. The minster's bells were wildly ringing, their clangs eerily echoing through empty streets. They were tossed in the gale until they reached the gate. Gytha's gatekeeper yelled at his boys to pull it open to allow them through. Padar kicked a rolling, thumping barrel out of their way and summoned all his strength to drag the Earl out of the storm and into the hall. He led him down the central aisle, past restless servants who were trying to snatch sleep, and behind a thick curtain into his own alcove.

'Here.'

He thrust a linen sheet at the Earl. When Earl Connor had dried himself off, Padar brought him soup from the cauldron that was always kept filled for Gytha's guard.

'What is it?' asked the Earl as he greedily grasped the bowl.

'Herbs, cabbage and onion. We are beginning to stretch the grain but the pot is never empty. Here, take this too.'

Earl Connor seized the spoon and ate. Finally, he wiped his

mouth with his sleeve and began to talk. He had come from the coast, he said. Half the south-west was on the move and he seemed just another destitute soul. Seeing no other way into the town he had skirted the town as the storm began to gather force. He had discovered the skiff abandoned where the River Exe widened as it flowed towards the sea, beyond the ship barrier, and had taken advantage of the storm to slip around the boom and get into the harbour. 'Simple as that, skald,' he said.

Padar lifted a skin bag and handed it to him. 'The messenger reached you?'

'More than a week past. I arrived back after Christmas to find the lady gone, King Dairmaid furious and Magnus distraught, but the messengers did come through.' The Earl wiped his mouth as he swallowed. 'Madness – she is mad, foolish, to make this journey in winter and alone.'

'She was not alone. What about the Danish ships?'

Earl Connor shook his head and drank again. 'Not before summer. The Countess will have to save herself however she can. Magnus has sent me for his mother and sister. The Countess will have to accept the Norman fealty, pay the tax, survive and wait. My task is to bring Lady Elditha and her daughter away from here.' He passed the skin back. 'The second I hope for; the first may be more difficult, and as I see it, the second depends on the first.'

'Get some rest,' Padar said, thrusting a blanket into Connor's arms. 'They are all trying to sleep. You can see them in the morning.'

40

Candlemas Day 1068

The flower of their youth, the older men, and the clergy bearing their sacred books and treasures went out to the king. As they humbly threw themselves on his mercy that just prince granted them pardon and forgave their guilt.

The Ecclesiastical History of Orderic Vitalis, 12th century, edited and translated by Marjorie Chibnall

By the following morning the storm had abated, but the besieged women awoke to further tragedy. As dawn was breaking, soldiers ran into the hall shouting for Countess Gytha. A messenger hurried to the chamber Elditha shared with Thea. They were already awake and dressed. 'Thank the saints Gytha is asleep,' Elditha said. 'Stay with your grandmother but do not awaken her, Thea.' She threw her furred mantle over her gown and, without even waiting to bind up her hair, rushed out of a side door into the garden, and climbed the orchard steps. Hair streaming behind her, she raced along the wall to stand with the soldiers who were gathered there to look at the grisly sight of a young man hanging from a gibbet outside the North Gate. His fair head had fallen onto his chest. His richly embroidered, saffron-coloured garments hung loosely from his bones.

Rumours raced through the morning. By Sext, the most important merchants had climbed on the walls behind the palace to see this horror for themselves. The Normans had hung a son of Exeter during the grey daybreak, while rain still pounded on the town's houses and as its citizens had begun to assess their damage. To the astonishment of the town burghers, in full view of those watching up on the walls, the Normans cruelly blinded another. The victim's screams could be heard penetrating the wet air. Below, rank-and-file soldiers competed with the jeering of their betters.

Elditha and Gytha received Earl Connor in Gytha's antechamber in the new hall. Alfred related the previous night's events. Gytha's relief that the merchant ships were not destroyed turned to anger when Alfred reported the massacre on the beach beyond the Port Gate. The murdered men who dangled outside the North Gate were hostages granted by her merchants to the enemy. Elditha's amazement at seeing the Earl, knowing he brought news of her sons, could not lessen the horror that had emerged early that morning.

'Why did the Normans have hostages?' Gytha said, clearly puzzled.

'Because those weasel merchants were treating with them behind our backs,' Alfred said.

'Send for Leofric at once,' Gytha ordered Alfred. 'Let us see what he has to say.'

An hour later, Bishop Leofric came stumbling breathlessly into her antechamber. 'Countess, we had no choice but to parley with them ourselves. The merchants ...'

'Are fools,' interrupted Gytha. 'And so are you. Even in parley we should be united, not divided. How, Bishop Leofric, how were there hostages?' Gytha demanded.

The Bishop looked down and said nothing.

'Speak,' Gytha raged. She waved towards a stool and Bishop Leofric sank gratefully onto it, his dark-gowned withers spreading over its edge.

He began with his excuses. 'These are my responsibility, my flock. They worry about their trade. The chief merchants of the town had granted King William six hostages – their own sons and even an elderly uncle – several days before the storm broke. It was proof of promise that they would bring an end to the siege. Then there was the slaughter by the river quay last night ...'

Gytha broke in, 'So they think you have broken faith, Leofric?'

'Broken faith, and let me remind you, you have not controlled your guards, Countess. King William gives a harsh warning.'

'That pack of bullies is no Christian army.'

'Countess, a son of Exeter is dangling at the gate. Another will die of his blinding. God has abandoned us and your people blame you. They say your stubbornness will be the ruin of them all. The burghers have banded together and ...' he stopped, and looked hard through popping eyes at the stranger by Elditha's side, '... once again, my flock brings their anger to me.' Not waiting for her to reply, Bishop Leofric rose off his stool. 'And now I must comfort their families.' He swept out of the chamber with a gawking monk attendant following, trying to snatch up the hem of his cloak as it swept over the puddled tiles.

'Their anger is nothing to my own,' Gytha shouted at his departing back.

Earl Connor climbed onto the ramparts with Elditha and Thea, saying he wanted to survey the Norman camp from the top of the town walls. Her joy at seeing Connor was spoiled by his news that King Dairmaid had called her a foolish woman, just like the rest of her kind. She felt that this must reflect Connor's own opinion. His words were chill. Unless they could stop the cataclysm, he said, there would be more hangings, more destruction. It was what she already knew. They must surrender. There could be no help before the summer.

There was a long, long silence. Elditha broke it. 'My lord, you have clearly come to bring us to safety.'

'If I can,' he said, 'but first Countess Gytha must pay the tax and then she must negotiate that you, Thea and I will leave. It is the only way to break this siege.'

'We must all leave,' Thea said. 'My grandmother, all of her ladies, everyone must leave. Grandmother has friends in Flanders, Denmark and Norway. We have cousins everywhere.'

'So, Earl Connor, you tell us to treat with Duke William?' Elditha said.

'Because we must, because Exeter has turned its back on their Countess. You know, two days ago I heard that the soldiers up on this very wall taunted the enemy and bared their arses to them. Then they poured oil and pitch down on them. They had courage.'

The Earl smiled at her story. 'Yet the Countess must now treat with the enemy. Pitch and boiling oil will not keep them from the gates.'

There were scalding tears in the back of her eyes. She turned away and began to descend the wall steps down into the orchard.

Later that day Earl Connor passed several hours alone with Countess Gytha. When they emerged from her antechamber Gytha's face was inscrutable. Elditha could not discern her intentions, nor did she speak of any, and nor did Earl Connor. He took himself to the Bishop's palace and did not return until well after night had fallen. That evening, although Elditha longed to be comforted by him – to talk about her sons – the Earl kept company with Padar and Alfred.

Before Nones on the following day, accompanied by the burghers of Exeter, Bishop Leofric came once again into Gytha's hall. Gytha descended the dais and banged her stick hard on the stone floor with such a fury that its gryphon head flew off and a second stick had to be fetched for her.

She then began a determined speech to the thanes and merchants that stood angrily before her. She reminded them of who they were; they were freemen of England. Englishmen were never subject to Normans. 'There will be no more of this. No agreement with the enemy. No talk with William. No fealty oaths. He'll give your trade to his own. Your daughters will be raped and married off to common soldiers. Your sons will be pressed into their army, like those foolish traitors in their camps out there. The bastard son of a bastard mother will hang you all.

And, if he doesn't, when my grandsons arrive to relieve us come sailing time, if even one of you betray this town, you will all be dead men.'

Elditha leaned forward from her bench. She could read their faces. She could see that the burghers of Exeter understood that in order to possess a future they must accept the new rule. Their old world was gone. It had gone two years before with the death of King Edward. The Normans had come and they intended to remain.

Bishop Leofric spoke up for the Normans. 'They rule much of Christendom, my lady Countess. They promise us cathedrals as grand as those in Normandy and in my heart I know that God wills it so.'

A chill penetrated Elditha. She gave her hand to Thea and whispered, 'What is she thinking? She must know it is over here.' Thea shook her head. Tears ran down her cheeks. The female members of the Godwin family, including four distant cousins, two ageing aunts and Hilda, all bowed their heads and sighed a collective sigh. Their resistance had run its course. They too must look to the future.

For a moment, the Bishop glanced their way. His eyes appeared to pop nervously from his loaf-like face. He lifted his hand, his plump fingers quivering, and pointed a fat ringed finger at the Countess. His voice quavered as he said, 'Countess. You are responsible.' He waved his hand towards the women. 'Think of your own family. Consider the fate that awaits these women if you continue to flout the rules. God have mercy on you.' With these words he turned and walked away, leading the band of grim-faced merchants and thanes. Their faces bore the sombre hardness of men who had had enough and would never bend to Gytha's will again.

As they sat abandoned by the Bishop, Elditha imagined the arching beams above pressing down, pushing them all into oblivion. Gytha's face seemed as if it was carved in stone, her anger frozen by the Bishop's retaliation.

Elditha rose first. 'Come, Mother, you need to rest; a draught of poppy perhaps.'

Slowly Gytha leaned down and retrieved her jewel-headed stick. She drew her back up straight and addressed Elditha, 'Go and find your distaff, girl.' Without another word, she tapped her way out of the hall.

Alfred was on watching duty again. The Normans moved their mangonels forward, closer than ever to the town. That night was so bitterly cold that even his sheepskin mantle felt thin. Alfred walked up and down, 30 paces forward and 30 paces back. A man beside a brazier looked at him as he passed, as if asking for reassurance. Rumour ran along the walls like a snake slithering through the tall grasses by the river below. The siege was close to its end. They feared for their future, but Earl Connor had assured the sergeant that no gate would open before a settlement was reached.

A roaring sound came from beneath them. It felt as if giants of ancient times were knocking on the door of the world. Something cracked and stones crashed. There were shouts from beyond the ditch. Alfred looked over. His men did likewise. Dust and soil rose up towards them.

'They are mining,' Alfred yelled.

He sent Padar to rouse the Countess. Padar raced along the wall and down the orchard steps and into the hall, shouting for her. She arrived wrapped in Godwin's bear-skin cape. When she heard that the mining had begun, she sent for Bishop Leofric and collapsed into her chair. For the first time since the siege had begun, Elditha saw Gytha's tears flow.

The next morning Earl Connor bravely rode from the palace, through the town gate and into the camp, carrying Gytha's pennant. By Sext the tunnelling had stopped. William pulled his mangonels back. Later that day, he entered the town escorted by Alain of Brittany and a small guard. The gates closed behind him. He met Countess Gytha, Bishop Leofric and the burghers of Exeter in the Bishop's palace. Elditha remained in the hall with the other women. She did not welcome an encounter with Alain of Brittany. Not long after, the Normans rode back to their camp. Negotiations for the women's exile had begun. The King agreed that part of the arrangement would be the removal of the Godwin women, their personal wealth in Exeter and their own servants. In return, he promised to guarantee the safety of Exeter's citizens.

When Gytha called her women together to tell them, Elditha left the hall by a side entrance to seek the quiet of the garden. She was coming to a decision of her own. She could not leave England, but she needed to consider Thea's future. Gytha intended to travel to Flanders, not Ireland. She might even continue to her native Denmark. Perhaps Swegne would make sure that the beautiful Thea married well.

Branches littered the pathways. Fencing, broken by the storm, had collapsed upon itself. Winter herbs had been flattened. Yet a tiny chapel dedicated to the Lady Mary had survived with its glass windows intact. Inside the priest had lit candles and now they glowed in two small haloes. As she watched them flicker she remembered that today was Candlemas. Later they would bring their old candles to the cathedral and distribute them to the poor. Bishop Leofric would announce to everyone that the siege had ended and they would give thanks that the town had not been sacked. As she thought of that, she anxiously paced the garden again. But she had made her decision. She would not return to Ireland and Thea would remain with Gytha.

She heard twigs cracking and looked to see Earl Connor approaching her. He was on her pathway. He had reached her. Bending down, he picked up a branch before she trod on it. 'Elditha, I must speak with you alone,' he said.

'My lord?' She was sure that she was making the right decision. She had heard him tell Gytha that although the Normans had won the battle they had not yet won England. Whether that was true or not, it had consoled Gytha. Now she must work out her own future.

She led Connor to a stone bench. He removed his cloak, a muddy-coloured serviceable garment, and spread it over the stone so she could sit. She looked up at the soldiers on the parapet above and said, 'The Normans have stopped the tunnelling, but if they wanted to they could break through our gates today. They could still break faith with us.'

'They believe that the Countess will give in to the wishes of her Bishop. If she changes her mind, she will see everything she cares for ruined. Your sons will come in the summer, but any attack we make then must be co-ordinated for it to have hope of success. If the English resistance lacks co-ordination, it is doomed. We must pull it together from every corner of the realm.'

'And King William says that the Countess cannot remain in Exeter,' she said sadly.

'None of you can.' He placed his hand over Elditha's.

'Connor, I have not seen my youngest child Ulf for so long that his face is fading from my memory. I won't return to Ireland now. I must find him.'

'Elditha, I would like to help you. Would you consider giving yourself over to my protection?'

She shook her head. 'We are friends, Connor, just that.'

He looked sorrowful and for a moment she thought she might change her mind, but he lifted her hand and kissed the yellow stone on the silver ring he had given her. 'So I do mean something to you, Elditha. And I shall always be yours in friendship. If you should one day ... if you could change your mind ... I can hope?'

But it was too late for love. Harold came between them. His memory hovered with her and about her. Though she did not say it and though he had hurt her deeply, so deeply she could not quite forgive him, her heart had always belonged to a fair-headed warrior who had borne a swan-shaped birthmark on his body and a bracelet tattoo on his thigh. Harold Godwin was hers alone, even where he dwelled among angels. The spinners at the foot of life's tree had spun her fate. She could not marry Connor of Meath, though he was more than worthy of her.

'You have never left him?' Connor asked, breaking their silence.

'You are a reader of thought, my Lord of Meath.' She

looked down at his hand that still held hers. 'But I believe that I have come to a decision. I shall enter a contemplative life here in the land I have loved.'

'There are safer nunneries in Ireland.'

'No, my lord, I shall ask permission to enter the convent at St Augustine in Canterbury. And, if that is permitted, my life will continue in a peaceful manner.' She slipped her hand from his. A smile played on her lips. 'There, I can pass my hours embroidering gold and silver copes for the Archbishop. But, in Canterbury, I shall be close to my old estate of Reredfelle. And there I shall wait to see Ulf set free.'

'What about Thea?'

'Thea shall remain with her grandmother and her aunt. I think if Gytha guides it, she might have a hopeful future. And maybe I can visit her.'

'And if your sons are restored to their kingdom?'

'I shall be in Canterbury waiting for them when they come.' She met his steady gaze. He was a good listener. 'And I pray that we too will speak with each other in better times, in a time when there is peace in the land and you can come to England.' There was such relief in this unburdening. She whispered, 'Thank you, thank you, Connor for believing in me. By listening to me now, you are helping me to understand myself.' She stood, leaned up and lightly kissed his cheeks, first one, and then the other. Then she walked back into the hall to tell Gytha and Thea what she had decided. Now was the time for her daughter to take care of the Godwin christening gown. Thea would travel with it to another land where her daughter and, in time, her daughter's eldest daughter, would protect this precious heirloom.

Two days later the sun shone in a flawless sky. The house-ceorl commander as well as Earl Connor and Ursula attended Gytha as they waited on the Bishop to hear William's agreement. Bishop Leofric made Gytha comfortable in his best padded chair, where she drank wine from a fine glass tumbler.

'So, Bishop, we are drinking the last of your English wine.

Send out your negotiators to William the Bastard. These are my terms.'

When she had finished, the Bishop nodded. 'My daughter, I believe that you are making the best decision. We can treat with the King.'

'King? Bastard he was born and bastard he remains.'

Leofric ignored that comment. Instead he said, 'The relics you promise will remain safe in the minster, and as part of our terms I continue as the Bishop of Exeter. Now, as for Lady Elditha,' he added after a discreet cough, 'was there not talk of marriage?'

'Yes, to God. You will see that her wishes are observed and that her safety in Canterbury is guaranteed. She is not the first and she will not be the last to choose the convent. Moreover, she brings to St Augustine a portion of my wealth. The Bastard has stolen her own.'

'Let us see what we can arrange.'

He made a steeple of his fat hands. Gytha noticed the opal Earl Godwin had given him, roosting like a small plump pigeon on his middle finger. She could feel Leofric gloating and, in that moment, she decided that if her grandsons regained their kingdom, Bishop Leofric would never enjoy Godwin favour again.

41

And here Gytha, mother of Harold, travelled away to the Isle of Flatholme, and the wives of many good men with her, and lived there for a certain time and so went over the sea to St Omer.

The Anglo-Saxon Chronicles, March 1068, edited and translated by Michael Swanton

Alain of Brittany set out for Wilton. There were some details concerning the ladies' exile that he needed to discuss with dowager Queen Edith. On his arrival, the abbey lay peacefully under a misty winter shroud. By Vespers he was comfortably closeted with Queen Edith in an antechamber warmed with charcoal that glowed comfortingly through lattice-worked braziers. On the table lay a manuscript. Edith followed his eyes as they lit on the parchment, noticing how he was drawn to the elegant acanthus stems that curled around the capital "E" of "Edward, Rex".

'It is very beautiful. My niece Gunnhild drew it,' she said with pride. In a brusquer manner she turned away from the manuscript and bade him sit and drink a glass of hippocras. 'Now, Count Alain, what news do you bring?'

'It is the King's wish that your mother must go into exile.'

'She is elderly and harmless.'

'Not so. She is dangerous and cannot be trusted. The King will allow her and her women their freedom if you send word to Flanders on her behalf. For now, they will go to the island of Flatholme, in the channel out of Bristol. But they are not to travel on to Ireland.'

Edith raised an eyebrow. 'Why ever not? Her grandsons dwell in Ireland.'

'King Dairmaid harbours traitors.'

'I see. My mother is a wealthy woman and she will want to see my niece, Thea, married out. Out of England, I mean, since Lady Elditha's lands and manors have been forfeit.'

'Arrange Countess Gytha's transfer from Flatholme to Flanders and the Countess may keep her treasures, but for her own use alone and not to be used to plot further rebellion. Her granddaughter's dowry is none of our concern.'

Edith paced the room. There really was no choice but to agree. 'I shall write it. And Elditha? My information is that she is in Exeter after all.'

'Indeed. I had understood her to be in Ireland, according to that rogue Beorhtric. And the skald too managed to escape Beorhtric's guard last year. One wonders about these English thanes' loyalty. But, as for the lovely Lady Elditha,' he paused, 'she is to enter a nunnery.'

'In the house at Wilton?' Edith raised a quizzical eyebrow. She was not so sure that she wanted responsibility for Elditha. The idea of her close to Gunnhild irritated.

'No, Canterbury.'

'St Augustine?'

He nodded and added with a hint of sarcasm, 'She intends to wed with Christ.'

'Ah, there lies a surprise. What of my nephew, Ulf?'

'Ulf will remain in Normandy and continue to be treated well, as long as his mother and the Countess conform. The boy is to be educated as a Norman.'

'His nurse, the woman Margaret?'

'The woman is to marry a merchant. She is still young.'

'And you, Count Alain, who will you marry now?'

He looked away. 'That remains to be seen.' He looked down at the scroll. 'Your little niece really has a talent. They say that once English nuns were calligraphers. It is not often you see that, nowadays.'

'And that is a pity. It seems that the world of men has encroached deep into our lives. One day they will be stitching in our bowers.' She reached out for a morsel-sized almond pastry.

'Not this one,' he replied with a hint of sarcasm in his voice and sipped his wine.

That night Edith wrote two letters and sealed them both. Things had turned out rather well. Her mother had survived. Elditha was to take vows in Canterbury. Who knew what Thea would choose? She smiled to herself. Gunnhild would remain here with her and that was enough.

Edith thought about her great work, her family biography. These new stories were for others to tell. Her scribes would write only her memories of her father, Earl Godwin, her brothers, Swegne, Harold and Tostig and, most importantly, those of her sainted husband who had ruled England for many peaceful years. Contented with this thought, she drifted into sleep. Over the abbey fields and beyond the distant hills, a last snowfall was cleansing the land, coating everything with virginal white. That night she slept peacefully.

Epilogue

October 1090

Sisters, you have long listened to this story and as we are nearing its ending let me tell you now about Ulf.

For many years Elditha dwelled in Canterbury. A long time ago she heard news of her older sons. They returned to the south-west in the summer of 1068 but had little support; they are now in Denmark. Her daughter Thea has married a prince of Novgorod. She is a great princess, with a child whom she has named Harold. Gunnhild, well, that is a story for another day. It is a great scandal, for she has eloped with that Breton knight, Count Alain – old enough now to be her father. No one knows where he has taken her; perhaps he has hidden her away in a dark, turreted castle in Brittany. If so, it is a terrible secret.

Two years ago, King William died in Normandy – cruel, old and despised by many. He divided his kingdom between his two sons, Robert and William the Red. Robert became the new Duke of Normandy. William, the favoured son, was crowned King of England. On the day of Duke Robert's accession to the Duchy, he knighted two young men; both had been royal hostages, nothing unusual there. One was Malcolm, son of the King of Scotland, but the other was Ulf, the youngest son of King Harold. These young knights were no longer hostages. They could travel where so ever they wished. When Elditha heard that her son Ulf was with Robert of Normandy, she decided to make a journey. She left Canterbury and crossed the Narrow Sea to the Norman capital of Rouen.

They met in the Archbishop's palace. Ulf sank to his knees and kissed the hem of her gown. As she raised him up and looked into his face she saw the lovely features she had known in the child of six. Her green eyes stared back at her from a countenance that was studious and kind. She reached up and touched his hair, as thick and flaxen as her own had once been so long ago. Why, he had almost reached the age she had been when they were in Winchester, before he was stolen from her.

That afternoon, Ulf and his mother sat together for many hours, eating honey cakes, sipping wine, remembering each other's memories; memories that reached far back into his childhood years beyond the time at Reredfelle. The evening shadows lengthened as they talked, since there was so much to say. My sisters, let us leave them there. In any case, this is where our tale ends. We must leave them together, happily accepting of their lives, talking long into the night, for they cannot have possibly imagined when it all began that the spinners at the foot of life's great tree had intended such a journey for them.

Yet, in the end, the spinners have spun my fate kindly and I am thankful. Close the shutters, Sister Elizabeth, I hear myself say. For there is a draught and I do believe that there is rain in the air tonight.

Author's Note

Edith (Elditha) Swanneck married Harold Godwinson circa 1050 when Harold was Earl of Anglia. There is no knowledge of who her family was and she could have been an heiress without brothers or sisters. They wed in a handfasted ceremony and may have been second or third cousins. This theory was explored by historian Frank Barlow. Marriage between cousins was not permitted by the Church. Equally, marriages between Danish families were often handfasted weddings in any case. Historians suggest that Harold married Aldgyth, the sister of the northern earls and widow of King Gyffud of Wales, in York during 1066. She is thought to have given birth to a child known to history as Harold. Since his marriage to Edith Swanneck was not sanctified by the Church, Harold, as had happened before with early medieval English kings, was able to make a politically advantageous marriage, by marrying a second time in a Church ceremony.

Little is recorded on the historical record with reference to Edith Swanneck herself. There were six surviving children from this marriage and a little girl who died. Harold and Elditha's sons were in Ireland at the time of the Conquest. Godwin, Edmund and Magnus used Dublin as a base from 1066 until 1069, from where they made raids into the inlets of Devon and Cornwall and stirred up risings. The historian Peter Rex considers that in the summer of 1068 their arrival with a fleet provided by King Dairmaid of Dublin was connected with Gytha's Exeter rising and was also intended as part of a general uprising in the south-west. Magnus died in a skirmish during this period. After their failed expeditions of 1068 and 1069 Godwin and Edmund joined Gytha, now exiled to Flanders. They travelled with Thea to the court of their father's cousin,

Swein Estrithson of Denmark and unsuccessfully harassed the north-west of England during the early 1070s. They probably lived out their lives at the Danish court.

I used the name Thea for Harold and Elditha's eldest daughter, Gytha, because it is confusing for there to be two Gythas so close together in a novel. In reality Thea-Gytha shared her grandmother's adventures. Saxo Grammaticus, a Danish historian (1150-1220) wrote that the young Godwin men travelled with Thea-Gytha to Denmark and that she was also chaperoned there by her Aunt Gunnhild, Hilda in the novel. Circa 1075 she was married off by King Swein to Vladimir Monomakh of Novgorod, Kiev and Smolensk. It would have been a fabulous marriage. They had many children, the eldest of whom significantly was called Harold. She died in 1107.

John of Worcester writes in the 12th century that Ulf, the youngest son of Edith Swanneck and King Harold, was taken as a hostage into Normandy after the Battle of Hastings and that he was released in 1089 and after his release he was knighted by Robert of Normandy, King William's successor to the Duchy. He may have accompanied Robert on his crusade to Jerusalem in the 1090s and not returned.

Edith Swanneck is recorded in *The Waltham Chronicle* as having identified Harold's body parts on the battlefield near Hastings by marks known only to her. The vignette depicted on the Bayeux Tapestry showing "The House that Burned", the firing of an estate before the battle and a mother and child escaping, was my inspiration for *The Handfasted Wife*. Interestingly, Andrew Bridgeford suggests in his book about the Bayeux Tapestry that the woman could be Edith Swanneck and the child, Ulf. The estate could, in fact, be Crowhurst. Only three women are shown on the tapestry and the other two are identified noblewomen. The theory carries weight. The estate at Reredfelle is to be found in the Domesday Book as a Godwin hunting lodge so I chose it as a location for the first section of my novel. *It is recorded in Domesday King William holds in demesne Reredfelle of the fee of the Bishop of Bayeux. Earl Godwin held it and then as now it was assessed for three hides ... There is a park. In the time of King Edward it was worth 16 pounds and afterwards 14 pounds. Now it is worth 12 pounds, yet it yields 30 pounds.* A park at this time was woodland set aside for hunting. What a wonderful source Domesday is! Edith Swanneck may be Edith the Fair, as identified as a wealthy landowner in the Domesday Book. Alain of Brittany fought at Hastings and he did take title to a portion of Edith the Fair's lands. He became very wealthy and was given the honour of Richmond after the northern rebellion. Count Alain was also related to William of Normandy through his mother, and also to the Breton duke who ruled from Nantes. His family lands were in Penthiévre, in the north-west of Brittany, and at some point during the decade before Hastings, his father, Count Odo of Penthiévre, had sent his two sons, Alain and Brian (who was Alain's older brother), to Duke William of Normandy's court to learn how to become knights. Alain had a half-brother, also called Alain, who has become known to history as Alain Niger, or Black, and who after his half-brother's death inherited his Yorkshire lands, the Honour of Richmond.

There is documentary evidence that Harold's daughter Gunnhild eloped with Count Alain from Wilton Abbey and that this was a scandal at the time. The date of the elopement is shadowy but letters from Archbishop Anselm of Canterbury to Gunnhild suggest 1090. Recent research documented in the annual *Haskins' Society Journal* suggests the 1070s for Gunnhild's elopement from Wilton Abbey, which is a more realistic date. My second and third novels in this trilogy *Daughters of Hastings* will fictionalise Gunnhild's elopement with Count Alain and Thea-Gytha's marriage to her Prince of Novgorod.

Now I come to where my imaginative speculation clearly exists within the pages of this novel. There is no evidence that Edith Swanneck, in actual fact, was King William's prisoner before or after Hastings, nor is there evidence that she was ever wooed by Count Alain of Brittany. Equally, I invented her journey to Ireland. However, as mentioned above, her sons are documented as having dwelled in Ireland during the years 1066-70 so it was logical that she just might go there. Importantly, the fact that Edith Swanneck disappears from the historical record allows for a degree of invention. I aimed to create a convincing world that was inhabited by English women during the years following the Conquest – one of loss and instability and one where marriages were arranged between widows and daughters of Hastings and Norman knights, to further the Norman land grab and cloak it in legitimacy. Edith Swanneck's story, as I have imagined it after the Battle of Hastings, becomes representative of what did frequently occur.

Edith Godwin's narrative and that of Countess Gytha follows the historical record because information is recorded in primary source material concerning them. The resistance of the women of Exeter is recorded by Orderic Vitalis. It also is mentioned in *The Anglo-Saxon Chronicle* that Countess Gytha went into exile from Exeter with a great treasure. The events of the siege follow Orderic Vitalis' account, inclusive of the proposed taxation resisted by Gytha, "mooning" on the wall, the massacre during the storm, the hanging of hostages and the divisions that emerged within Exeter during the siege. Padar, Ursula and Connor of Meath are imaginary characters but they are as real to me as the actual historical characters in *The Handfasted Wife*. This is, after all, a novel.

So what did happen to Edith Swanneck? A theory suggested by many historians is that she retired to a convent at some point after King Harold's death and this is the one I ultimately chose. However, the history of women at this time is shadowy and it is never really possible to pinpoint the truth. In conclusion, where there is recorded historical fact I stick to it, and I do not claim to possess or provide any new theories. I am writing here as a novelist, not a historian, and this story is, indeed, a work of historical fiction.

The Swan-Daughter

1

It had been so easy to take it.

As Wilton Abbey's bell tolled for her dead aunt's midnight vigil, everyone – priests, nuns, novices, postulants and girls – passed through the archway into the chill of St Edith's chapel. Gunnhild hovered near the back of the gathering. When the nuns' choir began to sing the first plainsong, she lifted a candle from a niche close to the doorway, cupped her free hand around it and slipped out into the cloisters. She hurried along a pathway through overhanging shadows until she reached her aunt's apartment, rooms that were set away from the main abbey buildings. Pushing open the doors, she crept into the reception hall, crossed her aunt's, the dead queen's, antechamber, the great bed-chamber and finally into Aunt Edith's vast wardrobe. *I must find it because when I do I shall have a suitable garment to wear when I leave this place. I must take it before it is given to that dwarf Matilda.*

She set her candle in an empty holder on a side table a little distance from the hanging fabrics and stepped into the space between wooden clothing poles. Frantically her fingers began fumbling amongst Aunt Edith's garments. *Which one was it? No, not those woollen gowns, nor the old linen ones either. No, look again.* Gunnhild moved along a rail by the wall fingering linens and silks until finally she found what she sought at the very end. She reached out and touched the overgown, pulled it down and took it out into the candlelight. Its hem was embellished with embroidered flowers – heartsease or pansies – in shades of purples and blues with centres of glistening pearls.

Her aunt had worn it when Gunnhild had first travelled to be with her in Winchester for the Pentecost feast of 1066. That was just after Aunt Edith's husband, King Edward, had died and Gunnhild's father was crowned king. Their family had risen and he had wanted his nine-year-old daughter to be prepared by her aunt for an education fit for a princess, to learn foreign languages, play instruments and embroider. She had remarked then to Aunt Edith that heartsease was her favourite flower and Aunt Edith had lifted her hand, smoothed it along the silk and said, 'One day, this dress will belong to you.'

She peered closer, examining the clusters of tiny flowers, noticing how perfectly they were edged with gold and silver thread. Her eyes darted about the fabric. There were no moth holes. The green silk dress was as fresh as it had been ten years before. She laid the overdress on a stool, returned into the depths of the wardrobe and with both hands shaking lifted down its paler linen undergown. With a cursory glance she saw that it, too, remained in perfect condition. *Make haste and hurry away.* She folded the over-gown into the linen shift and pulled her mantle over them both. She carefully closed the wardrobe's leather curtains, blew out the candle and sped from the apartment, fleeing back through empty cloisters to the Postulants' building.

Pausing to catch her breath, she pushed open her cell door with her back, slipped inside and spun around. Her every muscle tensed with fear. Eleanor was standing in the middle of the room.

'Christina sent me to find you ...' Eleanor, her friend since she had entered Wilton Abbey, broke off. 'What, by the Virgin's halo, are you hiding under your cloak?'

Gunnhild pulled out her bundle and dropped the garments onto her cot. Eleanor held up the silk overgown and then dropped it onto the tiles as if it were poisoned, her face pale with shock. 'This,' she gasped. 'Where did you get it?'

'I took what is mine by right,' Gunnhild said in a quiet voice.

'You stole it.'

'No I did not. My aunt promised that one day this gown would belong to me. All her clothes will be shortened to fit the dwarf queen. And...' Gunnhild glanced down at her grey postulant's robe and her hand flew to the hideous black cap that Christina, the assistant prioress, forced her to wear. 'I need something better than these.'

'Whatever for?'

'You will know soon enough, Eleanor, I promise.' Gunnhild scooped the gown into her arms, folded it and placed it back on her coverlet beside its linen undergown. Her mind working quickly, she searched around her chamber for a suitable hiding place. The garment chest had a strong barrel lock and a key, though she rarely secured it, but now ... She crossed the room, flung open the coffer's lid and bent down. For a moment she inhaled the pleasant scent of cedar-wood chips and felt around with both hands, rooting amongst her plain linen until she plucked out a green veil-band embroidered with a golden pattern and a pair of red deerskin slippers decorated with twisting fire-spitting Godwin dragons. Both had been gifts from Aunt Edith for her sixteenth birthday. She lifted the head band, turned it around and around in her hands and faced Eleanor again. 'These belong to the daughters of my family; my aunt gave them to *me* to keep, not to my mother who is in a convent, nor to my sister, Thea, who is far away in the lands of the Russ but to me,' she said, clutching her hands together so tightly her finger bones felt as if they would crack. 'No, Eleanor, the real sin is to imprison one of us in this abbey, to expect her to wear dull gowns day upon day, and order her to wed with God.'

Eleanor leapt up from the bed and pointed at the headband. 'Where in heaven's name would you wear that? Christina will find you out. No one is forcing you to take vows. You chose your own path. You have broken two vows already, obedience and poverty. If the abbess finds out ...' She caught her breath and rasped, 'Oh, for heaven's sake, Gunnhild, take them back to your dead aunt's rooms and leave them there for Queen Matilda before you break the third.'

'And that is unlikely here,' Gunnhild complained and tucked

the veil-band and slippers back in the coffer. 'No, I shall risk Christina's fury.' She plucked the gowns from the cot, laid them neatly on top of the fillet and slippers and covered the lot with two everyday shifts. Turning back to Eleanor she said, 'But, Eleanor, Christina must not find out. Please say you will not tell her. Besides, I have not yet taken any vows, nor shall I take them ... I have changed my mind ... My father, King Harold, remember how he was once king of the English. Never forget it, nor that the dwarf queen's husband, that bastard, William, killed him on the field at Senlac. Never forget that *King* William stole our kingdom.' She gasped for breath, almost choking with fury. 'My father never intended me for the church. He sent me to serve my aunt, to learn to read, write and embroider. Now Aunt Edith is gone to God's angels there is nothing left for me here. I intend to be free.'

'So, Gunnhild, how will that happen?' Eleanor's voice was very, very quiet.

Gunnhild found her calm again and equally quietly said, 'Eleanor, I am a princess. When my knight comes to claim me I shall be waiting for him in that dress.' She climbed up on to the chest and slipped her hand behind the statue that sat in the wall niche above it. She felt around for a small key and grasped it. Carefully, so as not to knock over her plaster St Edith, she climbed off the clothing chest. Kneeling on the cold tiles she secured the barrel lock with a loud clink, stood on the chest again, replaced the key and set the statue back into its original position. Looking over her shoulder she called down, 'Now it is hidden and only you and I know where. Promise you won't tell.'

Eleanor shook her head. 'Of course I will not. Gunnhild, I shall not betray you. Your secret is safe, at least on earth if not in Heaven.' As Gunnhild jumped from the chest Eleanor reached over and caught her hand. 'Hurry or you really will be discovered and I hope God will forgive you because if Christina finds out she will not.'

'Bah, I am not afraid of Christina.' Gunnhild hesitated momentarily, and added, 'No, not a bit, even though I know she will beat me with her rod through the cloisters and lock me in the ossuary if she ever discovers my intention to escape.' She reached out for Eleanor's hand. 'Thank you. You are a true friend.'

Eleanor drew her close and whispered. 'Be careful what you wish for, Gunnhild. Now let us slip back into the chapel before the dragon comes looking herself.'

Hand in hand they sped back to the novice stalls in the chapel where they took their places amongst the other postulants and novices and bowed their heads in prayer. The vigil was drawing to its end and the bell in the abbey church was tolling. It was only a few hours now until Prime. After morning prayers Gunnhild was to travel to Westminster because she was the only surviving Godwin heiress dwelling in England, but once Aunt Edith's royal funeral was over she would return to Wilton to be buried alive as deeply as the winter that was gathering about the cloisters. Touching the coarse hemp of her plain gown she sighed. No knight would ever look at her dressed in raiment as pale as the shroud that covered her aunt's once lovely form. Gunnhild's eyes swam with tears. She wiped them away from her cheeks using a corner of her cloak and whispered into the candle smoke, 'Aunt Edith forgive me. I want to be of the world, not apart from it.'

Bibliography

In addition to sources mentioned in chapter headings and in my Author's Notes I found the following particularly helpful when researching *The Handfasted Wife*.

The Bayeux Tapestry: New Approaches, Michael Lewis, Gale R Owen-Crocker and Dan Terkla (editors), Oxbow Books, 2010

The Bayeux Tapestry: The Life Story of a Masterpiece, Carola Hicks, Chatto and Windus, 2006

The Hidden History of the Bayeux Tapestry, Andrew Bridgeford, Harper Perennial, 2004

The Battle of Hastings, Sources and Interpretations, Stephen Morillo (editor), Boydell & Brewer, 1996

The Godwins: Rise and Fall of a Noble Dynasty, Frank Barlow, Longman, 1992

The English Resistance: The Underground War Against the Normans, Peter Rex, Tempus, 2004

The Trotula: An English Translation of the Medieval Compendium of Women's Medicine, Monica H Green (editor and translator), Penn, 2002

Medieval Women: A Social History of Women in England 450-1500, Henrietta Leyser, Phoenix, 1995

The Swan-Daughter

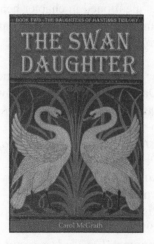

A marriage made in Heaven or Hell.

1075 and Dowager Queen Edith has died. Gunnhild longs to leave Wilton Abbey but is her suitor, Breton knight Count Alain of Richmond, interested in her inheritance as the daughter of King Harold and Edith Swan-Neck or does he love her for herself? And is her own love for Count Alain an enduring love or has she made a mistake?

The Swan Daughter is a true 11th-century tale of elopement, and a love triangle.